SATURN RUKH

Tor Books by Robert L. Forward

Timemaster
Camelot 30K
Saturn Rukh

SATURN RUKH

ROBERT L. FORWARD

TOR®

A TOM DOHERTY ASSOCIATES BOOK
NEW YORK

SATURN RUKH

Copyright © 1997 by Robert L. Forward

This book is printed on acid-free paper.

Edited by David G. Hartwell

A Tor Book
Published by Tom Doherty Associates, Inc.
175 Fifth Avenue
New York, NY 10010 USA

Tor Books on the World Wide Web:
http://www.tor.com

Tor® is a registered trademark of Tom Doherty Associates, Inc.

Library of Congress Cataloging-in-
Publication Data

Forward, Robert L.
      Saturn rukh / Robert L. Forward.—1st ed.
          p.   cm.
      "A Tom Doherty Associates book."
      ISBN 0-312-86321-7
      I. Title.
      PS3556.O754S28   1997
      813'.54—dc20   96-42527
                           CIP

First Edition: March 1997

Printed in the United States of America

0 9 8 7 6 5 4 3 2 1

Dedicated to Carl Sagan (1934–1996),
who inspired me to look at all planetoids
as potential abodes of life.

ACKNOWLEDGMENTS

Any hard science fiction novel depends a great deal on technical information generated by the research work of others. Those technical publications that I used the most in developing the scientific background to the story are listed in the bibliography. In addition, I would like to acknowledge the following for their technical help in various areas: Gordon T. Baker, Paul L. Blass, Darlene Draper, Steve Flanagan, Gary Flandro, David Folta, Eve Forward, Julie Forward Fuller, Tom Gehrels, David G. Hartwell, Robert P. Hoyt, Geoffrey Leet, Robert Maddock, Patrick Moore, G. David Nordley, Glenn S. Orton, James R. Powell, Carl Sagan, Nasser Shuwaier, James Stone, Ibrahim Wehishi, and Willie Wilson.

1

BILLION FOR THE JOB

GOT A JOB FOR YOU. PAYS A BILLION.

The message blinked at the top of the screen three times, then disappeared. Rod Morgan smiled. He had been hearing rumors about a quasi-multigovernment, quasi-commercial consortium that was raising capital to sponsor a risky trip to Saturn. He closed down his game of WARPWORLD, and switched to net-mail to read the rest of the message. He'd guessed right, it was from the consortium. The job must really be risky for them to be offering a billion dollars. Although the penny was no longer legal tender, a billion dollars was still a large fortune.

Rod read the message. They were asking him to be commander of the mission. That didn't surprise him, for after all, he *was* the best space pilot in the business. Without hesitation, he typed his reply.

JOB ACCEPTED. WHO ELSE IS ON MY CREW?

The reply soon made its way back over the ether and optical fibers of the SolNet. There were five names listed. Two—Seichi Takeo and Pete Stewart—were unfamiliar, while the other three were well known to Rod, since they were also involved in the project to build a resort on Mars. Sandra Green and Daniel Horning were stationed on Mars. Horning was one of the three medical doctors on Mars, and the best, besides being an excellent waste-handling engineer—an essential member of the engineering team on long crewed missions. Sandra was a biologist, part of the scientific team instructed to look for native Martian lifeforms. She was also the emergency medical technician for the small science group at Boreal Base. Fortunately for the consortium funding the Mars resort, but unfortunately for the scientists, it now looked like there *weren't* any native lifeforms on Mars. As a result, there hadn't been any major clamor by the greenie organization, the Peaceful Planet Protectors, against the further development of Mars.

The last of the three names, Chastity Blaze, was well known to Rod. He and she were part of the TransPlanet SpaceLines team that piloted freighters back and forth to Mars. Rod had finished his latest run two weeks ago and was taking a well-deserved vacation on the beaches in San Diego, working on his tan, while Chastity should be starting on her run home about now. If she was going to be part of his crew, this expedition was going to be fun as well as profitable. Rod closed his portable, being careful not to get any sand on it, put it away in its carry-bag, then ran down the beach and dove into the waves.

Fifteen minutes later, the same message appeared on a touchscreen console in a large cargo spacecraft just leaving on a high-speed trajectory from Mars.

GOT A JOB FOR YOU. PAYS A BILLION.

At first, Chastity thought it was someone's idea of a joke, so she searched carefully through the compressed linking-data at the end of the message for the address of the sender. It was art@sun.com.us.e—Art Dooley, president of Space Unlimited. Although Art probably didn't have a billion dollars himself, he knew where it could be found, so perhaps the message wasn't a hacker prank after all. The efficient, short-nailed fingers of Chastity's right hand flickered over the soft touchscreen and soon her reply was on its way back over the SolNet.

TELL ME MORE.

The Earth was on the opposite side of the Sun from Mars, so it would take the message over fifteen minutes to get to its destination. Then, it would take another fifteen minutes to get back. This gave Chastity plenty of time to think while she waited for the reply, for now that she had her ship under way, there was little for her to do. Pushing her bracelets up her left arm to get them out of the way, she returned to her work on the little finger of her left hand. The long nail had been wiped clean and Chastity was carefully painting on it the flag of Australia, with glued-on diamond chips for the stars. It would complete her collection of fingernail star-flags that she would wear on her left hand for a week before switching to another theme for next week. Each fingernail took a long time, but she had nothing but time now.

Chastity and her crew of two, copilot and scotty, were deadheading a Boeing-Mitsubishi freighter back from Mars after delivering a cargo of precision 3-D mechfabs, chemsyns, and specialized computer chips. There were plenty of raw materials on Mars, so instead of hauling food, fuel, habitats, and construction machines, she brought the specialized hardware that would allow the builders there to fabricate those necessities out of the Martian atmosphere and soil. All sorts of machines—including gigantic water well derricks, personal computers, bulldozers, Martian airplanes, and ballistic hoppers—were fabricated at Olympia Base using the precision mechfabs, with only the intricate computer chips—the brains of the machines—being imported from Earth.

While it was the precision mechfabs that made the machines, it was the chemsyns that made the fuel and food that kept the machines and humans fed. Chastity had even enjoyed a chemsyn-fabricated steak during her last evening on Mars. The artificial steak had been so tasty she had found herself reluctant to leave the mess hall table, wanting to order another rather than go off dancing with the muscular hunk that had been her date that evening.

The thought of her last date reminded Chastity that the only time she had met Art Dooley in person was also on a date. It was eight years ago. She was finishing her Ph.D. in astronautical engineering at MIT and Art was in his final year at Harvard Law School—specializing in space law. He had invited her to be his guest at an exclusive reception before the main banquet at the annual meeting of the International Astronautical Federation, which was being held in Boston that year. At that time in her life, she still wore long nails and multiple rings on both hands. She remembered that she had put on her best red-sequined strapless evening gown for the occasion. As the youngest and tallest woman there, she had attracted a lot of attention, and when the tuxedoed IAF brass found that the statuesque black-haired violet-eyed beauty could hold her own in engineering discussions, they had remembered her. She had impressed a lot of important people that night, including the Boeing-Mitsubishi CEO. That contact had resulted in a job as a spacecraft test pilot, which in turn led to her present job with TransPlanet—as she became a pilot of the ships she had tested.

She remembered that Art had been very supportive of her that night, making sure that she was introduced to the right people, then stepping back deferentially and listening, while letting her control the conversation. Strangely, he never asked her out again. Now, eight years later, here was this mysterious message from him.

It was at a similar IAF meeting five years earlier that the *real* space age had started. In an obscure paper entitled "The Properties of NHe_{64}^{*}", an optoatomic cluster-molecule chemist named George Phillips from the National Institute of Standards and Technology in Boulder, Colorado, had described to the aerospace engineers the structure and energetics of nitro-stabilized metastable helium, now called nitrometahelium by the atomic scientists, but "meta" by the aerospace engineers.

Meta was a strange molecule, with a structure somewhere between that of a buckyball and a bunch of grapes. At the core of a meta cluster was a single atom of excited nitrogen, surrounded by sixty-four helium atoms, each atom with one of its electrons raised into a more energetic metastable state. Metastable helium had always been easy to form—just pass some high-voltage electricity through helium gas. Large numbers of metastable helium atoms existed in every neon sign and the helium-neon lasers in grocery store checkout stands. It had long been known that if metastable helium could be stored, it would make a superb rocket fuel, since it contained more energy per kilogram than any other material known. If left to itself, a metastable helium atom would have a lifetime of two and a half hours, but if you crowded the atoms together in a fuel tank, the lifetime dropped to a fraction of a second, making the stuff useless as a rocket fuel.

Phillips had found that if you made a merged beam of helium and nitrogen atoms, and excited the atoms into their metastable states with lasers, the metastable helium atoms would cluster around the nitrogen atoms. The cluster constructed of sixty-four metastable helium atoms surrounding a single excited nitrogen atom turned out to be exceptionally stable. In some strange, still not understood way, the single nitrogen atom completely stabilized the excited helium atoms. The meta clusters were readily condensed into a liquid. Best of all, the liquid meta could be handled and stored over a wide range of temperatures without danger of explosion. Even the occasional cosmic ray couldn't trigger a chain reaction. When the meta was heated beyond twenty-two hundred K, however, the clusters disintegrated. Milliseconds later, the sixty-four helium atoms from the cluster would release their energy, creating a reddish-purple plasma of ionized helium gas along with the occasional nitrogen atom.

Specialized "magnoshielded" rocket engines had to be built to cope with the energetic new fuel, but fortunately, meta also had a high heat capacity, so it could be used to cool the exhaust nozzle before being "burned" in the reaction chamber. It wasn't long before the propulsion engineers had produced a rocket engine that got nearly all of the energy stored in the meta clusters turned into kinetic energy in the rocket exhaust. The exhaust velocities attained thirty kilometers per second, more than six times what could be obtained with the best rocket fuel up to that time, liquid hydrogen burned with liquid oxygen.

Now, instead of an Earth-to-orbit launch vehicle consisting mostly of fuel tank, the new MACDAC heavy lifters were mostly payload, with the meta fuel weighing only one-third the dry vehicle mass. Even Chastity's Boeing-Mitsubishi interplanetary freighter only required a fuel load equal to the vehicle mass, yet it still made the half-AU opposition run to Mars in less than two months. With that much propulsion margin to play with, any company that could build an airplane could build a launch vehicle or an interplanetary rocket. There were now three space hotels in Earth orbit and a resort on Luna. Soon, there would be a resort on Mars catering to the superwealthy clientele that wanted to climb the tallest mountain in the solar system—Olympus Mons. Unlike Chastity's slow freighter, the new Mars cruise liners for these customers would make the trip in ten days.

Three weeks later, Chastity walked into Art's office. When Art saw her, he felt a pang in his heart. *The only word that properly describes her is "magnificent,"* he thought to himself. She had dark-black curly hair, violet eyes, a sculpted strong-jawed face, and the body of a decathlon gold medalist. Art noticed that only her left hand still had the long, fantastically painted nails and the multitude of rings and bracelets. Her right hand was now bare and short-nailed, ready for its job at the delicate throttle controls of an interplanetary rocket ship.

Seeing the long, artistically painted nails took Art back to the time he had first seen them. It was eight years ago and he had been looking for a wife. He had approached that task with the thoroughness with which he had approached all the other tasks in his life. He was almost finished with law school—at the top of his class, of course. It was time for him to move on to the next phase of his life's plan. He knew he had good genes and he felt that the world deserved to have them passed on. He had set out to find a woman whose genetic abilities would complement his; someone with mathematical and analytic skills that would go with his social and artistic abilities, someone tall to compensate for his short stature, and someone who was willing to bear four children. Chastity had been only one of the many women Art had sought out and dated. But, on his first date with Chastity, it had been quickly obvious from their initial discussions that her primary goal in life was to fly spacecraft—and the radiation hazards of spaceflight and pregnancy don't mix—so instead of pursuing her further, he had introduced her around to his father's engineering friends at the reception and she had taken it from there.

Art had finally found a wife—a top-rank computer programmer—and he and Blanche were now expecting their fourth child while Blanche easily kept up with her career over the SolNet. He had remained faithful to Blanche all this time, but now he found himself wondering how it would feel to have long fingernails slowly scratching their way lightly down his bare back. . . .

"Hello, Chastity," said Art. "You're looking magnificent, as usual."

"What's this about a billion-dollar job?" asked Chastity, getting to the point.

"The job will take two-and-a-half years—thirty months—to accomplish. It's risky, and might cost you your life, so we feel that an appropriate payment for the task is a billion dollars."

"It must be awfully risky if you're willing to pay a billion dollars," said Chastity cautiously. "Is it legal? . . . and who is the 'we' that you mentioned?"

"I represent a consortium. It includes the governments of many

of the spacefaring nations, so the job is definitely legal. It also includes most of the aerospace manufacturers, space transportation
companies, and space resort owners. The long-term objective of the
consortium is to ensure an ample future supply of low-cost meta. Future growth in the space business depends upon the availability of
large amounts of meta at a reasonable price."

"I was beginning to worry about that myself," said Chastity.

Without waiting for an invitation, she made herself comfortable
in a large chair. "Helium is a pretty scarce element on this planet and
I throw a few hundred tons of it away into space every time I light
the candle on my freighter."

"You aren't the only one that's worried," said Art, perching on the
end of his desk. "The 'Save Our Helium League' is now holding
'SOHL-saving' demonstrations at Kagoshima and Baikonur as well
as Canaveral. We're used to handling kooks in America, but the
demonstrations are causing political problems in the other coun-
tries."

"Don't the demonstrators have a point?" asked Chastity.

"Not really," said Art. "We pump hundreds of millions of tons of
natural gas per year from the wells in Texas and the other western
states, and depending on the field, as much as seven percent of the
gas is helium. With the increased demand for helium to make meta,
the gas producers have been adding more helium skimmers to the
higher-concentration wells, so we have plenty of helium, even if the
SOHL-savers don't think so. But we still have to turn that helium
into meta and haul the meta up into space, which takes more meta
to get it there. The consortium is looking at a way of generating an
essentially unlimited supply of meta *in* space."

Chastity looked puzzled, her violet eyes seeming to turn darker
under her glossy black eyebrows as she tried to figure out what Art
meant. "Helium was named after the Sun, because that's where the
first spectroscopic evidence for it was found," she said. "But you can't
be meaning to capture the helium in the solar wind, or mine it on
Luna. Except for the Sun, where are you going to find significant
quantities of helium in space?"

"Saturn."

"Of course!" said Chastity, annoyed with herself for forgetting
about the outer planets. "Although Jupiter's closer . . . What are you
planning to use? Scoop-ships? It would be fun to fly one of those."

"Scoop-ships would scoop mostly hydrogen, with only a few percent of helium," replied Art. "Nope, what we are planning on doing is taking a meta factory down into Saturn's atmosphere and floating it there under a raft of balloons. The meta factory will separate out the helium and turn it into meta. Meta-fueled cargo ships will then haul the meta back to the inner solar system. This first mission will establish the feasibility of the concept by having a ship take a pilot-plant version of a meta factory down into Saturn and having the plant make enough fuel for the ship to make its way back. That's why we've chosen Saturn instead of Jupiter; the gravity well of Saturn isn't as deep, and besides, the gee level in the upper atmosphere is only one Earth gravity, while on Jupiter it's two-and-a-half gees. You'll find living on Saturn almost like living on Earth."

"I haven't said I'd take the job," warned Chastity. "Besides, I already have a job . . . with TransPlanet."

"TransPlanet is a member of the consortium. The CEO of Trans-Planet was the one who recommended you for the pilot slot on the mission."

"Pilot!" said Chastity, annoyed. "Who's commander?"

"Rod Morgan," said Art. "He's already accepted the job."

"Oh . . ." said Chastity, having to admit to herself that Rod was older and more experienced than she was.

"Why don't I have him come in and join us?" said Art, pushing a buzzer. "He's been working with the ship's engineers for the last three weeks while you've been on your way in. He can better answer any technical questions you might have, while I can answer the business and financial ones."

The door opened and Rod Morgan strode in, dressed in the tailored spaceman's jumpsuit and soft boots outfit affected by those who piloted TransPlanet ships. He was handsome and blond, with the same height and almost the same muscular build as Chastity, except her chest-circumference measurement involved different lumps from his. When people saw them together at TransPlanet functions, they often remarked what a cute couple they would make . . . and they *had* coupled occasionally.

"Hi, Rod," said Chastity, rising from her chair to give Rod's hand a strong shake. "The fact that you're going to be on this mission makes me more willing to consider it—besides the billion bucks, that is. What are we flying?"

"It's basically the same Boeing-Mitsubishi freighter-lander that you and I have been flying. That's why we two were at the top of the selection list. Instead of cargo modules, we'll be carrying more fuel modules, so we can make the interplanetary hop faster and still have enough fuel left to take us down into Saturn. Also, instead of landing struts, we'll be carrying a balloon."

"This sounds like a planetary exploration mission," said Chastity, turning to Art. "How come NASA isn't doing this? . . . or ESA . . . or, if it costs too much for one government, some multigovernment collaborative effort?"

"The reason a consortium has been formed to carry out the mission is to make the mission feasible," replied Art, launching into a long explanation. "If any one of the national governments were officially in charge, then the very idea of designing a mission with any significant risk to the humans on the crew would not be acceptable. In order to make the mission safe enough, the spacecraft would have to be made so heavy that it couldn't even lower itself into Saturn, much less carry enough fuel to take off again. By putting the burden—and any blame for failure—on a commercially led consortium, the spacecraft can be pared down in size so it can accomplish the mission. That's why Space Unlimited was chosen to be responsible for the operational phase of the mission."

"How risky are we talking?" she asked, blinking nervously.

"The fuel you need to get from Saturn back to Earth is going to be stored in orbit around Saturn," Art started. "You have to rendezvous with it to get home."

"Not much risk there," said Chastity confidently. "Rod and I have to do a rendezvous mission every time we refuel a freighter."

"You go down with only enough fuel to bring you to a halt under a parachute in the upper atmosphere. The balloon has to deploy and develop lift before the parachute drifts down to the level in the atmosphere where the pressure and temperature become too high for the spacecraft to survive."

"I won't ask the odds on that happening," said Chastity. "I'm sure the parachute and balloon designers will do as good a job as they can. And, taking along a little extra fuel to extend the hovering time will just postpone the inevitable." She paused and turned to look at Rod. "Will we fry or be squashed?"

"The walls of the crew quarters will collapse before the inside temperature reaches the protein coagulation point. They were designed that way."

"Good." She swallowed heavily and turned back to look levelly at Art. "What else?"

Art paused, not wanting to answer, and looked over to Rod for help.

"We have to make our own meta before we can leave," replied Rod.

"Suppose something goes wrong with the meta plant?"

"We have to make our own meta before we can leave," repeated Rod.

"That *is* risky." Chastity turned to look questioningly at Art. "I know it's because of the hours-long time delay between Earth and Saturn, that you need humans at Saturn in order to monitor and control the plant. But why aren't you just dropping the meta plant down into Saturn, and leaving the crew in orbit to run things through telerobots?"

"We priced out that option," said Art. "In order to cover all possible contingencies that might arise, the telerobot systems for the meta factory and its support facility became so complicated that the total mission costs ballooned to thirty billion. The project was a no-go at that price. Putting humans in for telerobots brought the price of the equipment down to an affordable three billion. That's why you'll be getting paid a billion dollars," explained Art.

"Is each crewmember getting a billion? Or is Rod getting more because of his age and experience?"

"You're not getting paid for your talent," said Art. "All the crewmembers are tops in their fields. You're getting paid for the risk. Same risk—same pay."

Chastity looked at Rod, who nodded his confirmation. She turned back to Art.

"How many in the crew?"

"Six," replied Art. "The consortium raised ten billion dollars for the mission—six billion for the crew and three billion for the equipment."

"Who gets the last billion?" asked Chastity, suspiciously.

The look in Art's eyes suddenly shifted from friendly to cautious. "Space Unlimited," he finally answered.

"What!?" exploded Chastity. "*We're* taking all the risk. Why should you get paid the same amount we are?"

Art knew that Chastity was in no mood to hear explanations of how much Space Unlimited had invested so far in putting this consortium together, and how much his business could potentially lose if the budget went over the ten billion target. A billion was a fair return for the business risk he was undertaking. If the project was successful and meta production started, he could then expect an even higher return, since Space Unlimited owned 5 percent of the consortium shares.

"If you're not interested in the job, I'll have to go to the next name on the list . . ." replied Art firmly. He then broke out his most ingratiating smile and tried again. "But Rod and I would *both* like you to be part of this mission."

Chastity thought for a long time. She didn't like it, but she couldn't complain too much. For the rest of her life she could live like a multimillionaire on just the interest from a billion dollars.

"Okay," she finally said. She turned and looked at Rod. "Let's go up and look at the ship."

The vehicle for the Saturn mission was being put together at the Boeing-Mitsubishi Assembly Station in LEO. After the trip up in the crew shuttle, Rod and Chastity put on spacesuits and went out on a Jet-Do, Rod at the controls and Chastity sitting behind him. They approached the crew capsule at the front of the ship. The capsule was in the shape of a cone seven meters high and seven meters wide at the base—like a gigantic Apollo capsule. There were three small view-windows toward the top of the cone, six larger ones in the middle, and an airlock door on one side near the bottom.

"Looks like a standard Boeing-Mitsubishi crew capsule," said Chastity as they approached. "Holds six—three in comfort. That's going to be pretty close quarters for a thirty-month mission."

"I don't mind if you don't mind," said Rod.

Chastity squeezed her thighs tighter against him. "I'll be fun the first few months," she agreed. "But by eighteen months I'll bet you'll be tired of having me around all the time."

"Never!" said Rod.

"Well, I may be tired of you!" she replied, giving him a punch in the ribs.

As they approached closer, she asked, "What's its name?"

"I've named her *Sexdent*," replied Rod. "After the trident that the god Saturn carries, only I changed it to 'sexdent' 'cause there are six of us, and when our habitats are installed in its side, the capsule has six 'teeth.' "

"You ninny!" Chastity shouted, giving him another punch in the ribs. "It's *Neptune* that carries a trident. You've got your gods and planets mixed up."

"Oh, well," said Rod. "At least the name has a nice nautical flavor . . . sexdent . . . sextant . . ."

Sexdent sat on a fuel tank module that continued the conical shape, so that the combined cone was eleven meters high and eleven meters wide at the base. At the base of the fuel tank module was an engine module with twelve large rocket nozzles spaced evenly around its base. This squat conical rocket ship was sitting on a large squat cylindrical fuel tank thirteen meters in diameter and eleven meters tall.

"The stack doesn't have the right proportions," said Chastity. "When we go on a normal mission to Luna or Mars, the conical crew capsule up front is followed by a stack of cargo or passenger modules, with the fuel modules and the engine module at the end, all the same diameter as the crew capsule. Of course, for this mission there'll be no cargo or passengers, but these certainly aren't standard Boeing-Mitsubishi fuel modules. They're too wide—and what's that donut-shaped thing floating over there at the end of that tether?"

"Since meta is so powerful, only a single fuel module and engine module stage is needed for a round-trip mission to the surface of Luna or Mars," said Rod. "For this mission, even though we have no cargo or passengers, we're going to need six stages. So things are built and stacked differently. The whole stack weighs a little over two thousand tons wet, most of it in the first two stages. At the base is the booster stage, with a fifty-ton tank and engine module, which holds a thousand tons of meta to get us up to speed. Sitting on that is the rendezvous stage, with a twenty-five-ton tank and engine module containing five hundred tons of meta to stop us at Saturn. Sitting on top of the rendezvous stage is the cone-shaped portion that we'll use to carry out the rest of the mission. It has the standard crew capsule on top, while underneath is a fuel tank and engine module that is not only our third stage, but part of our fourth, fifth, and sixth stages."

"How's that?" asked Chastity, not yet fully understanding.

"The fuel tank module gets refilled and the stage is reused," replied Rod. "When we arrive, the tank will be full of meta. We use up nearly all the meta to descend into the upper atmosphere of Saturn. We make more meta while floating around in Saturn's atmosphere, refill the tank, and use the same tank and engine module as the ascent stage. We then refill the tank again from the storage tank we left behind in orbit around Saturn, and use the same module as the return stage and the stopping stage."

"Storage tank?"

"The donut-shaped thing over there is the storage tank that holds the return fuel," said Rod, pointing. "It is the last thing to be added, and goes on top of the stack. It fits around the fuel tank at the base of the cone. We left it off until last, so Pete can get to the meta manufacturing facility underneath to check it out. Let me take you down there."

Rod zoomed the Jet-Do to the base of the house-sized cone, and tied it to a strut holding one of the meter-high magnoshielded engine bells. In free fall, it was easy for Rod and Chastity to float between the engine bells, where they found an airlock leading into a cylindrical structure tucked between the ring of engines around the base of the conical stage.

The airlock into the meta-manufacturing facility was a tunnel-like entrance that allowed only one person to cycle through at a time. As Chastity exited the inner port she was pulled through by a tall man with a balding head. He wasn't wearing a spacesuit, or much else for that matter, just the bottom half of his "cooljohns." She could feel the coolant in her own cooljohns switch to cold—it must be hot inside the facility. The man bent over the airlock door to start the cycle again and she looked him over from the back. He was built like a football tight end, with broad shoulders, muscular arms, slim butt, and long tapering legs. The only thing that destroyed the wedge-shaped symmetry was the roll of fat that jiggled over the elastic on his cooljohns.

With the cycle started, the man turned around and stuck out his hand. "You must be Chastity Blaze," he said. "I'm Pete Stewart, photochemical engineer. The facility is at normal pressure, but much too high a temperature, so if you want, you can strip"—a mischievous grin appeared at the sides of his mouth as he watched the annoyed look build on her face as the pause continued—"off your helmet and spacesuit to your cooljohns," he finished innocently as they shook hands.

She took off her helmet and put it under her arm. "I'll keep the suit on," she said. The airlock bell chimed. As Pete opened the inner door and pulled Rod out of the airlock, she took the opportunity to look around the room. They were at the end of a narrow corridor, which branched off into other narrow corridors. The walls of the corridors were formed of ceiling-to-floor racks of identical pieces of intricate-looking equipment with blinking indicator numerals and toggle buttons. There was a muted hum of electrical power permeating the hot dry air.

"I take it Pete introduced himself," said Rod as he removed his helmet.

"Yes . . ." said Chastity coolly.

"This is where we make the nitrometahelium," said Pete as he led the way down the corridor. "If this pilot plant can make the one hundred twenty tons of nitrometahelium we need to get off Saturn in less than a half year, then the consortium will send a full-sized factory that can produce a million tons a year—at a cost less than five percent of the price of nitrometahelium in LEO today."

Chastity was going to ask what would happen if the pilot plant didn't work, but she put the negative thought out of her mind by concentrating on Pete's bare back—it was a very nice muscular back and she wondered how it would feel to run long fingernails down that back and feel it twitch in response.

"These are the laser filters," said Pete, pointing to one wall. "The nitro-stabilized metastable helium clusters are only stable if there are absolutely *no* impurities in the cluster. Not one atom of hydrogen or any other foreign atom, not even an atom of helium-three, the lightweight version of normal helium-four. These racks of tuned lasers take the input gas flow of impure helium, which will have been extracted from the hydrogen and other stuff in Saturn's atmosphere by front-end physical and chemical filters, and clean all the impurities out of it, leaving pure helium-four gas." He turned a corner and led them down another corridor, which had similar racks of equipment, with slightly different arrangements of indicators and toggle switches. Most of them were dark. "These racks of tuned laser exciters take the helium-four gas stream, and apply pi pulses of laser light at just the right frequency and pulse length. The pi-pulses flip *every single one* of the helium atoms from its normal nonexcited state into the excited state at the same time. The stream of excited helium atoms is then merged with a beam of excited nitrogen atoms, here"—he pointed to the midsection of the illuminated unit—"tickled with another laser to induce the formation of the sixty-four-atom cluster . . . and out the end comes a stream of nitrometahelium, which condenses on the walls, is collected, and sent to the fuel tanks. If you look in this window you can see some droplets. They're pretty small, but that's all I have to show you, since for my helium source I only have a small pressure tank of a hydrogen-helium mixture pretending it's Saturn."

"Y'know," said Chastity as she moved to look in the window. "I've used tons of meta in my career, but I've never actually seen the stuff." She looked in the window at the tiny, almost spherical, metallic-looking drops collected on the far wall of the chamber. They had a silvery blue surface.

"Looks like blue mercury," she said.

"Acts like mercury, but it's a lot lighter," said Pete. "When we're in the cloud-tops on Saturn, the gravity will pull the droplets down the walls, where they will collect at the bottom of the chamber, then electromagnetic pumps will pump the liquid nitrometahelium into the fuel tanks."

"How come only this one unit is on?" asked Chastity, pointing to the dark units above and below the one they were looking at.

"The helium exciters are real power hogs," said Pete. "Since this stage is where the energy is put into the fuel, a lot of power is required to run each one. At Saturn we'll have Seichi's multimegawatt nuclear reactor up and running, and I can run all the exciters at once. Here, I have to borrow power from the Assembly Station, so I'm checking them out one at a time. So far I've only found one bad one."

"Make sure you find them all," said Chastity. "I don't want to spend the rest of my life on Saturn."

"Don't worry," said Pete with a wave of his hand. "I've designed this system so that it's not only redundant and failsafe, but is completely repairable by a person working in a spacesuit."

"You designed all of this?" asked Chastity, looking around. She was impressed.

"Every bit," said Pete with pride. "And it was assembled under my supervision. I'm now checking out each unit personally. After all, my life depends upon it working properly when we get to Saturn. If you two can get us down into Saturn safely, then I'll give you the fuel to get us back out."

"You can't ask more of the builder of a system than to bet his life on it," said Rod to Chastity. "Now let me take you to see another engineer who is betting his life on his system, but unlike Pete, he can't turn it on to check it out beforehand."

Leaving Pete to the task of checking out the facility, Rod and Chastity donned their helmets, exited the airlock, and leaving the Jet-Do tethered to the base of the conical ship, climbed up the rungs in the side of the crew capsule to the airlock at the center of the cone, where they cycled through together. This airlock was big enough for four people in their spacesuits. In a routine these two professional astronauts had gone through many times before, they turned their backs on each other, stripped down past their cooljohns, then redressed in the underwear and jumpsuits waiting for them in their personal lockers tucked into the wedge-shaped corners of the airlock.

"Ready, Chass?" asked Rod, his back still turned.

"Ready," Chastity replied.

As they turned around, Rod took a quick look at the altitude of the zipper up the chest of Chastity's jumpsuit. The zipper was well past mid-chest and almost no cleavage showed—she was all business today.

They entered the lower facilities deck in the crew capsule. The open space was a hexagon, two meters from side to side. Up the center of the room ran a ladder leading to the upper control deck. On the opposite side of the ladder from them was obviously the galley, with its preparation counter, compactor, oven, mixer, and microwave, and hatches above and below the counter leading to a freezer and refrigerator. Each of the six walls of the hexagonal room had doors. Three walls, the galley and two others marked FOOD and EQUIP-MENT, had multiple small hatches leading to storage areas. The food and equipment lockers were blocked by a large tube two meters high and a meter in diameter that took up nearly a third of the space in the hexagonal room. The opposite two walls, marked AIRLOCK and LIFE SUPPORT, had full-sized doors. The last wall, to the left of the airlock door, had two narrow doors, side-by-side.

"As Queen Victoria once said . . ." said Chastity, as she slipped into the nearest narrow door.

". . . never pass up a chance to visit a W.C.," continued Rod as he slipped into the other narrow door.

By the time Rod exited his bathroom, Chastity was already halfway up the ladder to the upper deck. He followed her up the rungs and through the half-circle hole in the grating that acted as a ceiling for the lower deck and a floor for the upper deck. The triangle-shaped open area in the top deck was slightly larger than the hexagonal-shaped open area in the lower deck, but it seemed more crowded since the conical shape of the ship caused the upper part of the walls to tilt inward slightly.

Rod and Chastity looked around at the standardized control deck arrangement. Both were glad that they would be operating familiar equipment during this new and dangerous journey. The triangular room had three touchscreen consoles, one at each apex of the triangle. Right above each touchscreen was a heads-up holoviewport. The holoviewport acted as a normal viewport providing a view of what was outside during the critical landing phases on the surface of Luna and Mars, while at the same time superimposing navigation and status information on that view. For other operations requiring pilot control, the holoviewport could replace the outside view with any other outside view obtained from cameras placed at strategic points around the ship, allowing the pilot to observe the process of docking the ship nose-first or landing the ship tail-first.

The seat before the engineering console was occupied. The person at the scottyboard swung around on the swivel arm that held the cushioned seat for the console and started to unbuckle himself.

"Don't bother for me," said Chastity, waving a hand at him. But he did anyway and floated free with a bow. He was a young Japanese man, wiry in build, with long artistic fingers.

A very handsome gentleman, mused Chastity to herself. *Reminds me of Mr. Sulu. It'll be a pleasure sharing watches with him!*

"This is Seichi Takeo, Chass," Rod said, doing the introductions. "And Seichi, this is our pilot, Chastity Blaze."

"I'm glad you're going to be part of the crew, Seichi!" said

Chastity cheerfully. Wanting to get things off to a friendly start, she pulled him over by their handshake, and touching his cheek with her long-nailed beflagged and bejeweled left hand, she gave him a peck on the other cheek. Seichi grinned widely in obvious pleasure and started to blush.

"I have read much about you, Miss Blaze," said Seichi eagerly, giving another bow. "You did the pioneering work on magnoshielded engines."

Rod turned to look at Chastity. "You did? I didn't know that," he said in surprise.

"I'm trying to forget it," replied Chastity grimly. "Just causes me ulcers. It was for my master's thesis. I came up with a design for an externally applied picket-fence magnetic field geometry that prevents a high-temperature plasma from reaching the walls of a reaction chamber or nozzle bell. That was in the days before meta. The only use for a magnoshielded engine at that time was handling the plasma from a fusion rocket, but no one had any good ideas for making a fusion rocket work—still don't. MIT didn't think it would be worth the money to patent the magnoshield concept, and I didn't have the money to do it myself. Two months later, a worldwide patent was filed in Japan under the first-to-file rule. What really jerks me is that large chunks of technical detail—even the drawings!—were taken directly from my thesis, which was available at the MIT library, but not yet published in the open literature."

"That doesn't sound fair . . ." said Rod.

"Fair or not, it's legal," said Chastity. "At least that's what the MIT lawyers said, pointing out that "improvements" had been made on my original ideas. There wasn't a damn thing I could do about it. How is one little person going to fight a big corporation like Mitsubishi?"

There was a long pause as Rod looked anxiously at Seichi. The pleased smile that had been on Seichi's face faded away.

"Seichi!" cried Chastity, concerned. "What's the matter?"

"Seichi is an employee of Mitsubishi," said Rod.

Chastity couldn't help herself—a frown flickered over her face. "What!?" she exclaimed angrily. She quickly tried to get herself under control. Certainly, Seichi would not have been involved in the piracy of her idea. But when Seichi saw the frown on her face and heard the angry tone in her voice, he stiffened and buckled himself back into the chair.

"It has been a pleasure meeting you, Miss Blaze," he said, swiveling away from them to face the console screen, "but Jeeves and I must now return to our task of checking out the reactor."

Chastity didn't know what to do or say next. She and Rod stayed silent and watched over Seichi's back at the holoviewport as Seichi's supple fingers played over the icons on the touchscreen. The image coming from the holoviewport was obviously not the direct view to the stars outside; instead, it was a close-up view of a cylinder about the size and shape of a large oil drum with a number of pipes and cables coming out of it. One end was connected through a flexible metal hose to another object about the same size, but instead of being a compact cylinder, this was obviously a rolled-up heat-pipe radiator array. Moving around among the plumbing was a small maintenance robot, looking like a metallic six-legged Manx cat with three-pronged flexible pincers for feet. It had the name TABBY painted on its back.

"Have Tabby remove the safety pin on the reactor controller, Jeeves," said Seichi.

"Very well, sir," said the voice persona of the ship's computer. The front paw of the robot reached for a metal rod with a red streamer attached to it and pulled it out of the cylinder. Seichi looked down at the display in the center of the touchscreen console in front of him. In the console display was a lower-resolution image of the view in the holoviewport, colored in the false colors of an infrared imager. Most of the image was in black and dark grays, except for the maintenance robot, which had a dark-red body and yellow leg-joints.

"Bring the reactor up to minimum level for checkout, Jeeves," said Seichi.

"How far away is that reactor?" whispered Chastity to Rod. "I don't see any shielding!"

"It doesn't have any shielding," said Rod. "But don't worry, Chass, the reactor is out in a compartment in that donut-shaped module, hundreds of meters away from us."

"Oh! Right . . ." said Chastity, now remembering the details of the briefing she had received on the nuclear reactor power supply. "That's far enough away for a checkout. When we get to Saturn, we'll be hanging a kilometer below it and the hydrogen in Saturn's atmosphere will do the shielding."

Slowly, as the three watched, the infrared image of the reactor on the touchscreen console changed color from black to gray to dark red.

"Radiation level nominal, sir," intoned the voice of Jeeves. "Generated electrical output power level within specifications."

"Start the pumps in the secondary cooling loops to the radiator," commanded Seichi. The rolled-up array of heat-pipe radiators now took on the dark-red glow as the outside of the reactor cooled down to a gray color again.

"That's as far as we can go with live testing, Jeeves," said Seichi. "Close it down and reinsert the safety pin." Seichi pointedly kept his back turned and his head down, staring fixedly at the infrared image screen and not turning around to talk to them. Rod coughed nervously during the hiatus while Chastity looked up at the ceiling. That was when she saw that something was missing.

"What's happened to the emergency escape hatch?" asked Chastity, pointing upward. "There's supposed to be a hatch here to let us out the nose in case the airlock malfunctions."

"The escape hatch in the nosecone was replaced with a tether reel," said Rod, glad that the subject had changed. He headed for the ladder. "Let's go outside again and I'll show you."

At the bottom of the ladder, the two astronauts entered the airlock, shut the inner door, turned their backs on each other, and started stripping down to get into their spacesuits again.

"I really goofed up there, didn't I," said Chastity, as she put her coveralls and underwear into her locker and reached for her cooljohns.

"Considering he's our scotty, you sure did," said Rod, repeating her motions. "Mitsubishi contributed the crew module and reactor to the consortium, so they got to pick one of their engineers as a crewmember. Seichi was the designer for the reactor—it's a specialized plutonium burner—and has spent the last six months getting briefed on the crew module so he can act as the ship's engineer."

"Plutonium burner?" queried Chastity, as she hooked up the plumbing inside her suit.

"According to Art, that's one of the reasons it makes financial sense to get meta from Saturn instead of overcoming the objections of the environmental freaks and extracting it from the natural gas wells. The Earth has an excess of plutonium, Japan especially. It would make sense to burn it in reactors to provide electrical power, but the antiwar, antinuclear, and green groups have made that politically impossible. So, Space Unlimited will be given all the plutonium it needs to provide the energy that will end up in the meta—and get paid to take it!—as long as the plutonium leaves the Earth and never comes back again."

"The radioactive waste is going to end up contaminating Saturn," said Chastity, hooking up her backpack. "I'm sure some planet-hugger is going to object to that."

"They already have," said Rod, closing his suit. "But Art just told the earth-huggers that they had a choice. Either convince the planet-huggers to shut up, or he was going to back out of the deal—and all that plutonium would be left on Earth. He got his way. The planet-huggers got something, however; they got to name the biologist for the crew."

"We have a greenie on the crew?" said Chastity, reaching for her helmet.

"Yep. Sandra Green. Apt name for her. She's a card-carrying member of the Peaceful Planet Protectors. Although there's a violent fringe group in the organization that has triggered off a number of 'peaceful' bombs, most of the members of the organization are reasonable people." Rod's voice now came over the suit-to-suit radio link.

"Ready," said Chastity through the link, not turning around.

"Me too," said Rod. They turned and headed for the controls to the outer airlock door. Chastity watched as the door lowered in front of them like a drawbridge. After the ship had landed on the surface of Luna or Mars, the open airlock door served as a useful platform when raising and lowering equipment. The cable supports to the top of the door acted as railings as they floated outside. They clipped their second safety lines to the cable and unclipped their first lines from the inside safety rings.

"Up we go," said Rod, pulling on the handholds up the side of the capsule. Chastity followed. At the top, Rod undid some latches and tipped over the nosecone portion of the ship on its hinge. The cone was a meter high and a meter in diameter at the base. A parachute was packed inside the cone. The shrouds of the parachute exited near the hinge into a channel that ran down the outside of the capsule. The one-meter-diameter hole revealed by removing the cone looked down onto a large reel of cable and a winding mechanism. One of Jeeves's mechbots was visible inside, its six paws clamped securely to a support post, waiting patiently for a command. The six-legged housecat-sized mechbot had the name MOUSER painted on its back.

"The reel and tether," said Rod. "Soon you'll be an expert in using it. Think of it as a reusable retrorocket with an unlimited supply of fuel."

Chastity commanded her suit to turn on her helmet light. Using the bright beam to illuminate the mechanisms below, she looked down.

"That tether looks mighty puny. Not even as thick as a clothesline."

"Isn't," said Rod. "Only a half-centimeter in diameter when collapsed, but it's made of the new hextube carbon polymer. Nothing but carbon-carbon bonds. It's also using the latest design in failsafe multiline Hoytether structures. It's so failsafe that it'll never need repair during its lifetime—which is a hundred years' worth of hits from micrometeorites and space junk. To prevent snags, the mechbot will clip off any cut strands each time the tether winds in. The first few kilometers are coated, to reduce chemical reactions with Saturn's atmosphere. We'll use that portion to hang the capsule under the balloon. The rest of the two hundred kilometers is bare, to cut down its weight. We'll use that part to climb down Saturn's rings."

"What are those long metal spikes racked up around the wall?" asked Chastity.

"Meta-propelled penetrators," said Rod. "When you want to make a temporary tether anchor to a passing rock or iceball."

Chastity commanded off her light and Rod tilted the nosecone back over the hatch and latched it. They returned to their Jet-Do and flew back to the Boeing-Mitsubishi Assembly Station.

"Using the tether is going to require some close teamwork between the capsule pilot and the tether operator," said Rod. "You and I are scheduled for a week or so on the tether whip simulator."

"I'm pilot, so I get to run the capsule rockets and you can run the tether," said Chastity.

"We're going to cross-train," said Rod. "At the end of the training, the testers will decide who is best at running what."

"Say, I just got back from a long trip to Mars. When do I get my vacation?"

"It'll have to wait. We leave in just four months."

"What's the hurry?"

"Launch window," said Rod. "We want to leave when the Earth's orbital velocity vector is pointing at Saturn—or at least where Saturn will be when we arrive one year later. That way we can take advantage of Earth's thirty-kilometers-a-second orbital speed."

"I see," said Chastity, understanding instantly. "If we miss that window then we have to wait a whole year to the next one."

"It's a pretty wide window. Shouldn't be any problem finding you a two-week vacation somewhere in there. The people that are going to get shortchanged are the two coming in from Mars. It's going to be especially tough on Dan Horning. He's got a wife and family on Earth that haven't seen him in almost a year."

". . . and we're going to be gone another two-and-a-half years. I wonder how she's taking it?"

"I'm sure glad I'm not married," said Rod with relief, as he started to slow down the Jet-Do with the front jets.

"I'd like to be," said Chastity, giving him a squeeze from behind. "But I'd never consider giving up my job, and it wouldn't be fair to my husband to be away all the time. Kids, of course, were something I had to give up thoughts of long ago. Those radiation resistance drugs they give us can repair tissue damage and keep cancers from spreading, but they can't repair the DNA damage in eggs."

"I've got a donation saved in a sperm bank," said Rod. "Good thing too . . . I must have logged over five thousand rems by now."

"Any takers yet?" teased Chastity.

"Almost," said Rod. "About five years ago."

"Prettier than me?"

"Impossible!" exclaimed Rod. "Besides, she wanted me to settle down to the Luna run so I would be home more often. That job's no better than being a bus driver." He paused. "So, when do you want to take your vacation? I need to schedule the simulator facility."

"It's more important that we cross-train," Chastity replied. "I'll just skip it."

"Don't you want to visit your folks?" asked Rod. "We won't be back on Earth again until three years from now."

"I don't have any 'folks' to visit," replied Chastity. "My dad still refuses to allow me to visit him and Mom. He kicked me out of the house when he caught me on a bench in the cemetery doing some heavy petting with a neighborhood boy—I had a bad case of 'minister's daughter' syndrome. I went to live with my Aunt Martha, but she died ten years ago."

"Oh . . ." said Rod. "Then, I guess we can start tomorrow."

Two months later, the two crewmembers who had been based on Mars—Sandra Green and Daniel Horning—finally arrived at Earth. They would have one month of leave on Earth, and then spend the last month living together in the crew capsule under simulated trip conditions, to make sure the members of the crew were compatible. Since they were all professional scientists, and four of them had been living in the close quarters of space habitats recently, no problems were anticipated, but if there was a serious incompatibility problem, it was important that they find out before they were committed to thirty months of living together.

After taking their vacation, Dan and Sandra met again on the shuttle that took them from Canaveral Spaceport up to the Boeing-Mitsubishi Assembly Station.

Doc had hardly seen Sandra on Mars, what with him being at the main base at the foot of Mount Olympus, while Sandra spent most of her time at Boreal Base looking for ancient frozen microscopic lifeforms in the polar ice field. The two had, however, worked together once over the medical emergency link on a nasty accident case. A technician had lost a forearm to the whipping end of a broken cable. Sandra had successfully stitched the arm back on under Dan's direction. He had gotten to know her better during their two-month journey back from Mars. Sandra was small and "pleasingly plump," with a cap of easily managed gray-flecked dark brown hair that Dan thought of as a "nurse's cut." Sandra was very bubbly and pleasant to live with, and was the life of the party at the weekly "socials" during the return journey, where everyone stopped working and gathered together for a special communal meal. Sandra was famous for her rum-flavored cinnamon rolls. Although she flirted a lot in social situations, she was usually reserved in her relationships with men, wanting to be treated as a professional colleague rather than merely as a person of the opposite sex.

"That month off certainly went fast, but I had the *greatest* time!" bubbled Sandra as they boarded the shuttle.

"What did you do?" asked Dan.

"Went on an expedition," said Sandra.

"Sounds like a busman's holiday," said Dan.

"I joined a team that was studying the whales in the Gulf of California. We think we have finally figured out how whales speak to each other, and this group wanted to check their theories by listening in as the mother whales taught the whale calves how to speak."

"Developing a dictionary of whale words?" asked Dan. "Do you mean that soon we'll have experts in whale language?"

"Not quite," said Sandra. "That was what held up research in cetacean communication so long. Whales don't use 'words' like humans do, so even the concept of a dictionary of whale words makes no sense. Although they use sound to communicate, they are capable of making many different sounds at the same time over a wide range, from clicks to groans to whistles. It seems that the sounds not only communicate concepts but feelings and relationships too. A very complex language, and we are only just beginning to understand it."

"Fascinating," said Dan.

"What did *you* do on your vacation?" asked Sandra, changing the subject.

"Spent time with the wife and kids," said Dan. "Took the kids out of high school and we all went to DisneyNation for a week. I told the principal the kids would learn some American history." The trip had been fun for the kids, but Dan and Pamela had argued most of the time. Although Pamela kept saying she didn't mind his going away on these long trips in space, she pouted and was unapproachable every time they were alone. Dan had done his best and fussed over her, spending much more than he had planned on the vacation, but Pamela liked fun and pretty things. Besides, he had told himself, what was the point of working so hard if it wasn't to spend the money on making his family happy?

After arrival at the Assembly Station, the two donned spacesuits, and they and their luggage were then taken out to the Saturn expedition vehicle by technicians driving Jet-Dos. After the lock cycled, the inner door opened and they were greeted by Rod and Chastity, waiting for them in the hexagonal-shaped lower facilities deck.

"Why don't you come inside with Rod for a while, Dr. Horning," said Chastity, motioning him inside, while she floated past him through the inner airlock door. "I'll help Sandra out of her suit and show her where to store her things."

"Let's drop that 'Dr. Horning' bit," said Dan. "Just think of me as 'Dan the plumber'—patching the pipes of personnel pods and people."

"Sure thing, Doc," said Chastity, as she traded places with him inside the airlock and shut the airlock door behind her so Sandra could get out of her suit in some semblance of privacy.

"Your locker is here," said Chastity, opening one of the six identical doors fitted into the corner of the airlock. "It's got a jumpsuit, boots, and a set of standard underwear—all in your size. And this is where you hang your suit." She put Sandra's helmet into its holder and turned to help her with the suit plumbing.

"I think I would prefer my own clothing," said Sandra, reaching for the large duffel bag she had hauled along. Chastity kept herself busy checking out Sandra's suit and hanging it up while Sandra got out of her cooljohns and got dressed. When Chastity turned around again, she saw that instead of a jumpsuit, Sandra was dressed in gray slacks and a white silk blouse tied at the throat. She looked very nice, very feminine, and very efficient at the same time.

As Sandra and Chastity changed places with Rod and Dan, Chastity saw that Seichi was talking with the two men. The minute Seichi saw Chastity appear, he excused himself, and turning away to the galley across the room, started to make himself a cup of tea. Chastity felt frustrated. Somehow, ever since their initial poor start, Seichi had managed to avoid coming into direct contact with her despite the close confines of the crew capsule. She desperately wanted to make friends, but she couldn't bring herself to just apologize— after all, she was the one who had been wronged.

"Seichi!" called Chastity to his turning back. "I'd like to introduce you to our crewmate, Sandra Green . . ."

Seichi turned, and avoiding Chastity's eyes, greeted Sandra with a free-fall bow.

"*Yoroshiku onegaishimasu*—pleased to meet you, Ms. Green. I must go now to my station." Leaving the two women and his tea behind, he pulled himself up the ladder where he took up the position at the engineering console in one apex of the triangular control deck.

Sandra gave Chastity a querying look.

"It's not you," said Chastity with disgust. "It's me. He thinks I'm mad at him, so he's been avoiding me. I'm not, though, really . . ." Sandra let it pass, so Chastity changed the subject. "There's a couple of things I need to explain to you, now that you are living in crew quarters instead of passenger quarters," she said. "When you came in on the passenger modules from Mars, you were traveling first class—crew quarters is like living in steerage. First thing is the toilets . . ." She pointed to the two narrow doors.

"Which one is the ladies'?" asked Sandra.

"Either . . . or neither . . ." replied Chastity. "First come, first served."

"I can get used to that . . ." said Sandra bravely.

"Normally, however, there is an unwritten rule that the men try to use the right-hand one first, leaving the left-hand one for the ladies." Chastity opened the left of the two small doors and ushered Sandra inside. She then stood in back of her to point out things inside.

"The shower stall is behind that watertight door. The washbowl is folded up into the wall there, to give you some dressing room. The urinal tube is there, with your own personalized cup in the compartment above it with your name on it . . . and that," she said, pointing, "is the dreaded zero-gee toilet."

"It certainly doesn't look like the toilets in the Mars passenger modules," said Sandra apprehensively.

"The passenger modules on the Mars rotate to provide a permanent quarter-gee artificial gravity," said Chastity. "So the passenger toilets are very much like airline toilets. *These* are designed so they will function with the gravity pointing in any direction including zero gee." Chastity reached over Sandra's shoulder and pulled on the back of the toilet. The whole toilet easily swung forward—rotating bodily on a pivot hidden in the wall.

Sandra's nose wrinkled. "I've heard about the problems with those zero-gee toilets . . ." she said, but then the biologist in her recognized something wrong. "Zero gee?" she said. "We can't be traveling to Saturn in zero gee. Although we've medicines to counteract radiation damage during long space journeys, we've yet to find a medicine that will prevent deterioration of the bones and vascular system from the lack of gravity."

"I know," said Chastity. "That's why the passenger module on a Mars liner separates into three compartments that extend out from the central passway. That way, just a slight amount of rotation gives a quarter-gee in the passenger module without a lot of Coriolis. The full-time quarter-gee is just enough to keep the body from breaking down, and it's also what keeps the toilets simple in the passenger module. That's also why passenger habitats mass so much. But we do things differently on a cargo run to keep the habitat mass down. Most of the time we fly along in zero gee. But once a day, in the morning, we put the capsule on slow spin to give a tenth-gee at the positions of the toilets. The Coriolis forces are nasty at these short radii, so some of us stay in bed and wait it out, while the others take their turns at the toilet. Then, after everyone is ready, we up the spin rate and do one-gee exercises for an hour to keep our bones healthy. During rotation the gravity force is toward the wall. When the capsule is sitting on Luna or Mars, the gravity force is toward the deck. The toilets *can* also work at zero gee, but they are best used at finite gees."

"What happens if you need to go when the capsule is in free fall?"

"I would recommend clinching your butt," said Chastity. "For the alternative is worse." She sighed. "But sometimes, 'when you gotta go . . . you gotta go.' So, open the door to the shower stall and step inside out of the way, while I come in and go through the motions so you can see how it's done." Sandra obediently scrambled into the shower. With a grimace, Chastity pulled the outer door shut behind her and stepped into the toilet area.

"That was most enlightening," said Sandra as the two exited the toilet. "You are right, clinching *is* the easier way out. I shall train myself for the morning elimination period."

"I'll take the evening," said Chastity.

They were both surprised to see that three of the men, Seichi, Rod, and Pete, were all congregated down in the lower deck. With the aluminum tube taking up a third of the floor area, the facilities deck was crowded with the five of them in it. As usual, Seichi was keeping out of the way of Chastity. As soon as she appeared, he activated the inner airlock door.

"I will make more room," he said, entering the airlock. Although he didn't need to, he closed the inner airlock door again.

Chastity wistfully turned back from watching Seichi avoid her again. The hurt look on her face changed as she glanced at Rod and

Pete. The two looked uncomfortable, and it wasn't because of her problems with Seichi. There was a loud voice coming from the control deck above.

". . . I've only been gone four days! How could you have spent ten million dollars in four days! That's my pay for a whole month! . . ."

"Dan had a call from his wife," said Rod, "so we came down to give him some privacy."

Dan tried to keep his voice down, but it still carried through the open grating from above.

"Pammy . . . please don't pout . . . Yes, I know I'm worth a billion dollars . . . but they are only paying me ten million a month while I'm on the mission . . . I get the rest when I return . . ." There was a long pause. ". . . Yes, it was nice of you to think of me . . . and I'm sure I will appreciate having a nice house on the Riviera . . . but it *could* have waited until I got back . . . Honey! Please don't be mad . . . I do *too* love you sweetums . . . and I'll tell you more about how much I love you once we get our habitats set up and I have some privacy. I hear someone coming . . . Gotta go now . . . Bye . . ." There was a heavy sigh.

Rod spoke up to break the strained silence that followed, his voice surprising him with its loudness in the reverberating confines of the capsule. "It's time to set up the habitats!" he said, giving the aluminum tube beside him a bang with his knuckles. The cylinder rang like a bell at the blow. "Seichi! Get out the checklist and take us through the procedure." Seichi exited the airlock, and avoiding Chastity's eye, went over to the engineering compartment and opened a hatch. He took out a checklist, a three-pronged holding fixture, and a tube of lubraseal.

"Remove grating between upper and lower compartments and store in the airlock . . ." he started, reading the first item on the checklist. The red square on the plastic sheet turned green as he pressed it. Dan, being above them, loosened the grating segments and passed them down to Rod and Pete, who passed them to Sandra and Chastity, who stored them in the back of the airlock.

"Remove console seats and store in the airlock . . ." continued Seichi. Soon the three console seats and their swivel arms had been removed from in front of the consoles and also placed in the airlock. Rod, having been through this routine many times before, took the three-pronged holding fixture from Seichi, and floated up to the upper deck to join Dan. With the console chairs gone, there was now a surprisingly large amount of room.

"Insert holding fixture inside inner habitat tube and turn central knob on fixture until it is firmly grasping the inner tube wall . . ." read Seichi. Reaching down from the upper deck, Rod inserted the fixture inside the aluminum tube on the lower deck and turned the knob. He was slowly lifting the massive tube as Seichi read the next instruction.

"Slowly remove the inner habitat tube . . ."

"The smallest one goes under the pilot console," Chastity reminded Rod, as she had gone through this routine many times too. Dan reached under the pilot console and removed a cover ring around the viewport window there and passed it down to Chastity to add to the stuff stored in the airlock.

"I see," said Sandra, watching things from inside the airlock. "The six habitat tubes are stacked one inside another."

"This is one time we discriminate among crewmembers," said Chastity. "The big ones get the big-diameter habitat tubes and the little ones get the smaller tubes. You're the shortest, Sandra, so that'll be your tube."

"*Shitsurei shimasu* . . . excuse me, Ms. Blaze," said Seichi, speaking directly to Chastity for the first time since their unfortunate initial meeting. His face was controlled and devoid of emotion as he explained his objection. "The smallest habitat tube is properly mine, for it is sufficient for my purposes, and I am sure that Ms. Green would appreciate more room."

"You are a true gentleman, Seichi," replied Chastity with a bright smile, seeing her chance to open up dialogue with him again. There was a flicker of response in Seichi's eyes, but then the curtain fell and he turned back to the task at hand.

"Easy does it," said Rod, as Dan moved to help him extract the smallest inner tube from the stack. "Don't nick the seals. That tube masses eighty-five kilos and with that much inertia, it can get out of control if you let it build up too much speed." The two got the cylinder out—it reached almost to the top of the control deck. Chastity pulled herself up the ladder, and locking herself in place on the rungs of the ladder with her knees and ankles, added her muscular strength to the task of moving the tube horizontal so one end was pointing toward the viewport window underneath the pilot console. While the three held the massive but weightless habitat tube in place and rotated it, Seichi applied lubraseal to the elastomer seals at both ends of the tube and the ring seal around the viewport window.

"Insert inner tube into sealing ring around smallest viewport window . . ." continued Seichi. With Seichi, Pete, and Chastity making sure the tube didn't tilt, Rod and Dan braced their feet against the opposite wall and pushed the tube into the ring seal. There was a series of loud clicks as latches grasped the ends of the habitat tube, connecting the tube firmly to the viewport window frame.

"Check seals for gas leaks . . ." said Seichi. He raised his voice slightly and changed to a command tone. "Jeeves. Have Kitty and Puss check seals for leaks." The computer's inside mechbot, Puss, scurried over the ceiling, around and down under the console and around the ring seal, then returned to its nest in one of the electronics compartments. The outside mechbot, Kitty, could be heard clicking its way along the outer hull, carrying out a similar check.

"No leaks observed in viewport seal," reported Jeeves.

"Push habitat into seal ring until fully seated . . ." read Seichi. Rod and Dan pushed harder, and slowly the habitat tube slid into place until the end seal was flush with the holding bracket. Where there had once been a window, there was now a two-meter-long, ninety-centimeter-diameter bedroom, with a window at the outer space–facing end and a soundproof hatchdoor at the inside end, ready to be "furnished" by its owner.

Soon the second habitat tube was in place. It was five centimeters larger than the smallest habitat, and Sandra could hardly wait to try it out.

"I'll pop into mine and get out of the way," she said, leaving the hatchdoor open so she could look out and see the activity as the rest of the habitat tubes were put into place.

"Say . . . this is roomy," she reported hollowly, some time later. "I can even sit up in here. That'll make it easy getting dressed."

"I've heard these habitats can hold three in a pinch," said Pete.

"That's about all you can do in them with three," said Rod. "I've heard two is more fun."

"Don't listen to them, Sandra," said Chastity. "Once you get the bedding in there, one is enough."

Soon all six habitats were installed, and despite Chastity's protests, she was given the largest one, 115 centimeters in diameter. The smooth outlines of the conically shaped crew capsule now bristled with six cylinders jutting out parallel to the base of the cone, the six "teeth" in *Sexdent*. Since the viewport that now formed the outside end of the habitat tube had once been set in the side of the conical spacecraft, it was set at a thirty-degree angle to the tube and was elliptical in shape. The fixture that held the viewport window to the end of the habitat tube could be rotated by a powered worm gear, so the occupant could not only look out, but look forward, aft, or to the side by merely activating the window control. Most of the crew went to sleep with their heads under the viewport, looking up at the stars. Rod and Chastity, having seen those views many times before, would sleep with their heads inward. In an emergency, they could be out the hatchdoor and into action instantly. Dan, however, turned his viewport down, so he could watch the Earth roll by underneath, watching the lights of Houston pass under, trying to determine which of those pinpricks of light was from the security floodlights illuminating the lawn of his home—with Pamela and the kids asleep inside. He even looked for his new vacation home on the Riviera, but he realized that he didn't know where the Riviera was, and by the time Jeeves had given him directions on how to find the location, it had passed over the horizon. He was asleep when it came by the next time—dreaming about winning the Solar Lottery. *Finally*, he would have enough money to satisfy Pamela. . . .

Chastity was the last one to use the bathrooms. She had taken advantage of the freedom of free fall and the luxury of unrushed time with no one waiting, and had given herself a complete spray-sponge scrubdown and pedicure. Glowing pink, she exited in her blue nightgown with the elastic band that kept the hem primly at her ankles. Springing lightly from her toes, she floated slowly up the ladder—guiding her way with her fingertips—to the top deck. Everyone was in their habitats, hatchdoors closed for the night.

"Dim the lights, please, Jeeves," she said, and the control deck turned dark except for the emergency alarm switch at the pilot's console. The ship passed over the terminator into the Earth's shadow and the stars came out. Chastity drifted over to the engineering console to look out for a while at the stars before going to bed. As her eyes adjusted to the darkness, so she could see fainter and fainter stars, her mind wandered back to the idyllic summer vacation evenings she had enjoyed when she was a young girl. She would climb out of her ground-floor bedroom window and leave the manse to wander next door into the cemetery of the country Baptist church that her father served. There she would lie on one of the wooden benches beside the path so she could look up at the stars and search for the planets.

She had dreamed, then, of somehow getting away from the tiny stultifying Idaho town she had been born in and going out in the world to see new and strange places, perhaps even going to the stars. Although she hadn't made it to the stars—yet—she had certainly seen new and strange places. Soon she would visit an even stranger place.

As she mused in the darkness and silence, eyes taking in the splendor of the night sky, she heard the faint sound of music. It was majestic in tone and matched the majestic beauty outside the viewport. At first, she thought that her brain was just recalling some music that she had heard in the past. But as she moved her head back and forth, she realized that it was her *ears* that were picking up the sound. It was coming from below. She pulled herself down to the grating floor, and grasping the slots in the grate with her fingers, slowly turned herself around in a circle until she located the source. It was coming from one of the habitats. In the darkness, she wasn't quite sure who it belonged to. She pulled herself over and put her ear to the habitat hatch. The music was definitely coming from this compartment. Then she finally recognized the melody. It was the "Saturn" movement from Holst's *The Planets*.

She tapped softly on the hatchdoor. The music stopped and the hatchdoor swung up. Inside was Seichi, lying on his back, bed strap over his chest. He turned on his side to look at her better, and his face grew solemn and distant as he recognized who it was.

"That was beautiful!" exclaimed Chastity softly. She looked past his head to see that he had an electronic keyboard up against his knees. "You were playing it! It sounded like an orchestra. You're wonderful!"

"Not so wonderful," said Seichi, and despite his attempts to remain distant, he began to blush at the compliment. "I only placed eighth in the Yamaha Keyboard International Competition, so I went into engineering. I'm sorry my music disturbed you. I will turn down the volume." He reached for the hatchdoor, but Chastity didn't pull her head back.

"But I want to hear more! Will you play for me?" she asked.

Seichi hesitated.

"Please?" she pleaded, reaching in her bejeweled hand to stroke his cheek with her star-spangled nails.

"I might disturb the others."

Chastity turned herself around above the grating floor, and slid feet-first into Seichi's habitat tube.

"I'll come inside then," she said, snuggling down next to him and pulling the hatchdoor closed behind her.

A few weeks later, it was time to leave. The crew had stacked away the habitats in the lower deck, and had rearranged their bedframes and cushions in a circle on the control deck floor where they would act as cushioned acceleration couches for the takeoff. Rod, Chastity, and Seichi, separated by 120 degrees around the circle, were each lying on their respective couches, looking up at one of the three holoviewports. Since they would be controlling and monitoring the ship during the takeoff, they had touchscreen consoles suspended above them by pantograph arms that came out of the side of the conical walls of the command deck. The three "passengers," Sandra, Dan, and Pete, were strapped into their acceleration couches between the other three. The six now looked upward at the three large holoviewports, each of which contained an image of Art Dooley and the crew at Space Unlimited's Mission Control Center who would be providing technical support for them up on their long journey to Saturn and back again. There were only three continuously staffed consoles at Mission Control Center for this mission: crew communications, vehicle telemetry, and science data handling. A large group of backup people were present today in the Control Center to witness the takeoff; some were at consoles, ready to monitor the takeoff itself, while the rest, who would be standing shift during the mission or who would be called in during the Saturn phase, were standing in the background to say good-bye. Even the observing gallery, normally empty, was crammed with newstapers and inquisitive members of the public.

"I wish I were going with you," started Art. "I've always wanted to go into space, ever since I was a little kid. The closest I've gotten is getting to say good-bye to people like you, whom I've arranged to send into space."

"Why?" asked Sandra, a little puzzled. "Certainly you could have *sometime* afforded to take a weekend trip to one of the Earth orbit hotels."

"Claustrophobia," replied Art, grimly. "My brother rolled me up in a rug when we were kids and wouldn't let me out. Now, even the passenger modules on the Mars liner have walls that are too close for comfort. If you six can show that we can convert Saturn helium into meta, and cut the cost of meta fuel in space to a fraction of its present cost, then it would finally be economically feasible to build passenger spacecraft to Luna and Mars with large staterooms in them. *They* would be big enough so I too could go into space."

The head of the science group standing in the background spoke to Sandra. "We know there's life on Saturn. The last few reentry probes NASA sent into Saturn returned distant pictures of a number of different creatures living in the upper atmosphere; we only have good pictures of one of them, a bubble-shaped floater, Latin name *Bulla volitare,* hundreds of meters in diameter. Being that large, it *must* be on the top of the food chain, feeding on the smaller species. Do your best to find them. Every bit we learn about the different types of lifeforms that exist on Saturn will help us in understanding our lifeforms here on Earth."

"I will," promised Sandra. "I'll get good pictures for sure, and perhaps bring back some samples. We'll be in the clouds for six months. I should be able to snare something in the nets I'm taking a—"

An agitated young man in the observing gallery interrupted her. "And make sure you determine the intelligence level of the Bubble People of Saturn. If they are intelligent, then the Peaceful Planet Protectors will *demand* that Space Unlimited terminate its plans to exploit the resources of Saturn, for they *belong* to the Bubble People."

"Don't worry, Jerry," replied Sandra, reassuringly. "I'll do my best. Don't forget, I'm a member of Triple-P myself. I doubt, however, that something that is as simple in structure as a large jellyfish is going to have any measurable level of intelligence. *Bulla volitare* is certainly a new species of animal, but I doubt it is an animal species smart enough to be called a 'People.' "

The CrewComm spoke to Rod. "Take care. Once you've escaped Earth, you'll be pretty much on your own. The round-trip communication time delay will soon become so long that any attempts on our part to run the mission or solve problems from a distance wouldn't make sense, since we have equally qualified and intelligent people, *you*, right there where the time delay is zero. You also have one of the world's best flight computers in Jeeves. We didn't skimp on his trajectory analysis programs and specialized parallel processing chips. He can calculate trajectories as accurately and as fast as our computers here can, *plus* give you the results instantly—instead of you having to wait an hour or two."

A chime rang and a countdown clock started on the upper right of Rod's screen. "Time to go," said Rod. "See you in thirty months." He turned and spoke over Dan, who was lying next to him. "All yours Chass," he commanded.

Chastity pulled down the pilot console a little, locked the pantograph arm that held it in place above her middle, and reached her right hand into a hand-sized compartment under the console touchscreen. Her trim-nailed fingers closed softly around the "joyball" floating in the middle of the compartment, suspended by magnetic fields generated by the highly sensitive sensing and feedback circuits. Twisting or pulling the joyball slightly would cause the attitude control jets on *Sexdent* to rotate or translate the ship, while lifting the ball forcefully upward would cause the main engines to fire, accelerating them forcefully ahead. When the countdown clock reached zero, she lifted up firmly on the joyball. The twelve main engines roared into life and they sank into the acceleration cushions behind their backs.

They left Earth when the thirty-kilometer-per-second velocity vector of the Earth was pointing to where Saturn would be a year later. The one thousand tons of meta in the booster tank boosted *Sexdent* away from Earth, adding another twenty-six kilometers per second. Now moving at fifty-six kilometers per second, they started their year-long climb out of the Sun's gravity well. The booster stage separated and used the last of its meta to deflect itself away from their course. The booster's next destination was interstellar space. *Sexdent*, its mass now less than half of what it was when she started, settled into its almost straight-line trajectory toward the ringed planet.

For the crew inside *Sexdent,* it was time to reinstall their habitats, which had been pulled back inside and stored for the duration of the three-gee boost phase. With plenty of large, heavily muscled crewmembers to heave and shove the bulky habitat tubes around, Sandra found she was more in the way than being of assistance. So, as soon as her habitat tube was installed, she stuffed her bedding and personal belongings ahead of her into the empty tube like a hamster remaking its bed and followed them inside to organize things in the comfy arrangement she had grown used to.

The bedboard frame attached by pinrods to holes in the wall of the tube. The frame was segmented and hinged, so that by raising a segment of the bedframe by the edge, one could gain access to the storage area formed underneath by the curved tube wall and the flat bedboard lid. Into other holes in the "ceiling" of the tubular habitat were plugged reading lights, personal computer consoles, squeezer holders, artistic decorations, and other necessities for making life comfortable in the aerospace equivalent of a sewer pipe, the holes supplying power and communication links as well as physical support.

Sandra finally finished laying away her clothing and other personal belongings under the lids of the bed. She could still hear the swearing and clanks of the habitat installation crew going on outside, so she stayed inside until they were done. She folded her console up against the ceiling and turned herself around in the tube so that her head was hanging over the "foot" of the bed where she could see out of the large slanted viewport window. The viewport was facing rearward and she looked "down" at the rapidly disappearing Earth-Luna system. They had passed the orbit of the moon only four hours after takeoff. They were now nearly eight hours into their journey and the Earth-Luna system was beginning to take on the familiar aspect that she had become used to on Mars. The two globes of the double planet were in half-moon phase because of their takeoff direction.

When she was a child, she had thought the Earth was flat, and made of "earth," while the Moon was a bright globe made of silver. Now, as a space traveler, she knew the Earth to be a globe covered with water and clouds, with an occasional splotch of "earth," while Luna was a globe covered with gray dust. When she looked at them both from a distance, especially during her travels to Mars, she also began to realize that the globes of Earth and Luna were not the typical "big planet with tiny moons" system typified by Mars, Jupiter, and the outer planets. Because Luna was comparable in size to its primary, the two really were more of a "double-planet" system, or perhaps a "mother-child" system.

The glaring orb of the Sun started to intrude through her viewport, so she found the window controls and rotated the viewport so that it was facing in the direction they were going. Ahead of them was Saturn, racing along in its orbit to meet them at the designated rendezvous point a year later. Sandra reached up into the tight corner formed by one end of the elliptical viewport window and the pointed end of the habitat, and pulled down the binocular viewer on the end of its pantograph arm. Setting the biviewer for "visual" and "motion compensation," she raised it to her eyes.

"There are strange lifeforms there . . ." she whispered to herself as the brilliant globe-and-halo swam into her ken. "And I'm going to see them. . . ."

Reentry probes dropped into Saturn over the past decade had sent back a few poorly resolved pictures of floating and flying lifeforms swimming in the thick air beneath the clouds of Saturn— "saganlife" some called them.

When the first lifeform pictures were returned, the scientific community had exploded with excitement. Even Sandra had been sure the discovery of life elsewhere in the solar system would reactivate the scientific exploration of the outer planets, leading to the establishment of crewed stations around each of the major planets and on the surface of the major moons. But when the politicians began to reckon the cost, and the scientists could promise nothing in return but better biological insight, no intelligent advanced technological species that would have new or different technological know-how that would pay back the massive investment that would be needed, then the dreams of crewed deep space stations evaporated, and the scientists had to be satisfied with the funding for a few more reentry probes.

Now, because of the needs of commerce, not the needs of science, there were going to be crewed space stations on and around at least one of the outer planets. There was room and need for a biologist on the first of those, and Sandra had been the lucky one chosen. She would be the first biologist to study these new lifeforms first-hand. With any luck, and the fishing nets she had arranged to have stored in the ship supplies, she would hopefully obtain a few specimens to bring back. She could hardly wait to get there. . . .

"For the first time, someone will be able to stay long enough to do a thorough job of finding and describing these air creatures." She, being the biologist who would find and describe them, would also have the privilege of naming all the new species that she found. "It'll be like starting over in the garden of Eden . . . getting to name all the creatures, one by one. I wonder what new and marvelous creatures I'll find there?"

Sandra released the biviewer so the pantograph could retract it back. She crawled under the restraint straps over her bed, and stretching her neck, nestled her head into its protective niche in the head-restraint pillow. Grasping the bedding restraints on each side of her with both hands, she closed her eyes and went to sleep, oblivious to the talk of the crew outside, to dream of meeting strange new creatures on strange new worlds.

Petra finished her climb with the rest of the flock. They had risen far into the sky during the long climb upward in the darkness. Bright was rising in the east and its warming light was streaming down through a break in the cloud layers above. That didn't happen very often and the flock circled in the beam of light, enjoying the warmth, singing gossip back and forth to each other. Petra could feel Petru's air sacs expand in the warmth. With the additional buoyancy of Petru's body, she could gain even more altitude for Petro, so she had Petru swallow another mouthful of bitterly cold rarefied air, and tilting the wings upward, she jetted Petru higher into the sky, the rest of the flock following along behind, maws opening and closing to feed the pulsing jets that drove them ever higher. As Petru climbed, Petra raised her head and gazed upward at Bright. Petra's large eye could see the flock of smaller lights that circled around the distant glowing sphere of warmth. She could easily see the larger red globe, Rexu, and the smaller red globe, Talu, that circled Bright at great distances. She knew there were three other globes closer to Bright, but usually they were so close they could not be seen through the glare. She raised a claw in front of her eye to block out the light from Bright and was rewarded for the effort by being able to observe two small bright spots close together—a larger blue-white light and a smaller gray light. It was Parent-and-Child. They must be at their farthest excursion from Bright, since the two globes were well separated from the glaring orb and were in their half-moon phase.

Petra knew that Rexu, Talu, Parent-and-Child, and the others must be globes, like the world Air that she lived on. Ancient long-dead elders of the flock had determined many dimmings ago that Air was a globe by reasoning its shape from the shadow Air cast on the rings of Arc. There was even a tale passed from flock to flock of one ancient and reckless young ruus that had left its flock flying east and had managed to fly all around Air, returning to the flock from the west, proving Air was round.

Although the smaller of the moons around Air were not globular, the larger ones were, and the illumination of Bright on the globular moons went through phases. The ancients had reasoned that since the lights circling Bright went through the same phases, they also must be globes. The globes were obviously far away, so they must be large compared to the moons of Air, perhaps even as large as Air itself.

"I wonder . . ." thought Petra.

"Wonder what?" replied Petro through their thinklink. Petro had woken early because the break in the clouds had let the light of Bright in early. He had remained aloof in his head, however, letting Petra control Petru, while he watched what was going on down below them.

"I wonder if there are creatures like us on the globes of light around Bright," said Petra back through the thinklink.

"If they are good to eat and we could catch them, then it might be worthwhile bothering to think about them," said Petro. "But since we can't fly there, then they aren't worth thinking about. Petru is cold and hungry, and I am ready to hunt. You have given Petru good altitude, so the hunting should be good. We will talk more when Petru is full and warm. Time for me to take over and you to rest. . . ."

Petra released Petru so Petro could take control of the giant body they shared. She crawled under the restraint feathers over her resting notch, and compressing her neck, nestled her head into its

2

CLIMBING DOWN THE RINGS

GOOD MORNING!"

The voice of Jeeves echoed loudly in the habitats. "Please awaken and lower your foot platforms. Rotational acceleration will commence in five minutes."

Pete groaned, and with his eyes still firmly shut, pulled his legs out from under the leg restraint band. Tucking his toes under the sides of the bed, he lifted the bottom quarter of the bed up on its hinge until the square panel was blocking the bottom end of the habitat. He then drifted back into sleep, to be awakened again when he felt his body slipping down the bed and his feet contacted the "floor" of his now "vertical" habitat. The first half hour of each day was spent spinning at six rpm, which produced a quarter of a gee in the habitats and a tenth of a gee in the toilets. Pete, eyes still closed, stood up on the panel and took off his pajamas. Pulling open the second of the cushioned panels on his now-vertical bed, he felt inside for a roll of clothing, and pulling it out, filled the hole left with the pajamas. In a series of motions that had become almost an unconscious habit, he donned his underwear, jumpsuit, and capsule socks with their sticky-patch bottoms. Back braced against the now vertically oriented "ceiling" of the habitat tube, and sock bottoms gripping the fabric of the cushioned bed, he chimneyed himself up to the top of the habitat tube, the downward pull getting noticeably weaker as he did so. By the time he had lifted the hatch, opened his eyes, and pushed protective niche in Petra's prow. Grasping the restraining feathers on each side of her with the myriad of claws along her neck, she closed her eye and went to sleep, oblivious to the talk of the flock nearby, to dream of meeting strange new creatures on strange new worlds.

his way into the near free fall of the control deck, he was wide awake.

After more than three months of living in close quarters with each other, the six members of the crew of *Sexdent* had developed a series of patterned behaviors that minimized the conflict of the crew, especially during the early morning. Pete, who hated to get up, was always the last one out of the habitats. He looked around at the hatchdoors. Rod's and Sandra's were closed. They were always the first ones up and had already been to the toilets in their nightwear and were back in their habitats getting dressed. As Pete started to crawl down the wall to the facilities deck, Seichi and Chastity crawled up the wall above him, Seichi in his kimono, and Chastity in her pale blue nightgown with the elastic ankle band. Pete knew that Doc would be in the "gentlemen's" toilet, which was confirmed by the green light on the "ladies' " toilet, so, as he had done practically every day in the past year, he opened the door to the ladies' and dropped in. He took a quick look at his wrist computer. He'd better hurry. Jeeves would be increasing the capsule rotation shortly.

Fifteen minutes later, everyone was back in their habitats, removing their exercise equipment from the cavity that had been exposed when the bottom panel on their bed had been lowered to make the floor of their habitat. Dual-purpose pieces of equipment, which in real life were spare parts for the life support systems, were called into play as "steps" and "weights" for their daily high-gee exercises. When Jeeves was sure that all were in their habitats and ready, the differential motor around the rotational joint that connected the crew capsule to the fuel module was energized again, and the rotation increased from six rpm to seventeen rpm. A chorus of groans arose from the open habitat hatches and mingled together on the control deck as the gee level in the habitats grew. The pull at the midsection of the habitats was now Earth-normal one gee, while the feet of the crew were at four-thirds gees and their heads were at two-thirds of a gee.

"Right step . . . back down . . . Left step . . . back down . . ." intoned Jeeves, taking them through the hour of daily exercises that would keep their bodies from deteriorating in the free fall of space.

Later that morning, over their communal breakfasts of microwaved fruit tarts and coffee, Rod made an announcement.

"Today, Saturn is in opposition—on the opposite side of the sky from the Sun—which means that the Earth is as close to Saturn as it's going to get this year—nine AU from Saturn and two AU from us. From now on, as Earth continues in its orbit, it's going to be moving away from us instead of moving toward us, so the round-trip communication time delay is going to start rapidly increasing from its present half-hour."

Dan winced inwardly a little at that news. Pamela was already upset about having to wait so long between her question or complaint and Dan's reply. He was rapidly losing control of the situation at home.

Six months passed. The Earth was now on the opposite side of the Sun from Saturn and *Sexdent*. With the Sun in the way, messages back to Earth had to take a dogleg around the Sun by way of Mars, which added to the round-trip communication delay, making it more than two hours. This was especially hard on Dan.

Pamela and the kids would normally call during breakfast from their home in Houston, telling him about what they did the day before and what they were planning for that day. He would get that message in mid-afternoon, since *Sexdent* was on Zulu Time. He would reply with a message for Pamela about family business, which she would get during her lunchtime. Her reply would come back early in his evening. He would conclude with a message to her and the kids about his day—which they would listen to around the dinner table. They didn't bother to reply to him then, because their reply would have arrived after he had gone to bed, so they waited until the breakfast session. With the family living the life of millionaires, Junior got a new "Tasmanian Devil" sports car for Christmas, while Helen got her own limousine and a chauffeur to drive it.

"I don't like the sound of that," said Dan, when he heard about the chauffeur. He trusted his daughter, but . . . He was relieved when the picture of the chauffeur came back. Instead of the young stud that Dan had envisioned, the chauffeur was a matron who looked like her last job was as bailiff in the Criminal Court Building.

The months continued on, with everyone finding their own ways to pass the time. Rod was using the large holoviewport at the pilot's con-

sole to get the full effect of the visuals on the fifty-first level of
WARPWORLD, when he sensed a warm presence behind his head.
He froze the action on the game and turned around. Chastity was
behind him. Her jumpsuit zipper was at half-mast.

"Just watching . . ." said Chastity, smiling cheerfully through lips
glistening with recently applied lipstick. "You sure are a good WARP-
WORLD pilot."

Normally, seeing that much of Chastity would cause Rod to shut
the game down and pay attention to her, but Rod had gone through
enough "slam-bam, thank you, sir" experiences with Chastity in the
past few months. He had tried to get romantic and stretch things out,
but she always wanted to get right down to business. He just smiled
back at her, then turned and continued his game. After a while she
left. Later she and Pete disappeared into her habitat tube. Knowing
what was going on in the tube changed Rod's mood, and he saved
the game before he got careless and got himself killed. He headed
for the ladder and climbed down to the galley to refill his coffee
squeezer. As his head came level with the habitat hatches, he noticed
that Sandra's hatch was open and she was inside, reading a novel. His
eye noticed a short line on her screen that ended in an exclamation
point.

"Colonel Montrose!"

After getting his coffee, Rod activated the ship's library program.
Knowing that Jeeves would not tell him what books Sandra had
asked for from the library, he had Jeeves search through all the novels for "Colonel Montrose!" It didn't take long for Jeeves to find it.
It was a trashy romance novel set in the Civil War period. Rod
skipped through the boring beginnings and got to the bodice-ripping
part. . . .

*It was a frosty winter's night in northern Virginia. Ruby Dar-
lington entered her bedroom carrying a candle, closing the door behind her to block out the loud voices of the Yankee officers quartered
in her mansion—enjoying the port from the cellars. The servants had
a small fire going in her bedroom fireplace. Standing in the shadows
beside the fireplace was a tall figure.*

"The woods are full of Yankees tonight," said the figure.

"Colonel Montrose!"

The tall figure in the gray uniform stepped into the firelight.

"Excuse me for intruding, Miss Ruby. But I had to see you once again before I head south to take up my new command . . ."

There was a commotion downstairs. Ruby cracked her bedroom door and listened.

"A Confederate spy has been seen entering the premises. Search the house!"

"I must go," said Montrose, putting on his hat and heading for the window.

"Wait!" said Ruby with a restraining hand. "There is one place even a Yankee is gentleman enough not to search." She pointed to her curtained bed and he headed for it. Quickly stripping off her dress and undergarments, Ruby slipped into her nightgown and climbed through the bed curtains to await the arrival of the searcher.

Rod started memorizing his lines.

That evening after dinner Rod got Sandra aside.

"The woods are full of Yankees tonight . . ." he started.

Sandra's eyes widened in surprise. At first, Rod thought that perhaps he had overstepped his bounds.

"Excuse me for intruding, Miss Ruby . . ." He started to back away, but Sandra restrained him with a hand. Her face broke into a pleased smile and she patted her hair with both hands as she stepped into her role.

"Colonel Montrose!" she answered. "You have no idea how *long* I have waited for someone like you."

A month later, Chastity watched in bewilderment from the galley as Rod went up the ladder to bed with Sandra once again. The two were always talking quietly together during the day, as though they were playing a game. It was not that Chastity was jealous—but she did feel left out. The sight of the two disappearing into Rod's large-diameter habitat brought Chastity twinges of desire. She knew that all she had to do was climb the ladder to where Pete and Seichi were watching sports programs in their habitats and tap on their hatchdoors and those twinges would be soon satisfied, but she desired something new and different. Doc had his back to her, doing maintenance work on something in the life support section. Deliberately lowering her jumpsuit zipper, Chastity floated over behind him and slowly drew the long fingernails of her left hand down Dan's back. When Dan first felt the fingernails, he twitched his back in annoyance, but as soon as he realized what was going on, he stopped work on the recalcitrant piece of equipment in front of him and arched his back into the caress like a tomcat. As the long scratch came to an end, he slowly turned around, to see two mounds of flesh trying to escape from their constriction. Chastity repeated her stroke on Dan's back with her left hand as she pulled his chin up with her right hand and planted a warm slow kiss on his upturned face. As their lips finally parted, she murmured, "I understand the fingernail tips feel even better on a bare back. Like to try it?"

For a long time, Dan considered the proposition. Finally, he gave a sad smile and shook his head. "I'd love to try it, Chass . . . but I can't—"

"I understand," replied Chastity with a smile. She gave him another kiss—a peck this time—and turned to head up the ladder, zipping up the front of her jumpsuit as she did so. She slept alone that night, just as Dan had done every night for the past year.

They were scheduled to arrive at Saturn exactly one year after they had left Earth's orbit. The Earth would be back around in its orbit to the point where they had taken off, so the distance to Earth was ten AU. A week before that date, Chastity was at the pilot console, watching the string of numbers that indicated the acceleration and velocity of *Sexdent* with respect to the Sun and Saturn.

"There it goes . . ." she murmured quietly to herself.

"There goes what?" asked Pete, who was floating around the upper deck sipping a squeezer of coffee.

"The acceleration went through zero," replied Chastity. "We left Earth going nearly fifty-six klecs. Ever since we left, our acceleration has been negative because of the pull of the Sun, and we have been slowing down as we climbed up out of the Sun's gravity well. We're now at thirty-nine klecs. But we just passed over the point between the Sun and Saturn where the gravity influence of Saturn takes over. Our acceleration is now positive as we fall into Saturn's gravity well and we're speeding up again. We should be there in about a week."

Pete came over behind Chastity and looked over her shoulder

out the viewport above her console. Saturn was no longer just an orange dot with "handles." It had grown until it was half as big as the Sun or Luna in the skies of Earth. The rings were nearly broadside toward the Sun and the northern hemisphere of the yellow-orange planet was fully illuminated, for it was "summer" on Saturn.

"How fast will we be going when we get there?" asked Pete, curious.

"Since we're on a fast-passage track rather than a Hohmann transfer orbit, we'll be coming at it at almost right angles to its orbital velocity," said Chastity. "We'll be meeting it going over forty klecs, and by the time we build up speed diving in over the rings, we'll be going almost fifty-four klecs. Once again we'll be the fastest spacecraft in the solar system."

The next morning, Pete was the last one out of the crew habitats.

"This free fall really feels good after all those gees," he said, as he pulled himself down the ladder and joined the rest of the crew for breakfast.

"Enjoy it while you can," said Rod. "Once we get down into Saturn, it'll be one gee all the time."

"Not quite one gee," Sandra reminded him. "Because Saturn is rotating so rapidly, the centrifugal force at the equator cancels out a portion of the gravity, so it's only ninety-three percent of one gee there, although it gets up to a hundred and twenty percent of Earth gravity at the pole."

"Any percent of gravity is too much," complained Pete. "Especially if you have to exercise in it."

"That's one thing you *won't* have to do," interjected Dan. "We can forget about the compulsory exercise period once we are on Saturn. We'll get enough exercise just going up and down the ladder while we're getting our day's work done. It'll be just like living on the Earth. That six months we're going to spend down there at Earth-normal is just what the doctor ordered for your bones and cardiovascular system."

"It *is* going to be a lot like living on Earth, isn't it," said Sandra. "To find the lifeforms, we'll have to go down to the water cloud level. Then, both the gravity and the temperature will be Earth-surface normal."

"Like Earth on a cloudy night," reminded Chastity, "there isn't going to be much illumination under three layers of clouds this far from the Sun."

"We will have much illumination from the lights on the reactor complex," said Seichi. "It will be like being at a baseball park at night."

"You're all forgetting the big difference between Saturn and Earth," said Dan. "The pressure. We'll be at ten bars."

"So the air will be a little thick," said Pete. "That just means my meta factory will be working at higher efficiency—the sooner to get us home."

"It'll be like living in an ocean of air instead of water," said Sandra. "I can't wait until I get to go out in my saturnsuit and collect some specimens swimming around in that ocean."

Later that evening, the crew gathered on the upper deck to listen to the latest report from Space Unlimited Mission Control. Art Dooley was there.

"Good work!" he said with a smile. "You've gotten there. Now comes the hard part, getting down and getting back up. Telemetry says that the ship is working fine, but of course you know that, with Jeeves right there monitoring everything as well as we can. Crew-Comm says that the microwave and laser links to the orbiters around Saturn are also working fine, so you should have no problem communicating with us as you climb down the rings—except, of course, for this blasted two-and-a-half-hour time delay." He turned around to look at the small group in the control room. "Anybody else have anything to say?"

The head of the imaging science team stepped forward from the group of scientists standing at the back. "Take your time going in," he said. "*Sexdent* has on board the largest, most sensitive, highest-resolution telescopic camera that has ever been to Saturn. Make sure you take the time to get *lots* of good pictures of the rings and all the moons, especially Iapetus—it's quite volcanically active, and we have yet to figure out how it maintains its two-toned color pattern."

"Will do," Sandra reassured him, then shook her head at the stupidity of her reply. He wouldn't hear her response for over an hour.

No one else stepped forward, so Art turned to look at the person sitting behind the CrewComm console.

"Take her down, Commander Morgan," said CrewComm.

✿   ✿   ✿

Three days later *Sexdent* reached the orbit of the outermost moon of Saturn, Phoebe. The small planetoid, in its highly inclined orbit, happened to be up near their incoming path, so everyone gathered at one viewport or another to watch as they passed over it. Chastity rotated the capsule until its nose was pointing at Phoebe so all of the ports had a good view.

"Looks like a small red version of Luna," said Dan, looking through one of the biviewers. "Dark reddish-gray dust with craters in it."

"It is a very much smaller moon than Luna," remarked Seichi. "Only two hundred twenty kilometers in diameter compared to Luna's thirty-five hundred."

"I wouldn't even call it a moon," added Chastity. "Its orbit is not only way up out of Saturn's equatorial plane, it's orbiting the wrong way. It's just a stray carbonaceous chondrite asteroid that Saturn probably captured in the distant past when it had an extended atmosphere."

Phoebe quickly passed out of view and Chastity turned the capsule back again to face Saturn. The orange planet was now a half a degree across in the sky—as big as Luna in the skies of Earth.

"I'm beginning to see bands," said Sandra.

"You should try these biviewers," said Dan, pushing the multispectral binoculars toward her on their pantograph. "I've got it set for wide-band visible with color stretching. The UV Spot in the lighter band about thirty degrees north of the equator really shows up well with that setting."

"Wow!" said Sandra, impressed. She flipped the setting back to normal visual band. "In real life, however, UV Spot is really kind of dull. Just an orange blob on an orange band on an orange sphere."

Three days later Saturn was much larger.

Sandra and Dan were at two of the consoles, while Chastity flew the capsule for them from the pilot's console. On Sandra's console screen was an enlarged image of some small features on the giant planet taken by a telescope looking out through a vacuum port in the engineering compartment on the facilities deck.

The rapidly rotating planet had a day of only ten and a half hours, so interesting features were at good viewing angles for only two or three hours. Since a good set of scientific images required a dozen images taken at different spectral bands, and the sunlight at Saturn was one percent as bright as sunlight at Earth, it took a good fraction of an hour to do the job right. So Dan, acting as spotter, used the biviewer above the scotty console to find interesting objects for Sandra to focus the large telescope on.

There were lots of features to be seen. Saturn had dozens of east-west bands of differing shades of orange. The bands moved with different wind speeds. Most of the winds blew in the direction that the planet rotated, so that features in those bands actually moved faster than the planet rotated. There were brown and white spots—various types of temporary cloud features—that moved along these bands. Some weather bands near the poles had repetitive swirls of clouds. In the northern hemisphere, there was one band that had what looked like a circumpolar river of clear air snaking back and forth through the center of the continuous cloud bank that made up the band. Strangely enough, there was no comparable feature in the southern hemisphere. With so many features to look at, and the rapid rotation of the planet that brought more features into view each minute, the real problem was to choose which features to take pictures of.

"Anne's Spot is now well over the horizon," reported Dan.

"I'm finished with White Spot Two," said Sandra. "What are the coordinates of Anne's Spot?"

Dan switched on the holoprojector for the viewport and Saturn suddenly had latitude and longitude lines superimposed on it. Two of the lines crossed near the center of a large oval red spot. A miniature version of the Great Red Spot on Jupiter, Anne's Spot was five thousand by three thousand kilometers in size, a third the diameter of Earth. Although nothing but a gigantic cyclonic storm, it was a very long-lived one. It was first seen during the flyby of the first *Voyager* spacecraft and had not changed much since. It could well be hundreds of years old.

Dan read off the numbers where the two lines crossed the red oval. "Anne's Spot is now at one hundred fifteen degrees east and fifty-five degrees south."

"You might want to consider an alternate subject," interrupted

Jeeves. "We are crossing the orbit of Iapetus. Closest approach will be in three hours. We will be flying by to the north of its leading hemisphere."

"Iapetus," said Dan. "Isn't that the yin-yang moon? One half black and the other half white?"

"Not quite half and half. More like one-third black and two-thirds white," replied Sandra. "Hmmm . . ." she added, obviously in a quandary. "During the last transmission the planetologists reminded me to take as many shots of Iapetus as I could. They're hoping to catch a dust volcano that is keeping the leading sector covered with dark material. It's their best guess as to what is causing the color difference, but there's no proof. But I'd hate to cut my photo session of Anne's Spot short—"

"We can do both," suggested Chastity. "I can rotate the capsule around the line of sight of the telescope so you can keep shooting White Spot, while Dan can take photos of Iapetus out his viewport using the biviewer."

"The biviewer won't have the resolution of the telescope, but it should be good enough to spot a volcanic eruption," said Sandra. "Do it."

Chastity stuck her right hand into the controller and carefully rotated the joyball inside. The capsule turned over so that Dan's up was now south instead of north.

"Got it!" he said shortly. He adjusted fingerwheels along the grips of the biviewer. "Expanding . . ." The tiny image in the biviewer grew into a picture of a cratered moon. The north pole was the bright white color of ice while the leading pole was almost a soot black. The demarcation between the white and the black was almost as if someone had used black spray paint to create a black crescent-shaped segment that stretched across the leading hemisphere from inner pole to outer pole. Dan looked carefully for the hypothesized "dust volcano" in the center of the black that would have acted as the spray can for the black paint, but it wasn't there.

"Sorry. No volcanoes today."

"Take pictures anyway," said Sandra.

The two were trying to collect as much scientific data about the giant planet as they could during this close approach to add to that already in the scientific archives back on Earth. Pretty soon they would be inside Saturn's atmosphere, and although they would learn a lot there, they would lose the synoptic overview that came from having the whole planet in their view at one time.

Saturn and its moons had been well explored by robotic probes and orbiters in the past, but the Earth scientists had emphasized that the images they were gathering would be useful for finding changes that had occurred since the last robotic visits.

After dinner that evening of macaroni and cheese, Rod made an announcement.

"We have less than twenty-four hours left. Get a good night's sleep. Tomorrow we pull the habitats in and go onto shifts. For the next few days we'll be using sleeping-bag hammocks in the airlock."

By noon the next day, all the habitats had been emptied of personal belongings, stripped of bedframes, and stacked one inside the next on the facilities deck. The bedframes had been rearranged into acceleration couches on the control deck for the high-gee maneuvers that would be coming next.

They were eight hours out when they passed over the orbits of Hyperion and Titan. Titan was on the other side of Saturn, which now filled six degrees of the sky, but Hyperion passed under them. They got some long-distance pictures of the oddly shaped object. Since they were moving so fast, Sandra was able to make a three-dimensional holographic strip from a series of images taken a few minutes apart. She had Jeeves display the reconstructed three-dimensional image on one of the holoviewports.

"Looks like a hockey puck," said Pete.

"Or a skipping stone," said Dan.

"Looks like a hamburger to me," said Rod. "A nice, big, juicy, flame-broiled, fat burger—"

"Stop it!" said Chastity. The crew had a choice of many excellent entrées for their meals on *Sexdent,* but grilled fresh-ground beef was not one of the options. All of them had agreed one evening that one of the first things they would do when they got home was visit a Mc-Donald's and have a Big Mac—although Pete held out for a Quarter Pounder.

Saturn grew in size until its disk was thirteen degrees across. It was tilted toward the Sun, with its north pole and upper ring surface illuminated.

Pete and Chastity were hanging in the sleeping bags in the air-lock. They were merely resting, for it was too early to sleep. Up on the operations deck, Rod controlled the orientation of *Sexdent,* while Dan and Sandra continued their photographic survey of the features on the planet. It was now obvious to Dan that they were heading for the eastern edge of the giant planet, right at the point where the shadow line of the Sun on Saturn passed under the rings.

"Doesn't look like there's much room between the D ring and the cloud deck," said Dan, using the biviewer to bring out the faint arcs of the innermost ring.

"Isn't . . ." said Rod. "Technically, there's zero margin because of the bits of junk spiraling in from the D ring. But it's pretty sparse—we'll just have to take our chances when we pass through the ring plane."

"That's going to be a very nervous couple of minutes."

"Milliseconds . . ." corrected Rod. "The rings are something like ten to a hundred meters thick. At our speed of over fifty klecs, we'll pass through the ring plane in less than two milliseconds. At the speed we're going, if there's something big in our way, we'll never know what hit us." He noticed Dan's frown. "But don't worry, Doc, I'm going to do my best to miss it. I'm going to have *Sexdent* kiss the upper atmosphere with its heat shield, so we should be below nearly all the junk."

"What about when we come out around on the other side?" asked Doc. "Will we still be able to make it through under the D ring?"

"Doesn't work that way," said Rod. "I'm going to make our new periapsis point right over the eastern terminator. That way, our new elliptical orbit will be at right angles to our incoming trajectory. Our track will stay well away from the rings because the peak of the new orbit will be high over the rings on the western side of Saturn. Our orbit will be in the ecliptic plane with its long axis at right angles to the Sun direction, while Saturn's rings are tilted at twenty-six degrees to the ecliptic and are facing the Sun. The only place the orbit gets near the rings is when it passes just under the rings over the eastern terminator. We plan on meeting Titan out at the apoapsis point and stopping there. Titan's orbit is also tilted, so we will be coming in at it at a steep angle, but by picking the right firing point I should have no problem stopping. Even if we miss that rendezvous, all we'll do is come back in and go under the rings at the same place over the eastern terminator where we started the new orbit."

Dan continued to search the western limb for new targets for Sandra to image. Because she now had a lot more targets to photograph, instead of a dozen different spectral band images of the same feature Sandra was now taking only four "color" shots of each one: red-infrared, blue, green, and ultraviolet.

"A small white spot is colliding with Brown Spot One at thirty-three degrees east and forty-two degrees north," reported Dan.

"We're starting over the E ring," reported Rod.

"I'd better switch targets then," said Sandra. "Saturn will have to wait. Rotate us around so I can see the rings, Rod."

Rod put his hand in the controller under his console and twisted the joyball inside. The capsule rotated until the telescope peering out the vacuum port in the engineering sector was pointed downward toward the rings. They were nearly fully illuminated by the Sun and quite bright. The enlarged telescope image filled Sandra's holoviewport with a multitude of arcs. For the next two hours Sandra took alternate shots of the E ring arcs and Saturn features. She also picked up some north pole images of Dione, Telesto, Enceladus, and Mimas, and an excellent shot of the braided F ring. They then started in over the brighter A, B, and C rings that were the only ones known to the ancient astronomers.

"Looks like the grooves on a phonograph record to me," said Rod, looking over Sandra's shoulder.

"We still don't know why they stay so distinct," said Sandra. "One would think over the millions of years they have been in existence they would have smoothed out more. Some people think there are lots of small 'shepherding' moons keeping the ringlets from spreading—I'm hoping to catch some of them in these photos. Haven't seen any yet, though."

"It would be hard for our eyes to pick out a single speck in all that clutter," said Dan, peering at the rings passing under them through the biviewer. At the speed *Sexdent* was traveling, they passed over each of the main rings in a few minutes, so Sandra only took single, high-contrast, black-and-white images of each view.

"A 'spoke' is starting in the B ring," Dan warned.

Sandra quickly shifted the magnification of the telescope from a

pulse passed down the tubes along the sides of the keel, pushing the air at higher and higher speeds until it jetted out the rear, driving the body of the giant bird higher. As one part of Petra's mind continued to direct Petru through the mechanical motions of the climb, the rest of her mind was looking upward to the heavens through her giant single eye. Bright had set below the western clouds and although stars could be seen between the breaks in the clouds above them, the cloud breaks were few and small in size. This would not be a good night for observation of the stars, so Petra joined in the gossip of the flock as they climbed.

"Ketra! Watch where you're going!"

"Sorry . . . Ketro swallowed a slimswimmer the wrong way during yesterday's hunt and Ketru has a sore left maw . . . left airtube sometimes halts in midpulse."

Suddenly a bright light appeared in the sky.

"What is *that?*" asked Hakra.

"Maybe it is Bright, rising again . . ." said Falra.

Petra looked to see what was causing the commotion in the flock. Streaking high above them was a bright light behind the clouds. Having memorized many facts about the lights in the sky she had learned from Elders, Petra knew that Bright was not rising again. Besides, not only was the light in the sky too bright to be the Godstar Bright, the color of the light was wrong. Instead of the yellowish-white color of Bright, this rapidly moving glow was reddish-purple in color.

"It's just a meteor," said Petra, to reassure the rest of the flock.

"The Ancients say that meteors can hurt you," said Conra. "Is it getting any closer?"

But as the glow continued and moved off to the southeast, Petra began to realize that this was not a meteor, but something else—something new in the sky.

"It is going away," said Petra. "There is no more danger."

The flock continued its climb, its gossip enriched by the recent event. Petra didn't join in as she added the information she had collected to her memory. She would visit the astronomers in the neighboring flocks during the next posthunt play period and see if they had been able to see the long-lasting purple light better than she had. Her mind couldn't help but speculate on what it might have been. If it was not a meteor, perhaps it was a comet. Comets grew bright and developed a long tail as they passed around the Godstar Bright. Perhaps this was a comet that grew bright as it passed around Air. Then again, it might be a strange form of lightning. Lightning sometimes gave off blue and purple light, but lightning moved very fast, while this purple light, although it moved rapidly through the skies, was nowhere near as fast as lightning. Petra couldn't think of anything else that might have been the cause.

After ten minutes, Rod announced through clenched teeth, "Only a half minute more."

The roaring finally stopped, and they went from three gees to free fall.

"Trajectory looks good," said Chastity, reading her pilot screen. "We took off nineteen klecs and are on track for Titan. We should get there in three days."

"If you wouldn't mind, Chastity," said Sandra, "I'd appreciate it if you would rotate us so our telescope port is pointing north so I can get some shots of the underside of the rings. We've already passed under most of the D ring, and the C ring is coming up."

"Okay," said Chastity, rotating *Sexdent* until the telescope had a good view of the rings above them.

"I see some spokes coming up on the B ring," said Dan, who had unlatched the biviewer and was spotting for Sandra again. "From the underside, the spokes show up brighter than the rings rather than darker."

"Forward scattering," said Sandra as she started collecting images. "The spokes are generated by small charged dust particles kicked loose from the bigger rocks by electrical currents. The dust particles scatter light better than the big chunks."

As soon as they cleared the backside of Saturn and could see Earth again, Jeeves set up a direct comm link to Earth through the high data rate laser communicator dishes. There were three dishes, each thirty centimeters in diameter, spaced 120 degrees around the ship so that one of them always had Earth in sight. The minute the receivers were turned on, they found a message streaming through space to them. It was from the Mission Control Center, congratulating them on their successful perigee burn, which had happened over an hour ago. Bemused, Rod responded. "Engines worked fine. We're on our way to Titan."

Three days later, they met Titan out at its orbit.

"Still just a featureless brown ball of smog," said Dan dejectedly as he scanned Titan through the biviewer.

"You're just looking in the wrong frequency band," said Sandra. "Both microwaves and near infrared can penetrate the smog clouds. Why don't you put down that biviewer and help me. You take the near-infrared telescope, while I set up the radar imager."

A few hours later they had moderately good images of the visually hidden surface of Saturn's largest moon—bigger than the planet Mercury and second only to Jupiter's moon Ganymede in size.

"Here it is—Titan undressed," said Sandra, as she gave the rest of the crew a tour of the orange smog moon on her holoviewport. "Since Titan is tidally locked to Saturn, it has six poles—the usual north and south spin poles, the inner pole that always faces Saturn, the outer pole that always faces away from Saturn, the leading pole that faces the direction of Titan's motion in its orbit, and the trailing pole on the opposite side of that."

She switched the holoviewport above the engineering console to show the infrared image of one side of Titan. It had a large dark splotch in the center that covered nearly the whole hemisphere.

"This is the trailing pole image," she said. "The dark regions are deposits of hydrocarbons all the way from simple compounds like methane—C-H-four—to complex carbon-chain hydrocarbons like oil and tar. Right here is a small ocean—mostly methane—but probably containing ethane and other stuff dissolved in it."

"How do you know it's methane?" asked Chastity.

"Because Titan's atmosphere still has lots of methane in it. It's ninety-five percent nitrogen and argon, and five percent methane. Since methane is easily broken up by sunlight to carbon and hydrogen, and hydrogen is easily lost to space, there must be a reservoir of methane on Titan's surface to keep the atmosphere replenished—in this case the reservoir is a small ocean. Besides, the surface pressure and temperature of one-and-a-half bars at ninety-four kelvin are in the range where methane and ethane are liquids." She switched to another view. This infrared image had a bright patch in it. "This is the leading pole image," she said. "That bright spot is a high-elevation continent of frozen water and ammonia ice sticking up out of the hydrocarbon-covered plains."

"Do you think there may exist lifeforms there?" asked Seichi.

"The landers haven't seen anything on Titan," replied Sandra. "Although there are a lot of hydrocarbons there, and even an ocean to get life started, the temperatures are probably too low for the chemical reactions to proceed at the necessary speeds. It's different on Saturn, where the temperatures get up to room temperature and higher. We *know* there are lifeforms *there*—and soon we'll have some on board to look at!"

They approached Titan from an unconventional angle. *Sexdent's* orbit was in the plane of the ecliptic, while Titan's orbit was tilted at almost twenty-six degrees because of Saturn's tilted axis. The burn at Titan was minor, only one minute at three gees. That burn put them into a long elliptical orbit about Titan that took them almost out to Titan's leading Trojan point. Another minor correction there, and they were stopped among the small collection of ice chunks that had collected at the weak gravity minimum region over the eons.

"There's a nice egg-shaped hundred-meter iceberg over there," said Chastity from her pilot's console. The acceleration couches had been removed from the control deck floor and stored in the airlock and the swivel-arm chairs had been installed in front of the control consoles. "It's tidally locked to Saturn in all three axes, so its orientation is perfectly predictable."

"Looks good to me," said Rod. He had rearranged the icons on the third console so that it was back to being the commander's console instead of a science console. "Are we ready for separation, Seichi?"

"Rendezvous stage safetied and vernier control tanks full," reported Seichi from the engineering console.

Rod tapped a red icon on his screen and the clattering sound of clamps releasing rattled through the hull.

"It's all yours, Chass," said Rod. "Take the rendezvous stage away a few hundred meters and hold it there 'til I back *Sexdent* out of the return stage."

Chastity activated her screen, flew the large empty rendezvous

tank out from behind them, and brought it to a halt in the distance.
Rod, using the vernier jets on *Sexdent,* brought the nose of the
spacecraft up close to the side of the iceberg. *Sexdent* still wore the
return stage fuel tank around its "waist," somewhat like the spare tire
Pete wore around his waist.

"Return stage ready, Seichi?" Rod asked.

"Ready."

Rod pushed another red icon, and another set of clatters indicated that *Sexdent* was now separated from the donut-shaped fuel
tank it had been carrying. Carefully, Rod backed *Sexdent* out of the
hole in the fuel tank, leaving it floating in front of them, about ten
meters away from the hundred-meter block of ice.

"Set the return tank module on autopilot, Jeeves," Rod commanded. "Maintain present orientation at ten meters' separation
distance."

"Very good, sir," said Jeeves, sending commands to a similar
semi-intelligent program in the computer that resided on the return
stage. Two of the vernier jets on the donut-shaped object fired to stop
a small amount of residual rotation that had been left from Rod's exit
maneuver and the tank full of meta became still.

"Now, stay there until we get back," ordered Rod.

"And don't get any holes," added Chastity.

"Okay, Chass," said Rod. "Fly the rendezvous stage in."

Chastity activated her control board and brought the nearly
empty rendezvous stage up until it was ten meters away on the other
side of the donut-shaped tank that contained the fuel that would take
them back to Earth. The autopilot on the rendezvous stage was set
to maintain station on the opposite side of the return fuel tank from
the iceberg. The two large masses would provide shielding for the
return stage from incoming space debris objects.

"Okay," said Rod, turning from the pilot console to look at the
watching crewmembers in back of him. "Time for a complete system check before we commit."

For the next few days, the crew was busy checking every system
and item of equipment on the ship—for their lives would depend
upon everything functioning properly.

Pete spent most of his time in the meta-manufacturing facility
nestled under the spacecraft proper. Since the thirty-five-ton factory
would be cut loose and left behind when the spacecraft lifted off

from Saturn at the end of their mission, no provision had been made to access the factory from inside the crew compartment. It would have added mass and decreased their chances of completing the mission, so Pete got lots of practice putting on and taking off his spacesuit as he moved back and forth from the factory and the crew compartment.

Mass was at such a premium that "plumber" Dan even emptied out the solid waste storage tank on *Sexdent*. The frozen vacuum-dried brown material was put into storage bags and sent out into space.

"Aren't you going to at least burn them up by deorbiting them?" asked Chastity primly as she saw the collection of bags growing outside one of the viewports.

"Nope," said Dan, as he prepared to exit the airlock with another odoriferous reminder of the excellent meals they had enjoyed in the past year. "When they set up a permanent manned station here at Titan to monitor the meta factories down on Saturn, this will be *just* the stuff to fertilize the hydroponics gardens." Chastity reminded herself not to visit the monitoring station.

After checking all the equipment inside the capsule, Rod, Chastity, and Seichi went outside to check everything there. Seichi examined the heat shield that covered the bottom of the ship. The heat shield had ports that swung aside to allow passage of the exhaust flames during their deceleration burn, then swung back to protect the nozzle bells as the ship entered the upper atmosphere. He activated the doors on each one of the twelve ports, checking to make sure that they seated tightly, then checked the release mechanism that would drop the five tons of heatshield after it did its job. He then checked out all the engine bells and magnoshielded nozzles. Each one took a number of hours, so he too was in and out of his spacesuit many times during the days of the checkout period.

Rod and Chastity helped Seichi with the engine checkout, activating the magnoshield from inside, while Seichi reached up into the nozzle bell with a magnetometer to check the field configuration. The two also examined the parachute, balloon, and shrouds that would bring them to a halt in the clouds and float them there during their six-month stay on the giant planet.

"That's the trouble," said Rod with a resigned shake of his head as he and Chastity looked at the neatly laid-out shrouds on top of fold after fold of tough fabric. "The only way to *really* check out a parachute is to jump with it."

Finally, they were ready. At dinner that night, Rod announced, "Mission Control says they are set up and ready to have us climb down the rings. As soon as Rhea is in the right position, we'll do a burn at Titan and drop down to our first 'rung' on the ladder."

Sandra, puzzled, asked Rod a question. "What I don't understand is how come if *Sexdent* is able to climb up out of Saturn's gravity well using its rockets, why can't it use its rockets to climb down?"

" 'Cause of the extra mass we have to carry down," said Rod. "If all we had to carry was the fifty-ton main capsule, the hundred and twenty tons of fuel in the tanks of the main capsule would do the job. But we also have to take down the thirty-five-ton meta factory, the five-ton heat shield, and the ten tons of balloon and shrouds—another fifty tons. We'd run out of fuel trying to slow down that load—and burn up. So we've got to take it in steps—using every trick in the book—to climb part of the way down the gravity well using the moons and rings—while saving our fuel for that last big step down into the atmosphere."

When the orbits were just right, Rod drifted *Sexdent* over to Titan and let it fall in toward the smoggy moon on an essentially parabolic orbit. At the point of their closest approach Rod fired the rockets for about half a minute at one gee.

"We're on our way," he reported. "We'll be at Rhea in five days."

"Let's have a party!" suggested Pete, but then he noticed that everyone had a concerned look on their faces. They were committed now . . . to a very risky mission . . . a mission that might cost them their lives. . . . He dropped the idea.

As they approached Rhea, Sandra got some good images of the bright, crater-covered moon.

"Just a well-worked ball of ice," reported Sandra, looking critically at the images she had collected. "Not much different from the bright side of Iapetus."

Rod brought them to a halt at Rhea with a half-minute burn at three gees.

"We'll have to wait here until the orbit timing of all the moons we're going to use is right," he said.

"Here we are . . . right outside the E ring," said Sandra, looking at the fine line across the sky that indicated the plane of the rings, "but I can't get any pictures—wrong angle. Have to make do with Saturn."

Soon she and Dan were back at their task of imaging features on the rapidly rotating face of Saturn. The giant planet now covered thirteen degrees of the sky—almost filling the holoviewports.

"Mission Control says the time for the next drop down is early tomorrow," announced Rod a few days later.

"What's the next stop?" asked Pete. "Dione? That's the next big moon inward."

"Not quite," said Rod. "We're going to leave sixty degrees early so we drop down on Dione's Trojan companion, Helene, instead. It's just the right size for Chass to try a tether whip maneuver. Save us some fuel."

The next day, at their closest approach to Rhea, Rod fired the rockets for only ten seconds. But that was enough to drop them downward again. Their trajectory skimmed only a few hundred kilometers above the E ring and Sandra got excellent pictures. For the next two days, they watched as Saturn loomed ever larger in their viewports.

"The white spot is catching up with Brown Spot One again," reported Dan from the biviewer. "You ought to get a shot of it."

"As soon as we stop, I'll take pictures of Saturn, but right now I'd better concentrate on the E ring," replied Sandra.

"We're not going to stop," said Chastity, who was controlling the orientation of *Sexdent* for the two scientists. "With a tether whip, you leave as fast as you came."

"Oh!" said Sandra. "Then you'd better turn us around so I can shoot Brown Spot now."

Sexdent soon caught up with Helene. It was a free-floating potato-shaped megamountain about thirty-five kilometers in diameter. Rod,

Chastity, and Seichi were at their stations, while the other three looked over their shoulders from their handholds on the ladder that ran through the center of the ship. The acceleration levels expected during this tether whip maneuver weren't large, only half a gee, so they didn't have to strap down on acceleration couches as they did for the rocket burns.

"We'll be catching up with her at eight hundred meters per second," reported Rod as the elliptical orbit of *Sexdent* started to intersect the circular orbit of Helene. "It should be a nice easy practice run for you. I'm ready with rockets in case you miss."

Chastity's long-nailed fingers flew over the keyboard to bring up a seldom-used menu on her screen. She touched the icon that flipped back the conical nosecone of *Sexdent,* exposing a metapropelled penetrator inside, its sharp tungsten-carbide tip pointing outward. Some hours ago, Jeeves had used its mechbot, Mouser, to move the penetrator from its storage rack on the wall to the launcher, and hook the flame-resistant metal-braid "tail" of the penetrator to the end of the two-hundred-kilometer tether stored on the reel.

Rod, working in concert with Chastity, used the attitude jets to direct the nose of *Sexdent* toward the still-distant moonlet.

"Launch," said Chastity quietly as the penetrator took off using a low-temperature exhaust of warm helium gas. After the penetrator was well clear of *Sexdent* the exhaust flame brightened into a reddish-purple plasma. The penetrator accelerated toward its target, dragging the tether behind it—the multiline structure automatically dilating to its extended shape as it was pulled from the reel.

Chastity had a plan view of the action on her console screen and a view from the penetrator's nose camera on the holoviewport. Her manicured right hand was in the controller's box under the console, directing the flight of the penetrator as her eyes alternated between the holoviewport and the console screen.

"We need to get a little closer, Rod," she said, tapping the image on the console touchscreen with the tip of a long glittering-gold fingernail. "I want a closest distance of a hundred and sixty."

Rod tweaked the joyball in the controller's box under his console. The vernier jets on *Sexdent* gave a short burst, the projected path line of the spacecraft shifted slightly, and the number indicating the distance between the trajectory of *Sexdent* and the trajectory of the asteroid at their point of closest approach changed from 210 to 160. He kept a close eye on that number and his hand ready around the joyball, in case the number started to change, but he couldn't help glancing out the viewport in front of him as they closed in on the slowly tumbling grayish-white mountain—growing larger each second.

The tumbling gray icerock was much larger in the holoviewport in front of Chastity. Knowing that Rod would keep *Sexdent* on course, she concentrated on the image in front of her, looking for the best place to put the penetrator. If it hit a hard surface, it might not penetrate enough and would be pulled out as tension was applied. If it was placed in a field of rocks, the rocks might cut the tether as it tilted over from the vertical during their turn. The best place was the middle of a small crater, as fresh as possible. She spotted one—and with minuscule adjustments to the joyball in her controller, the cross-hairs on the holoviewport shifted to the center of the crater.

"One hundred twenty kilometers . . ." intoned Seichi, reading off the length of tether that had been unreeled from the drum in *Sexdent's* nose. Chastity did a quick mental calculation and her fingers lifted the joyball, increasing the speed of the penetrator. "One-thirty . . . one-forty . . ." The small crater was now a large crater that filled the holoviewport . . .

". . . One hundred fifty kilometers . . . one hundred fifty-five kilometers . . ." reported Seichi.

"Contact!" said Chastity as the penetrator struck the icy surface of Helene and the image from the penetrator nose camera turned black. Sliding her fingertip across the tension control icon, Chastity began braking the still-unreeling tether. As *Sexdent* started to pull on the tether, gravity returned. It wasn't much, just four-tenths of a gee. The energy going into the electromagnetic brake was electrically shunted to resistance-heated radiator vanes that could be seen overhead out of the top of the viewports. The vanes glowed a deep red as they radiated away the energy that had been generated during the deceleration of *Sexdent*.

For thirteen minutes they swung around Helene, their nose pointing constantly at the icy planetoid, while Chastity carefully let out the tether. The pull of the lengthening tether winding around the surface of the icy rock caused their ship to lose speed.

"Slowing down nicely," said Rod. "Six hundred ninety meters per second . . . six-eighty . . ."

"Tether length reaching maximum," warned Seichi. "One hundred ninety kilometers . . . one hundred ninety-five kilometers . . ."

Just as Rod's velocity countdown reached 640 meters per second, and Seichi's length count reached 200 kilometers, they had swung 180 degrees around Helene and were now moving in the opposite direction.

Chastity watched her console carefully until the yellow line indicating the predicted trajectory for *Sexdent* rotated until it was parallel with the blue line for the optimum outgoing trajectory from Helene. When the two lines merged and became a single green line, she tapped a red icon on the screen marked "Tether Release." The tether was cut at the penetrator and snaked its way along the gray icedust surface as they left Helene behind and started their fall inward above the E ring toward the growing orange globe of Saturn—which was now eighteen degrees across.

"Nice job," said Rod approvingly as the ship returned to free fall. He looked at the image on his console screen. The yellow and blue lines weren't exactly parallel. They started to diverge at the edge of his screen. He could have brought them into exact parallelism with a short burst from the vernier jet, but decided not to. The small error wouldn't affect their arrival at the next moon significantly. He quickly wiped his screen so Chastity wouldn't see it.

"Perfect alignment!" he announced. "Nothing for me to do."

Chastity looked at her screen. It contained an identical image showing the small residual error she had left after her tether turn maneuver. She quickly wiped her screen so Rod wouldn't see it. With the screen now blank, she turned to grin her thanks at him, violet eyes glittering with pride at her successful maneuver. If he wanted to act like a gentleman instead of showing her who was boss, she would be lady enough to let him.

That evening she received a congratulatory message from Art Dooley over her personal comm link.

"That was an amazing demonstration of how powerful tethers can be," said Art. "For years, I have been trying to convince the venture capitalists I know to invest in space tethers for interorbit and interplanetary transportation. When meta was invented, however, all the early interest in space tethers went away, because meta-fueled rockets could do most space transportation jobs, and tethers were an untried and therefore risky technology. Although a space tether transportation system uses no fuel, and would cut space transportation costs way down, even below what we expect from using cheap Saturn meta, I could never get anybody interested. You just demonstrated that a good space tether can horse a two-hundred-ton payload around at a half-gee acceleration. The investors now believe that tethers are a 'proven' technology and are willing to put their money into it. Today I lined up enough of them to buy out this small business, Tethers Unlimited, that has the patents on the high-strength, failsafe Hoytether. We're going to pump a lot of money in it, turning it from a small business to a big business. Having someone as famous as you in the company management would be a big asset in our marketing efforts. Would you like to be on the board of directors?"

Chastity replied that she was flattered to be asked, but she would have to reserve her decision until she and the rest of the crew had completed their mission. After all, once one had a billion dollars in the bank, there was no need to work anymore, unless it was fun, of course.

A day later, they began to catch up with Calypso, the leading Trojan companion of Tethys.

"Hmmm . . ." said Rod as he set up his pilot board for the maneuver. "There must be something wrong somewhere, Jeeves. It says here that Calypso is sixty-five degrees ahead of Tethys. I thought that Trojan moons were always at sixty degrees ahead or behind their primary."

"The L4 and L5 Trojan points, which indicate the minimum of the gravitational well, are at exactly sixty degrees," replied Jeeves. "But if a small moon at that point is perturbed—which happens often in a moon system as complex as that of Saturn—then the small moon moves in an orbit around the minimum point. The orbit is not circular or elliptic, however, it is tadpole shaped."

"Tadpole shaped?" said Rod.

Jeeves changed the image on Rod's console screen from that of a telescopic view of Calypso to a plan drawing, showing the large moon Tethys and its leading and trailing Trojan moons. One was Telesto, a roundish potato-shaped moon about twenty-two kilometers in diameter. The other was Calypso, an elongated yam-shaped moon that was thirty kilometers by twenty-four kilometers by sixteen kilometers. Superimposed on the images were lines indicating the L4 and L5 points, with contours around them that were circular on the side toward the primary moon, and cusped on the side away. The circular portion looked like the head of a tadpole while the pointed cusped portion looked like the tail.

"As you can see," said Jeeves, using a blinking arrow to point out the moonlet on the screen, "Calypso is almost at the cusp point in its orbit around the leading L4 point, so it is sixty-five degrees ahead of Tethys."

"Now I see what you mean," said Rod. "The orbit does have the shape of a tadpole. What a weird shape. How far do those tadpole orbits stretch? Can the cusp point for the Calypso orbit go all the way around to the trailing Trojan point?"

"If Saturn were perfectly round, there were no other moons, and Calypso were given just the right perturbation, the cusp, or tail, of the tadpole orbit would reach all around to the point in the orbit opposite to the primary moon, where it would meet the tail of the maximal orbit from the trailing Trojan point. A tiny perturbation there could cause a switch."

"But in real life, switches don't happen," said Rod. "The perturbations of the other moons will kick it somewhere else long before it gets to the halfway point."

"Actually," replied Jeeves, "there is an example of such switching in the Saturn system."

"Really?" said Rod, intrigued. "Show me." His screen changed.

"There are two small inner moons of Saturn, Epimetheus and Janus, that are almost the same size, and share almost the same orbit. Janus, approximately two hundred kilometers in diameter, is about four times as massive as Epimetheus, which is about one hundred twenty kilometers in diameter. Since neither can be considered the 'primary,' there aren't the usual Trojan points with their tadpole orbits. Instead, both move in horseshoe-shaped orbits that lie on either side of the nominal circular orbit for their joint angular momentum. Janus, being heavier, moves in a small crescent that only covers a few tens of degrees of the circle, while Epimetheus moves in a large horseshoe orbit that stretches from plus thirty degrees all the way around to minus thirty degrees."

Rod looked at the diagram on his screen. "Say . . . Epimetheus is significantly inside the nominal orbit."

"That is correct," said Jeeves. "The nominal orbit for the combined system is 151,432 kilometers. Janus is presently orbiting at 151,422 kilometers—ten kilometers inside the nominal orbit—while Epimetheus is orbiting at 151,472 kilometers—40 kilometers outside. In a few years, the distances will be reversed. Epimetheus will be 40 kilometers inside, while Janus will be 10 kilometers outside."

"Curiouser and curiouser . . ." muttered Rod. "But right now we have Calypso to catch." He reset the pilot console to the telescopic image that he had started with, while Chastity settled in at the science console, setting up the screen icons for tether control. After some careful calibrations and consultation with Jeeves, Rod gave a short burst from the vernier rockets to adjust their incoming trajectory. The burst of noise and the slight acceleration brought most of the rest of the crew out of their habitats to see the action.

"Looks like a kid's first snowball," said Pete, looking at the rapidly approaching moon out the viewport over Chastity's shoulder as she prepared to fire her penetrator. "After this tether whip, I presume we'll be going to Enceladus next?"

"Nope," said Rod. "Enceladus is the wrong size—too large for a tether whip and too small for a gravity whip. Its diameter is five hundred kilometers, while our tether is only two hundred kilometers. If Chastity stuck one end of the tether into Enceladus and started to make a one-hundred-and-eighty-degree turn around it, we'd smack into the surface after only going ninety degrees. But even though it's five hundred kilometers in diameter, its escape velocity is less than two hundred meters a second—not enough to help a perigee burn significantly. So instead of burning something like a whole klec's worth of fuel to stop and start at Enceladus, we're going to bypass it. I'm going to add a burn to Chastity's tether whip at Calypso. That'll drop down past the orbit of Enceladus to the orbit of Mimas. But even then we can't use Mimas directly. Again it's the wrong size. Its diameter is only two hundred kilometers, but that's still too large for a tether whip. We're going to use a big boulder Sandra found tadpoling around its leading Trojan point."

They quickly caught up with Calypso.

"I'm going to do this one at one gee," said Chastity, "so make sure you hold on tight." She fired the penetrator and unreeled only fifty kilometers of tether before striking Calypso at its "waistline." This time Chastity hardly used the brake at all and the acceleration level quickly climbed to one gee as they started their rapid turn around the moonlet on the end of their short tether. Pete found his legs buckling under the unaccustomed acceleration and sat down on the grating. Chastity noticed the motion out of the corner of her eye.

"Only four minutes of this, Pete," said Chastity. "Then you'll be back in free fall."

"Don't forget my minute," Rod reminded her.

"Right . . . five minutes, Pete."

A few minutes later, Chastity turned to Rod. "Almost there," she warned.

"Ready," said Rod, his hand on the joyball in his controller.

"Cut!" announced Chastity as they completed their 180-degree turn around Calypso. The tether came free, and as the acceleration from the centrifugal force of the tether from the nose dropped off, Rod replaced it with the acceleration force from the rocket engines at the rear. For a full minute, the engines roared at one gee. The rockets stopped and they were back floating in free fall, freely falling even farther down into Saturn's immense gravity well.

A day and a half later, they reached the orbit of Mimas at the inner portion of the E ring and headed for the kilometer-sized moonlet at Mimas's trailing Trojan point.

"We're coming in much faster this time—one-and-a-half klecs," Chastity warned the crew that morning at breakfast. "So the gee level will be higher. You don't need to be strapped in acceleration couches—it'll only be one-and-a-third gees—but you'd better sit down."

After an eight-minute tether whip and a twelve-second rocket burn, they were on their way down again.

"What's our next stop?" asked Pete, as he floated upward off the grating in the free fall that followed the maneuver.

"We're going all the way over the A ring into the Huygens Gap," said Chastity, pointing to her screen. "There's a relatively clear region in the Cassini Division between the A and B rings. Sandra found out why—there's a pair of moonlets keeping it swept clean. We're going to use one of them. We'll be there in eight hours."

Six hours later, Chastity appeared again on the control deck. Rod, Dan, and Sandra were busy taking one shot after another as they zoomed just above the A ring.

"This next tether whip is going to be at high gees," she announced. "We're going to need acceleration couches."

"Lessee . . ." said Rod, switching gears. "Do I need to make a burn on this one?"

"No fuel needed for this one," replied Chastity. "We can do it all by braking."

The penetrator struck the Huygens Gap moonlet with the tether length at 140 kilometers. Chastity, lying on her back in the acceleration couch, used her controller to increase the braking on the tether while letting it pay out slowly. The acceleration level reached 2.6 gees, while the radiator fins sticking out of the sides of the capsule turned from red hot to white hot to blue hot as the kinetic energy taken out of the spacecraft was converted into heat and dissipated into space. For almost six minutes the crew endured the high acceleration, then suddenly it was all over, and they were back in free fall again.

"Next stop is the Maxwell Gap," Chastity announced. "We'll be there in four-and-a-half hours."

"We'll be going right over the 'spoke' region on the B ring," said Sandra. "With any luck, we'll actually be able to see what the spokes are made of."

Unfortunately, no spokes developed in the region they were passing over, so it was a disappointed Sandra who turned her console over to Seichi for the next maneuver.

"This one is going to be easier than the last one," said Chastity, as she set up her console. "It'll only be seven minutes at a little over a gee. Then Rod needs to do a burn of about a minute, and we'll be on our way down the next rung."

Confidently, Chastity sent out another penetrator toward the moonlet they had chosen in the Maxwell Gap. It was a perfect shot—

the penetrator hit right in the middle of the crater Chastity had chosen, just as the length of the tether reached its two-hundred-kilometer maximum length. The image in the holoviewport in front of Chastity turned black as the penetrator sank deep into the icy surface of the moonlet. She increased the tension on the tether, the gee level in the capsule started to rise, then suddenly the holoviewport image returned—the view was now that of a rapidly disappearing moonlet, almost as if the previous scene were being run backward. Then, as the shock wave returning down the cable hit the capsule, they suddenly found themselves back in free fall.

"*Damn!*" swore Chastity, pulling her right hand out of the tether controller and slamming both fists on the sides of the console in frustration, the metal bracelets on her left wrist clattering against the plastic. "The penetrator didn't hold! You'd better get us out of here, Rod."

"Damn again . . ." she said more softly, looking at the broken nail on the little finger of her left hand.

Sitting behind her, Dan heard the news he had been dreading. They would have to return home. Although they would be paid three hundred million for the thirty-month mission, they would not get the full billion unless they carried out the entire mission successfully— or died in the attempt. Pamela was not going to be happy.

Rod, right hand resting on his joyball controller under the pilot console, left hand poised over the touchscreen, did nothing for a while. His calm test pilot brain was going quickly through all the various options before he took any action. Then he made up his mind.

"I'm going down," he said softly. He turned the joyball, and *Sexdent* rotated until it was traveling backward along its trajectory. He lifted on the suspended sphere and the dozen jets in the base of the spacecraft roared into flame as ton after ton of meta was poured into their bellies to be exhausted as a high-speed reddish-purple plasma of ionized atoms.

When Chastity heard the rockets roar, she felt a tidal wave of fear rise from the pit of her stomach and flood through her body out to the tips of her fingers. She knew the fuel margins that were needed for this mission. The reason that they had climbed down the rings of Saturn using the tether was that they couldn't carry enough fuel to do the job entirely using rocket power. They would need more than two-thirds of their initial 120-ton fuel load for the final burn that would lower their velocity to match the velocity of the upper atmosphere. The number of tons of meta they were supposed to have in their fuel tanks before they attempted the final burn was etched in her memory—88 tons. She found the box on her console that indicated the fuel level. As the seconds passed, the number clocked quickly downward: 95 . . . 94 . . . 93 . . .

"How long is this burn supposed to last?" asked Chastity quietly after a full minute had passed and the number had gotten down to 91.

"Two minutes," replied Rod, holding the throttle steady at three gees.

The fear came back even stronger as the seconds ticked by and the fuel level dropped below 88 and continued down.

"I sure hope he knows what in hell he's doing," whispered Chastity to herself. She wanted to grab the control away from Rod and use the last bit of their fuel to get them out from the inexorable pull of the giant orange planet filling her viewport—out to Titan where they had fuel waiting to take them safely home. But her test pilot training kept her from interfering. She had failed on her part of the task and she now had to trust Rod's judgment.

"I bet you're wondering if I know what in hell I'm doing," said Rod over the roar of the dozen engines beneath them. "I'm just using a little of our ten-percent fuel margin to stay on the mission timeline, that's all."

Chastity watched wide-eyed as the numbers on the fuel indicator kept on dropping. Just as they were reaching eighty tons, Rod pulled down on the joyball and the roar ceased.

"There," he said calmly, monitoring his screen as Seichi checked out and shut down the auxiliary pumps and control systems of the dozen engines, one after the other. "We'll be hitting the upper atmosphere in about three hours."

"That's what I'm afraid of," said Chastity. "Is eighty tons going to slow us down enough?"

"I think we have a little more than that," said Rod. He used the differential motor between the crew module and the fuel module to put some rotational gees on the fuel tanks to settle the meta out around the periphery. "Eighty point three tons," he said finally.

"And we need eighty-eight tons to land without stressing the heat shields," she said. "They're going to get pretty hot—"

"It's not as bad as you think," said Rod. "Now that I've used up our fuel margin, we don't have to use fuel to decelerate that fuel, so we come out ahead."

"As long as I come out of it *with* my head," said Chastity. "How far will 80.3 tons take us?"

"Too complicated for this tired old head to figure," said Rod. "Jeeves? Could you calculate that for me?"

"Our arrival velocity at periapsis will be 27.3 kilometers per second," said Jeeves. "Since the surface velocity of Saturn is 9.9 kilometers per second, a burn of 17.4 kilometers per second will be required. That will necessitate the expenditure of 79.3 tons of fuel."

"See," said Rod serenely. "A whole ton of fuel left over."

"Less than one-percent margin instead of ten percent," said Chastity. "You cut that one pretty close. You'd better be equally good during the big burn."

"That's your job," Rod reminded her. "As commander, my job will be coordinating the activities of all the crew during the landing phase. Besides, didn't the simulator lab techs tell us that you were the better rocket pilot as well as better tether controller? I want the best person at the controls when we attempt the landing—especially since my life depends on it."

He was right, Chastity remembered. There would be a dozen things that needed to be done during the landing phase. Piloting the capsule was only one of them. "I guess I'd better brush up, then," she said, turning to the console and setting it up in simulator mode. "The real thing comes in three hours."

An hour and a quarter later, Rod got a personal video message from Art Dooley. Art was alone in his office. His face was stern.

"Are you alone?" said the image. "If not, restart this message when you are." There was a long pause, then Art looked up again. "I'm in business to make money. A *lot* of money. When you are trying to make a lot of money, you run some risk of losing what you have. I am ready accept that loss—of *money!* I am not willing to lose people's lives just to make *me* money! This mission is dangerous enough without you taking unnecessary risks. You should have aborted when Chastity missed her target. I would have lost a small fortune, but I wouldn't have minded a bit. Fortunately, you were lucky this time. But don't do anything risky again—not on my account, at least."

Rod had to agree that Art was right, and sent him a short apology.

*   *   *

Two hours later, everyone was strapped into their acceleration couches. Saturn filled the viewports as Chastity kept the ship's nose pointed downward. Her left arm, normally festooned with a multitude of bracelets, now bore only a single solid-silver-hinged bangle that held tight to her wrist where there was no chance that it would activate an icon on her touchscreen during their critical descent.

"The equatorial region looks pretty smooth," said Sandra. "You wouldn't think that the winds blow the hardest there."

"Smooth is what I'm looking for," said Chastity. She twisted the joyball and the nose tilted away from the vertical to look in the direction they were traveling.

"You can pick any target point you want, Chass," said Rod. "Saturn's so big that it really doesn't matter much when you do your burn."

"Everybody comfortably settled and ready?" said Chastity, checking the clasp on her bangle. "We'll be pulling three gees for almost ten minutes."

"Let's get it over with," said Dan nervously.

"Light the candle, little lady," said Pete.

Sandra's eyes were shut tight.

Chastity rotated the *Sexdent* around until it was traveling backward. The only thing in their field of view now was a thin line that marked the rings—almost directly overhead. Carefully lining up her yellow trajectory arrow on the console screen with the blue course line that Jeeves had plotted, she lifted up on the throttle and the main engines roared into life. They were pushed into the cushions of their couches at one gee.

"All engines at nominal performance," reported Seichi from the engineering console, his eyes scanning over his scottyboard.

"Thank you for your report, Mr. Takeo," said Rod, in his most commanderlike voice. "Increase gees, Ms. Blaze."

The incongruous formal commands brought a grin to Chastity's face as she raised the joyball even higher in the controller and the acceleration level rose to three gees, and stayed there. . . . After a number of minutes a groan escaped Sandra's lips, followed by a mild curse from Dan. Then there were more minutes of strained silence overlaid on the continuing background rumble of the roaring engines. The black sky outside the viewports started to glow. The ship shuddered slightly as the air thickened and flakes of glowing dust streaked off out of view. Still the engines roared and the pressure on their bodies rose as Saturn slowly added its gravity pull to the slowing spacecraft.

"Heat shield at one thousand kelvin," reported Seichi. "Twelve hundred . . . fifteen hundred—"

"Twenty seconds to cutoff," interjected Chastity over Seichi's reports. "Ten . . . nine . . . eight . . ."

"About time!" added Pete through clenched teeth.

Suddenly the rockets faltered.

"Out of fuel!" yelled Chastity, hastily pulling back on the throttle.

"Good enough!" replied Rod. "Seichi—close the heat shield ports over the engine nozzles, then shut down those main engines carefully, we'll need them to get back up. Chass—switch your controller to the vernier system. We've got a few hundred kilograms of meta in those tanks. Keep the heat shield below five thousand K if you can."

The intense pressure of the high deceleration forces disappeared. But in their place was not the pleasant sensation of free fall that they had all grown used to. Instead, there was the fractional-gee acceleration that came from being in a falling elevator—an elevator that wobbled erratically back and forth as it dropped through the air, leaving a glowing trail of ionized gas and melting ablative material behind it. They passed quickly through a thin cloud layer.

"The heat shield temperature has peaked," said Chastity. "We've reached terminal velocity at this altitude."

"Time to pop the chute," said Rod, pressing an icon on his console. The nosecone of *Sexdent* took off in a jet of hot helium gas, pulling the parachute with it. Everyone held their breath and watched upward through the viewports as the streamer of cloth climbed skyward . . .

. . . and blossomed into a beautiful white flower.

"The prettiest sight I've ever seen," said Pete with relief.

The shock of the opening parachute rattled through the structure, as the multiline tether from the parachute pulled up another, thicker skein of fabric, this time made of clear plastic. On and on it unwound around the conical capsule. It ended with two thumps as two metallic canisters followed it up to the sky, pulling along after them the multiline tether from the nose of the ship. The clear plastic also inflated and slowed their fall, but although they fell more slowly now, they still fell . . . and would continue to fall until the balloon inflated.

"Get that reactor up and running, Mr. Takeo," commanded Rod, but Seichi was already active at his scottyboard. Chastity punched a red icon on her screen. There was a jerk upward as the load was lightened. "Heat shield away!" she announced.

Far below and far away, Petro heard a strange sound through the ultrasensitive hearing chamber that stretched along the leading edge of Petru's wing. It was a screeching sound that started high in the clouds and then softened to a whistling sound, somewhere above and off in the distance. As time stretched on, a second sound started below the slowly falling whistling sound. The second sound grew louder and more shrill as it fell straight downward until it disappeared into the distant depths of the hot hell below them. It moved much faster than any other falling object that Petro had ever heard.

"What was that?" said someone in the hunting formation.

"Nothing you should scan," replied Petro irritably. He had yet to have his first turn in the feeding region near the center of the hunting cone, and the hunger twinges in Petru's gizzard made him easily annoyed. "Keep your pings focused ahead—where the food is!"

Petro thought for a while of reporting the falling object to Petra when she woke at the end of the day. It might be one of those meteors that she was always talking about. But Petro's mind was focused on the hunt and he soon forgot all about the incident.

Minute after minute, the crew felt the uneasy feeling of being once again under gravity instead of free fall, but this gravity wasn't steady and comforting; it had the uneasy variability of something falling. . . .

Chastity used the vernier jets to keep the capsule from tilting or rotating while Seichi got the reactor going. The reactor was hanging below the heat radiator and flexfan complex up at the mouth of the balloon above them. As the reactor started to generate electricity and heat, it passed the waste heat through secondary cooling loops to the radiator fins. The fins started to glow as they radiated away the waste heat, while the electricity from the reactor started to rotate the flex-fans. The fans pulled cold Saturnian air past the glowing radiator fins, turning the high-density cold air into lighter-density hot air that flowed into the mouth of the balloon and started to inflate it.

The crew, still in their acceleration couches, looked upward at the nearly transparent strip of plastic stretching upward above them as it slowly expanded. Sandra read off the altitude, while Dan read off the outside pressure.

"Sixty thousand five hundred," said Sandra.

"One bar," said Dan.

"We're still falling . . ." whispered Pete.

"But slower . . ." added Sandra. "Sixty thousand."

The minutes passed. The balloon above them began to take on a more rotund look. The sinking feeling in the pits of their stomachs slowly faded away as the random motions of the capsule damped out. Rod had half expected a spontaneous cheer to rise up from the crew. He had experienced many such from the passengers after successful landings on Luna and Mars, but this "landing" in the soft clouds of Saturn took so long and arrived so slowly that no one could really tell exactly when the event occurred.

Pete was the first one to acknowledge their safe arrival. Even though the altimeter was still dropping, he unbuckled his couch restraints and got to his feet.

"I don't know about the rest of you," he said, heading for the ladder to the deck below, "but I'm going to have my first worry-free shit in over a year!"

3

LIVING IN THE CLOUDS

ALTITUDE STABILIZED.

Rod read the situation message from Jeeves on the console screen. He gave a small sigh, generated by a combination of relief and pride in a job well done. The balloon had inflated enough to keep them aloft and they were safe. He could now relax, get out of his safety harness, and put away his acceleration couch. Rod had noticed, with a slight bit of annoyance, that most of the others had left their couches some time ago. The others, not having the burden of command responsibility, were off wandering about the ship, making coffee and gawking out the viewports at the scenery like a bunch of hick tourists.

Another message appeared in the box for messages that reported nonurgent but out-of-nominal situations.

EXTERNAL PRESSURE DIFFERENTIAL 1.8 ATMOSPHERES. The number *1.8* was in yellow.

"How many atmospheres can the hull take, Seichi?" he asked, turning his head. Like Rod, Seichi took his responsibilities strongly and he too was still lying supine on his acceleration couch, safety harness snugly keeping him in place, scottyboard hanging above his midsection.

"Four is the nominal limit, sir," Seichi replied, "but it can hold off more than that."

"I don't want to get anywhere close to the limit, nominal or not," said Rod. He turned and hollered down through the grating: "Doc! Is it okay for Seichi to boost the air pressure inside here?"

"Sure," Dan hollered up from the galley. "We planned on doing that anyway, but let me come up and monitor things." He clumped heavily up the ladder in the nearly Earth gravity of Saturn, one step at a time, encumbered with a squeezer of hot coffee that kept squirting hot brown liquid out its straw and onto his wrist as he grasped it tightly to keep it from falling. It would be some time before the crew got used to living under gees again.

"I've already started the pressure increase," said Seichi, as Dan appeared and went to the science console to check on the life support system. By the time Dan had clumsily made his way up the ladder to the control deck, Seichi had reinstalled the scottyboard in its normal position below the holoviewport and was taking his acceleration couch apart.

"Fine," said Dan, reading the pressure gauge on the console screen. He didn't really need to read the gauge, for he could feel the pressure change in his ears. He brought up a copy of the scottyboard on the science console and started to push some icons. "Let me slow it down a little to give our ears a chance to adjust."

Down in the airlock, Chastity was helping Pete into his saturnsuit.

"These saturnsuits are sure a lot easier to put on than vacuum suits," said Pete, shivering in his underwear as he pulled the long flap between his legs and snapped it closed in front. Chastity then shook him into his tight-fitting insulated bright yellow-green pants from behind. She finished by giving the "love handles" spilling over his belt line a pinch for luck, then helped him into his oxygen tank harness. It was much lighter and less bulky than an underwater scuba tank harness, since all Pete had to carry was his oxygen. The inert hydrogen-helium atmosphere of Saturn would take the place of the inert nitrogen that makes up 78 percent of Earth-normal air. Last thing on was his helmet, which regulated the oxygen flow and kept the small amount of ammonia gas in the Saturnian air from getting to the wearer's eyes and face. The helmet had other functions as well. Because it is always dark underneath the multiple cloud decks of Saturn, the helmet had an infrared video camera built into the crown and a light-amplifying holovisor built into the visor. For communication with the ship, there was a high-bandwidth radio link that could transmit video as well as audio.

Chastity cycled Pete through the airlock and stayed just inside the door, watching on the airlock console display a copy of what Pete was seeing in his helmet visor. She kept the volume on the display down so as not to disturb Sandra, who was trying to go to sleep on the facilities deck so she would be fresh and ready to hunt for biological specimens when sunrise came to this part of Saturn. Now that they were in Saturn's gravity field instead of free fall, the sleeping sacks had been arranged to hang like hammocks. The Sun was just setting and Sandra would be able to sleep until sunrise. Saturn had only a ten-and-a-half-hour day, however, so sunrise was five short hours away.

The outer airlock door swung downward in front of Pete with a hiss. He stopped at the threshold of the large opening in the side of their conical ship and looked upward. It was dark, for they were under the ammonia cloud layer and the Sun was setting. He thought he saw one or two faint patches of light in the cloud deck. Probably the light from some of Saturn's moons. He would let Jeeves figure that out later. He looked straight up at the balloon, far above them. In the infrared band of the holovisor, the balloon glowed with a warm red false color from the temperature of the hot air inside it. At the mouth of the balloon was a glaring white spot that was the waste heat radiator for the lesser white spot below it—the plutonium reactor and its electrical generator. The reactor, with its load of twenty kilos of Japanese plutonium, was the "Sun" for this little portion of Earth floating in the cold air of Saturn. The photons from the hidden glowing-hot surface of the nuclear reactor were turned into electricity by the thermophotovoltaic cells that surrounded the reactor. The photons that didn't get made into electricity were reflected back to the reactor, where they were converted into heat again and recycled, while the waste heat generated by the photovoltaic cells went up the secondary cooling loops to the radiator to heat the air in the balloon. The megawatts of electricity generated were shipped down the tether on wires made of room temperature superconductors. Some of the electricity was used to supply power and heat to the crew inside *Sexdent*, but most of the electrical power went to the meta plant, where it was to be turned into fuel. Since the meta plant had not been turned on yet, nearly all of the reactor power was going into making hot air to fill the balloon that was their sole means of support. A small amount of electrical power went into operating floodlights that illuminated the balloon above, and the tether and capsule below.

Pete next stepped out onto the open airlock door, and holding on to the cable attached to the door, he looked over and down, turning his head slowly from side to side so that Chastity and the all-absorbing memory of Jeeves could see what was below them. Far below he could see the next layer of white clouds, illuminated partially by the glow of the setting sun, and partially by the floodlights from the reactor complex above. They looked like water clouds, but he couldn't be sure. Then he spotted a thin cloud formation off in the distance. It hung midway between the ammonia cloud deck above and the cloud deck far below.

"What's that in the center of my view, Jeeves?" asked Pete, holding his head still. "A cirrus cloud?"

"I suspect it is an ammonium hydrosulfide cloud," replied Jeeves. "According to the calculations of the atmospheric physicists, that compound is expected to condense out into clouds at an altitude higher than water vapor but less than ammonia vapor. The ammonium hydrosulfide cloud layer seems to be sparse in this region at this time."

"Good thing, too," said Pete. "Ammonia is bad enough, but ammonia *and* hydrosulfuric acid combined sound like bad news to someone outside in their skivvies."

The cold of the below-freezing atmosphere was beginning to penetrate through the insulation in his suit, so Pete stopped gawking and started the short climb down the rungs built into the conical side of the capsule, being careful to always have at least one safety line attached to either a rung or a safety ring.

As he came to the level of the meta plant and started in on the catwalk between the engines, he could see the heat exchangers for the meta plant hanging below. They had automatically deployed when the heat shield had been dropped. They were glowing dark red in the infrared band of his holovisor, cooled by the nearly two atmospheres of dense, cold hydrogen gas surrounding them. He entered the small airlock in the meta plant with relief, for the walls of the metal tube were warm from all the equipment heating up the inside of the plant. It wasn't long before Pete had every unit in the complex plant busily turning Saturn atmosphere into meta.

When Pete returned an hour later, both Rod and Chastity were waiting for him at the airlock door.

"How does it look?" asked Rod, although he was already relieved at the bright, confident smile on Pete's face.

"You can start planning on how you're going to spend your money, you billionaire," said Pete. "All the units are operating perfectly and pumping out meta by the liter. We're making over a ton a day. We should have the hundred and twenty tons we need well before the hundred and eighty days we planned." He turned to Chastity and started opening his mouth again, but she put a long-nailed index finger in front of her lips and pointed to the hammock behind him. "Sandra's still asleep," she whispered. "We'll see you upstairs and you can tell us more."

"First things first," whispered Pete, pulling open the door to one of the toilets and going in.

Later, up on the flight deck, Pete, Rod, Chastity, and Dan discussed their plans for the next few days.

"I can operate the plant up here at this altitude," said Pete, "but the meta production would be improved if the input gas were at higher pressure, so the partial pressure of helium would be higher."

"Sandra and I would like to get down in the water cloud layer," said Dan. "I doubt we'll find any significant lifeforms up here where it is dry and cold."

"Cold is right!" said Pete. "That's the other reason I want to go where the pressure is higher—the air will be warmer and I won't freeze my balls off every time I check on the meta plant."

"I'll start a descent trajectory, then," said Rod. "But at the same time I'm going to head north. We had to land near the equator so we could take advantage of Saturn's rotation. But the trade winds are high near the equator and high wind velocity means high turbulence. We've been lucky so far, but the farther we get out of this region the better I'll feel."

"Take the descent portion real slowly," said Dan. "It'll make it easier for all of us to readjust. I'm also going to have to change the mixture. Nitrogen is okay up to a few atmospheres for short periods, but since we'll be down here six months at even higher pressures, there's the problem of nitrogen narcosis. I'm going to switch us over to a deep-diving mixture of helium and oxygen. Fortunately, there's plenty of helium outside, and with all the electrical power coming down from the reactor, we can make all the oxygen we need by electrolysis. I'll also set up the science console so when we exceed six atmospheres it will slowly change us from a helium-oxygen atmosphere to a hydreliox mix."

"Hydreliox?" asked Chastity.

"A mixture of hydrogen, helium, and oxygen," replied Dan. "It's what the deep-sea divers use for saturation dives, where you stay down for days at a time. Even though it has hydrogen mixed with oxygen, it won't explode, since above six atmospheres the oxygen content needed to keep the partial pressure in our lungs at twenty-one percent Earth normal is less than four percent. The record for hydreliox breathing is sixty-six atmospheres' pressure for forty-three days. It was set by a group of researchers in a dry tank, sort of like the conditions we're working under. They came out fine."

"But we're going to be breathing that mixture for a hundred and eighty days," said Chastity. "More than four times longer."

"But the highest pressure we plan on using is ten to twelve atmospheres," Dan reminded her.

"It's still risky," murmured Chastity.

"That's why we're getting paid a billion each," said Rod, ending the conversation. "Let's get to our scheduled shift tasks."

Pete punched an icon on a nearby console. "Jeeves says I should be asleep," he announced, reading the screen. "I think I'll join Sandra on the sleeping deck."

"I'm on pilot duty," said Chastity, who always knew her scheduled duties.

"Then rotate the flexfans to horizontal and take us north, Ms. Blaze," ordered Rod.

"Aye-aye, sir," said Chastity, swiveling around to the pilot console.

Soon, far above them, four huge electrically powered fans swiveled in their frames, unrolled their large flexible blades, and started to turn, pushing cold Saturnian air past them to the south while dragging a giant balloon and a tiny encapsulated bit of humanity to the north.

Four hours later, there was a high-pitched cry from one of the sleeping bags on the facilities deck. Sandra unzipped the sound barrier and stuck her head out, concern on her face. She saw Dan at the galley, having another squeezer of coffee.

"Something's happened to my voice, Doc!" she said. "I squeak! I must be coming down with laryngitis! I thought we were through with those Earth bugs!"

"You're perfectly fine," Dan reassured her in a tenor voice.

"You squeak too!" Sandra exclaimed.

"I've changed the air mixture," Dan replied. "The velocity of sound is three to four times higher in helium than in air, so your voice box has a higher natural resonant frequency. You'll get used to it."

They all did—after a long time—but sometimes, especially after a long period of not talking, such as right after waking up, hearing the voice of Donald Duck squawking from their mouths was a rude surprise.

Both Dan and Sandra were busy soon after daybreak. Dan was scanning the horizon for any sign of flying lifeforms from the scotty console holoviewport, while Sandra was operating the high-resolution telescope from the science console. Rod was piloting the ship from the pilot console, turning the capsule at Sandra's direction so she could get a panoramic record of the clouds around them in the multispectral camera.

"Just as expected," said Sandra as she took a quick look at the data piling up in Jeeves's almost-bottomless memory. "With the multispectral camera we can get the chemical components of the various cloud formations. We've got orange-tinged ammonia clouds above, white water clouds below, and an occasional gray ammonium hydrosulfide cloud in between. See anything out there more interesting for me to focus on, Doc?"

"I'm afraid not," said Dan, lowering the biviewers with a sigh. "We need to get down to the water cloud layer."

"We're on the way," promised Rod. "But it will take us a day or so. Do you two want to do another scan?"

Dan looked at Sandra and she shook her head.

"It would be a waste of time," said Dan. "We might as well do something else."

"Like make ourselves a decent place to sleep!" suggested Sandra.

"Lunch first," said Rod, putting the balloon on autopilot and heading down the ladder.

After a quick lunch of green pea soup with microwave "puffed" croutons expanded from compact cubelets, the crew set to work making their "house" a "home." The habitat tubes were pulled up out of each other and reinstalled. The last time they did this, they were in free fall. Back when they were in space and in free fall, the habitat tubes were massive—nearly eighty-five kilograms—but they were not "heavy," and could be easily wrestled into place by hand. Now, the near-Earth-normal gravity pull of Saturn made the habitat tubes dangerously heavy. The crew had to use a winch, along with plenty of muscle power, to install them in place.

"Last one!" said Rod with relief as he cinched down the last of the seals.

"Now we can sleep like civilized beings again," said Sandra, watching out her open habitat hatchdoor from her recently installed bed, "instead of hanging in a sack."

The light through the viewport windows faded swiftly as the Sun set once again on the rapidly rotating planet.

"Well," said Rod. "I guess it's too dark now to get any work done on the outside. We might as well go to bed and get started early tomorrow morning."

"It's too early to go to bed," complained Pete. "Besides, the night is only five hours long here—you'd just barely get to sleep before you'd have to wake up again. Let's have a party and stay up all night instead!"

Rod looked dubious.

"That sounds like fun!" said Sandra with a giggle.

"It would be a great way to celebrate our safe arrival—and our billion dollars," Dan added.

"I could make some hors d'oeuvres," said Chastity. "On those long trips out to Mars and back, I developed a number of ways to turn our standard entrées into something different—and tasty."

"I could contribute some music," said Seichi. "I played keyboard in a dance band during college."

"And I can contribute the drinks," said Pete. "I've had the chemsyns in my lab busy producing ethanol. I mostly use the stuff to clean the optics on my lasers—but I've got plenty of bottles to spare. It won't take me more than a few minutes to go outside and get some."

"Now that's beginning to sound like a real party!" said Rod, finally convinced. "Let me help you on with your saturnsuit." The two started down the ladder to the airlock.

"I think I'll go take a shower," said Dan, following them down. "I'm all smelly and sweaty from fighting those habitats."

"I'll get my keyboard," said Seichi, crawling headfirst into his habitat.

"And I'll put on my party dress," said Sandra, ducking back into her habitat and pulling the hatchdoor shut. "It's got a real skirt—great for polkas!"

"Party dress!" said Chastity, shaking her head to herself as she was left alone on the control deck. She looked down at her utilitarian jumpsuit—the only costume she wore in space. She had brought along three more outfits for this trip—all the same. She thought briefly of putting on one of her nightgowns for the party. They were pretty—although a little thin—but the elastic band at the ankles would make it impossible to dance. She thought for a bit, then reached up to her chest and lowered her zipper a little. Now dressed for the party, she climbed down the ladder to the galley on the facilities deck to start work on the party snacks.

As Chastity arrived on the lower deck, Rod was shutting the inner airlock door on Pete, who was putting on his helmet, ready to go out. Rod's eyebrows rose when he saw the level of Chastity's zipper. He hadn't seen that much of her cleavage in weeks. He turned to the airlock controls and cycled Pete out.

Dan came out of the head. From his wet hair it was obvious that he had opted for a complete shower instead of a sponge bath. Chastity was pleased to smell the aroma of Old Spice in the air—the chemsyns did a good job on that aroma. It was going to be nice consorting with "male" men at a party this evening, instead of the "guy" men she worked alongside every day. She was beginning to look forward to the party. While the reconstituted hot dogs were plumping in the microwave, she ducked into the "ladies' " and opened her personal locker. Some of her large collection of bracelets were there. She put them all on, decorating both wrists this time. She would be maneuvering men, not spacecraft, for the next few hours, so bracelets would be more of a help than a hindrance. While freshening up her lipstick and putting on some perfume, she had another thought and got out her nail polish collection. Soon the short nails on her "astronaut" right hand were decorated as prettily as the longer nails on her left hand. She took a look in the mirror at the level of her zipper.

"Don't want to look too eager," she said to herself, pulling the slider up a few teeth.

As she exited the ladies', she looked up to see Seichi coming down the ladder. He too had "dressed up," in a brightly colored "Hawaiian" shirt. He was followed close behind by Sandra, wearing a bright red skirt, red stockings, and black Velcro-bottomed slippers.

"No peeking now," said Sandra, as she stepped out onto the open grating above them and headed for the ladder. The men studiously avoided looking up until Sandra was stepping off the last rung.

Humph, thought Chastity to herself as she saw how deeply the front of Sandra's blouse was scooped. *I wonder why she was so concerned about them peeking up her skirt—they can see almost as far peeking down her front*. Still, she was relieved to see Sandra's low neckline—she wasn't the only one being a little naughty tonight.

As Sandra let loose of the ladder, Rod stepped forward, and giving a gallant bow, asked in his most gentlemanly manner, "Ah would be most pleased if you would honor me with the first dance, Miss Ruby . . ." The gallant effect was slightly spoiled by Rod's high tenor voice.

"Wye, certainly, Colonel Montrose," said Sandra, limping her hand at him. She turned to Seichi. "Can you do a polka?" Then she had another thought. Miss Ruby—the vixen—disappeared and Sandra Green—the scientist—took her place.

"Say, I wonder how that's going to sound? Will it be pitched up in tone like our voices?"

"I don't know," said Seichi. He played a chord, then a short tune. "Sounds the same to me—"

"It is," said Dan. "Since that keyboard has no resonant structures, it'll sound pretty much the same. The reason your voice changes is that your vocal cords just make a buzzing sound. It's the resonances in the voice box that pick out the frequencies that get emphasized, and, for a certain-sized box, the resonant frequencies change with the speed of sound."

Seichi quickly segued into a polka, and Rod and Sandra started to dance, trying to avoid the ladder in the middle of the facilities deck as well as the spectators trying to keep out of the way in the "corners" of the two-meter-diameter hexagonal room.

When the tune came to an end, Sandra was beaming but Rod

was tired from the strain of trying to avoid hitting something. "Once we get Pete back, we can use the airlock for the wallflowers, and let the dancers have the floor."

"In the meantime, there's room for two couples on the floor if we slow-dance," said Dan. He came up to Chastity and bowed. "May I have this dance?"

Seichi switched to a slow waltz and Dan took Chastity in his arms, his eyes carefully avoiding looking down as he did so.

Pete soon returned with a number of plastic bottles. While Pete set up the bar in the airlock and Chastity arranged the hors d'oeuvres on the galley area, Rod and Dan removed the ladder so they would have more dancing room. It took some effort, but they finally got the ladder sections unhooked and shoved up on the top deck grating, out of the way. Soon all were drinking various fruit juices spiked with Pete's "laser juice," and nibbling expanded bread wedges spread with liver pâté or cream cheese and hot sauce, and dipping hot dog chunks into a barbecue sauce and mustard mix.

After a number of dances, Dan asked Seichi to show him how the keyboard worked.

"My mother made me take piano lessons when I was a kid," said Dan. "Maybe I can make enough music so you can have a turn dancing with the girls." The keyboard had a number of features, including instant memory, so shortly Dan was blasting out a loud polka, while Seichi and Sandra twirled violently around the room.

After an hour, it soon became obvious that Pete had skimped on the food and loaded up on the laser juice. He was too drunk to either dance or talk. Dan and Rod wrestled him into a sleeping bag and hung him in the back of the airlock to sleep it off.

The next time Dan locked arms with Chastity for a slow dance the liquor made him lose control of his eyes and they looked down. Chastity caught him doing it, but instead of ignoring it, she smiled and winked at him. So far on this trip he had resisted her invitations. Maybe this time . . .

"Like what you see?" she asked, moving closer so that her long fingernails were scratching lightly at the back of his neck. "You can have more—"

"I like what I see," replied Dan. "And I like you . . . but I can't have you . . . I'm sorry." He started to back out of her arms, but she pulled him back.

"Stay and dance anyway," she said, snuggling into his chest. "You're nice . . . and I like you . . . even if I can't have you. . . ."

The party slowed down. The dancing stopped and they all just sat on the floor, finishing off the last of the food and talking. Rod had Sandra giggling in one corner, and Dan, Seichi, and Chastity sat on the dressing benches in the airlock and talked about Earth.

A little while later, Rod put up the ladder, then loudly said, "Well, goodnight all . . ." as he and Sandra headed up to their habitats. After a polite interval, Dan left too, leaving Chastity and Seichi alone.

"Can you make that keyboard play automatically?" asked Chastity as she and Seichi finished off the last of the liver pâté.

"Certainly," said Seichi, reaching for it.

"Then have it play something slow for one last dance—just you and me," said Chastity.

Over the next few days, Rod and Chastity took turns "driving" the balloon north using the electrically powered flexfans.

"Whoops!" said Chastity as the balloon suddenly dropped a few hundred meters, producing a sinking feeling in her stomach. "I'll sure be glad when we get out of this equatorial jet stream with all of its turbulence."

"Pete will be glad too," said Rod, feeling queasy himself from the swinging motion of the capsule. "He's taking a risk every time he goes outside to check on the meta plant. One of those 'whoops' at the wrong time and he's gone. . . ."

The next day they entered the white clouds below. Sandra and Dan were carefully watching the readings of the chemical analyzer monitoring the composition of the air outside. As they entered the cloud deck, the readings shifted slightly.

"Water," said Dan. "Ice at these temperatures, but mostly water."

"A little bit of ammonia and ammonium hydrosulfide, but not much," added Sandra. "With the helmets to protect our eyes and noses, and the saturnsuits to protect our skin, it shouldn't be too bad, although I wouldn't want to stay out in it too long."

"Once we get down under the cloud deck where it's dry, it shouldn't be bad at all," said Dan. "Except when it rains."

"Once we get down under the cloud deck, I'm counting on seeing some saganlife forms and perhaps catching a few specimens," said Sandra. "Something *really* alien."

"Although you can't *see* any lifeforms up here in the clouds," said Dan. "You might be able to *catch* some . . . small ones . . . riding on the water droplets."

"You're right!" said Sandra, getting up. "Help me get in my saturnsuit. I'm going out to set up a dew net and see what I can collect."

"If you wait until we drop below the freezing point so we are collecting water droplets rather than ice crystals, I'll come with you," said Dan.

A few hours later, Dan and Sandra were standing out on the open outer airlock door in their neon-bright fire-engine yellow-green high-visibility saturnsuits. On their arms, legs, and helmets was a highly reflecting colored identification band. Sandra's color was green, of course, while Dan's was orange. Each had a safety line attached to rings on opposite sides of the door. They peeked over the edge. The water cloud layer they were in was thick and dark. The 1 percent of Earth-level sunlight that made it across the ten AU of distance to Saturn was now almost completely absorbed by the thick mist. Dan turned on the floodlights that illuminated the exit opening of the airlock, but the intense beams were swallowed up a few meters away by the dense white fog.

Sandra and Dan threw out a net made of absorbent string. After letting it hang over the side for about fifteen minutes, while *Sexdent* plowed its way through the mist, they pulled it back up, soaking wet, and stuffed it in a large plastic bag.

"Look!" said Sandra, as she held the bottom corner of the bag up into the bright beam of the floodlight. "A tiny jellyfish!"

Dan looked carefully at the tiny struggling creature. "Looks like it's drowning to me."

"Drowning?" said Sandra, taking another look.

"It may be built like a jellyfish," said Dan, "but I think it prefers air to water."

Later, inside, after fishing out the larger specimens that were visible as tiny specks in an intense light beam, and putting them into

separate containers, Dan and Sandra went into a routine. Down on
the lower deck, Dan would prepare a slide from some water drop
that had something interesting floating in it, and hand the slide to
Puss, who would clamber into the constricted confines of the engineering sector on its six feet, and insert the slide into a nanoimager
there. Meanwhile, up on the command deck, Sandra, with the aid
of Jeeves, would quickly scan the slide using the large display on the
science console. Jeeves would save a detailed digital image for later
analysis, while Sandra would look quickly at the larger specks to see
if any of them were significantly different from the others. After a
couple of hours, Sandra called a halt.

"My eyes have had it," she said. "Let's let Jeeves and Puss do the
rest. There's nothing but simple sinkers here—no floaters or swimmers—too small."

"Sinkers?" asked Seichi, who was watching over her shoulder.

"The simplest of saganlife," said Sandra. "Even if a creature is
heavier than air, if it is small enough, the viscous drag of the air is
high and its rate of fall is slow. These small sinkers are easily carried
upward by convective air flows, such as the thermal that is lifting the
warm wet air below us, where it condenses to form the cloud around
us. The small sinkers use the thermals to rise up to where there is
light and they can use photosynthesis to grow. But as they grow, they
become heavier and are no longer buoyed up by the air currents.
They sink deeper and deeper into the atmosphere until they get to
the depths where the air is so hot they are pyrolyzed."

"Pyrolyzed?"

"Cooked to a crisp," said Sandra.

"That does not sound like a viable mode of living," said Seichi,
dubiously.

"It takes a month or two for the mature sinkers to fall," said Sandra. "As long as they can reproduce a new generation of tiny sinkers
in that time period, then life goes on. The more successful lifeforms
have learned to float or swim, although most swimmers also have
flotation bladders."

She cleared the screen. "I think I'll go get a cup of coffee." She
clambered down the ladder to the galley on the deck below, while
Seichi returned to his post at the scottyboard.

When Sandra turned away from the galley, sucking on the hot

squeezer, she saw Dan standing at the door of the engineering sector, holding a glass tube with stoppers at both ends and hoses running into the stoppers.

"I rescued him," said Dan, holding up the tube.

"Who?" asked Sandra, bewildered.

"The drowned jellyfish," said Dan. "Fortunately, the water protected him from the oxygen in our atmosphere until I could transfer him to this tube and evaporate the water away with some oxygen-free outside air. Nearly blew him away in the process, but now he's stabilized. See him . . . up near the top . . . swimming upward toward the light."

Sandra looked at the pulsating microscopic glitter floating in the air inside the glass tube.

"Half-balloon, half-jellyfish," she said, looking carefully at the tiny speck. "A toroidal bladder of hydrogen to provide buoyancy and hoop stiffness, a mouth that gulps air into the top of the hole in the toroid and squirts it out the bottom to provide jet power, and fine sticky tentacles waving in the jet exhaust to capture anything worth eating. Awfully tiny for a floater."

"Floater and swimmer," Dan reminded her. "Saturn's air is ninety-four percent hydrogen and only six percent helium, so there isn't much density difference between the pure hydrogen in his flotation bladder and the hydrogen-helium air mixture outside. When he stops gulping, he starts sinking."

"Needs to get a lot bigger before he becomes a true floater," said Sandra. "What should I call it, Jeeves? It's a ring-shaped creature that swims to keep alive."

"The Latin name for a ring- or annular-shaped swimming creature is *Annulus natare,*" replied Jeeves.

"Sounds good to me," said Sandra cheerfully.

"The motto for these tiny guys is 'Eat to live,' " agreed Dan. "I wonder how big a ringswimmer can get?"

The scientists back on Earth were overjoyed that Sandra and Dan had not only identified a new species on Saturn, but had actually captured a sample of it, which could be frozen and analyzed later on Earth. They were slightly disappointed later when they learned that

Jeeves and the nanoimager onboard had been able to determine the chemical makeup and genetic structure of *Annulus*. It wasn't too much different from life on Earth.

"Not surprising," said Dan, after Jeeves had given its initial verdict. "Asteroids strike all the planets all the time, and some of them are powerful enough to throw off large blocks of rock or ice into space, with microscopic spores hidden inside the cracks. It would take just one rock, blasted off from the Earth's surface billions of years ago, to infect Saturn. After all, as we have found, the environment under the clouds of Saturn isn't that much different from the environment a few hundred meters beneath the surface of Earth's oceans."

"A detailed study of the gene pattern should be able to determine *when* the Saturn genetic pattern deviated from the Earth genetic pattern," said Sandra hopefully.

"I'm sure it will," said Dan, reassuringly.

"I'm afraid that is not going to be exciting enough to get the Congress-critters to spend more money to come here for scientific purposes," interjected Rod.

Rod was right. Although the scientific community was very excited over the finding, the public and Congress soon relegated the discovery to the category of: "another kind of jellyfish," although some of the more intelligent ones added: "on Saturn."

The dawn of the next day found the *Sexdent* hanging below the water cloud layer. The balloon itself, a kilometer above them, was still inside the clouds.

"Wake up, you sleepy heads!" called Chastity through the intercom to the habitats. She had been standing watch at the pilot console while the rest of the crew slept through the short Saturnian night. "Wake up and look out your viewports! I can see down! And I mean *down!*" She adjusted the multitude of floodlights on the outside of the capsule so they were all pointing downward. Inside their habitats the rest of the crew woke from their five-hour night's rest and rotated the tilted viewports in the ends of their habitat tubes so they too could look down. The view below them was free of visible clouds, but they could see no surface. The floodlight beams just faded out in the distance far below them.

"That sure is a long way down," said Pete over the intercom as he stared down into the blackness from the comfort of his bed.

"And the lower you go the hotter it gets," said Dan, who was also looking down from inside his habitat. "Say, Chass," he added. "What is the temperature outside? Should be above freezing now that we're under the cloud layer."

"It is," replied Chastity. "Temperature is eight degrees C. That's warm enough that we don't even need to wear our saturnsuits anymore. We can go outside in our coveralls. Almost like being on Earth—nearly one-gee gravity and room temperature air."

"You must like to live in colder rooms than me," said Rod from his habitat. "Besides, we still have the high pressure to cope with." The reminder of the high-pressure environment they were in made everyone notice once again Rod's high tenor voice from the hydreliox mixture they were all breathing. "What *is* the pressure anyway?"

"Just under ten bars," replied Chastity.

"That's a lot," complained Rod.

"Ten bars is like being under only one hundred meters of water," said Dan. "People have gone a lot deeper."

"But not for as long as we will be doing," Rod reminded him.

"That's why we're getting paid a billion each," retorted Chastity. "Hurry up and get dressed, so you can take over this pilot console. We're already ten minutes into my sleep shift."

"Set it on autopilot and go to bed," said Rod. "I'll be up and take over as soon as I've had my coffee."

Sandra was the first one dressed. While the others were gathering around the galley for breakfast and coffee, she skipped breakfast and took over the science console. Pulling down the biviewer, she set it on maximum photon amplification and maximum zoom, and started a scan.

After a while Rod came up the ladder, a breakfast bar in one hand and a squeezer of coffee in the other. After checking all the settings Chastity had left on the autopilot, he left the pilot console alone and went over to the science console to see how Sandra was doing.

"See anything?" he asked, then realized how dumb the question was. If Sandra had seen something, she would have announced it immediately, and everyone would be crowding around one of the holoviewports trying to see it too.

"Hard to see anything when it's as dark as it is," replied Sandra.

"With the sunlight cut by a factor of a hundred by the ten-AU distance, and what sunlight there is left being absorbed by the three cloud layers above us, there's practically no light left to see with."

"I guess the creatures out there must be blind," suggested Rod. "Like the creatures that live in caves or the bottom of the ocean."

"Either that, or they would have to have eyes as big around as *Sexdent* to collect enough light to see at all," replied Sandra. After a while, she finally whispered, "I think I see something. Get this bearing, Jeeves." She lined up the biviewer crosshairs and pushed a button on the handgrip.

"I have both a radar and a sonar return from that point," said Jeeves. "The object has a significant Doppler shift and width. It is coming in this direction and consists of a multitude of smaller objects moving in formation."

Now that her brain had the clue, Sandra was finally able to "see" what she was seeing. "It's a flock of snakes!" she cried loudly. Dan, resting in his habitat, trying to compose in his mind his next long-distance message to Pamela and the kids, suddenly flipped ends in his habitat, grabbed his biviewer from its holster in the end of his habitat, and with the guidance of Jeeves, soon had the biviewer focused on the long, narrow cloud.

"Or I guess I should call it a school of snakes," said Sandra, as the cloud grew closer.

"Ribbonsnakes," said Dan. "Like the ribbonfish on Earth . . . swimming in formation like a flock of geese, except they are swimming vertically instead of horizontally."

The school of animals were indeed shaped like ribbons, very thin and very long, but wide all along their midsection. They swam through the air with a vertical waving motion. They looked like a ribbon waving in the wind, but instead of merely responding to the wind, they were the ones doing the waving, moving themselves along by pushing on the pockets of air they had crested. On each side of the "leader" ribbonfish, and one "wavelength" behind, were two other ribbonfish, riding on the "wake" the leader fish had made. The vertical "V" formation looked very much like those formed by migrating geese.

"Hey! What's happening!" complained Dan, as the capsule suddenly spun on its axis, rotating the ribbonfish formation out of his line of view.

"They're flying by, and aren't going to get any closer, so I'm having Rod rotate the telescope around," replied Sandra over the intercom link. "I want to get a close-up view of those creatures. I don't see any eyes or mouth and they're too thin to have a big gut."

After the flock had flown away, Sandra and Dan had time to look closely at the enlarged images of the *Infula natrix,* or "ribbon-shaped swimming-snakes"—the name Jeeves and Sandra had given the creatures in order to avoid confusion with Earth ribbonfish.

"No sign of a mouth," agreed Dan. "And awfully thin. The big ones are hundreds of meters long and four meters wide, but only a few centimeters thick. They certainly aren't floaters. That's a lousy surface-to-volume ratio for a balloon."

"Pure swimmers," said Sandra with certainty.

"With no mouths, they can't be 'hunters' in the usual sense," said Dan, highly puzzled.

"Maybe there *is* a mouth, but we can't recognize it," suggested Sandra.

"Well, *I* sure can't," said Dan. "And with no eyes they wouldn't be good hunters anyway."

"There are a number of dark spots spaced along the edges of the creatures," said Sandra. "There seem to be more of them at the 'head' portion than along the sides and at the tail. Perhaps those are the eyes."

"There could be a lot of small eyes like those on a scallop," suggested Dan. "More for detection of shadows than for imaging."

"Scallops have eyes?" interjected Rod, who had been listening to the two scientists while keeping the balloon headed north.

"Scallops have a couple of dozen cute little baby-blue peepers stuck up on stalks, all around the perimeter of the tasty part—the better to see you with," said Dan. "If they spot the shadow of a predator, they snap their shells shut and the water squirting out between the two closing shells jet-propels them away from harm."

"Scallops have *eyes!?*" exclaimed Rod again, more loudly this time. "I didn't know they had eyes! I don't think I'll ever eat scallops again!"

"Then again, the ribbonsnakes may see by sonar," said Sandra, ignoring Rod's histrionics. "And those dots are some other organ."

"Or maybe the spots are just pure decoration," added Dan. "That's the trouble with *real* alien lifeforms . . . it's hard to interpret what you observe."

They finally gave up and stored the images away in the bottom-less depths of Jeeves's memory, remembering to send copies to their scientific colleagues back in Mission Control on Earth. The five-hour-long "day" was over, so they went back to bed for a nap, in order that they would be ready to search the skies when sunrise came again.

The next day's search was highly successful. There were breaks in both the ammonia and water cloud layers, and yellow sunbeams would shine down to their level. In many cases the distant sunbeams would illuminate creatures floating through the air. Fortunately the telescope had motion compensation, so high magnification could be used, and they obtained brightly illuminated high-quality images of a number of different air creatures.

"This one looks familiar," said Dan as he zoomed the telescope in on a large creature illuminated from above by a beam of sunlight. "It's a bigger version of the *Annulus* ringswimmer that I rescued from the drop of water."

"You're right," agreed Sandra as she looked at the jellyfishlike creature. There was a large toroidal balloon that provided basic flota-tion. Hanging down from the outer perimeter of the fat ring was a cylindrically shaped, slowly pulsating thin membrane that pushed the creature upward with each pulse. Acting in synchronism with the outer membrane was a smaller, conical membrane hanging down from the inner perimeter or "mouth" of the creature. When the outer membrane was contracting, the inner membrane collapsed, blocking the hole in the ring and forcing the thick air out the bot-tom to produce the jet pulse that pushed the creature upward. When the outer membrane was expanding, the inner membrane opened, drawing fresh air, laden with microscopic bits of food, inside for the next pulse. Both membranes were covered with long cilia that cap-tured the food out of the air as it passed through the creature.

"Those pulsation cycles are taking almost a whole minute to complete," said Dan. "That must mean that the creature is quite large. It's hard to tell at this distance. Jeeves?" he asked. "What's the size of that thing?"

"The outer diameter of the flotation ring is ten meters, while the total length from the top of the ring to the base of the outer mem-brane is about fifty meters," replied Jeeves.

"That's as big as the *Sexdent!*" exclaimed Dan. "It's amazing how big the thing is, compared to the tiny specimen that we captured in the cloud net. You'd think a creature that large would spawn larger children."

"For all its size, it is still very primitive," replied Sandra. "There are jellyfish almost that big back in the oceans of Earth, and they too have microscopic spawn."

"But you would think that because it depends upon a flotation ring to keep afloat, there would be a minimum size for survival. The membrane of the flotation ring can only be made so thin. The smaller the volume enclosed, the greater the proportion of the membrane mass to the total mass. There has to be a minimum size below which a 'floater' turns into a 'sinker.' "

"You're forgetting that the ringswimmers can swim as well as float. When they're small, they keep afloat by swimming, which is easy when you're a tiny creature. At that size, swimming through the thick air here on Saturn is like swimming through molasses—you sort of 'crawl' through the air. Later, after they get bigger, and swimming is less effective, the flotation ring keeps them up between strokes."

The short "sunlit" day was nearly over when Dan noticed a large water cloud forming in an otherwise clear patch of sky.

"Looks like a thermal column is forming over there," he said, marking the angle to the cloud using the direction-finding ability of the biviewer he was using.

"Where?" asked Seichi with some concern, for he was acting pilot for this shift. "I want to make sure I avoid it." Jeeves marked it on the situation display. It was well off to the east, far from their planned track northward.

"A thermal column means hot air rising up from the lower depths," said Sandra. "There's bound to be some critters rising sunward along with the air. Rotate the telescope viewport around to that side, Seichi."

"It's a pretty big cloud," Dan warned her. "Must be pretty dark underneath it."

Fortunately, with the Sun setting in the west, the illumination was nearly perfect for viewing the contents of the rising column of air in the thermal.

Dan increased the zoom on the biviewer. "Specks!" he announced. "Thousands of specks!"

"Come on!" Sandra swore impatiently as she shoved the telescope drive icon to its maximum slew speed. Finally the specks showed up on the imager—greatly magnified compared to the maximum zoom available through Dan's biviewers.

"Balloons!" she exclaimed as the slewing stopped and the images steadied on her screen. "Thousands of balloons!" Slowly she scanned the telescope up and down the rising column of iridescent spheres. "Big balloons rising fast near the top of the column until they disappear into the bottom of the cloud and smaller balloons rising more slowly down below."

"That makes sense," said Dan. "The bigger the balloon is, the better the lift-to-mass ratio."

"What are you going to name them?" asked Dan.

"It's already been named," said Sandra. "This is one of the few saganlife species where the images returned from the Saturn penetrator probes contained enough information to allow firm classification. This species is the *Bulla volitare,* or 'bubblefloater.' Just to make sure, I'll need to take a closeup view of the underpinnings." She zoomed the telescope in on the bottom part of one of the larger balloons rising up above them. Dan came over to look at the expanded image in the display.

"Yep, *Bulla volitare,* all right," she murmured, pointing at the screen. "A multitude of long sticky tendrils hanging down from the perimeter to catch the food, just like on an Earth jellyfish."

"What is that long tubelike thing hanging down inside the fringe of tendrils?" asked Dan.

"Looks like a penis to me," said Rod, who had come to the upper deck to take over the pilot duties from Seichi.

"It's *not!*" said Sandra primly. "It's a proboscis—used for sucking up the food bits that land on the sticky tentacles—at least that's what was deduced from a series of images we got from the last imaging probes. Let's watch it in action and see if they got it right."

As they watched, the proboscis made a spiraling motion around the inside of the curtain of tendrils, occasionally stopping as it coped with a particularly large "bite."

"Look!" said Dan. "One of the smaller balloons has been captured by the tendrils of a larger balloon." The impact of the large prey on the tendril curtain caused the proboscis to halt its spiral search pattern, and it swung across the interior of the curtain of tendrils to the other side. By the time it arrived, the balloon portion of the captured bubblefloater had deflated.

"I bet it deflated in an attempt to make itself too heavy to hold up," said Dan. "But it doesn't seem to have worked. Those tendrils must be really sticky."

"Yet, the fact that the bubblefloaters have evolved an escape strategy indicates that they have at least a modest intelligence," remarked Sandra, who was already planning her next hyperpaper. This would be a spectacular one, with all the video images she would be able to include along with the text.

"Looks like the proboscis is going to get a nice big chunk of meat to eat for a change," said Rod, fascinated by the scene, "instead of a constant diet of little tidbits."

"It would really be a shame if such pretty creatures as the bubblefloaters turned out to be cannibals," said Sandra. She then felt a little ashamed at making such a judgmental statement. Certainly these creatures were so limited in intelligence that they could be forgiven for eating their own kind. Nevertheless, she was relieved when the proboscis, instead of tearing away at the captured balloon, lifted off the sticky tendrils one by one and allowed the captured balloon to drop free.

"Let's look at some of the other bubblefloaters," said Sandra, using the icon control to slowly slew the telescope from one target to another. There was enough light that she could split the incoming beam into two different images with different magnification, one of which showed the swirling cloud of rising balloons as small glistening dots, while the other gave the expanded image in a window superimposed on the broader view. She stopped at one pair of dots, then quickly swerved past.

"Say!" exclaimed Rod, who had been watching a copy of Sandra's screen on his console. "Go back to that one! Are they doing what I think they're doing?"

Sandra's face turned beet red as she hesitated. "Very well," she said, the scientist in her annoyed with herself for having acted so prudishly. She swerved the magnified window back until it was centered on the two dots. There were two bubblefloaters rising together, side by side, holding "hands" by their tendrils. The proboscis of each was extended over underneath the tendril curtain of the other, with the tip of each proboscis buried deep within the dense "core body" at the base of the flotation sphere.

"I told you those long things looked like a penis," said Rod loudly.

"They *could* be feeding each other," said Sandra, but even she didn't believe that.

They kept the telescope on the rising coupled pair, but nothing happened.

"They really make it last a long time," said Rod, impressed.

That remark was enough for Sandra, and she swerved the telescope off to other targets. Just before the Sun set behind an ammonia cloud, they spotted a bubblefloater with babies. Below the large spherical float of the "mother" bubblefloater were a dozen smaller balloons. Each seemed to be fixed to a number of the sticky tendrils, up near the base of the tendril where it came out of the equator of the flotation sphere. The proboscis of the mother not only brought food to the mouth of the parent, but occasionally would take a tidbit up to one of the babies, where it was eagerly grabbed by the proboscis of the little one and transferred to its tiny mouth.

"That makes evolutionary sense," said Dan approvingly. "Pure floaters can't start out small—the mass-to-volume penalty for small floaters makes it impossible for them to stay up. So Momma grows them up to a good size and lets them out when they are big enough to float on their own."

All of a sudden, the proboscis pointed downward, stiffened, and a spray of liquid shot from the tip, driving the mother bubblefloater upward and off the top of the viewing window.

"What's going on?" exclaimed Sandra. She was reaching for the telescope slew icon to recapture the magnified image, when a winged creature flashed through the high-magnification window and back onto the low-magnification background view. The creature was so large that its shape was easily seen even at low magnification. Sandra quickly raised the background magnification so they could see the interaction, even if they could not see the details of the participants.

"Looks like a hawk among the pigeons," said Rod, as the large winged shape closed in on another balloon, a small one this time. The bubblefloater deflated and dropped, but the flying wing shape had expected that maneuver and easily scooped up the dropping bubblefloater into its cavernous maw.

"Looks more like a manta ray or devilfish than a hawk," remarked Dan. "Body built like a flying wing airplane, and a long whiplike tail—except this creature has big horizontal and vertical fins at the end of its tail—probably to give it better turning radius."

"Flaps its wings just like a manta ray," remarked Sandra in awe as the winged devourer hunted down another balloon. This was a large one, and it successfully avoided the first rush by using the water jet from its proboscis to jet out of the way, but also pointed the jet so the cloud of water blinded the onrusher.

"I bet that stings the old eyeballs and nose," said Rod. "A faceful of shit and piss."

"The balloon can probably only do it once," remarked Dan as they watched a second winged hunter go after the same balloon. Dan was right. The balloon had expended all of its "ballast" in the first encounter. This time its options were limited to the "deflate and drop" maneuver. It was not enough. With a few strong flaps of its decameter-sized wings the winged hunter drove itself downward faster than the balloon could fall and it was all over.

Dan turned from the screen and looked at Sandra, who had a grim look on her face. "What are you going to call that devilfish-shaped winged hunter?" he asked.

"You just came up with a good name for it yourself," said Sandra. "Jeeves? What is a good Latin name for a devilfish-shaped winged hunter?"

"One suggestion would be *Diabolus alavenator,*" replied Jeeves.

"*Diabolus alavenator* it is," said Sandra. She turned to Dan. "But we'll use 'winghunter' for short."

After the attack, the winghunters circled as a flock as they digested their catch, and Sandra got a chance to look over the creatures at high magnification. The typical adult was three meters thick at the middle and had a twenty-meter wingspan, with a long tapering quadruple-fluked tail for steering. There were large eyes, almost two meters in diameter, built into the wing-shaped body on each side of the cavernous mouth.

"They need eyes that big if they are going to be good hunters during the typical dark Saturnian day," remarked Sandra as she and Dan documented the images they had selected for their hyperpaper on *Diabolus alavenator.*

"The wings must be full of inflated compartments to give them the size needed without too much weight," remarked Dan, "but they are definitely not floaters—not even partial floaters. I have yet to see one of them stop flapping. They must use up an awful lot of energy."

"They seem to be very efficient hunters," said Sandra. "As long as the supply of balloons holds out, they'll do just fine. I noticed that they aren't leaving the area. They're keeping this cloud of balloons in sight."

"Probably saving them for tomorrow's breakfast," suggested Rod. Suddenly a worried look appeared on his face as his command responsibility thought up scary scenarios that he might have to cope with some time in the future. "Say . . . there isn't any possibility that there could be specimens of these winghunters big enough to cause us problems, is there?"

"I doubt it very much," Sandra reassured him. "The adults we saw are probably at their optimum size. If they got any larger, their wings would be too big to flap quickly and they would be poor hunters."

"Good. If they got any bigger—I'd start to worry about the balloon," joked Rod.

Two months later, Rod was giving his weekly status report to the crew at the Space Unlimited Mission Control Center.

"Things are going fine. The meta plant is working well. The fuel tanks are over half full with sixty-two tons of meta in them out of the one hundred and twenty needed. I have used the fans to move us out of the strong wind bands at the equator, and we are now at twenty degrees north where the winds are lower. I will continue to move us north, primarily to make sure we are clear of the equatorial region where the Great White Spot phenomenon is known to occur. Although the predicted time of occurrence based on past records will be sometime after we will be leaving, I want to make sure we are well clear of that turbulence if it arrives early. I will stop at about twenty-four degrees north to stay below the turbulence features like the UV Spot that show up at higher latitudes. Other than that, we have no plans. Will report in again next week. In the meantime, we are glad the scientists and the news channels are enjoying the pictures we are sending back of the weird lifeforms we have found here."

✿   ✿   ✿

They were all gathered around the galley having breakfast of coffee and fruit bars—or in the case of Seichi, who had just finished the night watch on the control deck, a late supper of green tea and sweet bean cakes.

There was a sudden jolt as the floor rose under them, followed by a deep humming sound. Within seconds, Rod, Chastity, and Seichi were up the ladder and at their posts, their squeezers leaking their contents onto the lower deck floor.

"Report, Jeeves," commanded Rod as he scanned the pilot console screen. He didn't want to take over from the autopilot as long as Jeeves seemed to have things under control.

"Something struck the balloon tether at a point about five hundred meters up from the capsule," replied Jeeves. "I suspect it was a ribbonswimmer."

"Tether status?" asked Rod, concerned that their link to their support might be jeopardized.

"Tether seems okay," replied Seichi from the scottyboard. "Two secondary strands were stressed past their elastic limit at the five-hundred-fifteen-meter point, but they are still intact."

By this time Sandra had climbed up the ladder to where her head was above the opening in the upper deck grating. The loud humming noise that had started with the jolt continued on, fading only slowly with time.

"Ribbonswimmer?" she asked. "Are you sure?"

"That's right!" said Rod, slightly perturbed. Certainly Jeeves could not be accused of slacking off on duty, but it was still strange that the semi-intelligent ship's computer had let something large hit the ship without taking evasive action. "I thought ribbonswimmers always flew in large flocks. Didn't you see them coming?"

"My radar and sonar detect many flocks of ribbonswimmers flying past each day," reported Jeeves. "The trajectory of the flocks is normally very predictable. The flocks also seem to avoid not only the balloon and the capsule, but also the tether. I am certain they can detect its presence with their sonar, since I can detect the side scatter from their location pulses. Although this flock was passing very close to the tether, they had already adjusted their track to miss it, so I assumed they would pass by without incident, as had happened many times before. This time, however, they were attacked by a formation of winghunters diving down out of the cloud deck above. The ribbonswimmers scattered in panic and one of them struck the tether."

"Must have sliced the poor creature into pieces," said Chastity.

"Not completely," said Jeeves. "Although one end of the creature was severed and has fallen away, the remaining portion is still entangled in the tether strands."

"How can you tell?" asked Chastity. She quickly figured out the answer. "Of course, your sonar is getting a stronger return signal from that point on the tether."

"The sonar evidence is additionally corroborated by analysis of the vibratory modes of the tether," said Jeeves. "The vibrational frequencies that make up the humming tone you hear are consistent with a three-hundred-kilogram mass being attached to the tether at the five-hundred-fifteen-meter point."

"A three-hundred-kilogram sample of a ribbonswimmer!" exclaimed Sandra in delight. "I'm going to climb up and get it!"

"A half-kilometer climb in a saturnsuit!" objected Pete from the deck below. "You're crazy. Let one of the outside mechbots do the job, either Tabby riding up on the balloon, or Mouser in the nosecone tether compartment, whichever one Jeeves needs least."

"Pete is right, Sandra," said Rod. "Let Mouser bring back some chunks for you to cut up and analyze."

"My one chance at a biopsy of a major Saturn lifeform is not going to be done at long distance using Mouser's clumsy claws," replied Sandra, as she started down the ladder. "Help me on with my saturnsuit, Doc."

"Sandra!" exclaimed Rod, concerned. "I forbid you to take the risk."

"I'll go with her, Rod," said Dan up through the grate as he put his empty squeezer into the galley dishwasher. "Seichi? Would it be possible for you to fix us up with some half-kilometer-long emergency lines in case we need to get back down in a hurry?"

"I can easily accommodate your request," said Seichi. "There are spare reels of tether lines in the nosecone for use in repairing broken strands on the main tether."

Sandra and Dan put on their saturnsuits and donned backpacks containing extra tanks of oxygen, and Seichi cycled them through the airlock. As the outer airlock door opened, Mouser clambered down the side of the conical capsule on four legs, holding two small spools of string in its two front claws. Sandra looked at them suspiciously. "That looks like kite string!" she exclaimed. "I'm not going to trust my life hanging from that stuff! I want a rope!"

"Those lines will most certainly hold you," said Seichi. "They are rated for three metric tons. They are made of the strongest tensile material known, macromolecular hextube polycarbon. Each molecule is a minimum of a meter long, so the strength is nearly that of a pure carbon-carbon bond. Your real problem will be handling the line without cutting your saturnsuit or yourself. That is why I used the mechfab to fabricate this reel controller for you." He took the reels of line from Mouser and snapped them into the mechanical contraptions. They consisted of a handle to hold the reel, with a thumb brake that controlled the payout of the reel.

"When you are ready to come down, attach the free end of the line to the balloon tether, hang on to the handle at the bottom of the reel, and press the friction controller with your thumb to control your rate of descent."

Sandra looked at the contraption dubiously and tucked it into her chestpack, which was already full of sample bags and various biopsy instruments. Dan's chestpack contained more sample bags and some surgical tools from his medical kit, including a bone saw, in case the ribbonswimmer surprised them and had hard portions in its internal anatomy.

Moving their safety lines along in front of them, Sandra and Dan made their way to the nosecone tip of *Sexdent*. The twelve main lines of the balloon Hoytether were fastened to twelve capture hooks that encircled the one-meter-diameter hole that led to the tether compartment. Stretching between adjacent main lines of the tether were pairs of slightly thinner secondary lines. The two secondary lines connected to the primary lines crossed over to form an X before they reached the connection point a meter higher up on the adjacent line. The whole multiline tether looked like a tubular cat's cradle a meter in diameter and a kilometer long. Dan and Sandra squeezed their way between two of the taut primary lines that were carrying the main load of the eighty-five-ton load of *Sexdent* and meta plant, and its slowly increasing multiton load of vital meta fuel. The way was made easier since the secondary lines were slack. The secondary lines would only be called upon to carry the load if the primary line segment they bridged was cut. Because the primary lines were taut while secondary lines were slack, there was no tendency for the tether to neck in, so Sandra and Dan had a clear path to the top with almost no danger of falling, since they were surrounded by tether strands and had only to stick out an arm or a leg to break a fall.

Sandra took a look upward, trying to see her target. It was too far away to discern in the slightly bent column of white lines that curved gracefully away in response to the wind far above. Holding on to two of the taut primary lines of the Hoytether, she placed her instep into the narrow V-shaped notch between the two crossing secondary lines a half-meter above and pulled herself up. Her next step was in the notch formed at the connection point between a primary line and a secondary line.

"Two rungs is one meter, so a half a kilometer is one thousand rungs," she said as she continued her way upward. "Only nine hundred ninety-eight to go." After letting her have a head start, Dan started climbing up after her on the other side of the tether.

They made a number of stops, during which Sandra was glad that Dan had insisted on hauling drinking water along. The saturnsuits were designed to conserve body heat—not necessarily the best idea under the present circumstances. Finally, they came to their goal.

The ribbonswimmer had been deeply slashed by its impact with the taut primary strands of the tether. As Jeeves had predicted, one end of the ribbonswimmer had been cut off, but the other end was there, and hung down alongside the Hoytether where it could easily be examined by the two scientists climbing up the inside of the tether.

"The skin looks like the surface of a starfish. Covered with cilia," said Sandra as she stroked the surface with her gloved fingers, making sure that the image intensifier in her helmet camera got a good closeup view so the video images transmitted down to *Sexdent* and stored in the cavernous memory of Jeeves were of high scientific quality. "Probably works the same way, too." She pointed to the converging pattern on one portion of the skin. "Probably is a mouth right here in the center." She pulled apart a mat of longer cilia to expose a pursed mouth, then took out a scalpel and poked the handle inside, not wanting to risk her finger—gloved as it was.

"No teeth or tongue," she remarked as she poked around. "Not very deep. Can't seem to find a throat. Strange . . ." A few quick strokes with the other end of the scalpel and the mouth had been removed. She looked it over and looked into the hole that had been left.

"The reason I couldn't find a throat is that there isn't one!" she exclaimed.

"No throat?" said Dan.

"Look for yourself," said Sandra. "Underneath where I removed the mouth is nothing but air bladders. There is a whole network of them, with valves connecting each one to the next. But there doesn't seem to be any central gut or central anything." She took another look at the "mouth." "In fact, I suspect that this mouth is nothing but a stomach. The skin gathers any food that happens to strike the surface and directs it to the mouth, which then digests it."

"But what about excretion?" asked Dan. "What goes in must come out."

"Once you've sucked all the good out of it, you spit it out and wait for the next meal," said Sandra. "Or, if you have a mouthful that you are working on, just have the cilia hold the morsel until you are done."

"So the ribbonswimmer is a gigantic flying mouth," said Dan.

"More like a collection of flying mouths working together for the common good. Any one of them couldn't come up with enough flotation or flying ability to hunt prey by themselves, but by joining together, they can survive. Each mouth and its surrounding cilia are like a single cell in a multicellular animal or plant on earth, like sponges and coral.

"That philosophy probably also applies to the whole school of ribbonswimmers. They swim so close to each other that any prey that doesn't get stuck to the skin of one ribbonswimmer gets pushed by the backwash onto the skin of a nearby ribbonswimmer."

They clambered up and down the tether, looking at different portions of the remains of the giant creature. Although the creature as a whole was dead, some of the less-damaged sections responded in a desultory fashion when prodded, giving Sandra and Dan some clues as to their function. Each portion looked very much like the next, but there were differences.

"Look here," said Sandra, pointing to an area where the region of inward-pointing cilia around a mouth was very much smaller than the regions around it. "Here's a tiny mouth fed by a small region of cilia, while next to it is a very large mouth supported by a very large and very old region of cilia."

"Old?" asked Dan, puzzled. "How can you tell how old it is?"

"Look at the cilia, especially the larger ones close to the mouth. Some of them are scarred or are missing their tips, like they have been damaged in the past by contacting something sharp."

"Probably from trying to grab something that bit back," murmured Dan.

"You don't see any of that damage on the small region with the small mouth," said Sandra. "The small region must therefore be younger. I would bet that it's a bud off the older region. Sort of like a bud on a coral reef. The creature not only gets bigger by having its cells grow bigger, it buds off new cells too."

"So, like a coral reef, it keeps on growing bigger and bigger."

"Probably not," said Sandra. "We've seen large and small ribbonfish in a flock, but not tiny ones and not huge ones. If you are too small, you don't have enough flotation volume and wing area to fly fast and hunt well. If you are too big, the feeding surface-to-body volume ratio becomes unfavorable. I suspect that once a ribbonfish gets to an optimum size it divides in two."

They continued their examination of the gigantic creature. Sandra found, by poking some of them, that the membranes between the flotation bladders were contractile.

"So instead of using muscles to move stiff bones, they use pneumatics to move rigidized bladders," she concluded.

"Certainly is alien," said Dan.

"Not really all that alien," said Sandra, calmly. "I'm sure you can recall a human organ that works in a similar fashion, although it uses hydraulics instead of pneumatics . . ." She paused, certain that it wouldn't take a medical doctor very long to figure out what organ she was talking about, especially a male medical doctor. But the pause grew longer as the look on Dan's face grew more puzzled. She finally decided she would have to give him another clue—Dan was so naive in many ways.

"That is . . . if you think about it *long* and *hard* enough." She giggled when Dan's face suddenly grew red behind his visor.

They spent some time looking at one of the dark "spots" on the creature, trying to figure out if they were functional or purely decorative.

"This black segment looks pretty much the same as the tan segments around it," remarked Dan. "A circular pattern of cilia surrounding a mouth. I think it's just a 'spot.' A decoration, like the spots on a leopard, same type of fur, just a different color."

"You might be right," said Sandra as she combed through the black cilia with her gloved fingers, "but these black cilia *do* have a different shape and texture, as well as color. They look more like feathers than fingers." She lifted up a fan of some of the larger ones. "They're linked together with tiny hooks like the feathers on a bird, so they always overlap." Underneath the larger circle of "feathers" were smaller circles of smaller feathers. It was dark under the fan of outer black feathers so Sandra switched on her helmet lamp. Instantly, there was a reaction as the smaller feathers raised and turned their tips toward the bright source of light. Sandra found herself looking into a myriad of dark "eyes," each surrounded by dark feathery lashes that formed a hollow cone that restricted the incoming light to only those rays coming from a single direction. The involuntary reflective response of the feathers to the strong light only lasted for a few seconds as the retractile tissues used up their last reserves of energy. The feathers collapsed again.

"Must be an eye," concluded Sandra. "A crude eye. There's no lens to form an image. It basically operates like a pinhole camera, with the feathers able to form the 'pinhole' in many different orientations so there is directional information provided. Yet not too crude, since it's a compound eye, like that of a bee. The multitude of different eyes looking in slightly different directions must be able to give range information too."

"Quite adequate for detecting predators, considering the basic simplicity of the creature," said Dan.

"Not quite adequate for spotting tethers, though," remarked Sandra as she cut out a section with a couple of eyes in it.

Loaded down with samples, the two worked their way up the inside of the Hoytether, clearing away the rest of the ribbonswimmer's body from the tether lines. They were joined by Mouser, who carefully inspected the lines in the struck region and replaced two of the secondary lines that had been stretched past their elastic limit. They were able to load up Mouser with a few kilos of ribbonswimmer tissue to lighten their load, but they had to carry most of the rest of the twenty kilos Sandra had collected down the half-kilometer "rope ladder." They were both tired and hungry as they finally entered the airlock, just as the Sun set on another day in the clouds of Saturn.

"I'm making dinner tonight," said Pete, as he helped them pack their samples in the freezer. He held up a sealed bag containing a large chunk of flesh; it was very lightweight for its bulk because of the flotation bladders. "Would you like me to pan-fry up some of these ribbonswimmer filets for you?"

"No! Thank you!" replied Sandra with a grimace. "I can just imagine the aroma—ammonia and methane mixed. I *will* have a filet, however. I'm hungry enough to eat a cow, so I'll have one of my special beef filet dinners. Be careful how you grill it, I like it medium— no red on the inside and no black on the outside."

"I'll set Puss to work on it," said Pete cheerfully. "It'll be ready by the time you finish with your shower. Don't forget to save room for dessert, I'm making cherries jubilee, complete with flaming brandy. I think I have finally found the right settings on the chemsyns to get it to produce cognac!"

"Nix on that, Pete!" said Dan. "Don't forget we're breathing a mixture that includes both hydrogen and oxygen. Although the percentage of oxygen is theoretically too low for the mixture to explode, I don't want to take any chances."

That night at dinner Rod announced, "Tomorrow is the tenth of June; we're halfway through the mission."

"As far as the meta production is concerned, we're more than halfway," remarked Pete. "We reached ninety tons a few days ago— only thirty tons to go for a full load. Then we can go home and collect the rest of our billion."

The mention of money sent Dan's mind wandering away from the excitement of the day—hanging from a windblown tower of string while trying to figure out how a dead alien worked when it was still alive. Now all he could think of was the chore of composing this week's message to Pamela and the kids. The kids now led very active lives, and by cutting the calls down to once a week, Pamela said she could count on everyone being there. With Saturn in opposition to Earth, they were only nine AU away, which cut the round-trip communication delay to only two-and-a-half hours. It was still too long for him to cope with the situation back at home. During the 150-minute interval between the time he had coped with one question or problem and supplied an answer or a suggestion, Pamela or one of the kids had usually generated another question or problem. Right now he had a more serious problem, and Pamela would be no help in solving that one. If tomorrow was the tenth of June on Earth, then his second quarterly estimated tax payment was due to the IRS on the fifteenth. He would have to talk to the loan officer at the bank again—for certain Pamela hadn't left much in the checking account. The minute they were inside, Dan went to his habitat and sent out messages to the loan officer and Pamela. Those difficult chores done, with a heavy heart he clambered back out to join the rest of the crew for dinner.

The sight of Pete preparing the cherries jubilee brightened Dan's spirits, even though Pete had to forego lighting the brandy. The cherries were slightly mushy from being freeze-dried and reconstituted, but the total effect was delicious. Dinner done, for all of the crew except the one on night watch duty it was off quickly to bed for three-and-a-half hours of sleep followed by another day shift of five-plus hours. Technically 3.5 hours of sleep every 10.7-hour Saturnian day worked out to 8 hours of sleep every 24-hour Earth day, but every once in a while, one of the crew felt the need for a longer, deeper sleep session. After declaring that the next daylight period was going to be a personal "Saturnday," he or she would take the day off and sleep in, while the others covered their shift duties. Both Dan and Sandra had just experienced a tiring day and Dan offered to let Sandra announce a Saturnday, but she turned him down.

"There's no way I could stay asleep knowing that all these specimens were waiting for me to slice them up and put them under the nanoimager," said Sandra. "Why don't you declare a Saturnday instead." Dan, tired from the day's exertion, agreed and headed for his habitat. Instead of dropping off to sleep, however, he switched ends and stuck his head out under the tilted viewport that made up one end of his tubular habitat. Since he would be sleeping in tomorrow, he could afford to spend some time gazing at the stars. There weren't any stars visible tonight since the ammonia cloud deck, although thin, was unbroken, but the water clouds were patchy, allowing him to see the brilliantly illuminated rings arcing overhead, tinted orange by the ammonia layer. For the next few months, the rings would be at their maximum inclination to the Sun's rays, and would be a brightly lit bridge from horizon to horizon every night. He stayed awake, calming his tormented soul with the majestic sight, watching the rising or setting of Tethys, Dione, and Mimas. He finally fell into a troubled sleep just as Titan loomed over the horizon, to dream once again of winning the Solar Lottery . . . only this time, instead of receiving a check, he was handed a "Payment Overdue" notice from the IRS.

Petra, riding in her usual position along the ridge of the central keel, urged Petru to open the gigantic maws on either side of the keel and take another large gulp of cold middark air. The giant body rippled along its sides as it sieved the air clean with its mouthfeathers and pushed it out forcefully in twin jets from the rear, driving the winged being upward against the prevailing winds. Petra urged again and Petru responded with another burst of power.

"The nights are very short now," Petra thought to herself. "I must hurry to get Petru to the clouds before Bright rises, so Petro has a good hunt tomorrow." She raised her head on her long neck and looked around. Only a few of the flock were at a higher altitude than she was. Holding on to the wingfeathers with some of her claws, she looked down over the leading edge of the gigantic wing that composed most of the body of Petru. Most of the flock was below her. She was certainly doing her part to get them all to a good hunting altitude. She had been hoping that the skies would be clear tonight so she could continue her studies of the skies, but the orange-tinted highclouds prevented her from seeing the stars and the globes. The only things visible in the sky were the Arcs and the moons. Largemoon was now rising. It would be brighter for the rest of the night. She greeted Largemoon with a song, a multitude of tones generated by passing air from one flotation cavity to another through an orifice, a process that usually was silent, but which could be made to generate a tone by careful control of the tension in the orifice. In a range of tones that varied from the rumble of thunder to the whistle of a pierced roundfloater, Petra started the rising song. Soon the entire flock joined in, waving their long colorful tailfeathers in wide swooping and rising motions that imitated the swooping and rising tones of the song.

```
                    s   s     s
          r  r  r   c      c
             a      a  a  a  a
          i  i  i  i      i
          s  s  s  s  l  l  l  l
          i  i  i  i  i  i  i
          ngngngngngngngng
                C  C  C  C  C
                U  U  U  U  I
       R  R  R  R  R  R  R  R  R
          A  A                 C  C
                L     L  L  L
       I  I  I  I                 I
       S  S  S  S  V     V        M
       I  I  I  I  I  I  I  I  I  I
       NGNGNGNGNGNGNGNGNGNG
                F  F  F  F  F  F  F  F
       R  R  R  R  L  L  L  L  L  L  L  L
       A   A   A   A   A   A
       I  I  I  I     I   Y   Y
       S  S  S  S  TTPPTTPP  PP    PP
       I  I  I  I  I  I  I  I  I  I  I
       NGNGNGNGNGNGNGNGNGNGNGNG
```

Petra didn't notice it at first. She was too engrossed in singing with the rest of the flock. It was at times like this she felt herself greater than herself alone, part of a community of spirits that had gone on long before she was born and would go on long after she had died. Now she was part of it and enjoying it. Finally, the sensory input from the giant body under her control became too noticeable to ignore. The air Petru was swallowing had no taste! She knew what that meant and quickly stopped singing. She used the giant wingspan of Petru to send a single chirp of sound out and up. After a long wait, a faint echo returned and was picked up by Petru's wing, acting as a giant ear. The return was fuzzy in tone, depth, and width. She had been right, there was a flock of slimswimmers ahead of her, who were also climbing during the night. As they flew, they left a trail of empty, tasteless air behind them. All Petra needed to do was follow the path of tastelessness and it would lead her to a middark meal. Petra would be the hunter for a change instead of Petro. She quickly informed the others in the flock and they went into their slimswimmer formation. In the daytime, when the males were diving from high altitude, the jet-powered winged bodies of the ruus could outfly anything in the skies. During the nighttime climb upward, however, the slimswimmers could fly fast enough to easily evade the maws of a single ruus. The slimswimmers had poor sonar. They depended upon their eyes to detect predators at a distance. At night, however, when there was little light, they could be taken by surprise if the attacker remained silent during the attack.

"You all heard the return from my chirp, so you know where the slimswimmers are," said Petra, directing Petru's voice downward so the slimswimmers above would not hear. The gigantic area of the wing of each ruus made a supersensitive sonar detector, and the return from her single pulse had been quite strong, so she knew everyone in the flock, even the children still on wing, not only knew the location of the flock of slimswimmers, but had already used their giant eye to pick them out against the Arc-lit orange highclouds. "We six highest will set a silent trap. The rest of you know what to do."

Petra looked around. Hakra and Conra were above her. Hakra was highest and would take the top dive position. Conra would duck under the prey and attack from the front, while Petra and the others below would attack from the sides, rear, and bottom. Silently, using their excellent eyesight to keep each other and the prey in sight, they closed the trap on the slimswimmers, while the remainder of the flock noisily talked amongst each other as they flew off in the opposite direction, always climbing as they went.

The females didn't often get a chance to hunt. Despite that, tonight they were very effective at coordinating their attack even without talking to each other. As each one moved into position, far distant from the unsuspecting flock of slimswimmers, but keeping pace with them, their tailfeathers would twitch up and down, indicating to the others they were ready. All waited until Hakra had Hakru in the top position. Hakra waved Hakru's tail once, then dove straight down at full jet power, screaming and roaring and yelling from every interbladder orifice, while the other five closed in from all the other directions, as silent as their pulsating jets allowed, maws wide open. The flock of slimswimmers, attacked by a screaming monster from above, scattered in panic in all directions. Each ruus in the attack party had at least one gullet full of slimswimmer before the attack was over, while some more-fortunate ones had both maws full. Grinding their gizzards contentedly, they rejoined the rest of the flock and continued the long climb upward, singing as they climbed.

```
                    s  s  s  s  s  s  s  w  w  w  w  w
              r  r  r  r  c     c     c     c
              a     a  a  a  a  a  oaa  oaa  a  a  a  a  a
                                r     r     r  f  r  f  v
        i  i  i  i  i
        s  s  s  s  l  l  l  l     l     l  p  t  p  t
        i  i  i  i  i  i  i  i  i  i  i  i  i  i  i  i  i
        ngngngngngngngngngngngngngngngngngng
                 C  C  C  C     C     C     C
                 U  U  U  U  I     I     I     I
     R  R  R  R  R  R  R  R     R     R     R
        A     A           C  C  C  C  G  C  G
                 L     L  L  L  L  L  L  L  L
     I  I  I  I                 I     I     I     I
     S  S  S  S  V     V        M     M     D     D
     I  I  I  I  I  I  I  I  I  I  I  I  I  I  I  I
     NGNGNGNGNGNGNGNGNGNGNGNGNGNGNGNG
        F  F  F  F  F  F  F  F  F  F  F
  R  R  R  R  L  L  L  L  L  L  L  L  L  L  L
     A     A     A     A     A     A     OA     OA
  I  I  I  I     I     Y     Y     Y     Y
  S  S  S  S  TTPPTTPP     PP     PP     T     T
  I  I  I  I  I  I  I  I  I  I  I  I  I  I  I  I
  NGNGNGNGNGNGNGNGNGNGNGNGNGNGNGNG
```

Back on *Sexdent,* Jeeves heard a multitoned sound through the ship's sonar. It was obviously very far away because it faded and drifted in direction as though it had passed through many different density strata and had been blown about by the winds. It was a long, variable, complex sound, unlike any other Jeeves had detected since their arrival on Saturn. The recording of the strange sound was filed away in Jeeves's still nearly empty memory, and Jeeves turned its attention to the tasks that started each morning on Saturn: preparing breakfast, lunch, or supper for each member of the crew, depending upon which shift they were on; cycling Pete Stewart through two airlocks and assisting him in his daily checkout of the meta plant; and a myriad of other chores.

Bright was illuminating the eastern horizon as Petra and the rest of the flock finished the climbing song and brought their bodies to a halt at a common altitude. All of the ruus in the flock were hungry from the exertion of the long climb during the night, but Petra and some of the others had some of the hunger pangs dulled by the middark snack. This was the time for socialization and grooming, while the males woke up and took over control prior to the daily hunting dive. With Petru flying at constant altitude at low speed, the wind across the wing top was slow enough that Petra could leave her perch on the top of the keel and start her morning grooming of Petru's topside.

Down below, snuggled in his niche in the bottom of Petru's keel, Petro awoke. He stayed in himself, letting Petra retain control of their giant body. Even though he was not operating Petru, he could still groom his side. Since gravity was constantly attempting to pull him off, he had to be more careful with his clawholds on the feathers than Petra did. So while the female head and neck groomed one side of their joint body, the male head did the other side. Occasionally, when they were both putting things into the same maw, they would look at each other, eye to eye.

"I can sense something tasty in Petru's left gizzard," said Petro to Petra through their thinklink. "You must have had good luck during the darkclimb."

"A slimswimmer school," replied Petra. "Six of us ate, while the others acted to deceive the slimswimmers into thinking we had left."

"Well done," said Petro. "I will take the outer position in the hunting cone when we start the dive, so the others of the flock can be fed." They parted and returned to their grooming tasks.

Extending her neck, Petra used her multitude of neck claws to crawl along the wing top, combing out feathers, collecting small prey that had impacted on the giant body, and using her large eye to find the tiny vermin that burrowed into feather roots. The vermin were laboriously extracted, pierced if not too tough, then taken to the wing edge and dropped into the maw below, where eater became eaten. The attack on the slimswimmers had resulted in some bits of slimswimmer flesh being caught between feathers. This, too, was scraped from the feathers and dropped over the wing edge, where it impacted the mouthfeathers and fell into the all-devouring maw. By pumping up the inflation sacs in her neck, Petra extended her reach all the way to Petru's wingtip, then down the wing to the tail. Only the tips of the tailfeathers were out of reach of the long flexible neck, but that was what flockmates were for. Toward the end of the grooming session, the flock formed a lazily flying circle, while each one tended the colorful tailfeathers of the one ahead of it. Over the tops of the circle, the female heads gossiped about the night's rare hunting interval and the progress of the children of the flock, while down below, the male heads bragged about yesterday's hunt and what they intended to accomplish in the upcoming hunt.

One by one, the female heads relinquished control over the gigantic winged body they had directed during the long climb to hunting altitude and allowed the male heads to assume command. The females contracted their necks, lay them in the crevasse along the top of the inflated keel that ran the length of the giant body, held their neck in place by grasping the roots of the feathers on either side of the crevasse with the claws extending from each neck segment, closed their large single eye, and went to sleep for the day. Those that had children on wing made sure their babies were snuggled under their necks, while the older children were tucked well under the upper wing feathers of their parents. During the hunting dive the airspeed across the top of the gigantic flying wing bodies would sweep off anything that wasn't securely shielded from the gale. Some of the older children settled down under the feathers right at the leading edge of the wing. The wind was much stronger there, but from that position their male heads could look out over the wing and pretend they were the ones controlling the gigantic body that supported them. After enough hunting dives as passengers, they would gain enough experience from watching their parent operating in coordination with the rest of the hunters in the flock that they would be able to participate in future hunts, as a free-flying "wingmate" to their parent, keeping up with the flock by gliding on the air blast from the parent's leading edge.

As the male heads took over each body, they broke from the grooming circle and checked out their control of the twin jet-powered body by zooming upward at high speed. They then rejoined the rest of the group as they chased each other in mock prey-predator aerial combat. Soon all the winged bodies were controlled by the males. At the command of Conro, the eldest of the flock, the cloud of circling bodies formed themselves into a hunting cone and dived. At first they fell mostly by the pull of gravity, but as their speed through the air grew and the air friction rose, they gulped larger and larger mouthfuls of frigid high-altitude air into their twin maws on each side of their keel. Their wings rigidized, grew thinner, and began to sweep back, as internal pressure changes moved air from one wing-bladder to another. The sides of their bodies pulsed faster as the inward-gulped air was passed rapidly through the long body and spurted out in twin jets from the rear. Slight changes in jet strength from one jet to the other, combined with slight adjustments of the angle of the wingtips, and flicks of their long steering tail, directed the large bodies closer and closer together until the whole flock became one gigantic flying maw. The combination of gravity and jet power gave the formation of flying hunters a speed that was greater than that of any of its prey.

Since Petru had been one of those in the flock that had eaten during last night's meeting with the slimswimmers, Petro joined the hunting cone as one of the outer-edge "gatherers." His job, along with the others at the leading open edge of the cone, was to drive the prey toward the center of the cone, where it would become fodder for those in the eating positions near the tip of the conical formation. The long shallow dive took them into warmer, moister air. There had been sunlight passing through this portion of the air for some time now, and the air had a rich taste. There was nothing that Petro's eye could see or Petru's sonar could detect, but the mouth-feathers in Petru's maw, which screened the air before passing it back to the air passages, were now dripping rich-tasting drops into the gizzard at the base of the maw. With the air this rich in food, there should be a flock of slimswimmers in the region. Petro increased the intensity of the sound pulses generated by Petru, scanning the beam in a spiral in the forward direction. A faint return came from far ahead and below; Petro tightened the spiral scan and concentrated it in the direction of the faint return. Soon there were enough returns that all in the flock could hear that there was worthwhile prey in that direction. Slowly, the hunting cone shifted in direction and headed for the source of the distant return. The jets from each body increased in strength as the flock added speed. Sonar searches were stopped and even conversation ceased as the silent swift hunting cone closed in on its victims.

Soon the prey was in sight. Petro's large eye could now make out the individuals in the flock of slimswimmers. They had not moved significantly from the position at which Petru's sonar had detected them. Usually, when a flock of prey animals heard the distant ping of a searching ruus, they headed in the opposite direction as fast as they could go. These slimswimmers had not done so. The reason was obvious. They were under attack by a small flock of wingflyers, who were keeping the main school herded together while consuming the outer victims one by one. Neither the wingflyers nor the slimswimmers had eyesight as good as a ruus, so the silent hunting cone would sweep down on them unnoticed, until it was too late.

"This time we will have a variety of tastes in a kill," thought Petro to himself. He and the others in outgatherer positions passed the cluster of slimswimmers and wingflyers and began to circle inward, closing the way in the forward direction. Suddenly the prey and their small predators became aware of the onrushing cone of death. Together in panic they fled in all directions, but it was too late. The high-speed divers in their close-packed cone scooped shrieking bodies into their gigantic double maws, maws with orifices ten times bigger than their prey. The bodies collided with the sharp edges of the stiff mouthfeathers inside the maws, where they were sliced into strips of bleeding flesh that slid down the feathers into the gizzard below, to be sucked dry and ground to pulp by pulsating minibladders covered with hard, viciously sharp toothfeathers. One of the older children was lucky this hunt. Its parent, at a good point in the hunting cone, was the recipient of many of the slimswimmers, so when a less-tasty wingflyer came along, it adjusted its trajectory with a flip of its tail and directed the incoming wingflyer into the maw of the child. The wingflyer was a good-sized bite for the child, but it had no problem in swallowing the wingflyer whole.

The hunting formation did such a good job of capturing most of the slimswimmers and wingflyers in the first pass that there was little to go back for. Leaving the remnants of the prey to re-form and build up into worthwhile targets for the future, the hunting cone regrouped and headed downward again. As they headed downward, the flock broke into the diving song.

Petro, having missed out on the food because of his position as an outgatherer, now switched positions in the hunting cone with one of those that had captured their fill. As the flock dove, the outgatherers sent out loud, forward-directed pulses and the whole cone listened for the returns. Soon they could hear something far away and down below. From the purity of tone and the amplitude variation of the returns, it had to be a cloud of roundfloaters, rising up on a thermal. Since the roundfloaters had no rapidly moving portions on their bodies, the return tones were not shifted in frequency, while the elongated, variable-amplitude shape of the return, in contrast to the sharpness of the ping that had been sent out, indicated that the return signal had bounced off a large round object. It was a good-sized cloud of good-sized roundfloaters and Petro could feel hisses and rumbles in Petru's gizzard as the giant winged body prepared its digestive tract for some input.

This hunting interval would last longer than the previous one and the tactics would be different. Although the roundfloaters were of low intelligence and had no eyes to see with, they were exceptionally good at detecting sound. They made little sound themselves when they were floating upward on a thermal, and the extremely large sound detection area provided by their flotation balloon meant that they could hear things at greater distances than even a ruus could. Not only could the roundfloaters detect the search pulses of the outgatherers before the outgatherers could detect the returns, but they could even hear the muffled roar of the jets shooting out from the rear of each of the gigantic flying-wing bodies. Since the roundfloaters could not fly, high-speed chase was not needed; stealth was more effective. The flock stopped their jet-driven high-speed dive and went into a silent gliding formation, where the only noise they made was due to the air rushing over their wings. Each gigantic flying-wing body fluffed up its leading-edge feathers, softening even that noise. The silent deadly hunting cone increased in diameter as the dive continued.

The cloud of roundfloaters soon came into view of Petro's giant eye. This area was full of thermals, each containing a cloud of spheres, slowly rising upward in the circling heated air column. The hunting cone converged on the nearest food cloud. As they drew nearer, Petro could begin to see the spicy-tasting fringe that hung from the globular flotation bladder of the roundfloater. Inside that was the meaty portion of the roundfloater, the foodgatherer and the gizzard. The trick in swallowing a roundfloater was to make sure the heavy meaty portion at the base of the balloon passed over the lower lip of your maw. That way you swallowed the roundfloater whole. If you missed, then the heavy portion would drag some of the balloon shreds back out of your gizzard and you would be left with nothing but a mouthful of hot air and a few shreds of flotation bladder.

The hunting cone dove silently on the columnar cloud of blind roundfloaters. The wing noise of the outgatherers on the hunting cone was finally detected by the roundfloaters nearest them. The roundfloaters shrieked a warning to their cloudfellows and took evasive action. Those roundfloaters that were above an outgatherer dropped their ballast load of waste and water they had been saving for just such an occasion and shot rapidly upward, while those roundfloaters that were below a detected outgatherer deflated their flotation bladders and dropped downward. Although this saved those already outside the cylinder of death that the hunting cone bored out of the sky, it did little to save those in its path. The ruus had made the size of the hunting cone large enough that neither maneuver allowed the roundfloater to escape the double-mouthed maws of the ruus in the base of the cone. One by one, the giant balloons were swallowed by the much-larger maws.

After the first cloud had been passed through, the hunting cone shifted in direction toward the next thermal and its drifting cloud of food. Petro, who had filled both gizzards during the last encounter, left the tail of the cone and took over the upper outgatherer position while Petru digested its meal. Since they were still far from the next thermal, and silence was not necessary, the flock broke into song again.

"My sonar receivers are detecting strong infrasound signals from the west," Jeeves reported to Chastity and Sandra on the control deck.

Sandra took down the biviewer and looked out the science console viewport.

"Oh my God . . ." she whispered.

"What *is* it!" shouted Rod, coming up from below as rapidly as he could. He banged his head on the grating again and swore.

"It's a flock of the largest birds I have ever seen," said Sandra. "They look like a winghunter with two air intakes, but they're much larger. They could swallow a winghunter in a single bite. But unlike the winghunters, they aren't flapping their wings—I guess they're too large for that. They must be jet powered! They're in a conical formation. Probably optimum for hunting."

"Hunting?" said Rod, grabbing the viewer.

"There are four of them ahead of the others, on the outside of the formation, like beaters, while those trailing behind are arranged in a conical shape."

They watched in awe as the hunting cone dove on a distant columnar cloud of bubblefloaters.

"The cone of birds has become silent," said Jeeves. "I cannot even hear their wing noise."

"Stealth hunters!" said Rod in admiration, as he watched the hunters approach their prey through the biviewers.

"The floaters are fleeing in panic," reported Rod. "Some are deflating and dropping as fast as they can, while some are expelling their gas and jetting upward."

"And I bet the flock formation is just big enough from top to bottom to capture them no matter what tactic the bubblefloaters use," Sandra observed.

"The birds in the base of the cone only move away from their nominal positions to capture an incoming bubblefloater, then they move back again," reported Rod. "There is no way for a floater to escape that trap."

"How big are those birds, anyway?" asked Chastity from the pilot console.

"Hard to tell," said Rod, still hogging the biviewer. "They are so far away it's impossible to estimate the distance."

"My radar returns indicate that the wingspan is four kilometers," reported Jeeves.

"*Four kilometers!*" shouted Chastity. "That's as big as Central Park!"

"An accurate analogy," confirmed Jeeves calmly.

"Those aren't birds," said Rod. "They're rocs! Like the one in 'Sinbad the Sailor.' "

"*Rukh,*" interrupted Sandra, annoyed because Rod was hogging the biviewer. "The proper name for that mythical giant bird is spelled with a *u* and ends in the Arabic consonant *kh*. It's pronounced with one-and-a-half syllables—*Roo*, like in *kangaroo*, and a guttural *kh*, like in Genghis *Kh*an. It's *Roo-kh,* not *Rock*—the arrogant English-man that first did the translation of the name got it wrong."

"Whatever it's named, they're *big!*" Rod raised the biviewer again. "And they're coming this way. We ought to get a good look at them as they pass by. I'll go get the high-res IR camera." He gave Sandra back the biviewer and headed down the ladder to the equipment storage locker.

Chastity tapped some commands onto her pilot screen. When Jeeves's reply came back, she gave a concerned frown.

"Rod?" she called. "I think you had better forget the camera and come up here."

"What's the matter?" Rod called from down below, over the sound of an equipment drawer being shut.

"Jeeves says that the rukh formation isn't going to go *by* us, it's going to go right *through* us, and the altitude of the center of the formation is right at the altitude of our balloon."

Soon Rod was back up the ladder. All the previous excitement over finding a new species on Saturn had evaporated from his face. In its place was the serious, veiled-eyed look of a test pilot in trouble. He looked at Chastity's screen and grunted as his eyes took in the details of Jeeves's presentation. He turned to look at Sandra.

"Any chance they'll avoid the balloon instead of eating it?" he asked.

"With the nuclear reactor inside, the balloon is probably hotter than most bubblefloaters," replied Sandra. "But its size is well within the typical sizes of floaters. They would avoid eating our capsule—their sonar would tell them it's too dense for them to handle, but the balloon is going to look like a nice big fat juicy bubblefloater to them."

Rod didn't reply. The random flickering motion of his eyes showed that his test pilot brain was trying to find a way out of their predicament. Sandra noticed that Chastity was in the same trance. Leaving the two pilots with the problem of extricating them from their problem, Sandra turned to the science console and quietly fingered in commands to Jeeves to warn Pete down in the meta plant and wake Dan and Seichi in their habitats. When she turned back from the console, Rod and Chastity were each busy at one of the other two consoles. She pulled over the biviewer and took another look at the oncoming formation of giant birds.

The formation now completely filled the greenly glowing screen of the biviewer. Each rukh looked like a flying island. At this distance she couldn't see any evidence of eyes, but then, you can't see the eyes of a whale until you are up close either. The mouths, however, were easily visible. There were two of them, like two large oval intakes built into the wings of a flying-wing type of jet bomber. The mouths were two hundred meters high and nearly twice as wide. As she watched, the rukh at the "feeding point" apex of the conical formation pulled out and its place was taken by another one. The satiated bird increased its speed and assumed one of the four "beater" positions ahead of the feeding cone. The rukh did not beat its wings during the maneuver that took it ahead of the flock. The thick balloon-like wing structures were obviously only for flotation and gliding, although the tips did warp during turns to assist the long tailfeather rudder. She could see pulsations going down the sides of the body behind the intake regions. After separating out the food from the incoming air, the creature probably compressed the air and jetted it out the rear like the water jet on an octopus or squid.

Sandra was having Jeeves feed her earphones frequency-shifted versions of the tones that the sonar picked up. The shifting of positions within the formation involved a great deal of "talk" among the giant birds. The rukhs were obviously social animals with enough intelligence to communicate with each other and plan hunting strategies. Sandra wished that she could have met them under better circumstances than that of hunter and prey.

"They're at sixty kilometers and closing," reported Chastity.

"What's the ETA?"

"Fifteen minutes."

"Sixty kilometers in a quarter hour! Those things *can't* be moving at two hundred forty klours!"

"They're hunting, they're diving, and they're jet powered," interjected Sandra.

"Then there's no time left for trying to *think* our way out of this predicament," said Rod firmly. "I'm going to see if I can *fly* us out of here!" He punched an icon on his screen and suddenly his breathing could be heard loudly throughout the ship and in each habitat. "Pulling gees in thirty seconds. Buckle in!"

"I have the meta production line going through emergency shutdown," reported Pete from inside the meta plant. "Should be completed in ten."

"These habitats weren't designed to take gees," objected Doc, his voice echoing inside his cocoon.

"I'll be right out" came Seichi's voice from the habitat beneath Rod's console.

"No time for that, Seichi!" replied Rod. "Chass! Take over the scottyboard!"

"I sure hope in *hell* you know what you're doing!" growled Chastity as she pulled up the shoulder harnesses from the seat back and clicked them onto her seat belt. "With the meta plant attached, we mass eighty-five tons dry, but we've only got ninety tons of fuel in our tanks. That'll only get us halfway to Titan. After that, we drop back and burn up!" She paused as she tried to figure out what Rod was thinking of. "Unless, of course, you're planning on dropping the meta plant. . . ." Having voiced her objections, her trained left hand obediently flickered over the icons on the scottyboard screen and two bright red flickering icons appeared.

BALLOON JETTISON SWITCH
PLANT JETTISON SWITCH. WARNING! PERSONNEL STILL IN PLANT.

"Let me know when you want the balloon cut," she said grimly, glad now that she didn't have the decision-making responsibility that went with the job of commander. "But you'll have to push the meta-plant jettison switch yourself."

"*Hey!*" yelled Pete over the comm link. There was a long pause, followed by a resigned "I don't like it . . . but I'll understand if you have to do it."

"Cancel the icons," Rod replied. "We're taking the balloon and meta plant with us." He took one last look at the formation of birds plotted on his screen. Jeeves had plotted an escape corridor for him to follow. He stuck his right hand into the throttle cavity below his console and nestled his wrist into the restraint while his fingers closed on the joyball.

Rod didn't bother with a verbal countdown of the last seconds. He lifted the joyball and the rockets roared into life. With plenty of fuel but very little time, he ran the engines at maximum thrust. That thrust level would normally have pushed *Sexdent* at greater than ten gees, but with the drag of the balloon and the mass of the meta plant, the *Sexdent* seemed to be merely crawling. Rod knew that he couldn't follow Jeeves's escape corridor since it went almost straight up. As soon as they gained any altitude and the shrouds started to hang down below them, the exhaust would melt the shrouds and disconnect them from the balloon. He was forced to improvise by flying in an arc that kept the exhaust away from the tough but temperature-sensitive polymer strands that were their lifeline. There was a violent twist at the nose of the ship as it rose up above the balloon and the tether tightened again. Chastity was ready for it and expertly controlled the tether reel so they were actually hauling in tether line at the same time they were pulling on the balloon at the maximum tension the tether could take. There was jerk after jerk as the weaker portions of the main strands parted—their places taken by the four secondary strands, two on each side, which bridged the broken strand and "healed" it, making that section stronger than it was before the main strand broke. The jerks tapered off in number as the weaker strand segments were eliminated.

"Twenty tons of fuel left," announced Chastity after they had been pulling for a number of minutes.

"Going to use it all," answered Rod. "We can make more later if we get out of this." He looked at the display Jeeves had arranged for him. The ship and the balloon were both moving slowly toward the edge of the "cylinder of death" that was being carved out of the sky by the gigantic maws of the flying cone of rukhs. At first, the speed of the capsule—and the balloon it was dragging—had increased with time under the constant acceleration of the rockets. The speed now seemed to be stuck. Despite the constant strong thrust of the dozen roaring engines there was no further increase in speed. The viscous drag on the balloon had increased as their velocity had increased, and they had now reached their equivalent of terminal velocity through the thick air. Rod could only watch with concern as the two tiny dots that indicated the rocket hauling the balloon slowly crawled their way to the edge of the "cylinder of death," while the formation of rukhs glided inexorably toward them, eating everything within that cylinder.

At the science console, Sandra was keeping all of Jeeves's sensors busy, gathering every piece of data she could on the giant birds, making sure at the same time that a copy of all the data being collected was being transmitted up to the commsats for relay to Earth. The leading dot on Rod's screen, which indicated the position of the crew capsule, switched to yellow, then green, as it broke out of the gray-hatched cylinder of death. The balloon, trailing a kilometer behind, was still red. The leading edge of the "eating cone" was still ten kilometers away, with the four "beaters" about five kilometers out ahead. The nearest beater was on a trajectory that would take it about three kilometers below them. Sandra prepared her cameras to take images of the rukh as it flew under them.

"Green!" exclaimed Rod with relief. "The balloon is clear of the cylinder! We're going to make it!"

"Good thing, too," said Chastity. "We've only got three tons of fuel left."

Petro was quite amazed at what he saw ahead. There was a tiny dense object emitting a glare like the Sun. It was rising rapidly upward, while following behind it was a strangely shaped roundfloater, moving much faster than any roundfloater Petro had ever seen before. What was most peculiar was that the roundfloater was below him, but had chosen to jet upward instead of dropping downward. Petro had been sending out strong hunting sounds, and although the roundfloaters were very stupid, even *they* knew that when the hunter is coming at them from above, it is foolish for the prey to rise to meet the maw that intends to devour it. If the roundfloater had deflated and dropped like all the others before it, Petro would have left it alone, for he had recently been gorging at the tail of the cone and would leave the roundfloater for those in the cone to eat. But since this one was rising up above the cone, where those in the cone could not reach it, it became fair game for him. Pulsing his sides harder and lifting his tail to tilt himself upward, he rose in pursuit of the morsel.

"Rod . . ." said Sandra from the science console. Rod was throttling down the engines, letting the ship drop below the altitude of the balloon, so its buoyancy could take over the task of keeping them from falling. Sandra's voice had a worried tone. "The outrider rukh is leaving its position in the formation and is coming up after us."

"She's right, Rod!" said Chastity, watching on her screen as the trajectory of the giant bird changed to meet theirs. "It's going after the balloon!"

Rod started up the engines again and was just at the point where he was starting to pull up on the balloon again, when the rukh met the balloon.

Sandra screamed:

"It's swallowed our balloon—whole!"

4

SWALLOWED BY THE MAW

PREPARE FOR SHOCK!

Jeeves's voice bellowed throughout the ship. Red warning messages flashed on all the consoles. The shock wave generated by the strike of the fast-moving rukh traveled swiftly up the taut Hoytether and pulled violently on *Sexdent's* nose, jerking the capsule end for end. Rod's seat broke away under the strain and he went flying back into the ladder.

Under the inexorable pull of Saturn's gravity, the capsule started falling . . . spinning . . . tumbling . . . out of control. Chastity, her breath knocked out of her by her harness, grimaced as she rubbed ruefully at what she hoped weren't broken ribs. The tumbling, twisting fall and the continued silence of the engines soon made her realize that Rod was out of action—quickly confirmed by a glance over her shoulder. Rod was still strapped in his broken seat, trying to wrestle free from his safety harness and bumping into things as the capsule twisted and twirled in its fluttering free-fall drop.

"Rod!" yelled Chastity from the scottyboard. "Shall I switch to jets?"

"No!" came Rod's reply as he struggled free from the seat and pushed it through the passway hole to the deck below. "Keep your joyball on tether control. We're going to need both rockets and tether if we're going to get out of this mess. We don't have enough fuel to stop our fall for more than a few minutes."

He fought his way back to the pilot console. Holding on to the broken seat support with one hand, he stuck his other into the joyball controller. With a few expert blasts from the attitude control jets, he brought the spinning and twisting motions of the capsule to a halt. He was tempted to use the main engines to halt their fall, but he knew better and let the fall continue. Now that the scene outside his holoviewport had steadied, he could see the giant body of the rukh growing larger below them as they fell down toward it. Their fall would take them behind the long tail of the massive bird as it flew by underneath. By looking up, he could see the Hoytether that had previously connected them to the balloon, trailing away into the distance from its connecting point on the nose of the capsule. The track of the Hoytether arched upward and out across the back of the rukh to a point at the front near its left mouth, over a half-kilometer away.

Rod knew that when they came to the end of the Hoytether, they would experience another jerk. The next one might be strong enough to snap the tether, leaving them to fall into the crushing-hot hell that was lower Saturn. With almost no fuel left in the tanks, there was only one thing that could keep them aloft.

"If Sinbad could do it, so can we," he said loudly.

"What?" asked Sandra from the science console, her voice small with fright as their continuing free fall went on, second after second.

"We're going to hitch a ride on a roc."

"It's *rukh*," persisted Sandra. "With a *u*."

"Rukh or roc. I don't care. As long as it's a rock that floats." He turned to Chastity. "Chass! We'll run out of slack soon. Let the tether run free at first, then turn on the electromagnetic brakes and bring us to a fast halt."

Chastity nestled her right wrist in the restraint in the controller cavity under her console and gently grasped the joyball inside with her trimmed astronaut hand. The long painted fingernails of her left hand flickered over the soft surface of the touchscreen, pulling up information. The Hoytether was at only the twelve-hundred-meter point so there was plenty still on the reel. She would have no problem bringing them to a halt at a reasonable gee level. The fuel gauge showed there were only two thousand kilos of meta left. She frowned.

It might as well be zero. Rod was right. Their only hope lay in the Hoytether. She hoped the giant bird was up to coping with the load the tether was going to put on it.

They fell in altitude below the rukh. The Hoytether now lay across the rukh's black-feathered back and off the trailing edge of its winglike body. The tension increased as the slack Hoytether snaked its way across the rukh's wingfeathers and more Hoytether started to pay out from the reel in the nose of *Sexdent*. Chastity engaged the electromagnetic drag brakes on the reel and gravity came back to the ship.

"Pull more gees!" said Rod.

"I was going to control the tether payout and bring us to a halt under the bird," said Chastity.

"We'll just be an easy target for an attack by another of those fly-ing killer whales," replied Rod. "Pull gees and swing us around un-derneath the bird and up in front of it. I'll then fly us to a safe spot right in the middle of its back. At least we'll be safe from another at-tack there."

"Penguins do the same thing when they are attacked by a school of killer whales," said Sandra. "I hope the poor rukh is able to carry our weight—its body is nothing but a big balloon, despite its great size."

"If it has trouble carrying us when we're centered on its back, then it'll have even more trouble carrying us hanging from its mouth," replied Rod brusquely. "It would be like a snagged trout hav-ing to haul a fishing weight around all the time."

Chastity increased the braking level and the gees rose as they began their giant swing ride underneath the gliding airbird.

"That sure is a big monster," said Dan from the inside of his habi-tat as he looking out his viewport at the rear end of the rukh rising above them, its long, brightly colored tailfeathers stretching out be-hind it. "I was watching him during his strike and saw him swallow that balloon like the *Sesame Street* Cookie Monster eating a cookie."

Sandra looked upward through the science console holoviewport. She could now see the pale orange-white belly feathers as the cap-sule swung underneath the rukh on the end of the Hoytether. "A good match for the cloud layers above," she murmured, admiring the effectiveness of the hunter's camouflage. She quickly rechecked the science console to make sure that the science imagers were still tracking the bird and getting pictures to radio back to Earth. Even if they didn't make it back themselves, the knowledge they had gathered would.

"We'll be at the end of our swing in about ten seconds," warned Chastity.

"Seichi," commanded Rod. "Get out here quick. We may need you."

Seichi came out of his habitat and took over the science console as Sandra ducked into her habitat to get out of the way. Seichi made a few quick flicks at some icons with a forefinger and the science console turned into a copy of the scottyboard in front of Chastity. Leaving the control of the Hoytether in Chastity's hands, Seichi quickly checked all the engineering systems.

The capsule finished its swing underneath the rukh and passed in front of it. With much of the Hoytether now wrapped over the back and around under the kilometer-sized bird, they were now only a half-kilometer away from the prowlike keel that stuck out in front of the body between the two giant air-scoop mouths. Inside the mouths could be seen hanging featherlike structures.

"Looks like the inside of a baleen whale's mouth," remarked Sandra from inside her habitat.

"Form ever follows function," remarked Dan from his adjacent habitat. "These air whales occupy the same niche here on Saturn as our water whales do on Earth. They need the same types of equipment to survive in the same type of niche."

"Featherbones instead of whalebones," murmured Sandra to herself.

The swing of the capsule brought them level with the head of the flying creature.

"They have two eyes," said Sandra, as the top of the head portion came into view. "One on top of the prow and one below. It must have binocular vision in the vertical direction."

"Those eyes are monsters," said Doc, impressed. "Must be ten meters in diameter. As big around as a small house."

"But still small compared to the size of the beast," said Sandra. "Just like Earth whales again."

"They may be small in comparison to the body size," said Dan, "but they're still large in an absolute sense. They must have excellent night vision with all that photon collection area as well as extreme range capability during daylight. I wouldn't be surprised if they hunt by sight."

"Will you two *shut up* so I can *think!*" yelled Rod, continuing on in a muttering tone that brought forth a throaty chuckle from Chastity. "Here we are, about to die, and all those two can say is: 'What big eyes you have, pretty birdie. . . .' "

They reached the end of the swing, started upward, and went into free fall. Gingerly using their main rockets, Rod flew them over the top of the bird, the Hoytether trailing along behind. With the last of the fuel, he brought them to a halt above the back of the giant bird. He had to keep some of the horizontal thrusters operating in order to counteract the strong wind flow across the rukh's back as they flew in formation with it. They were now so close to the surface of the rukh that they couldn't see its full extent.

"It's like flying over a forest," complained Rod, looking for a spot to land.

"A forest of huge black feathers," remarked Chastity, awe in her voice.

"A truly gigantic forest," agreed Seichi. "Many feathers are nearly one hundred meters long."

Rod, carefully watching an image on his console produced by a camera pointed downward from the base of the capsule, lowered *Sexdent* on its rockets until he could see the feathers below starting to wilt.

"Don't want to burn my way through my landing pad," he muttered as he cut the engines. But instead of the expected silence as the rumbling roar of the jets faded away, they could now hear a different deep rumbling noise. It was a multitoned roar that arose around and through them as the *Sexdent* dropped heavily downward. . . .

It was like crash-landing on an island covered with black palm trees. The heavy capsule fell through the canopy of tree-sized feathers and came to a rest, the broad base of the conical capsule nestled among a forest of nearly transparent quill shafts.

"Look at those tree trunks," said Chastity as *Sexdent* settled itself in amongst the feather quills. "Most of them are over a meter thick."

The deep roaring noise continued. All during their long fall and crash landing, the rumble had become louder. It had started out with tones so deep that they were more felt than heard. The roar rose in intensity, as higher and higher tones were added to it, while the deeper tones continued on, as if someone were pulling out all the stops on a gigantic organ while simultaneously pressing on all the keys, in rolling chord after rolling chord that started at the bass notes and ended with the highest-pitched pipes. As the organlike roar grew louder, a rolling and bucking motion started underneath them, shaking the capsule on its base.

"The poor creature is suffering!" screamed Sandra from her habitat. "You must have burned him with the rockets."

"The rockets were off long before I made contact," replied Rod. "It must be something else."

"It's the reactor!" said Seichi. "It's still operational! The radiators must be burning the inside of its mouth! I hope I still have control. . . ." Seichi quickly brought up the icons he needed on his scottyboard and closed down the reactor. The lights in the capsule flickered slightly and then resumed their normal glow.

The roaring of the giant beast slowed and finally halted.

"We're on internal backup now," Seichi announced.

"How long are the batteries good for?" asked Dan from his habitat, concerned about the future health of his charges.

"We have some small batteries for emergency lighting," replied Seichi. "But our primary backup power supply is a thermophotovoltaic cell similar to that used on the reactor. This one, however, is powered by heat from the decomposition of meta." He took a quick look at the fuel gauge. "We have enough meta fuel for a number of days."

"Days!" exclaimed Chastity, now discouraged. "Perhaps I should have cut us loose from the tether and gotten it over with—"

"What are we going to do now?" squeaked Sandra, her small voice echoing in the silence.

Petra and Petro were both awake. The pain signals radiating out from the stinging sensation in Petru's gullet had wakened Petra from her normal deep lighttime sleep. After a quick thinklink to make sure Petro was awake and functioning, she let him continue to control Petru while she merely tapped off feelings from the stream of nervous impulses coming from various parts of their body.

Petru was hurt badly. There was a hot heavy lump in its left airtube. The giant body was roaring involuntarily in response to the intense pain, its voice sounding like a thousand ruus singing the deathdive song in a thousand different dialects. Fortunately, the stinging sensation soon stopped. Petru's body calmed down and came back under full control of Petro. Although the heavy lump no longer hurt, it was still stuck inside Petru's airtube.

"That was a close call," said Pete from inside the meta plant. "Calls for a celebration. I think I'll have some laser juice."

"No you don't!" said Chastity in a firm voice. "We're not safe yet! We're going to need every clear head we've got to figure a way out of this predicament."

Rod, who had been thinking through every possible future scenario that could evolve from their present situation, finally spoke.

"We're not falling—that's good—we have hours to solve our problems instead of seconds. Seichi has the backup power operating—that's good—we have a few days to solve our problems instead of hours. Seichi has control over the reactor and it's still in working shape—that's good—but he can't turn it on without damaging our means of support—that's bad—but we should be able to figure out a way to free the reactor in a few days' time. We have no meta in our fuel tanks—that's bad . . ." He raised his voice and turned toward the pickup for the radio link to the meta plant. "Pete! Provided Seichi can get the reactor going again, can you make meta riding on top of a rukh?"

Sandra was pleased to hear that Rod had pronounced it right this time.

"Almost positive," Pete assured him. "The meta production units were designed to stand higher gee loads than our landing, so they should all be working. I'll need to check and make sure the heat radiators weren't damaged during the landing, but even if some of them were damaged or we have to limit their temperature to avoid toasting our host, it would just slow the production rate a little."

"Then there's still a chance we can get home!" said Dan, face lighting up. The good news cheered everyone.

"And collect our billion!" added Pete.

Suddenly, everyone was thrown to one side as the floor beneath them tilted and the capsule slid sideways. Black feathers now filled two of the holoviewport windows.

"Provided we don't fall off this bird first," said Rod, suddenly galvanized to action. "Seichi! Tell Mouser to cut us a bunch of ten- and twenty-meter-long tie-lines from the tether mending reel. Then have Jeeves use Mouser and Kitty to fasten *Sexdent* to the quill roots. Chass and Doc! Follow me to the airlock. We've got to get outside and help the mechbots tie this capsule down before this bird realizes it can get rid of us by simply doing a barrel roll. Sandra! Come down and cycle us through the airlock! Pete! Meet us outside!" He headed for the ladder and the airlock below.

The outer airlock door lowered and Rod, Dan, and Chastity stepped out onto it. Although the air was relatively warm, Rod had insisted that they be fully protected, so they wore the full saturnsuit: neon yellow insulated jacket, tights, gloves, boots, and helmet. It was dark under the canopy of layered black feathers, and they had to activate the image intensifier holovisors in their helmets. They looked around. The large black feathers dominated the scene; their quills, a meter or more in diameter, rose up out of large follicles in the semi-transparent skin and arched off to the rear. Underneath were smaller down feathers.

"Not quite like a forest," said Dan. "The feathers are layered and pointing toward the rear of the bird. More like a forest that's been blown over in a windstorm."

"We won't have any problem in determining direction, anyway," said Chastity. "South is the direction the feathers are pointing."

They climbed down the rungs in the side of the conical capsule that led from the airlock door platform to the base of the ship where Pete was waiting for them on the catwalk between two of the engines.

"This heat radiator is in good shape," Pete said as he patted an array of metal vanes located behind one of the main engine rocket bells. It was now obvious that the capsule had landed on one of the down feathers, squashing it flat. Pete stepped off the catwalk onto the "ground."

"Look at this!" he said in surprise, as he jumped up and down. "It's like a trampoline!" The others soon joined him.

Jeeves and Seichi already had the two outside mechbots busy. As they watched, Kitty would first tie a line to an engine mount or safety ring, then scurry off across the smooth skin to fasten the other end of the line to the base of a quill root. Mouser came scuttling down from the nose of *Sexdent* carrying a number of coils of line.

"Let's get busy and help Kitty get *Sexdent* secured," said Rod, handing out segments of line to the others. Soon the four were bounding back and forth across the rukh's skin, threading lines between tie-down points on the capsule and the nearest quill roots. The crew experienced an occasional fall when they got too exuberant with their bounds and came down off balance, but they bounced right back up again unhurt. The quill roots were hollow, very much like the hollow quills on Earth bird feathers, except that the outer surface of the rukh quills was a thin membrane rather than a thick shell. The rukh quill used high internal pressure to achieve the rigidity needed to serve as the shaft of the long feathers.

"Hey, Dan!" called Rod from where he was attaching a line to a quill. "Look at this. Is it a new feather sprouting?"

Dan came over to look. Right beside a large quill, seemingly growing out of the same follicle, was an elongated balloon.

"It's a balloon—inflated until it's rigid—just like the feather quill," said Dan. "But the color and texture are different." In order to compare the internal pressure in the two objects, he tapped first on the quill and then on the strange object. At he touched the small balloon, the strange object moved! It quickly burrowed down deeper into the follicle, then inflated itself until it was tightly wedged between the quill root and the follicle wall.

"It's the rukh equivalent of a louse!" said Dan, pleased at the discovery. He started to reach down to drag the vermin out of its hiding place so he could obtain an image to be stored in Jeeves's ever-accepting memory.

"Watch out!" warned Rod. "It may bite!"

Dan paused. They finally settled on the technique of working two lines around the creature's body, forming each line into a lasso, and pulling the two loops tight around the "waist" of the vermin. By standing on opposite sides of the opening, Rod and Chastity now were able to use the lines to pull the creature out. Once out, the two long lines pulling in opposite directions kept the creature from reaching either Rod or Chastity, while Dan could safely get close. Dan was just starting to collect images with his holovisor when the vermin gave off a loud whistle and shot straight up in the air. Startled, Rod and Chastity let go of their lines and the vermin shot off into the sky, trailing the lines and a fine stream of particles behind it. Dan managed to track down one of the particles and picked it up.

"What'd you find?" asked Sandra, who had been watching from the holoviewport window high up on the nose of *Sexdent.*

"A tiny version of the jet-powered rukh louse that just left," said Dan, putting his find into a sample bag. "When the parent gets big enough, it jets off into the sky and spreads its young to the winds. If they are lucky, they land either somewhere else on the rukh that the parent just left, or perhaps on some other rukh in the flock. I suspect they usually time their seeding flight for the right conditions, but since we disturbed this one, it decided to jet off now."

"Jet-powered rukh louse . . ." repeated Sandra. "Succinct description. Jeeves? What's that hard-to-pronounce Latin name for louse?"

"*Phthir . . .*" replied Jeeves. "If you would like a proper Latin name for the creature, I would suggest *Phthirjactus rukhester,* or louse-jetter rukh-dweller."

"That's enough science for now," said Rod. "Let's recheck and tighten up all the tie-downs, then get back inside and plan our next step over lunch."

"You three check the tie-downs," said Pete. "I'm going back inside the meta factory and check out the production equipment. See you at lunch."

"Don't come back with laser juice on your breath," warned Chastity. "We'll have a party *after* we get the reactor out and running."

Petra could sense that the injury to Petru's windpipe had been a strange one. Sometimes, during a hunt, Petru would swallow a slimswimmer that managed to fly between the sharp mouthfeathers hanging down from the roof of Petru's mouth. When that happened and the slimswimmer struck the back wall of Petru's airtube, its sharp-edged body would inflict a cut on the airtube wall before the slimswimmer escaped through the jet outlet. This was not a slimswimmer cut. It hurt too much for that. Also, the stinging hotness was caused by a very dense and very heavy object. The object was much too dense to fly, so it must not be a normal prey animal that the flock would hunt.

"Hot . . . dense . . ." mused Petra. The stargazer in her makeup then remembered the time, many dimmings of Bright ago, when she, in her nightly climb into the heavens, had seen the fall of a meteor out of the sky. It had passed right through the flock, glowing brightly as it fell. From the speed of its fall it had to be dense. Perhaps Petro had chased one of those meteors and had Petru swallow it. She would query him about it later. Right now he was busy deep inside Petru's left mouth, trying to dislodge the object from Petru's airtube.

Petra could feel there was something else bothering Petru. There was a heavy weight sitting right in the middle of its back. This was a minor problem compared to the painful object stuck in its airtube, but it was annoying Petru, so Petra decided to investigate. She lifted her head and extended her neck until her eye was high in the air. She looked back over Petru's wing but could see nothing at the point where the sense of heaviness came.

"It must be under the feathers," she thought to herself. "I'll go see." From the sides of her head arose two air bladders shaped like wings. The headwings cut into the air flowing over Petru's back and lifted her head into the air. Using the headwings to control her direction of flight, she let her head be blown toward the rear. As the head left its normal cradled position at the top front of the keel, her neck sacs inflated, one after the other, causing the compressed neck to expand and extend. At each joint between the neck segments, the two clawed feet for that joint released their grip on the featherroots on either side of the long cradle they had lain in. The head glided to a landing in the feathertops of Petru's wing and Petra started the long crawl back to the rear across the top of the forest of black feathers that covered Petru's back, the claws along her neck reaching and grabbing the feathertops in synchronism. Soon all of Petra's neck was out of its normal cradled position and each segment sac was filling, as Petra elongated her neck to reach the position where Petru reported heaviness. She used her four large front claws to part the feathers above the heavy spot, and adjusting her eye for near-vision, she peered down.

"*Eeeee . . . !*" screamed Sandra. The tops of the feather trees had parted and a huge eye was peering down at her. From her position at the holoviewport high up in the conical tip of *Sexdent*, she could see that the eye was connected to an elongated segmented body, with a pair of clawed feet between each segment. "It's a giant caterpillar!"

Outside, Rod, Dan, and Chastity looked up. Each quickly ducked behind the nearest quill.

"Don't move," said Rod over their helmet radio link. "I don't think it's spotted us yet. It seems to be looking at the capsule."

"What the hell is a giant caterpillar doing on the back of a rukh?" whispered Chastity.

"It's not a caterpillar," said Dan. "That's the head and neck of the rukh itself. I recognize the eye. The neck must be collapsed and hidden when the head is in its normal position near the front."

"The long neck makes sense," added Sandra over the radio link. "Since it can never perch and bring its wings up to its head for grooming, the head must be able to reach every part of the body, all the way out to the wingtips. But where's the other eye? There were two eyes, one on top and one on the bottom."

"Maybe each eye has its own head and neck," suggested Dan.

"That doesn't make sense," said Sandra. "Eyes have to have a large brain right behind them to function at all. If there are two independent eyes, that means two independent brains. Which one controls the body?"

"Maybe they take *turns! Shut up,* so I can think!" said Rod brusquely, annoyed again at the two scientists as they calmly discussed the construction details of a creature that was about to attack them.

The giant eye parted the feathers further, reached down with its two front pairs of two-meter-long claws, and tried to lift the capsule by grasping the habitat cylinders sticking out from the sides of the ship. The claws slipped on the smooth rounded surfaces as they attempted to pick up the heavy metal capsule. Sandra shrieked again as the capsule tilted slightly, but it was soon obvious that the capsule was too heavy for the eye to lift.

"Didn't even budge it enough to put strain on the tie-down lines," said Rod with satisfaction. "At least we won't have problems from that quarter."

Chastity took advantage of the eye's preoccupation with the capsule on the other side and tried to clamber up to the safety of the airlock door. The eye, however, saw her neon yellow suit, and with surprising swiftness, Chastity soon found herself in its grasp.

How embarrassing, she thought to herself, her initial flush of fear dissolving into annoyance as she realized that she was living out a cliché. *Heroine caught in the clutches of a bug-eyed monster . . .*

Clinging desperately to the climbing rungs with her knees, she pulled with both hands at the hard inflated hollow claw that had encircled her waist and was trying to pull her off. The claw pinched her waist hard, but couldn't penetrate the tough yellow fabric of her saturnsuit. She struggled hard, trying to break the grip of the claw, but it was an even match. Rod started forward to help her.

"Stay back, Rod!" shouted Chastity. "We can't afford to lose both pilots." Suddenly, there was a short burst of flame from somewhere nearby and she was free.

"I hope I did not singe you," came the voice of Seichi over the radio link. "I reasoned that a short burst of hot meta from the nose jets might drive the monster away. It seems to have worked."

The giant eye had reared back in surprise at the flame. One of its neck claws was rubbing the side of one of its neck segments. The creature had obviously felt the effects of the flame. The eye started down again to attack Chastity as she finished her climb into the airlock. Another blast from the nose jets drove it back.

"Just the thing!" exclaimed Sandra. "Now at least we're communicating with the monster. It's not much in the way of communication. Simply, 'If you get anywhere near us you'll get burnt.' But at least we're communicating. Too bad it's punishment instead of reward. I've trained mice to climb ladders using nothing but treats."

"You'd have a hard time using treats on this thing," said Rod from behind one of the quill trunks. "No mouth."

The giant eye circled around the *Sexdent,* looking at it from all angles. It noticed the lines holding the capsule down. It reached a claw toward a line on the other side of the capsule from where the first attitude jet was fired, but Seichi gave a blast from the jet on that side. The big-eyed caterpillar soon got the idea and backed away.

"Do you have your finger above the icon for the nose jets, Seichi?" said Dan from behind another quill trunk.

"Yes," replied Seichi.

"Then I'm coming out," said Dan. He stepped forward and started walking slowly across the bouncy "ground" toward the capsule. The eye started down again, but another short burst by Seichi drove it back again. Dan slowly climbed the outside rungs up to the airlock door and joined Chastity inside.

"You may come out now, Rod," said Seichi. "My finger is poised."

Rod stepped out hesitantly. Now, instead of reaching down for him, the eye actually backed off slightly, its large foreclaws closed and folded up out of the way.

"I do believe it's *got* it," said Sandra excitedly. "It's learned to leave humans alone after just a few training sessions. I wonder how intelligent it is."

When Petra parted the feathers over the place where Petru felt something heavy sitting on its skin, she hadn't really thought about what kind of animal she would find there. The last thing that she would have guessed, however, would have been an animal in the shape of a mathematically perfect truncated cone with six obliquely truncated cylinders sticking out from its side. The creature had three large eyes near the top of the conical body, with additional eyes at the ends of each of the six cylinders. The mouth of the creature hung open. The large lower jaw was not moving and the creature didn't try to fly away, so it was probably dead. There were also some bright yellow vermin there, hiding behind the featherroots, but she would take care of those later. Right now she needed to take this dead animal off Petru's back and put it in Petru's mouth where it belonged. She attempted to pick up the cone by grabbing four of the cylinders with her foreclaws, but the cone was heavy and the surfaces of the cylinders were hard and slippery. Try as she could, her claws kept slipping off and she was unable to budge the conical creature.

One of the vermin tried to climb up the cone to go into the cone's mouth. Petra reached for the four-legged pest, intending to burst its body with her sharp claws and then toss the deflated remains to the winds, but the vermin proved to be solid and also heavy for its size. The body of the vermin was resilient instead of hard like the body of the cone, but although resilient, its yellow skin was very tough and her sharp-pointed claws were unable to puncture it. She pulled at the pest, trying to dislodge it from its perch on the cone so she could toss it away, but it clung to the cone with two of its legs and fought Petra's claws with the other two.

Suddenly, a bright flash of light came from the tip of the cone, and Petra felt a stinging sensation on her third segment. She quickly let go of the vermin and backed off to safety, rubbing the hurt spot with one of her segment feet. She started to reach down again, but another burst of light warned her away. The light had a unique reddish-purple color. The last time she had seen that color was many Largemoons ago when she had seen a long-lasting meteor passing through the upper skies just under the Arcs. She had long wondered if there were strange creatures that lived on the other globes in the sky. Perhaps this creature came from one of those globes and had flown here to visit.

A moment's thought rejected that conclusion. The creature had no wings and no flotation bladders. It obviously couldn't fly in the clouds of Air, so it certainly would not able to fly above the clouds where the air became thin, or between the globes where there was no air. This was obviously a specialized kind of vermin—a nonflying parasite that rode on true animals that had their own means to maintain themselves afloat.

Petra next noticed the fine tendrils coming from the nose and base of the conical creature, somewhat like the tendrils hanging down from a roundfloater or a ringgulper. The creature had fastened its tendrils firmly to the base of the many featherroots surrounding it. Petra now understood why the creature had been so hard to lift. She bent down to cut away the tendrils with her foreclaws, but another burst of light from the tip of the cone drove her back.

Another of the small vermin moved toward the cone. It moved on its hind legs only. The front legs were not up in a defensive posture, but swung loosely at its sides. Petra bent down to grasp the brightly colored creature before it could reach the cone. Although Petra's interaction with the first of the vermin had convinced her that her claws could not burst the strange dense pest, she knew that she was strong enough to lift the creatures bodily and toss them over Petru's trailing edge into the hot depths of hell below. As she reached for the vermin, a blaze of light and heat came again from the cone. Petra reared back, convinced now that for some reason the conical creature was protecting the four-legged yellow vermin. When the last of the three vermin ventured forth, Petra left it alone.

All three vermin were soon inside the mouth of the conical creature, obviously unafraid that the mouth would swallow them. The vermin took turns coming to the entrance of the mouth and peering up at Petra with their single large eye at the top end of their bodies. It was now obvious to Petra that the smaller vermin somehow belonged to the larger conical parasite. Perhaps the conical parasite had parasites of its own!

Petra was trying to figure out what to do next when a thinklink call came from Petro.

"I have found the thing that injured Petru's airtube. It is too heavy for me. If you come and help, together we may be able to remove it."

"I'll be there soon," Petra thinklinked back.

Leaving the dense vermin as a problem to be dealt with later, she raised up her head and crawled back over the feathertops to Petru's left mouth.

Over a hot lunch of instant soup and noodles, the crew made plans to recover the reactor and get it operational again.

"The reactor is somewhere inside the rukh's mouth," started Rod. "Exactly where, we don't know. Although we can't see it, we have contact with it through the control and power lines built into the Hoytether and we know it's still operational. My plan is to hike to the leading edge of the rukh by following under the Hoytether lying on top of the feathers overhead. We then move along the leading edge of the wing until we find the loop of the Hoytether that leads to the reactor. Then, standing just behind the leading edge of the wing, we use the Hoytether to haul the reactor back out of the rukh's mouth. We then lower the reactor down until it's hanging over the front edge of the wing, turn it on, make meta for a few months, and then leave."

"Sounds simple," remarked Dan. "Unless the rukh objects to having heavy objects hanging from it on lengths of line."

"Hmmm . . ." said Rod with a nod of his head, agreeing with Dan. "We may have to set up guard on the Hoytether until Sandra trains it to leave the tether alone. If she could train a tiny mouse to climb a ladder, she should be able to train a giant bird to leave a Hoytether alone."

Sandra didn't look perturbed at Rod's assumption. "My classmate taught her mouse to sweep the floor with a tiny pushbroom," she said. "Should be a snap to teach the rukh to leave the Hoytether alone. After all, we have already taught it to leave humans alone using the meta jets on *Sexdent*." She thought for a bit. "We'll need a portable meta jet, though."

"We already have such an instrument," said Seichi. "It is a meta-energized welding torch. Very simple. If needed, I could easily make a number of copies using the three-D mechfab in the engineering sector."

"How much does the nuclear reactor weigh, Seichi?" asked Rod. "I'll need to take along enough hands for the task of hauling it out and lowering it down."

"The reactor proper masses only one hundred kilograms," replied Seichi. "The thermophotovoltaic converter that surrounds it to produce the electricity is another fifty kilograms, while the heat radiators are another fifty kilograms, for a total of two hundred kilograms mass or four hundred forty pounds weight."

"Need at least four people then," said Rod.

"Unfortunately," continued Seichi. "The reactor-converter-radiator system is quite firmly connected to the large electrically powered flexfans. They mass well over a metric ton. They will need to be cut loose from the reactor before you can pull it out. Fortunately, I have confirmed that the mechbot Tabby is still with the reactor-flexfan complex and operational," reported Seichi. "Given a meta torch, it is capable of disconnecting the flexfans from the reactor."

"Good!" said Rod. "It would be instant death for any person to get anywhere near the reactor. Even though it's turned off, it's still radioactive."

"It would not be an instant death," Seichi corrected him. "Although the radiation dose received after only a few minutes of work would be fatal, actual death takes a number of days."

"Bleeding from every organ in your body," grimaced Dan. "Not a pleasant way to go."

"I'm concerned about the poor rukh," said Sandra. "The radiation dose it's getting can't be any good for it."

"Fortunately," interjected Dan, "the radiation dose received by an organ is proportional to the density of the organ. Most of a rukh is air, so not only is the radiation dose spread out over a wide volume, most of the dose is absorbed by the air, not the body tissue. The rukh will have a nasty burn where the reactor is now lying, but the rest of it shouldn't suffer too much."

"We should get it out as quick as we can, anyway," insisted Sandra. "The first rule of being a good symbiote is not to harm your host."

"I'm afraid we're more parasite than symbiote," said Dan, handing his soup bowl to Puss to put into the dishwasher. "But I agree. Let's get a move on."

"Right!" said Rod, taking command. He looked at Seichi. "You'll have to stay here, of course, Seichi. We'll need an expert at the scottyboard to give commands to Tabby and get the reactor started once we have it free. Just to make sure we have enough hands to handle the reactor, all the rest of us will be going to haul it out of the rukh's gizzard."

Seichi wished that it were otherwise. He would greatly enjoy the experience of trekking across the back of a being as large as the Imperial Palace Gardens. But he knew he must subjugate his personal desires for the greater benefit of the entire crew. He now began to appreciate the feelings that the American *Apollo* command module astronauts must have felt—the ones that stayed up in their lonely orbit about the Moon while their comrades had the opportunity to visit the lunar surface.

"I shall be at my assigned post when needed," he replied, bowing. "First, however, I shall make you additional meta torches." He opened the door to the engineering sector and started touching the icons on the mechfab console inside the door.

"And I'm going to have Mouser braid us some decently thick climbing lines," said Chastity, heading for the scottyboard on the control deck above. "Those hextube strings may be strong enough for a safety line, but they're too thin and slippery for climbing and belaying."

While Seichi serenely watched their departure from his post behind the holoviewport high above them, the remainder of the crew exited out on the airlock door and made their way onto the quiveringly alive "ground" in their bright yellow saturnsuits with their different-color reflective identification bands. Each carried extra tanks of oxygen, bottles of water, and as much line as they could shoulder. He or she bounced through the forest of feathers in a ragged column. While the tailenders would wait under a break in the feather cover through which could be seen the Hoytether passing overhead, the leaders would bound ahead to the next break where the Hoytether could be spotted again. After hiking along the bouncy surface for about half a kilometer, they began to notice that the canopy overhead was now closer to the ground, and the rush of air across the tips of the feathers became so loud they could hardly hear each other through their radio link. They were approaching the leading edge of the wing of the giant bird. They turned up the volume in their helmet earphones and continued on.

Once they had reached the leading edge of the wing, they turned and headed inward to pick up the end of the Hoytether attached to the reactor. Their search was aided by Seichi, who had jury-rigged a radio transmitter to the power line, causing it to give off a signal that they could home in on with their helmet radios. It didn't take long to find the other loop segment of the Hoytether and they started along it.

"The ground is starting to really slope downward here," said Rod as he gathered the group together under a break in the canopy. "Drop your empty tanks and water bottles here. Tie them to a quill so they'll be there when we come back. We'll then lash to each other and head on downhill, anchormen tied to a quill while the climber is belayed to the next quill."

The surface got steeper and the feathers got smaller and more dense. They were in no danger of falling off since there were so many quill roots to grab on to. But that also meant that the Hoytether leading to the reactor stayed out of reach at the top of the feather canopy. Rod called a halt.

"It looks like my idea of hauling the reactor out by pulling on the Hoytether from on top of the wing isn't going to work. We're too tiny. We're dwarfed by all these gigantic feathers. Even if we climbed a feather and pulled the tether down to ground level where we could anchor our feet against a quill and pull, the tether would just get caught in the feathers somewhere between us and the reactor." He took a big breath. "I'm afraid we're going to have to climb down into the mouth of this beast and work inside where there aren't any feathers to snag the tether."

They found a break in the black feather canopy where the Hoytether was only a few tens of meters overhead. With a boost from

Rod and Pete pulling on long lines from higher up on the wing edge, and Dan and Chastity helping her keep her balance with lines from the side, Sandra, chosen because she was lightest, managed to shinny up a feather and tie a line to the multiline Hoytether passing overhead. The Hoytether, which was normally cylindrical in shape when hanging freely, had collapsed into a double-sided tape, draped from one feather top to the next. They climbed up the line to the Hoytether and soon were traveling over the top of the feather canopy, climbing partially downward and partially horizontally with the Hoytether acting as a multiline rope ladder.

"Look over there," said Dan during a rest stop. He pointed to the inflated keel at the center of the giant bird. They still were too close to the rukh to get any sense of how big it was, but the keel stuck up out of the flat forest of black wing feathers like a small feather-covered ridge, making it visible at a distance.

"I don't see anything," said Chastity.

"It's what you don't see that counts," said Dan. "When we flew over this bird earlier, there was a large eye perched at the front of that keel ridge. Now it's gone. Instead there is a bunch of neck segments running down the ridge and heading over the leading edge of the wing and down under the left side."

"I bet that top eye is inside the mouth," said Sandra. "Trying to do something about that nuclear reactor."

"That could be a problem," said Rod. "I don't fancy meeting a giant caterpillar face to face in a dark cave."

"We have it trained, Rod," said Sandra confidently. "Just make sure you take your meta torch with you and you'll be perfectly safe . . . probably."

They finally came to the place where the Hoytether parted from the feather tops and hung freely downward. Instead of being collapsed into a tape as it was in the feather canopy, the twelve primary lines of the Hoytether had sprung open to form a hollow cylinder a meter in diameter. At intervals, the primary lines were cross-connected by secondary lines that gave them "rungs" to climb on.

"What a wind!" exclaimed Sandra as she clambered into the comparative safety of the inside of the one-meter-diameter Hoytether. "Good thing we have these helmets." She was even more glad that she had a helmet on when her visor was suddenly splattered by a jellyfishlike flying creature. Sandra thought it might have been a ringswimmer, but there wasn't enough of it left for accurate determination.

Now that they were out from under the feather canopy, they could look around and see that the rukh was still flying in formation with the large flock of rukhs that had formed the hunting cone. They were no longer in the hunting cone formation, but instead were flying around in lazy circles.

"Dan," said Sandra. "Notice that nearly all the other rukhs have their two eyes settled in their niches at the top and bottom of the keel."

"Also notice that both eyes are open," said Dan. "When they were in their hunting cone formation, only the bottom eye was open. The top eye was closed. Probably asleep."

"Makes sense," said Sandra. "Especially if they have highly intelligent brains. For some reason, intelligent brains need to have rest periods—probably to take care of computer housekeeping functions like erasing garbage bits, firming up memories, and rearranging files. Dolphins sleep that way. One eye and one brain hemisphere at a time. One eye-brain set keeps watch and keeps the dolphin swimming and coming up for breath, while the other eye-brain set takes a nap. Then they switch. The rukhs must do the same thing with their pair of eye-brain systems."

Climbing rapidly down the inside of the multiline tether, the group soon cleared the wing edge and hung in space in front of the gigantic mouth of the amazing winged beast. The mouth was an oval cavity some two hundred meters high and four hundred meters wide. The opening pulsed slowly as it gulped in air, sparsely laden with food. The illumination from the setting sun allowed them a glimpse inside.

"Works just like a baleen whale, all right," remarked Dan, as he made sure that images of what he was seeing through his visor were being broadcast back to the massive memory banks of Jeeves while simultaneously being broadcast back to Earth. The wingtips of the rukh tilted slightly, sending the giant body off in pursuit of a larger-than-normal morsel. At the same time deep pulses of sound could be heard coming from the leading edge of the wing.

"That proves that they don't just hunt by eyesight," said Dan. "Both eyes are inside the mouth, but the creature just sensed a large piece of prey and changed course to get it. It must be able to see by sonar as well as light."

The prey was a medium-sized bubblefloater. They watched as the balloonlike creature passed below them and into the maw of the giant bird. The balloon portion of the bubblefloater burst as it struck the sharp edges of the long stiff feathers hanging from the roof of the mouth. Although the feathers were long, they were not very wide. The barbicels that kept the feather barbs locked together must have been numerous and strong, for the barbs did not separate under the impact.

"Although they may look like feathers, they act like a knife blade," remarked Sandra. "Featherblades instead of featherbones."

They watched as the shreds of balloon, strands of tendrils, and pieces of bubblefloater body dripped down off the featherblades into a conical cavity at the base of the mouth. At the bottom of the cone could be seen pulsating bladder sections covered with what looked like black shark teeth, which ground away at the dripping fragments, turning them into a pulp that drained into the gullet at the center.

"Thank heaven the reactor didn't go in there," said Rod, looking at the pulsating gizzard with its grinding shark teeth. "Where did it go, anyway?"

"After the rukh sieves the food out of the air with the featherblades, it channels the air to its exhaust jets," said Dan. "Since the reactor hasn't come out of the end of the jets, it must still be inside the rukh's windpipe, hanging from the end of the Hoytether."

Below them, the Hoytether described an arc that went through the featherblade curtains and into the dark recesses of the mouth. They continued their climb down the inside of the tether and started to approach the featherblade curtain.

"Look over there at the bottom of the keel," said Dan, pointing. "When we swung by here a few hours ago, there was an eye there. But now it too has left its perch and gone into the mouth. All that's left outside is the base of the neck."

They could now see where the neck segments from the lower eye joined up with the neck segments from the upper eye at a point where the featherblade curtain met the inner wall of the mouth. The slender inflated necks didn't move in the turbulent wind. They were securely attached to the wall by the pairs of claws between each neck segment. The two necks went around the curtain and past the gullet into the windpipe, heading in the same direction as the Hoytether.

"Looks like they're in there waiting for us," said Rod, concern in his voice. "But there's no helping it. In we go . . ." He continued the climb down the swinging Hoytether.

By the time they passed over the lower "lip" of the mouth they were traveling almost horizontal. It was now possible to slip and fall through the large gaps in the Hoytether, so Rod made sure that everyone used a safety line as well as a climbing line attached to the person ahead and the person behind.

"Pit stop!" Rod announced as they came to the baleen curtain.

"What!?" shouted Chastity, who was leading the way.

"Whatever it is we're going to run into in there, it's more than likely to scare the piss out of us," said Rod. "So to make sure that doesn't happen, we're going to piss right here before we go in. Downwind first. That's you, Chass. The rest of us will look the other way. When you're done, give a holler, and the next one will take the upwind position."

"This is crazy," said Chastity in protest. But despite her protest she started to roll down the top of her saturnsuit pants.

Soon the necessities had been taken care of. They started through the featherblade curtain, Rod first, meta torch at the ready, and Sandra last.

"I wonder if the gizzard noticed the new taste among all its usual tastes?" mused the scientist in Sandra as she looked down the one hundred meters of dripping featherblades into the grinding gizzard below. As she watched, another small cloud of miniature bubble-floaters struck the featherblades and were sliced to dripping shreds that became grist for the living mill below.

Dan was in front of Sandra and stopped to look at the featherblades that had been parted by the Hoytether.

"Seems to be just a specialized feather with an edge as sharp as a razor," said Dan as he felt the edge with his yellow-gloved finger, then looked at the undamaged glove. "Not as sharp as a razor—more like 'as sharp as a knife'—a slightly dull knife."

"Sharp enough to do the job," said Sandra. "Especially when your prey impacts at a hundred klours or more."

"We're lucky it wasn't sharp enough to cut the Hoytether," added Dan. "But then, of course, even a razor has a hard time cutting a macropolyhextube line."

They passed through the curtain into the darkness to join the others. The sun had set, so it was extremely dark inside. They had lights in their helmets and image intensifiers in their holovisors, but it was still hard to make out the far walls of the gigantic windpipe, which were dozens of meters away. The walls were pulsating. The portion near them would first expand away under the force of the air rushing in through the featherblade curtain, then the featherblades would fold shut, like a vertical venetian blind, the walls would contract, and the trapped air was forced out the rear of the windpipe as a high-speed jet.

"Works just like the old V-1 flying bombs," said Pete, as they watched the creature go through a few intake-exhaust cycles.

"I notice that the inner wall is covered with feathers, while the outer wall is a thin transparent membrane," said Chastity. "Why isn't it all one or the other?"

"Rukhs have feathers for the same reason Earth birds have feathers—to keep them warm. In the case of the rukh, however, not only do the feathers keep the bird at optimum working temperature, the higher temperature causes the hydrogen flotation bladders to produce more lift. The rukh is a flying hot-air balloon. The inside wall has feathers to insulate the main body from the cold air in the windpipe. But feathers produce a drag and mass penalty, so the outer parts of the windpipe evolved to be featherless and optimized to operate adequately while cold. Sort of like the feet on a penguin."

The humans continued on down the sloping tether, moving quickly when the rukh was drawing its "breath," and holding on to the lines of the Hoytether with both arms and legs when the jet blast started. The windpipe narrowed and curved as it came to the midsection of the giant bird. The Hoytether, never designed to stay expanded when subjected to side forces, was now again a flat double-layer tape collapsed against the inner feathered wall, still some ten meters off the floor.

"We'll have to do some hand-by-hand along the outside," said Rod, squirming out between the lines of the Hoytether. He waited, hanging on tight with both arms and legs, until the fierce jet blast of the exhaust cycle was over. In the comparative calm that came when the rukh was "drawing its breath" he quickly clambered around the bend, trailing a safety line behind them.

"I'm inside the Hoytether again," he reported a short time later.

"Come on around, one at a time. The last one is to leave a safety line connected to the tether."

Soon they were all safely around and ensconced in the comparative safety of the multiline Hoytether. They turned their helmet lights down the long wind tunnel. The Hoytether stretched away from them and continued on downward toward the living floor, which also had an obvious downward slope. The far end of the wind tunnel was pitch black.

Their helmet lights were seen by other eyes, which turned to look at them from the blackness. The five humans, literally hanging by a few threads high in the air on the inside of the mouth of a gigantic monster, found themselves staring at the reflection of their lights coming from two ten-meter-diameter eyes.

What was most disconcerting to the humans was that the two eyes, which the brain wanted to interpret as staying a fixed distance apart, moved around independently of one another, causing the bewildered human brains to imagine the invisible creature behind those eyes going through bizarre gyrations. Rod and Pete had their meta torches at the ready, but the eyes didn't attack. Instead, one of the eyes continued to stare at them, while the other turned away.

"Did you feel that?" said Chastity. "The tether just gave a twitch! Everybody hold still and feel one of the primary strands!" They all stopped moving.

"The primary lines seem to be more taut here on the other side of the bend," said Rod. "But I don't feel anything else."

Suddenly, they all felt another twitch.

"That was stronger than the last one!" said Chastity. "Those bug-eyed monsters are fooling around with the tether!"

"That was a pretty strong twang," said Pete with a concerned voice. "Like one of the lines was cut."

"It would make sense," said Dan. "The eyes have probably located the reactor and fan, found they couldn't drag it back up the windpipe and dump it out the mouth, so now they're concentrating on cutting the tether so the annoyance can slide out the rear."

"Those multiline Hoytethers can take a lot of cuts," said Pete, now alarmed. "But they're designed to withstand random cuts, not a deliberate attack. I wonder how many lines they cut before we got here?"

"However many it was," said Rod, "they aren't going to cut any more!" Unfastening his safety lines to Pete and the tether, and putting the meta torch on low, he starting crawling down the center of the Hoytether as fast as he could go. Pete started to unfasten his safety lines to follow Rod, but Chastity prevented him from disconnecting from her.

"With Rod off, I'm in charge," she said with a stern voice. "We'll only take risks when we must. Rod is going to need us all to haul the reactor out, so we are *all* going down to back him up—*together!* Now leave those safety lines connected and get a move on!"

Seichi's voice came over the radio link. "You are approaching the reactor. Although the reactor is unshielded, it has been off for some hours. It is safe to approach within fifty meters, but any closer and you will start to accumulate a perceptible radiation dose."

The downward-sloping Hoytether finally reached the floor of the windpipe and they could now crawl faster because their knees and feet were less likely to slip off the lines and down through the large gaps in the Hoytether. When they reached Rod, they found him at a tattered section of tether, holding the two eyes at bay with his meta torch.

Sandra noticed that one eye had raised up its head and pulled back away from Rod, with its four extralarge front foreclaws folded to its body. "That must be the eye we met on topside," she thought to herself. "We had it trained to keep its claws off humans." The other eye, however, was still feinting an attack. It tried to reach toward Sandra, at the end of the crawling group of humans, but Pete quickly drove it away with a long flame from his meta torch. After foiling a few more feints at the humans and the tether, the humans soon had both eyes trained to stay off at a distance with their foreclaws folded.

"The first eye desisted from the attack on the tether right away," said Sandra. "We trained it to keep its claws off humans up there, so it was easy to extend the training to keep it away from the tether. The other eye took longer to train. That probably indicates that each eye has a separate intelligence behind it."

"A being with two brains," said Dan, musing.

"I remember being told in grade school that the real big dinosaurs had many brains," added Pete. "I always wondered which brain ran things."

"For Christ's *sake*, Pete," said Rod, annoyed again. "You're beginning to talk like a scientist instead of an engineer. We've got more important things to do now than discuss the number of brains needed to run this flying monster. Keep those eyes at bay while Seichi and I get the reactor free from the flexfans. Seichi? Is Tabby ready?"

"I have instructed the reactor mechbot to come to your position," came Seichi's voice over their radio link. "It should arrive shortly." The mechbot soon appeared out of the darkness, its six clawed feet crawling nimbly along the primary lines of the Hoytether. Rod handed his meta torch to Tabby, who took it off down the Hoytether in one claw, its five remaining legs working just as effectively as six had done on the way up.

"What is Tabby going to do?" asked Sandra, a little puzzled. Her query was answered by a bright light as Tabby lit the meta torch and started to cut through the mechanical connections linking the flexfan system to the reactor complex.

"Careful!" warned Sandra. "You're likely to burn the poor creature! All our training could go for naught!"

Her warning was augmented as the two eyes took notice of the distant light and started toward it. A quick blast of flame from Pete's meta torch drove them back, but instead of staying motionless, the two eyes now wavered back and forth as if uncertain what to do next.

"I have the mechbot positioned so that any molten drops of metal fall on it, rather than the creature's skin," Seichi reassured her.

The Hoytether gave a jerk as the load on it lightened. A short time later they felt a shift in the slope of the floor of the windpipe.

"Feels like the rukh got rid of some excess weight," said Rod in a pleased tone. Tabby soon reappeared and returned the meta torch to Rod.

"Now comes the hard part," said Rod. "Pulling the reactor back out. Hope you're all in good shape."

Chastity and Pete had been active during the interval when Tabby was busy. They had restrung one of the braided climbing lines so that one end was hooked firmly on the upslope portion of the Hoytether, while all along its length were tied stirrup loops.

"Don't try to lift using your arm muscles," warned Rod as the five crewmembers spread themselves along the multilooped line. "Just put your feet firmly into the stirrups, bend your legs, reach down to the nearest tether connection point and pull it up using your leg muscles." They all reached down and grabbed adjacent connecting points on the Hoytether. "All together now . . . pull!"

"It's moving!" said Sandra excitedly, but her gloved fingers slipped and the shock of losing her support caused the others to also lose control. The reactor slipped back to the end of the tether with a jerk.

"This is going to be harder than I thought," said Pete with concern. "We've got a half kilometer to go. All uphill."

"We need to have some method of holding the load while we reset ourselves," said Chastity. Soon the lower Hoytether segment they were pulling on had short segments of safety line attached to it. After each lift, the four larger crewmembers kept their legs stiffened to hold the half-meter gain they had made, while Sandra moved the hooks to consolidate that gain. They would then wait until the jet exhaust phase of the rukh's breathing pattern had passed, so they didn't have to fight wind drag as well as gravity, and then lift again for another gain of half a meter. After each ten meters, the multi-loop climbing line was reset higher up the Hoytether, and the crew took a sip of water or a nibble on an energy bar and started again.

"That's the last of my water," said Pete at a rest stop after they had progressed about another hundred meters. "I wish it had been filled with laser juice—calories as well as refreshment. As it is, I'm pooped."

"I hate to admit it, but I am too," said Dan.

"We can't give up! Now that we've come this far!" said Chastity.

"I agree," said Rod, emptying his water squeezer and putting his feet into the stirrup loops. "Okay, crew. Tote that barge."

Groaning, they bent to their task. The first pull was successful, but on the second one, both Sandra and Dan slipped and the reactor fell back.

"I'm afraid it's no use," said Dan.

"Damn!" said Rod. "We'll just have to tie it down here and go back to the ship and come back when we're rested. Bringing more water and energy bars this time."

"That isn't going to work," said Chastity, pointing to the two eyes still watching them from a distance. "As soon as we're gone, those eyes are going to complete their tether-cutting job."

"One of us will have to stay and keep them at bay with a meta torch," said Rod.

"Perhaps we can have Seichi do the job by giving Tabby the meta torch," suggested Pete.

"Neither one of those ideas is going to work," said Chastity. "There are two eyes. They could attack the tether at two widely separated points and there would be no way to stop one or the other of them from sooner or later cutting the tether and dumping the reactor."

"There's got to be *some* way out of this mess," said Rod, going silent as he went into his test-pilot-in-trouble mode. Chastity did the same. The others grew silent to let them think.

"What are the yellow vermin doing now?" asked Petro.

"They're not moving. Must be resting," Petra replied. "They have obviously been working very hard at pulling the heavy hot thing up Petru's airtube."

"It is amazing to see vermin cooperate like that," said Petro. "Why don't they cut the multitendril with their hot light and let the heavy thing slide out Petru's jet? They got rid of the other heavy thing that way."

"They must want to keep the heavy thing for some reason," said Petra.

"Perhaps it is some sort of food," suggested Petro.

"Your suggestion is probably correct," said Petra. "But instead of food for them, perhaps it is food for their host. When I left the vermin, they were all inside the mouth of the heavy conical creature that is sitting in the middle of Petru's back. Perhaps the vermin go out and drag in prey for the cone. The hard mouth of the cone can no doubt crush the hard shell of the heavy thing, and they all share in eating what is inside."

"Food or not, the vermin are doing what we want them to do," said Petro. "Getting the heavy hot thing out of Petru's airtube before it becomes hot again and causes more pain."

"They seem to be having trouble. Perhaps we should help them," suggested Petra.

"How can we?" replied Petro. "We have already found that we could not pull the heavy thing up the airtube, even when we two pull together."

"And the five vermin do not seem to be able to move the heavy thing," said Petra. "Even when they all pull together." She paused as she reconsidered the strange idea that was forming in her head. "Perhaps if we two *helped* pull, then all of us, working together, could remove the heavy thing from Petru's airtube."

"Help?" said Petro incredulously. "I can understand helping others of the flock, for they are family. But helping *vermin?!*"

"It will get the heavy thing out of Petru's airtube," Petra reminded him.

"Perhaps it is a good idea," replied Petro, always a pragmatist. "But how? Every time we come close to the multitendril they start their hot lights and threaten to hurt us."

"They seem to be relatively intelligent—for vermin, that is," said Petra. "And they do seem to understand the idea of mutual cooperation. Although we can't talk to them, they do have that big bulbous eye at the front of their heads to see us with. Perhaps I can show them our intent by example." She elongated her neck and stretched it out down the airtube, foreclaws reaching out like she was attempting to grasp something.

Sandra suddenly broke the enforced silence of the thinking group of humans. "Look! One of the eyes is doing something funny."

"Doing what?" said Rod, coming out of his trance with his meta torch at the ready. As all their helmet lights focused on the two eyes, they could see that one of them was stretching its neck downwind, parallel to the Hoytether, but a good distance away from it. The neck then contracted, pulling the head back along the same path. It repeated the motion a number of times, each time reaching out with its foreclaws as if it were grasping something and pulling it back.

"What is it doing that for?" said Rod, bewildered. "Could it be some kind of trick? Keep a watch on the other eye—"

"Looks like it's digging a ditch," said Pete.

"Tote that barge . . . lift that bale . . ." murmured Dan in time to the motions of the eye, also puzzled.

"Haul that Hoytether!" said Sandra. "It's making motions like it was pulling on the Hoytether. Like it wants to help us pull!"

"That sure makes sense," said Dan. "I'm sure they want the reactor out of their body's windpipe as much as we do."

"How do you say yes in rukhese, Sandra?" asked Chastity.

"Perhaps this will do it," said Rod. He stuffed the meta torch out of sight in a pouch on his backpack and raised both his hands to show they were empty. Pete did the same.

Watching him carefully, the eye that had been doing the hauling motion came closer to them and reached slowly for the segment of Hoytether below them. It touched one of the main strands, grasping it firmly without trying to cut it. The line was slightly slack since the load of the reactor was being carried on some of the adjacent primary lines that were anchored onto the multilooped pulling line. Chastity reached out to grab the same strand and pulled on it too. Together, human and alien felt each other pull . . . cooperating . . . working together to bring the line taut . . . getting it ready for the next lift. The other eye joined with the first eye. The humans scrambled into position on the climbing line.

Now certain that they all agreed on what needed to be done, Rod, Chastity, Dan, Pete, and the two eyes pulled on the Hoytether. The reactor moved readily and Sandra scrambled to readjust the holding hooks for the pause between lifts.

At first the two eyes kept their necks far from the humans and the Hoytether. Only the foreclaws directly under the head actually touched the Hoytether lines, and then only when it was time for the next pull. But the necks found that they were pulling at an awkward angle, and as the effort went on, the smaller neck claws that extended from between each neck segment shifted their anchor positions on the airtube wall from one feather to the next, a feather more in line with the direction in which they were pulling. Then, some of the claws found a better purchase on the upper sections of Hoytether. Soon the humans found themselves practically engulfed in legs, as neck claws obtained purchase on the Hoytether lines all around them. The stronger, but only two-legged, humans and the weaker, but multilegged, alien heads soon jointly worked out a routine. The five humans and two eyes would climb the taut upper portions of the Hoytether for about ten meters, pulling the reactor with them, while the Hoytether piled up below them. Then, while four of the humans and the two eyes held their gain, Sandra got the limp section of tether out of the way and readjusted their climbing line, and they prepared for their next burst of effort.

To coordinate the effort, Rod took to yelling commands and encouragement. "Everybody ready? Everybody bend . . . everybody

PULL!" Soon his command of "Pull" was matched by a deep bass note that arose from deep within the air bladders of the giant body. Sandra noticed that although the body of the rukh could make sounds, the eyes were strangely silent. She had hoped that there would be an opportunity to speak more with these creatures (*creature*—she reminded herself—two eyes and two brains but only one body and one "individual"), but it was going to be difficult to hold a "conversation" with one of the eyes when it couldn't speak.

With all of them working together, it didn't take long to pull the reactor up the windpipe to the inside of the featherblade curtain, Tabby riding shotgun on the reactor itself. Rod had given his meta torch to Tabby, and any time one of the eyes tried to approach the reactor, Tabby warned it off. The humans didn't need warning.

"Now what do we do?" said Chastity as they called a halt with the reactor still a hundred meters downhill and downwind. The slope of the windpipe had become shallower, and it was now possible for just two humans to haul the reactor along by pulling on the Hoytether attached to it. "We need to get the reactor up over the lip of the mouth. We can't get near it, so we can't push it over the edge, and we can't pull on it, because the Hoytether goes *up* from here." She pointed at the inflated keel of the giant bird. The prow of the keel stuck out ahead of the intake port of the mouth. "Looks like we need a few people to climb out to the end where they can anchor themselves and pull the reactor from there." She didn't sound very enthusiastic about the prospect. Pete gave a heavy sigh of weariness and sat down heavily in the floor of mouthfeathers. There was a long silence as everyone tried to think of some other option.

"We already *have* two of us anchored out there!" said Rod in a brightening tone. Holding on to the safety line connected high up on the hanging portion of the Hoytether, he waited until the breathing cycle of the rukh reached the point of minimum wind, and walked across the mouthfeathers to where the two eyes were watching them. As the tiny human approached the giant caterpillars, their bodies now contracted significantly in length, one of the giant ten-meter-diameter eyes bent down to Rod's level. Rod bravely reached upward and grabbed the sharp claw at the end of one of the four large forearms. The eye, instead of pulling the claw away or using it to grab him, allowed the tiny creature to lead it by the claw. Rod brought the eye back to the section of the Hoytether where they had all been pulling, and made pulling motions toward the front of the mouth. He even went so far as to lean out over the downward-sloping lip of the mouth, held up solely by his grip on the Hoytether.

The two eyes started to pull on the Hoytether as he had shown them and the reactor actually moved a few meters, but suddenly they quit pulling, dropped the Hoytether, lifted their heads, and started contracting their inflatable neck segments.

"Shucks!" said Rod in disappointment. "I was sure they had got the idea. But instead of helping, they're leaving."

"As their neck segments contract, they sort of 'back up' their feet," remarked Sandra bemused.

"Like a moving picture run backwards," added Dan.

The humans watched as the multitude of legs underneath the contracting necks climbed the feathered keel and nestled into place in the notchlike "cradle" that just fit it. The last segments, however, didn't settle down into their niche. Instead, they inflated again and lifted the eye up into the incoming wind. Small fins rose up from the head in back of each giant eye and the fins guided the eye back across the gap from the keel to the mouth, where the Hoytether and the reactor waited.

"They have built-in canards!" said Pete, impressed by nature's engineering skills as he watched the neck and head fly the eye in for a perfect landing. With their necks now in the right orientation, the two eyes started pulling on the Hoytether again. The humans climbed up on the hanging portion of the Hoytether in order to be far away from the reactor when it passed under them. Although the humans could not advance the position of the reactor from their position, they could lighten the load that the eyes had to move, by lifting up on a line Rod had directed Tabby to tie to the reactor.

With their necks now pulling from the right direction with a good anchor, and the lift from the humans decreasing the friction load, the two eyes of the rukh had no problem pulling the reactor, Tabby still riding on it, over the high point in the floor of the mouth. Once the reactor was past the rise, it slid slowly down and off into space. The fall was carefully controlled by the humans, who changed the reactor anchor point from primary line to primary line on the Hoytether, slowly spiraling the reactor down, while adding in slack sections of Hoytether that had been gathered in during the trip of the reactor up the windpipe.

Their portion of the job done, the two eyes pulled back their necks and Sandra got to see how they deflated their neck segments until their intersegment neck claws were practically side-by-side next to each other, holding on to the feathers that ran along the sides of the two grooved niches, one running along the top of the keel and a similar one below. With all the neck segments collapsed and tucked into the groove, there was just room for the two heads to settle down at the very tip of the prow, one eye at the top of the prow and one eye below, each swiveling around independently as they jointly scanned the skies. The Sun started to set and the lower eye closed in sleep. The breathing cycle of the giant mouth increased in pace, the ever-present rush of wind increased in strength, and they felt the rukh start its nighttime climb into the darkening skies.

Finally the chore of lowering the reactor was done. It now hung safely below the rukh at the end of nearly a half-kilometer of Hoytether. The weight of the reactor caused a depression in the dense feather forest where the Hoytether passed over the feather-tops, but the spread-out pressure was easily borne by the stiff high-pressure bladders that formed the leading edge of the giant wing.

"She's down, Seichi!" Rod reported over the radio link. "Turn her on!"

"I have been checking it out while you have been lowering it," said Seichi. "One of the three secondary cooling loops seems to have been damaged. We will have to run at reduced power."

"How much reduced?" asked Pete, concerned. Dan felt his heart skip a beat as he waited for the answer. They had been too busy the last many hours for him to even consider attempting a call to Pamela. He was sure that the Space Unlimited crew monitoring their voyage were aware from the telemetry and video relays that their balloon had been destroyed and they were in deep trouble. But if they hadn't gotten around to telling Pamela until they were sure of their exact status, she would be furious at him for not calling in as scheduled. She probably was now so mad that she would somehow find a way to blame him for the rukh eating their balloon. . . .

"Two-thirds of maximum," replied Seichi.

"That's still four tons of meta a week," said Pete. "Thirty weeks and the tanks will be full. We may get home a little late, but we're on our way to collecting our billions."

"Restarting reactor," reported Seichi.

✸   ✸   ✸

"There is something wrong," said Petro sleepily through the think-link. "Bright is coming up in the wrong direction."

"That is not Bright," said Petra, as she bent her neck down over the side of Petru's keel to look down at the redly glowing object hanging below her. "That is the heavy thing we took out of Petru's air-tube. It is hot once again. Go back to sleep." She felt Petro's mind disappear from the thinklink. Through Petru's wing she could hear others in the flock as they commented on the new source of light. Now proud that she was the possessor of something that caused so much comment, she flew off to show the others of the flock Petru's new "things": the glowing cylinder hanging below Petru on the end of the multitendril, and the strange conical creature and its intelligent vermin sitting in the middle of Petru's back.

5

JOINING WITH THE FLOCK

REACTOR OPERATIONAL. CAPSULE PRIME POWER RESTORED.

The reassuring voice of Jeeves boomed inside the helmets of the five crewmembers outside, and echoed throughout *Sexdent*, with Seichi its sole inhabitant. Hanging from their windblown perches on the inside of the multistrand Hoytether, itself hanging from the leading edge of the giant wing of the rukh, they looked down at the reactor a half-kilometer below them. From their viewpoint high above, they could see the radiator fins glowing a bright red in the gathering dusk.

"Good job, men," said Rod with relief. The two women were too tired to object to the choice of words, while the men didn't even notice Rod's slip of the tongue. "Let's get back to the ship and get a well-deserved good night's rest." He started the hundred-meter climb up to the safety of the wingtop, the Hoytether tilting slightly as the rukh changed its course. It was now dark and the rukh had started to circle upward into the night sky, the pulsing motions of the dual windpipes along its sides increasing their thrust and tempo as the giant bird climbed. As they rose through the darkness, lit only by the red glow of the reactor below, the speed of the wind over their bodies increased. Fortunately the heavy weight of the reactor at the end of the Hoytether kept it from swinging as badly as it had during their climb down.

They finally reached the wing edge where the Hoytether col-

lapsed from a rope tube into a crude rope ladder at the point where
it touched the black canopy of feathers. They continued their climb
over the curved leading edge of the wing, brushing the feather tips
aside as they clumsily tried to keep their balance on the tether lines.
In the darkness, they missed the place where Sandra had tied the
climbing line to the Hoytether.

"We're too horizontal!" complained Sandra as she once again fell
through the open mesh of the collapsed Hoytether and had to be
hauled back up by Chastity and Dan. "When I climbed the feather
tree and hooked our line onto the Hoytether, the tether was nearly
at a forty-five-degree slope."

"You're right," agreed Rod. "Back we go. If we keep following
this section of Hoytether we'll fall off the back end of this bird."

The strong wind over the top of the rukh's wing was against them
now and they had to take turns at the front as "windbreakers." They
soon found the point where they had climbed up, and one by one
slid down the line onto the living floor of the feather forest. Chastity,
having had some mountain climbing experience, rappelled down
first, then she used a spare length of line to arrange a simple sit-sling
"chair" to lower the others down.

"I thought it was dark when I was up there," said Rod as he
landed next to Chastity. "But being in a forest of black feather trees
is worse than being underground in a coal-pit on a cloudy, moonless
night." He added his helmet-light beam to Chastity's and together
they guided Sandra as she was lowered down into Rod's arms.

"There you go, Miss Ruby," said Rod, putting her gently on the
living surface of the feather forest while helping her get her legs out
of the sit-sling.

"Wye, thank you, Colonel Montrose," replied Sandra with a faked
accent, seemingly oblivious of the roving hands removing the sling
lines from between her thighs. "You're *such* a gentleman."

"Gaaack," muttered Chastity over the radio link as she hoisted
the sling up again.

The way back through the forest went quickly, since all they had
to do was keep one hand on the guide line they had laid down
through the feather forest during their journey out to the front of
the rukh's wing. They cycled through the airlock in two shifts.

"Girls first, then the boys," said Rod. "We could all fit in the airlock at once, but then we'd all have to wait with our backs turned

until the last one was dressed, so it wouldn't be much faster. Besides, there's only two toilets."

"A toilet! That's what I need first," said Sandra, quickly climbing up the rungs to the airlock door. "I'm not going to even bother getting dressed in the airlock, I'll take my clothes with me into the bathroom. No fair peeking down through the grate, Seichi!"

As soon as he could get to his habitat, Dan sent a message to Pamela telling her what had happened. He then spent long hours alternating between catnaps, the coffee dispenser, and long hours in his habitat, alternately explaining and comforting and arguing with Pamela, while simultaneously trying to arrange his financial affairs at long distance so that she and the children would be properly cared for. Pamela was no help.

"I'm really furious at you for putting me in this position!" she yelled at him, tears of fury pouring down her face. "You should have stayed home and taken proper care of me and the children! You're nothing but a selfish bastard, running off for years to play macho Buck Rogers space games—with a couple of floozies along to boot."

Dan listened through her tantrum, then tried again in his reply to get the conversation back again on a more reasonable tone. But it was difficult to come up with something to say that was nonconfrontational when she would tearfully say, "Don't you trust me to spend the money wisely?" when the correct answer to her question was no.

"I *am* taking care of you and the kids. I've been sending messages to the bank and the finance office at Space Unlimited to set up an annuity so that the kids will be sent to college and given a substantial stipend to get them off to a good start in their lives, while you'll be well taken care of for the rest of your life." He changed his tone. "And Pammy dearest, I want to reassure you that Miss Blaze and Miss Green are just professional colleagues. I love you, and only you. It has been a long and lonely time for us both, but when I get back I will love you like you have never been loved before."

But Pamela didn't buy his reassurances. Her face was still furious when her reply came back two-and-a-half hours later.

"I don't want to be stuck with a miserly annuity for the rest of my life. I want all the money turned over to me now!" The fury on her face turned into a sneer. "And, as for 'Miss' Blaze, everybody in Houston knows how randy that 'preacher's daughter' is. Do you really expect me to believe that in the whole year you two have been cooped up together, you haven't even slept with her *once!?*" Her eyes glared at the camera and her voice took on a menacing tone. "This insistence of yours about setting up an annuity shows that you don't trust me! Well . . . I don't trust *you!* I'm getting a divorce!" She thrust the remote control at the camera and the screen went blank.

For the rest of the day and into the night the tired crewmembers who had worked for hours in their saturnsuits slept, while Seichi, eyes occasionally blinking, kept watch. Nothing eventful happened, for the living platform they were riding on merely continued its slow circling climb to altitude. The flock finally rose above the water clouds into the crisp clear frozen air just as the Sun peeked over the horizon.

"Daylight!" said Rod, struggling out of a deep sleep as his command responsibilities took over control of his body. His head had been resting on a pillow in the viewport end of the habitat tube and the sunlight now fell full on his upturned face.

"Mmmmf," said Sandra, who had scrunched to the opposite end of the tube to get away from the snoring, her head buried underneath her pillow. Rod climbed out over her, closed her habitat door softly behind him, and went to his own tube to get a change of clothing from the storage area under his mattress. As he made his way down the ladder to the toilets, he saw Dan standing at the galley, drinking coffee. Dan's eyes were red from lack of sleep, and his face looked so woebegone that Rod almost wished he were a woman so he could take Dan in his arms and comfort him.

"What's the matter, Dan?" he asked.

"Having some problems with Pamela," said Dan. "Nothing you can do . . . or should do . . . I'll take care of it . . . you take care of this ship." He deliberately turned his back and started making another cup of coffee. Rod shrugged; Dan was right. He did have more important things to take care of. He opened the door to the bathroom and went in. A short while later he was up on the control deck.

"Status report, please, Seichi," said Rod as he activated the pilot console and brought up a copy of Seichi's scottyboard.

"The rukh has taken us thirty-five kilometers up in altitude, while slowly drifting northward a half-degree," replied Seichi. "The reactor is now operating at only sixty-three percent of nominal because of the slightly lower air pressure here at altitude."

"That's not good," said Rod with a frown. "Is the bird taking us still higher?" He looked down at the altimeter icon on his screen as he asked the question. The indicator numerals were only slowly varying.

"No," Seichi replied. "The flock stopped climbing at sunrise and are now just circling."

"Very good," said Rod. "Why don't you take a Saturnday and sleep in. You must have been up for at least twenty-four hours."

"Twenty-eight, sir," replied Seichi. "But I will be fresh after a few hours' sleep and will be back to assist you."

"Assist me in doing what?" said Rod, annoyed with their predicament. "There is nothing for us to do for the next six months except wait. Wait until our meta tanks are full and we can fly out of here and back home. We might as well have plenty of sleep while we're waiting." Rod's voice turned gruff. "Take a Saturnday, Mr. Takeo. That's an order."

"Very well, sir," replied Seichi with a formal bow, his normally pleasantly smiling face now firm-lipped. He turned to make his way down the ladder, but Rod put a hand to his shoulder and restrained him.

"I'm sorry, Seichi," said Rod, apologizing. "I guess I let my feelings show. It's just that I'm supposed to be commander of this mission. But I can give any damn command I want, and this damn bird will do just as it pleases. Fortunately," he concluded, "it seems to want to be cooperative." He looked out the holoviewport window through the gaps in the black feather canopy at the wheeling formation of giant birds all about them. "I wonder what they're going to do next?"

Fortunately, the twice-daily chore of cleaning the topside of Petru didn't take Petra too long this time. The flock had engaged in no hunting during the night's climb and the air had not been rich in food. Petra also made short work of cleaning the tailfeathers of Balru, who was ahead of her in the grooming circle. She then flew Petru to the center of the flock, where she could show off Petru's "things." Once at the center, she turned over the control of Petru to Petro in preparation for the daily hunting dive. But before the dive, while the others were still busy finishing their cleaning chores, there was plenty of time for socializing. One by one the members of the flock dove down to where both eyes could look at the strange glowing object hanging below Petru on a long multitendril.

"It is extremely dense," said Galro as he probed the object with Galru's sonar. "I cannot see inside it."

"It also seems to be hot," exclaimed Galra as she extended her neck toward the glowing red object, foreclaws extended.

"Don't touch it!" warned Petro from above. "It is so hot that it can hurt you. Unlike a hurt from a cut, the kind of hurt it gives you lasts a long time."

"If it can hurt you, then why do you keep it?" asked Galro. "It's so dense it must also be heavy. That will slow you down in the hunt. Let it go."

Petro didn't want to admit that he couldn't let it go. If he attempted to cut the tendrils holding the heavy hot thing up, the tiny dense vermin with the six legs would come rapidly up the multitendril waving its hot light maker. Petra saved the situation by suggesting that the flock come see the strange conical creature riding in the middle of Petru's back. Petra inflated her neck sacs and, using her headwings, flew her head over the back of Petru's wing to the spot where the dense creature and its four-legged vermin lay. She parted the wingfeather canopy over the cone, tucking the feathers back under other feathers nearby where they would stay out of the way. The conical creature was still there, but its mouth was closed and there was no sign of the vermin. They must be inside the mouth. Petra hoped they had not been eaten—she wanted so much to show the brightly colored tiny creatures to her flockmates. Wouldn't they be amazed to see one of them "grasp foreclaws" with her! Right now it would be sufficient for her flockmates to see and sound the dense conical creature riding on Petru's back.

When the canopy parted over *Sexdent* and the giant one-eyed caterpillar once again peered down at him, Rod quickly called Dan and Sandra up from the galley.

"We have visitors!" he explained to Dan and Sandra as they clambered up the ladder onto the control deck, followed quickly by Chastity and Pete. "The upper eye must have invited its friends over to take a look at us."

"How do you know it's the upper eye?" asked Dan.

"The third neck segment is inflated," replied Rod. "When the eyes were helping us get the reactor out of the rukh's windpipe, I noticed that the third segment of the lower eye didn't inflate like the other segments. Must have been injured sometime in the past. Anyway, the upper eye must be showing us off to the others, because it's holding down the feathers around us while keeping its head back so the other rukhs can fly over one at a time and take a look at us. Here comes another one . . ."

With the feather canopy pulled back out of the way, the humans could get a good view as another member of the flock flew down to fly in close formation over their rukh. For the humans, it was like reexperiencing the opening scenes of the first trilogy set of the *Star Wars* videos. The prow of a large wedge-shaped flying wing appeared over the tops of the feather canopy. Set in the prow of the flying wing were two gigantic eyes. Slowly and ponderously the rest of the flying wing made its way into view, the massive four-kilometer-long wingtips stretching far out of sight from horizon to horizon. Once the giant body was in position, both eyes used the canards on the sides of their heads to fly their long necks in for a closer look. After looking, the eyes withdrew to their perches and the giant visitor would move forward until its massive body blocked out the sky. Then it would lift up and away. Only after it had moved a number of kilometers upward could the humans see the whole creature through the gap in the canopy above them. Sandra made sure that the holoviewports were capturing high-resolution images of the giant birds as they passed overhead.

The humans quickly found names for the individuals in the flock.

"That big one there with the bald keel looks like a condor," remarked Rod. "While the other big one where the feathers on the keel are turning white looks like a bald eagle."

"Those would be good names for them," said Sandra. "The rukhs seem to be at the top of the food chain, so the names of raptors would be most appropriate. In fact, I think I'll name the species *Rukh raptosaturnus.*"

Soon a number of the rukhs in the flock had been named. Besides Condor and Eagle, there were Kestrel, Hawk, Falcon, Merlin, Buzzard, and Harrier, while the rukh they were riding on had been given the name Peregrine.

"What's that long tubular thing coming out of the belly and trailing along behind Harrier?" asked Dan, as the most-recent visitor flew up and away. "It's not a tail—there's a long plume of feathers coming out the rear end for a tail."

"Unlike the rest of the body, there aren't any feathers on it," said Chastity. "Looks like a penis to me."

"Everything looks like a penis to you," retorted Sandra. Just then a jet of liquid shot from the end of the tube they were watching and disappeared behind in the wind.

"I guess that answers my question," said Dan. "At least it serves one function of a penis."

"What's going on now!" said Rod with alarm as the floor tilted underneath them. He lowered his gaze to his command console screen.

"Feels like we're going into a shallow dive," said Chastity as she quickly activated the pilot screen.

"They're forming the cone arrangement they use for hunting," Sandra said as she watched the formation take place in the distance. Their rukh was near the base of the cone.

"How do you know it's a hunting formation?" asked Pete.

"Because that was the formation they were using when they hunted *us* down," replied Sandra.

"Oh," said Pete, somber for once. He had been in the meta plant during the attack and had missed seeing the flock on the hunt.

Dan had pulled down the science console biviewer on its pantograph and was using it to look at the individual rukhs in the kilometers-wide formation.

"Most of the rukhs have their top eye closed, while their lower eye is wide open and looking ahead and down," he reported.

"The lower eye must stay awake during the day during the hunting dive, while the upper eye sleeps during the day and flies their joint body to altitude for the next day's hunt," suggested Sandra.

"Peregrine's upper eye isn't going to sleep," said Chastity, peering upward out the holoviewport window. "In fact, it's coming down closer to get a better look at us." She activated the icon for the meta jets on the nose of the *Sexdent.*

"If it doesn't have to participate in the hunt, then it probably is giving up some of its sleep time to satisfy its curiosity," suggested Pete.

"Well, if it's curious, I'm curious too," said Sandra. "I'm going to go out and see if I can find out how to talk to it." She quickly clambered down the ladder to the airlock door below.

"I'm coming with you," said Dan, following close behind.

"Make sure you wear safety lines and carry a meta torch!" yelled Rod behind them.

The eye bent down slowly toward the viewport window while carefully keeping its large foreclaws closed and tucked out of the way. Chastity kept her finger poised over the nose-jet icon, but held off.

"It *is* curious," said Pete, intrigued.

The eye peered into the windows at the ends of each habitat, and then into the larger holoviewport windows. Pete backed away from the science holoviewport when the ten-meter-diameter eye drew close to him. Rod held his ground and just stared back when the eye shifted to the command holoviewport. Chastity waved when the eye appeared in her window, causing the eye to jerk back on its pneumatic neck. It returned slowly as Chastity waved again; then she turned around and got Pete to join her in the window.

"I'd give a pretty penny to know what is going on in that mind right now," said Chastity with a chuckle.

Petra was puzzled when she finally realized what she was seeing. She had looked into the eyes of the conical creature trying to figure out if it was alive or dead. She found that what she thought were eyes were really pieces of skin that were so dense they reflected the sonar pulses that she had directed at them, yet so transparent that you could see through them to the inside of the creature. The inside of the creature was hollow, which didn't surprise Petra much, since everything floating in the atmosphere of Air was hollow. What was surprising was to see that there were small four-legged vermin living inside the hollow portions. Although the inside vermin were the same size and had the same number of legs as the outside vermin, they had different skin color from the bright yellow-green outside vermin, and two small eyes and strange string-feathers on their heads instead of the single large eye and bald head of the outside vermin. The inside vermin must be very powerful vermin indeed if they had that much control of the conical being. Just then the mouth of the cone opened, and one of the brightly colored outside vermin stepped out on its hind feet.

Sandra stepped out onto the lowering airlock door in her neon bright fire-engine yellow-green saturnsuit, safety line firmly tied to her air-pack harness. Dan, similarly garbed and carrying a meta torch, stood guard behind her. The opening of the door had put tension on one of the tiedown lines that ran from the rungs on the side of the *Sex-dent* to the root of a nearby feather-tree quill. The waiting caterpillar with the large single eye went to the quill root and reached out a foreclaw toward the knot. Chastity gave the nose jet a short blast. The caterpillar eye quickly backed off and went into its foreclaws-closed position.

"The door is resting on the line to that root," said Dan, looking over the side where the problem line passed under the platform. "It must be pulling on the quill root and hurting."

"I made sure we had plenty of tie-down lines," said Rod over the radio link. "You can cut that one loose if it's causing problems."

"Do it," said Sandra. "We owe this creature a lot of favors."

With a flick of the meta torch, the macropolyhextube was burnt through and the feather tree above the quill root vibrated noticeably in response. The line, which had snapped back toward the quill root after being cut, now lay limp on the ground. The eye watched the nose jet carefully as it slowly reached a foreclaw toward the line.

"Let it have the line, Chass," said Sandra. "Maybe we can move from punishment training to reward training. I wish we had some method of communicating with it other than the threat of a meta torch. Do you see anything that looks like ears, Dan?"

"I don't see any obvious ears, but it certainly has an eye," replied Dan. "A big eye . . . the better to see you with. Why don't you try sign language?" He stepped back into the airlock and came back out with a short length of coiled safety line. Sandra dropped the coil of line, then picked it up. She waved her right hand at the nearby eye, palm up, not knowing what other gesture to use. The caterpillar waved a foreclaw in imitation of Sandra, and keeping its eye focused on the nose jet, slowly bent down and retrieved the dropped piece of line.

"Not much of a gift," said Dan. "One end is still tied to the quill root. Perhaps I'd better go down and cut it off."

"You stay on that platform," commanded Rod. "We can afford to lose our doctor, but we can't afford to lose our plumber. Besides, I used a bowline loop lasso to encircle the quill. It should be real easy to pull off."

Rod was right, it didn't take long for the eye to figure out which line to pull to undo the lasso. Once the eye had the line in its grasp, it backed away and began examining the line, holding it up to its eye, running it through its claws, pulling on it to test its strength, picking at the bowline loop at one end, and attempting to coil it up like the line Sandra was holding. It was obvious that it had never handled anything like this before. It tried draping it around its head at the first segment joint. The attempt ended when the line fell off, so it finally settled on winding the line around its "neck" a few times like a long muffler, then tucking the loose end through the bowline loop and pulling it tight.

"A shoestring necktie!" exclaimed Pete.

Seemingly pleased with the result, the eye rose up on its neck and went off.

"Shucks," said Sandra. "I guess it's going off to get its sleep. I was hoping it would stay and talk so I could get to know it better."

"What are you going to talk with?" Dan replied. "You certainly can't carry on a conversation from inside that helmet. The only reason I can hear you talking is because we have a radio link. We're going to have to devise a loudspeaker system. A bass one, considering the deep sounds we have heard coming from the creature."

"We'll need some kind of blackboard too, so I can draw pictures," said Sandra as she followed Dan back into the airlock. The door rose shut behind them.

It was soon realized that Sandra's "blackboard" would have to be a console screen, since there was nothing on *Sexdent* that could be used to write with, except catsup and mustard. Fortunately, the three main control deck consoles for the commander, pilot, and engineering positions were designed to be detached and hung above the acceleration couches during high-gee maneuvers. The high-data-rate fiber-optic cables that connected Jeeves with each console were the same cables as those used to send data up and down the Hoytether to the reactor, so Mouser delivered a long segment of fiber-optic cable from its repair reel. Soon the airlock had its own portable console for Sandra to use the next time the upper eye came for a visit. The fiber-optic connector for the portable console plugged into a data port in the outside airlock control panel so the airlock could be used by one member of the crew while another was outside using the console to converse with an eye. In the process of setting up the communications console, Rod lost his job, for it was obvious that if one of the three control deck consoles needed to be sacrificed for use in the alien communication system, the commander's console was certainly less important than the pilot's or engineer's console.

Rod finished his second cup of coffee and looked around at the organized confusion. Sandra was in the airlock programming the portable console with simple large pictures. Chastity and Seichi were putting together a "woofer" speaker and checking it out with Seichi's keyboard, while Dan and Pete were building an ultra-low-frequency sound detector using a large diaphragm of reflective Mylar with a laser beam readout. Seichi should have been asleep, but Rod knew there was no use trying to make him get some rest while there were so many interesting things to do.

Might as well get out of the way, Rod said to himself. "Going out to get some exercise," he announced to the crew. "Chass. You're in charge."

"Make sure you wear a safety line and take a meta torch," replied Chastity, not looking up.

Sandra cycled Rod through the airlock and he stepped outside onto the platform door. The upper eye was nowhere in sight. The wind whistled across the feathertops and gusts billowed down into the clearing that the eye had made around the capsule. A strong gust of wind swirled through the airlock door and blew a forgotten sock out onto the platform. Rod stomped on the sock as it went by, picked it up, and returned it to its proper place in his locker. His first task was to check the tie-downs that held *Sexdent* to the back of their giant host. Some were loose, so he tightened them. Some were taut, the lines singing as he plucked them, so he loosened them slightly to take the pressure off their host's quill roots.

"Might as well make myself a useful symbiote," said Rod as he searched each quill root for inflated vermin. Once he had set the helmet's image intensifier visor on infrared, the vermin were easy to find, their active bodies being much warmer than the passive quill roots. Each time he found one, he would first pierce its jet bladder with a short burst from his meta torch. With its bladder gone, the gigantic louse was then easily hauled up out of the quill follicle, its pneumatic-operated gripper claws no match for Rod's bone-backed muscle-powered grip. Rod was thorough. Holding the squirming creature at arm's length, he lit his meta torch again. After making sure the head portion was well toasted, he torched the egg sac to make sure no descendants of this particular louse would ever bother the rukh or its flock again. Once he had cleared the quill root lice from the area surrounding the capsule, he started hunting for more. Trailing a length of macropolyhextube line behind him, he would set off on a path leading directly away from the capsule, searching each quill root for lice. After clearing one radiant for some fifty meters, he would backtrack to the capsule, shift directions, and start off again.

On one of these "hunting trips" he was walking through a "clearing" where there was a break in the feather canopy above, letting some sunlight in. He saw a glint in front of him. The glint was caused by a fine transparent fiber, running nearly horizontally from feather to feather.

"Looks like a spider web," he said to himself.

At the thought, he quickly lit his meta torch and looked carefully all around him. If the giant bird harbored giant lice, it might harbor giant spiders that would be more than a match for a mere human being—meta torch or no.

"Never liked spiders," he muttered, looking carefully through the dim forest around him, helmet light on high beam and image intensifier on maximum sensitivity.

He didn't see any giant spiders, so he took another look at the shiny thread in front of him. Being careful not to touch the thread, he followed it to the next feather. There, at the end of the fine line, was a tiny insectlike creature sitting on the edge of the feather. There was a semicircular notch in the feather where the creature had obviously been nibbling away.

"Got something for you to see, Sandra," Rod reported over the radio link. He turned on his helmet light to illuminate the specimen and set his image intensifier on image transmit.

"*Eeeee!*" yelled Sandra over the link.

"Sorry," said Rod. "Had the image intensifier lens on high magnification. Here's my finger for comparison. See . . . it's not much bigger than my little fingernail. Looks like a daddy longlegs to me. There's this small central body with real long jointed legs."

"Twelve of them," said Sandra. "The better to grab you with."

The creature ignored the increased illumination from Rod's helmet light and continued eating away at the edge of the feather.

"A feather mite, certainly," said Sandra. "What shall I call it?"

"How about 'longleg spidermite' for a name?" suggested Rod.

"Kind of long," complained Sandra. She paused to think about it. "But 'longleg' *is* a short, self-descriptive term. I'll let you get away with it for the common name. If it's like most vermin, it only infests one species of host. Jeeves? What is the Latin name for a long-legged rukh-spider?"

"*Longicrus rukharanea,*" Jeeves instantly replied.

Sandra went on. "One thing concerns me. I can understand how the longleg survives in its present form, but I can't understand how it evolved. It has no air bladders, so it can't float, and it has no wings, so it can't fly. It must have evolved with one or the other, and lost them once it developed its parasitic lifestyle. Even so, how does it get from one host to the next?"

"It does have the ability to spin a thread, like an Earth spider," said Rod, trying to adjust the position of his head to pick up the glint from the fine line in the visor imager.

"That's the answer!" said Sandra, pleased to hear the information. "Once a longleg gets ready to leave the host, it just climbs to the top of a feather and lets out a long line into the breeze coming over the top of the rukh's wing, and when the line is long enough, the air drag pulls Mr. Longleg Spidermite off its perch and off the back of the rukh, where it slowly falls down through the flock. If it's lucky, it finds a new feather forest to eat through. They must have started evolution as sinkers, but very slow sinkers because the thread gave them a high surface area-to-mass ratio. Did you remember to take sample bags?" she asked. "I'd like to look at that thing under high magnification."

"Sorry, no bags," replied Rod. "I was just going out for a walk, not a scientific expedition." He thought for a while. "I've got it! I'll empty my water bottle and bring the wee beastie home in that."

"Don't forget to bring a sample of the thread," reminded Sandra as the radio link went back on standby.

With the longleg tucked safely away in his backpack, Rod continued his vermin-clearing operation, now careful to look for vermin on feather edges as well as featherroots. He came to a patch of feathers that were badly infested with quill lice. Soon the meta torch was almost in constant use as he methodically cleared out one louse after another, making sure than none of their spawn survived.

Suddenly, the canopy opened above him and Rod looked up to see a giant eye peering down at him. This had to be the lower eye, since the third air sac segment was collapsed and the creature wasn't wearing a hextube string tie. When the giant caterpillar saw the meta torch flaring quietly in Rod's hand, it rose up, first set of foreclaws drawn up out of the way, while the second set of foreclaws kept the canopy held open. Rod finished off the louse he had been working on. Holding the deflated, but still-squirming, body of the quill louse by his gloved left hand, he fried its brain and cooked its egg sac. He added the body to the stack he had been collecting. Then, turning off his meta torch, he stepped back. The gigantic eye came down to look. It picked up one of the bodies, held it close to its eye, and put it back on the pile. Then, one of its foreclaws extended, it slowly approached Rod. With the meta torch at the ready in his left hand, but hidden behind his back, Rod extended his right hand and grasped the tip of the large, stiffly inflated, balloonlike claw. Once, when Rod had needed help to pull the reactor out over the lip of the mouth, he had led that very claw to the Hoytether and asked for its assistance. Now, he found himself being led by the claw, as the eye contracted its neck, clearing the way for them both through the feather forest. They came to a large quill that had five large quill lice jammed down into the follicle pore. The pore was oozing and the skin around the follicle was swollen and scabby. Rod could see from the thickness of their bladder skins that three of the lice were mature and well dug in. There was no way the pneumatic-powered claws of the eye could extract them. Protected by the bladders of their larger mates, two smaller lice had also forced their way into the pore. Even when the mature lice had jetted off, the pore would still remain infected. For all Rod knew, this particular pore might have been under attack for weeks or months.

"I bet that's sore!" said Rod, letting go of the claw and bringing out his meta torch. "You once helped me, so I'll help you." He quickly burst the five sacs to make sure the mature lice didn't jet off, spreading infection through the forest. Then, one by one, he extracted the creatures and torched them thoroughly. As he finished each one, the eye would pick up the corpse, raise it up to the top of the canopy, then use its canards to fly its head high above the back of the still-diving wing and let the burnt body of the vermin fly off on the wind, to fall into the hot depths below.

The task done, Rod looked up at the giant eye and the eye looked down at him. Rod raised his hand. The giant eye bent down, one of its foreclaws extended in imitation. Rod "shook hands."

"Any time you need help in getting rid of some more bandits, partner," he said, "just give me a call." Dropping the claw, he headed off into the forest, following the macropolyhextube guide line he had been paying out during his journey. By the time he made his circuitous way back to *Sexdent* it was getting dark. Sandra, Dan, and Seichi were waiting on the surface outside the airlock, hoping for a nighttime session with the upper eye. Seichi was holding his keyboard, which was connected to a large "woofer" speaker standing beside him. Dan was monitoring the output of his similarly large-sized low-frequency microphone. As they waited they could hear deep rumblings from inside the rukh as the eyes used the giant body to "gossip" with the other members of the flock during the changeover period between the daytime hunting dive and the nighttime altitude climb. Since the human ear had difficulty hearing such low tones, the actual "listening" was done by Jeeves, who analyzed the signals coming from the laser beam motion detector monitoring the vibrational oscillations of the low-frequency microphone, and raised the frequency of the oscillations to the middle of the humans' hearing and speaking audio range. Similarly, when Seichi would play a note on the keyboard, or any of the humans spoke, Jeeves would down-translate the frequency spectrum to the middle of the rukh's audio communications band.

Sure enough, once the nighttime climb of the flock started, the upper eye came visiting again, wearing its "shoestring tie." It was carrying the loose end of the string tie in one foreclaw. As the eye approached them, it extended the foreclaw proudly to show what it had done.

"It's tied a bowline in the loose end!" exclaimed Dan. "It must have figured out how to do it from looking at the knot at the other end. Let me get another segment of line and teach it a square knot."

"Dan!" said Sandra. "We're not at a Boy Scout camp. Let's concentrate on the language lessons." She turned to Seichi. "The rukh body is still talking. Can you imitate the sound?"

A complex rumble was rising up from the air sacs of the beast below them. The sound vibrated the soles of their boots and their bowels quivered in sympathetic response. Seichi listened to Jeeves's frequency-translated version of the multichordal sound through his helmet phones, while at the same time he tried to "feel" what the rukh was saying with the whole of his body. The rumble stopped temporarily and Seichi repeated what he had heard using his keyboard, some of his fingers often having to hit more than one note at a time, then sliding off on another note while sustaining some of the others. Fortunately, the keyboard was designed so he could key in the permanent notes of the chordal phrase as a "drone," then remove his fingers from those keys and use them elsewhere to bring in other notes. The large ultrabass speaker beside Seichi vibrated visibly as it responded to Seichi's playing. The deep rumbling sounds coming from the speaker caused the eye to jerk back in surprise, and the surface they were standing on became quiet.

"I think it heard something familiar," said Sandra, holding her breath in excitement. "Play it again."

Before Seichi could respond, the eye moved closer to Seichi and the speaker, and the surface below them rumbled again. At the same time the eye used a foreclaw to touch the surface they were standing on.

"It's the same chordal pattern as before, but just part of it," said Seichi, repeating the chordal phrase with his keyboard. "Much less complicated and easier to play."

"But what does it mean?" asked Dan, bewildered.

"The eye pointed down with its foreclaw as it said it," said Sandra. "Perhaps that's its name. Let's try and make sure. Are you ready to repeat that chord?"

"Easy as cake," said Seichi. "I had the keyboard in record mode."

Sandra pointed down, making sure she touched the taut skin of the rukh below their boots, while Seichi had the keyboard play the simpler phrase over again. The eye bobbed rapidly up and down in excitement and confirmed the identification by pointing at the body below them while repeating the chord once again. The eye then pointed a foreclaw at itself and again the body rumbled a chord. The eye looked expectantly to see how the humans responded.

"We must have got it wrong," said Sandra, disappointed. "That was the same chord."

"Maybe it's just trying to make clear that the body and the eye are one person," suggested Dan.

"I do not think so," said Seichi after a long pause. "Jeeves? Wasn't there a different note in that chord?"

"You are correct," replied Jeeves. "The lowest note shifted three hertz upward. Would you like me to repeat it through the speaker? I have a perfect copy in my memory."

"If I had you do that, then I would not be learning to speak the language," replied Seichi, fingering the difficult chord once again, with the lowest note now slightly higher. He finished by pointing a finger at the eye.

The eye bobbed excitedly up and down, then inflated the canards on the sides of its head. The wings caught the air and raised the head high in the sky on a rapidly inflating neck while at the same time an organ chord of rising tones emerged from the beast below them. Then, just as suddenly, the canards brought the head back down again and the chord stopped.

"I think that was the upper eye's equivalent of saying 'It's *got* it!'," said Sandra, smiling at the eye's antics.

It was now Sandra's turn. "Sandra," she said, pointing at herself. Jeeves repeated the word a few octaves lower through the woofer speaker. The huge body of the leviathan strained below their feet as it emitted a short, multitoned, almost stuttering sound.

```
      s   s   s   s
       a  a  a  a  a
        nd nd nd nd nd
          r   r   r   r
           a   a   a   a
```

And the language lesson started.

The computer console turned out to be of great help in getting many concepts across, especially once Sandra had shown the eye how it could draw pictures on the touchscreen with the end of its foreclaw. Soon they jointly knew words for many objects, including the Sun and its planets, and many actions, such as "come" and "go."

After five hours of lessons, the sky started to get light as morning came. They were joined by the lower eye, which had snaked its way upward from its perch below.

When the upper eye didn't introduce the newcomer, Sandra decided to take care of that herself.

"Are you ready with the keyboard, Seichi?" she asked.

Going back to the beginning of the language session, she pointed down at the surface below them and Seichi played the chordal phrase that the aliens used for the body of the rukh. She pointed at the upper eye wearing the string tie and Seichi played the same chordal phrase with the single note three hertz higher. Then Sandra pointed at the recently arrived lower eye and waited. The upper eye pointed at the lower eye and the body below them gave out a chordal phrase that was almost identical to the ones Seichi had played.

"The changed note is lower in this chord instead of higher," said Seichi. "Am I right, Jeeves?"

"Correct," said Jeeves. "Three hertz lower."

"It sort of makes sense," said Sandra. "They are really just different parts of the same animal. They must share the same root chord for their names but have slightly different added notes to indicate which part is which."

Since the humans couldn't easily produce chords, they chose the nicknames "Uppereye" and "Lowereye" to distinguish between the two eyes. The string tie of Uppereye and the nonfunctional third air sac on Lowereye made it easy for the humans to tell the two apart.

Sandra tried to talk to Lowereye, but it was soon obvious that what Uppereye had learned during the night had not been passed on to Lowereye. She sighed and started in over again.

"Sandra," she said, pointing to herself.

```
        s  s  s  s
        a  a  a  a  a
        nd nd nd nd nd
          r  r  r  r
          a  a  a  a  a
```

came the reply. But instead of the rolling chord vibrating up from below in an ultrabass rumble, it came as a bass chord directly from Lowereye's head.

"The eyes *talk!*" yelled Sandra in surprise.

"That is only logical," replied Seichi. "We have already observed that the rukh's body is controlled by only one eye at a time, so only one eye can use the body to speak with. It must often be necessary for the intelligence behind the other eye to be able to communicate. They have air sacs in their neck, so they certainly could have developed the necessary vibratory control over their bladder orifices needed to produce speech. The speech tones of the eyes are necessarily pitched up a few octaves from the speech tones of the body because of the smaller bladder size."

"That's going to make it a lot easier to talk with them," said Sandra. "If we can get them to use eye-talk rather than body-talk, then we won't have to always have Jeeves in the loop to hear those sounds we can't hear with our own ears."

"Sun come," said Uppereye, pointing to the direction of the rising sun. "Uppereye go."

"Wait!" said Sandra. When Uppereye didn't halt, Sandra realized she would have to teach that word to Uppereye in the next lesson. She searched around in her memory for a phrase that contained words that Uppereye *did* know. She finally found them.

"Not go!" she blurted out, and Uppereye came back.

"There is one more thing I need to show them," she said to Seichi. "I'm going to climb up onto the airlock platform. You two stay down here and *don't look up.*"

"What are you going to do?" asked Seichi.

"They think that humans have hard heads with one big eyeball, like they have, and tough elastic neon yellow bodies. All they've seen of us is the outside of our saturnsuits. I'm going to show them what a human being *really* looks like."

"Sandra!" interjected Dan. "Don't do it! It could be dangerous!"

"I'll be able to hold my breath long enough for the airlock door to cycle," said Sandra, as she climbed the rungs to the platform door.

"But someone needs to keep an eye on you in case you get into trouble in the airlock," replied Dan in a concerned tone.

"I volunteer!" interjected Pete over the link.

"Don't worry, Sandra," said Chastity. "I'll make sure that I'm the only one watching you through the airlock window."

Once in the airlock portal, Sandra unfastened her backpack with her oxygen supply and hung it from a safety hook inside, where the umbilical could reach her helmet intake. Leaving her helmet on, she proceeded to strip in the cold and gusty Saturn morn, dropping her clothing on the door of the airlock in her haste. She had originally been thinking of pointing out the various parts of her body as she unclothed them, but the "wind chill" factor from the frequent gusts billowing through the clearing around *Sexdent* made her drop that idea. Tomorrow she would name the various body parts to Uppereye using drawings on the portable console. Now completely naked in front of the two giant staring eyes, she took a deep breath, and deliberately blinking her eyes often to help protect them from the ammonia fumes in the atmosphere, she lifted the helmet from her head, shook out her hair, and pulled on it with one hand to show its structure. Holding the helmet aloft she quickly turned around so the eyes could see her from all sides. As she turned, she could hear and feel sonar pings from the two eyes as they looked inside her. Her pirouette finished, she dropped the helmet back on her head, turning the air supply to high as she did so, to flush the ammonia-laden Saturnian air out of the helmet. Once she could safely do so, she used her held breath to say: "Close that airlock door, Chass! It's *cold* out here!"

Before the door could rise shut, however, an errant gust of wind whistled through the airlock and Sandra's pink silk panties flew off the door and sailed across the clearing to land in front of Lowereye. The massive foreclaws of the giant caterpillar picked up the limp piece of underclothing. Solemnly the giant eye inspected the item, marveling at the three openings and their elastic bands. After toying with the object awhile, Lowereye realized that its whole foreclaw would fit into the larger opening, while the individual pincers would fit through the other two smaller openings. Using its other foreclaws to help, it drew the underpants snugly onto its upper left foreclaw like a rock singer pulling on a fingerless glove.

With the show over and the airlock door closed, Uppereye waved good-bye to Seichi and Dan and left. Imitating the wave with its "gloved" hand, Lowereye followed.

"Looks like a one-eyed, two-fingered Michael Jackson," said Pete from an upper holoviewport, making sure the viewport imager got a good picture of the dressed-up alien. "I bet I can sell this to the InterRock magpage."

"Say," said Chastity loudly through the echoing confines of *Sexdent* as she watched Sandra get dressed through the inner airlock window. "The eyes have seen only one half of the human race. How about one of you guys imitating Sandra for the education and amusement of Peregrine's eyes tomorrow night?"

"No way!" "Not me!" came the rapid responses from Rod and Pete.

"Just as well," concluded Chastity with a wry smile. "It's so chilly out there, the important bits would be all shriveled up anyway."

"Disgusting!" remarked Petro as he and Petra made their way back over the feathers to their nesting niches on Petru's keel. "The four-legged vermin were almost pleasing to the sight with their bright yellow-green skin, their large shiny eye, and the bright light they emitted from the top of their heads. But it was all false. A visual lie! Hidden under that beautiful exterior is nothing but a bluish-pink blob with hair-feather patches in strange places and two tiny squinty eyes. They look like deformed gizzard worms with legs."

"They must realize they are ugly," said Petra, trying to defend her newfound friends. "That is why they cover their ugly bodies with beautiful things. Look at you. Doesn't your claw look better now that it has that shiny pink thing on it?"

"It does look nice," Petro had to admit, rotating his panty-covered foreclaw in front of his eye.

"What a marvelous new idea," mused Petra as she settled into her niche. "Putting things on your body to make yourself more beautiful."

When the news about the successful language lessons with the obviously intelligent rukhs reached Earth, there was mixed reaction. The scientists, news channels, and the general public were thrilled that another intelligent species had been found for the human race to talk with. Within just hours, you could buy rukh tee-shirts, rukh baseball caps, and rukh-shaped gliders and balloons. Within days, the Peaceful Planet Protectors were petitioning the United Nations to put the Rukh People of Saturn under a UN protectorship, with Triple-P as its sponsor, since none of the commercial nations could be trusted. Within weeks, there were video games and animated television shows featuring battles between fleets of human-powered airplanes and dirigibles against flocks of gigantic, man-devouring rukhs.

Art Dooley, however, was very unhappy, as he watched his major investment in the mission evaporate away. "That *sinks* it," Art said, when he first heard the news from the chief scientist of the mission team. "There's no way we're going to be allowed to set up meta production facilities on Saturn. Although the most suspicious greenie has to admit that full-blown meta production for the next million years won't even begin to deplete the large stock of helium gas on Saturn, even I have to admit that it would be a very bad idea to operate unshielded nuclear reactors in the living space of friendly intelligent beings. Besides, we were planning on dropping the used reactors when we were done. That would only make it worse. After the reactors have gone down where it is hot enough, the reactors would melt, releasing volatile radioactive waste products, which would then be brought up by the next thermal column carrying the food supply for your intelligent friends. As soon as the crew makes it back home, they'll be paid off and the Saturn meta project will be closed down."

"I admit it is bad news for Space Unlimited," said the chief scientist, "but it's good news for the science community. Now that we have identified a good reason to visit Saturn, the science budget for manned deep space exploration to the planets will have to expand. Soon, we will be searching all the outer planets and moons for signs of life. Perhaps even the planetoids in the Kuiper Belt."

"That's where you're wrong," said Art grimly. "Finding an intelligent species on Saturn may sound like good news to you scientists, but in reality it's bad news for both of us. Yes, for a few years you scientists will get increased funding to send orbiters and balloon probes to Saturn to continue conversation with the rukhs—with the two-and-a-half-hour time delay between sentences that implies. But as for setting up a crewed orbital station around Saturn, forget it. Just to set it up will cost tens of billions—we know, we've priced it. And to keep it running will cost more billions every year. What you scientists don't realize is that governments have to make a profit on their investments—not immediate profits, but profits sometime in the foreseeable future. Those governments that ignore the forces of the marketplace don't survive over the long run. Look at the former Soviet Union and its flirtation with communism and state-sponsored military expansion and space exploration—it took over seventy years for the market to exert its forces, but it did. Tell me, Doctor. What is the human race going to get back from its investment of billions of dollars per year to talk to the rukhs? Do the rukhs have any advanced technology that we can use?"

"No," replied the chief scientist. "They seem to have no technology at all. They are intelligent enough, but they haven't had access to any materials with which to make tools."

"You forgot to make the case that we might learn some new biology from them," Art reminded him. "How different is their biology?"

"Since they live at the same temperature we do, they use the same carbon chemistry that we do. In fact, the information Sandra obtained using the nanoimager on some of the samples seems to indicate that they use the same DNA helix and genetic code that we do. It is now suspected that life on Saturn was seeded from spores in rocks blasted off from Earth billions of years ago." He paused as he tried to think of *something* that would make further interaction with the rukhs worthwhile. "But . . . their culture and language are unique—"

"And you expect the U.S. government, or any government, to spend billions of dollars a year on 'cultural exchanges'?" retorted Art. "I'm afraid not. Without the motivation of a commercial return from the production of meta, there will be no permanent base orbiting Saturn, and no realistic way to maintain communication with the rukhs. It looks to me like these initial conversations between the rukhs and the humans are going to lead nowhere, as soon as the beancounters controlling the government purses realize the rukhs are nothing but noble savages."

"We've just passed the forty-ton marker in the meta tanks," Pete announced two months later as he came in from checking out the meta factory. "Four more months and we'll be on our way home to collect our billion."

That night at dinner they were all talking about what they would first buy with their riches. The only one who wasn't there was Seichi, who had taken the last nighttime shift and was starting a long Saturday by sleeping in. Rod and Pete were arguing over which was the better sports car, a Toyota-Benz Tsunami or a Rolls-Skoda Rocket.

"You guys can keep your sports cars," remarked Chastity. "I'm going to get me an armload of diamond bracelets and rings, and go back to Idaho and dazzle my daddy right out of his pulpit. He said I'd never amount to anything."

"I thought you said he wasn't speaking to you," said Rod.

"Mom finally got up enough spunk to tell him otherwise," Chastity replied. "Knowing Dad, the fact that I'll soon be a billionaire probably made it easy for him to 'forgive' me."

"I'm going to buy a big mansion on the Mississippi," said Sandra dreamily. "And wait there until my colonel comes for me . . ." She looked coyly at Rod, who was trying to figure out what he should say in response when the voice of Jeeves boomed throughout the ship. "EMERGENCY! REACTOR EXCEEDING THERMAL LIMIT! INITIATING SHUTDOWN!"

Rod was up the ladder in an instant, with Chastity right behind him. With the commander console gone, Rod went to the scottyboard. The console was already activated and a red warning icon blinked rapidly on the screen.

"Damn!" Rod exclaimed as his test pilot eyes scanned the rest of the screen, looking for other problems. "Just when things were going so good . . ." The lights flickered as the power from the reactor failed. The console screen dimmed, then recovered. There was now a change in the icons in the power sector of the console. The icon for the prime power was now red, while the icon for the meta-powered internal backup power now had a green ON in it.

"Jeeves! Wake Seichi!" he commanded. "We've got to get that reactor going or we're as good as dead!"

There was a clang as a habitat hatch was shoved open and Seichi scrambled out onto the control deck in his underwear, eyes blinking as he tried to wake up. Within seconds his fingers were flying over the screen on the scottyboard as he analyzed the situation. When he turned to look at Rod, his face was grim.

"The reactor is not in good condition. I am sorry to report that the impacts from the larger prey of the rukh have finally damaged it. Another of the secondary cooling loops has lost pressure. It must have a leak somewhere. I can bring the reactor back up using the last remaining cooling loop, but I'll have to cut the power level to compensate in order to keep the reactor temperature within its thermal limit."

Rod was relieved that it wasn't more serious. "Do it," he said. "As long as we can keep making meta, we still have a chance."

Seichi carefully took Jeeves through the procedure of completely closing down the reactor, taking it from its emergency shutdown state to its dormant startup state, with the emergency shutdown rods removed and back in their primed position. Once that was done, he used Tabby's camera eyes to explore the damage to the failed cooling loop and to check out the condition of the remaining loop. The coolant had leaked from a crack at the base of a cooling fin. The fin had been bent sharply back by a strike from a large animal hitting it at high speed. What was worse was that further inspection showed that the remaining cooling loop pipe had dozens of similarly damaged fins, many with cracks. None of them was leaking—yet.

Two hours later, Seichi had the reactor back on-line with Rod, Pete, and Chastity anxiously looking over his shoulder. The lights flickered again as Seichi switched from the internal backup system that burned meta to the reactor prime power system that generated excess electricity to make meta.

"We're back up at one-third design power," Seichi said finally.

"I'd best go down into the meta factory and shut down some more meta lines," said Pete, heading for the ladder leading below. "The individual production lines are slightly more efficient if they are operating at peak power instead of reduced power. That'll give me a chance to clean the optics on the resting ones. Every percentage point in efficiency is another liter of meta."

"Concerning percentage points . . ." remarked Seichi. Pete stopped on the ladder and looked up at him. "You should shut down all but thirty percent of the meta lines—not thirty-three percent. Since the power to operate the crew capsule comes first, the amount left over for making meta dropped to less than a third."

"Oh," said Pete, a slight frown creasing his forehead. "Right, thirty percent it is." His head dropped below the grating floor as he headed for the airlock—stopping off at the toilet first. It would be a long day.

"I'll cycle you out," said Chastity, following Pete down the ladder.

"Well, at least we're still producing meta," said Rod to Seichi, trying to put a positive note on things. "It'll just take us a little longer to get home. Fortunately, we have plenty of food."

"I didn't want to tell the others, since it is useless to worry about things you cannot control," said Seichi in a quiet voice so that those down below would not hear. "But as commander, there is something you must know, even though it increases the burden you must carry."

"What is it?" said Rod, not really wanting to know.

"The failure was probably caused by hydrogen embrittlement widening and deepening the stress crack until it leaked. The stainless steel tubing normally isn't affected by hydrogen, but stress cracks, especially in welded portions of the tube, allow the hydrogen to get inside the metal and cause it to fail. The cooling fins were designed to operate under a floating balloon, not a high-speed flying wing. The remaining cooling loop has many similar cracks. It won't be long before it fails also, especially if it experiences additional strikes from prey animals."

"I see," said Rod. "Any time estimate?"

"With only one data point, it is difficult to estimate," replied Seichi. "But this loss took place in two months. The next one will likely be in weeks rather than months."

"And we need four more months of meta production to fill the tanks. It's going to be close."

"Nearly six months," Seichi reminded him. "The factory is now operating at only thirty percent capacity."

"Right," said Rod, lips firm. "But, as you said, it is useless to worry about things you cannot control." He paused, then turned back to look at Seichi with a quizzical expression. "*Is* there any way you can control it? Can we somehow plug those cracks?"

"If we could drain the cooling lines and take them apart, then it is possible to weld the weak points in the heat pipes, reassemble the line, and recharge it with coolant," said Seichi. "But that complex task cannot be done with Tabby. Its crude manipulators were not designed for such delicate work, and its small size means it cannot handle large pieces of equipment in the gravity field of Saturn. It requires a much stronger and more sophisticated robot—or a human being."

"Which is out of the question," said Rod. "A human wouldn't last an hour in that radiation environment, rad-drugs or not." He sighed. "You're right. We'll not tell the others. We two will do the worrying for them."

Rod did, however, report Seichi's finding back to the Space Unlimited Mission Control Center. They started working on contingency plans. Unfortunately, there weren't many options available since the problem was occurring so far away from Earth.

The language lessons with Uppereye continued during each nighttime altitude climb. Sandra and the rest of the crew now had outside bass "speakers" built into their backpacks so each could talk directly with Peregrine's eyes, while Uppereye was learning to speak a crude form of pidgin English using sounds generated by its neck sac orifices. Seichi had learned enough of the rukh chordal language to communicate with not only Uppereye, but Lowereye and the other rukhs who occasionally came by to visit the humans during the socializing periods that occurred at morning and evening when both eyes were awake. Seichi's range of tonal ability was limited to the seven octaves of the keyboard, whereas a rukh's multibladder voice covered twenty octaves, from whole-body breathing modes that generated notes that took many tens of seconds to complete one cycle to a "falsetto" generated by the neck sacs that was too high for the human ear to hear. Still, Seichi could generate the names of everyone in the flock, adding to the name chord the chordal patterns that meant "Hello," "Good-bye," "Please come and talk to me," "How are you feeling?", and "Did you have a good hunt?", as appropriate to the situation.

As the giant winged body of the latest visitor, Eagle, lifted upward, its body booming out deep tones and Seichi responding with his own keyboarded chords, Sandra waved good-bye and turned to Seichi.

"It is really amazing how well you can converse with the rukhs in their own language, Seichi," she said.

"It is a little like the art of writing hiragana, but you do it with chordal patterns instead of strokes of the brush," Seichi explained. "You start with the chord that represents the basic root concept and add other chords in other octaves that represent additional concepts, adjusting all the concept chords so they blend rather than conflict, then modify that combined chord with either changed notes or additional notes that signify the context and tense of the meaning you are after. The rukhs carry it much further, however. A typical single Japanese hiragana character can be either a word or a long phrase, while the rukhs speak the equivalent of sentences or paragraphs with each chord. I am sure my feeble attempts at speaking their language sound to the rukhs like 'Me Seichi say hello to you Upperye' spoken in baby babble."

"Still, they must understand you," replied Sandra as she watched Eagle bank away. "The others in the flock do so like to come and talk with you."

"I would suspect they find me amusing," replied Seichi. "I notice that each time I try to generate a new phrase by combining chords that I have never combined before, the visitors and Upper-

eye repeat the chord back and forth to each other, their heads bob-
bing up and down in amusement, before Uppereye takes the time
to pronounce the chord correctly for me a couple of times until I get
all the nuances correct. I can't complain. With their willing help, I
am rapidly becoming proficient in the language."

"I notice that you now know the name of practically every bird
in the flock," said Sandra.

"What I find interesting is that every name chord has a common
deep bass subchord," said Seichi. "I believe it is a root chord meaning either 'rukh' or the 'family name' of the flock. I will have to try
it out when the elder of the flock, 'Condor,' finally gets around to
visiting me. I'll chord 'hello' and the root chord with the family
name, with the little high-pitched twittering bit that means the chord
is a question, and see what response I get."

Sandra noticed that Uppereye's eye was blinking sleepily, the nic-
titating sheet sliding downward over the surface of the lens, wiping
away bits of flying food creatures that had been blown into the clearing by the wind gusts and splattered against the high-pressure balloon optics. She had learned from experience that Uppereye was almost addicted to using the portable console to bring up new pictures
of life on Earth and the other planets and would stay at the console
all day if Sandra permitted it. Sandra turned off the console power
at the airlock junction panel.

"Now is time for Uppereye to sleep," she said firmly.

"Sandra turn on console? Again? Please?" said Uppereye, its
neck sac orifices putting a querying rising tone and pause after each
of the last three words.

"No," replied Sandra, being firm. She had once let Uppereye stay
up all day playing on the console, and the next night the language
lesson had to be canceled because Uppereye could barely stay awake
enough to keep Peregrine flying upward.

"Sandra goes to sleep. Uppereye goes to sleep," she said as she
took the dark console from Uppereye's lower set of foreclaws. "Sandra see Uppereye when darkness comes again. Good-bye, Uppereye."

"Good-bye, Sandra. Good-bye, Seichi," said Uppereye, raising its
head canards and lifting off in the constant wind that passed overhead to fly back to its sleeping notch at the top of Peregrine's keel.

As Sandra and Seichi gathered together their equipment
preparatory to climbing up the side of *Sexdent* to the airlock door,

they could feel the living surface beneath their boots tilt slightly, as the body of Peregrine started the long downward hunting dive with the rest of the flock. Simultaneously, the surface rumbled as Low-ereye had Peregrine's body join in song with the others.

```
d d d d s  s  s  s  s  s  s  s  s
      l l l l l  l
      u   u   a  a  a  a  a  a  a
i i i i   i   i   i   i   i
      v   v   d  d  l  l  l  l
pp  pp  mp  mp  n t  n t  gg  gg
i  i  i  i  i  i  i  i  i  i  i  i  i  i  i
n g n g n g n g n g n g n g n g n g n g n g n g n g n g n g
  D D D D D D D F F F F F F F
        R R R  L    L L L L L
        O  O        O  O
  I I I I O O O O A Y A Y A Y A Y
  V   V   P   P         T   T
  PP  PP  PP  PP  LL  LL
  I  I  I  I  I  I  I  I  I  I  I  I  I  I  I
  NGNGNGNGNGNGNGNGNGNGNGNGNGNGNG
    D D D D S S S S S S S S S S S S
        L L L L L L L L L L L L T
    I I I I I I I I O I O I O O O O O
    V   V   D   D   D   D   W   W
    PP  PP  PP  PP  P  P  P  P  PP
    I  I  I  I  I  I  I  I  I  I  I  I  I  I  I  I
    NGNGNGNGNGNGNGNGNGNGNGNGNGNGNGNG
```

"I wish I knew what that all meant," said Sandra as they both stopped to experience the song, for they found themselves feeling it with their bodies more than hearing it with their ears. Seichi let the multitone chord flow into the section of his memory where he stored the language of the rukhs. He had taught himself the trick of not thinking of the chords as words, or even phrases, but as "feel-ings" and "inclinations" and "impressions."

"It is about going down," he finally concluded, "but a swooping pleasurable exciting daring down."

They climbed up the rungs to the airlock where they traded places with Rod and Pete. Pete went to check out the meta factory, while Rod took advantage of the daylight to resume his vermin removal patrols.

Still groggy from having only three hours' sleep during the previous five-hour "day," Sandra yawned behind her visor as she waited in the clearing outside the airlock door for Uppereye Peregrine to arrive. There was still plenty of daylight, for it was summer in the northern hemisphere of Saturn, but darkness would be on them soon.

"That's strange," Sandra remarked to Seichi as she finished her yawn. "Usually, Uppereye is already here when we come out, eager to start the next language session."

"There is something else strange," said Seichi, who was adjusting the low-frequency sound detector. "Body Peregrine is singing a new chord that I have never heard before. It isn't too complex. Basic in chordal pattern . . . almost primitive in nature . . . more like a 'feeling' rather than a 'thought.' "

"I noticed," said Sandra. "It's been going on for a long time." She looked upward to the holoviewport at the top of *Sexdent* that looked out over the clearing. Pete was in the window, keeping a security watch on the two outside, finger always ready above the nose jet icon in case Sandra or Seichi inadvertently said something that would rile Uppereye into attacking. From the higher viewpoint, Pete could see a relatively long way across the top of the feather forest that surrounded them.

"Pete," she called. "Do you see Uppereye coming?"

"No sign of Uppereye," replied Pete through the radio link. "But there's something strange going on. Maybe that explains why Uppereye is late."

"What kind of strange?" replied Sandra, annoyed at being kept in the dark.

"Normally about this time the flock is circling about in a big horizontal ring, head to tail, the heads of one bird grooming the tail section of the one in front. Now they are circling in a big vertical ring." Sandra and Seichi looked up at the formation of rukhs that were flying along with Peregrine. Pete was right. Peregrine was flying along leisurely but was slowly sinking in altitude. Right above Peregrine was Hawk, who was also sinking downward, keeping a roughly constant distance from Peregrine. Above and going off to the right were Eagle, Buzzard, and other members of the flock, keeping pace with Peregrine, but at different distances. Altogether they formed a giant arc that "set" in the forest canopy to the "west" over where Peregrine's right wing would be.

"I now see what might be the reason for the vertical ring," said Pete, as Peregrine flew lower and started moving to the right, bringing more of the upper part of the ring into the narrow view cone Sandra and Seichi had at the bottom of the clearing. "In a minute or so, Peregrine will be at the bottom of the vertical ring and you'll see two rukhs at the center of the ring. I don't know exactly what they are doing, but it looks naughty to me!"

"Make sure the holoviewport imager is on record!" yelled Sandra, frustrated that she couldn't see a thing, while Pete had a front-row seat. "And don't just sit there watching! Tell me what's going on!"

"It's Falcon and Harrier," replied Pete. "Harrier is flying in close formation with Falcon, just below and a little behind." He paused.

"And?!" said Sandra, exasperated.

"You know that penislike thing that trails out of the bottom of a rukh's body?"

"Yes, the elimination tube," she replied.

"Well . . . this may be just my dirty mind . . . but I think the upper eye on Harrier is 'tickling' it."

"It *is* your dirty mind," replied Sandra with scorn. "You're anthropomorphizing—a typical problem with people who don't have the proper training you get in the life sciences. What exactly is the upper eye doing to the waste tube? Don't forget, these birds groom each other. Perhaps the upper eye on Harrier is just grooming Falcon's waste tube to get rid of some vermin or something."

"Perhaps so," replied Pete. "But to me it looks more like groping than grooming. The upper eye on Harrier is extending its neck and climbing up the underside of the tube with its neck claws, then contracting the neck sacs to pull the tube closer to Harrier's body, then climbing upward again to repeat the pulling motion. And I'm not sure, I guess I could be anthropowhatsing again, but I could swear the tube was expanding and getting longer. Too bad you're not up here to see it."

Sandra couldn't stand it any longer. She dropped the portable console she had been going to use to talk to Uppereye and quickly climbed the rungs up the side of *Sexdent* until she was standing at the top of the cone.

"Oh my gosh! You're *right*," she said. "It *is* bigger."

"And longer," added Pete, as Peregrine continued slowly sinking as it circled with the rest of the flock around the two rukhs in the middle. "Here comes the lower eye on Falcon. I wonder what it's going to do about Harrier's upper eye pulling on his privates."

As they watched, the lower eye of the upper rukh expanded its neck sacs and crawled along the bottom of its body. When it came to the elimination tube, it took the top side of the tube, crawling down to the tip while the upper eye of the lower rukh climbed up the bottom side of the tube toward the tube's root in the upper rukh's body. The lower eye stopped crawling as it came near the end of Falcon's elimination tube. In front of it, the tip of the tube started to expand.

"Look at the tip swell up!" said Pete in astonishment. "It's developing wings! Just like the canards on the heads, except there are four of them. If Falcon's lower eye is going to act as pilot for the penis, it'll have control in both pitch and yaw!" The engineer in him was impressed by the design evolution had developed. "You've got to admit now that it isn't just an elimination tube. It's sure acting like a penis to me."

"You're right," admitted Sandra, her crotch cinching up in involuntary reaction as she saw the giant penis develop a wicked-looking barbed tip as the canard wings inflated. She tried hard to return to a mood of scientific objectivity. "Of course, there are many Earth species where tip expansion is used to maintain coupling after initial penetration."

"I know about dogs," said Pete. "Where the tip of the dog's penis swells up after penetration, but barbs?"

"Snail penises have barbs," replied Sandra. She thought for a moment. "And snails are hermaphrodites! Every single rukh we've seen has a similar elimination tube. I wonder . . . are the rukhs also hermaphrodites?"

"Men have nipples too," Pete reminded her. "That doesn't mean they can have babies. Got to watch out that you don't anthropize there, Sandra."

Sandra ignored his jibe.

"I guess we're going to miss the climax," said Pete with a resigned tone as Peregrine's altitude continued to drop. Soon all they could see was the bottom side of Harrier, its elimination tube a mere withered imitation of the giant one approaching Harrier's top side.

Sandra was disappointed, but was still glad that they had been able to get some images of what for most species is a rare and usually private act. While she waited up on the top of *Sexdent* for Peregrine to rise up on the other side, she had time to listen again to the primitive chordal patterns coming from Body Peregrine. She looked down at

Seichi. He was lying flat on the surface of the giant body. The first time he had done this, Sandra had been concerned that something was wrong, but it was just his way of "feeling" more of the actual chordal pattern notes in their natural octave to augment the frequency-shifted versions of the notes coming into his helmet phones from Jeeves.

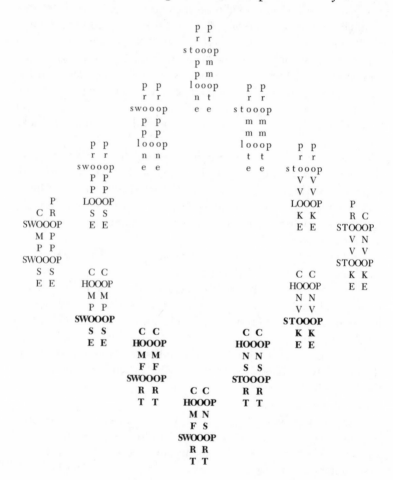

The group experience the flock was undergoing was beautiful, sensuous, friendly, pleasurable, rejuvenating, and exhilarating. Petra slowly switched her chordal patterns as her position changed in the rotating ring surrounding Falru and Renru. The sound of the flock enveloped, surrounded, and encouraged the couple at the center. Petra knew that the two in the center of the ring were experiencing stronger and more intense sensual and pleasurable feelings than the others flying in formation with them, but the whole flock enjoyed the experience, vicariously feeling twinges of pleasure while enjoying the beauty and friendliness of the act taking place. Most important to the flock as a whole was the strong feeling of group rejuvenation that came with the realization that soon a new baby would be joining the life of the flock.

By the time Peregrine had risen up in the circling ring to the point where the humans could once again see over the top of Harrier, the two rukhs were fully coupled together. The lower eye of Falcon had ridden down with the tube as it had penetrated Harrier and had crawled off onto Harrier's back and was using its neck claws to grip tightly onto Harrier's tailfeatherroots in order to hold the two giant bodies together, while the upper eye of Harrier was doing the same by holding on to the featherroots on Falcon's lower prow.

"Now we know what that notched clearing Rod found on Peregrine's back is for," said Sandra.

"They sure make it last a long time," remarked Pete, almost wistfully.

Sandra ignored his comment. "I notice that on both rukhs, the eyes that are not involved in the sex act are closed. Has that been true all during this interaction, Jeeves?"

"That is correct," replied Jeeves after an almost imperceptible pause during which it extracted and examined in detail every image stored that day in its incredibly cavernous memory. "The upper eye of Falcon and the lower eye of Harrier have been asleep. I conclude they are asleep because their eyeballs will occasionally jerk rapidly under their eyelids in the same manner as human eyes do when they are asleep."

"I'm sure the sleep researchers back on Earth will find that interesting," Sandra mused, looking at the others in the flock as they circled around the coupled couple. "All the rest of the flock have both eyes open, like they usually do during the morning and evening socializing periods. They all seem to be busy watching the event. No wonder Uppereye didn't come for its language lesson."

"Bunch of voyeurs," interjected Pete.

"Except for the one closed eye each on the two rukhs involved," Sandra mused further. "Only one eye controls the body at any time. I guess during intercourse the eye not actively involved goes to sleep to avoid complicating the interaction with its thoughts. I'll have to ask Uppereye all about this. Wonder if it'll be reluctant to talk about sex."

Darkness finally came. With the darkness the primitive chord coming from Body Peregrine faded off and was replaced with the more complex and varying chordal patterns that indicated "gossip" between members of the flock. Body Peregrine tilted and started the long nighttime climb to altitude.

"Well, we didn't see the ending, but I guess it's all over," said Pete. "I wonder, will Peregrine be tempted to try something like that with us still on its back? It looked kind of interesting from a distance, but I don't think I would really enjoy seeing a winged penis flying right over my head and coming in for a landing, no matter how scientifically interesting it might be to you."

"Hmmm," mused Sandra. "I think I'd better query Uppereye about that possibility as soon as it arrives."

"Do you want to come inside and play some mommy and daddy rukh games while you're waiting?" Pete asked, switching to a private channel to do so.

"Don't be silly," Sandra replied. "Besides, seeing that barbed head is going to put me off playing any kind of games for a long time."

Shortly afterward, Uppereye appeared for the long-delayed language lesson. It turned out that Uppereye was quite willing to talk about what they had seen, and rukh sex life in general. It soon became clear to Sandra that the rukhs were indeed hermaphrodites. The upper eye on each rukh was the "female" half of the hermaphrodite bird, while the lower eye was the "male" half. When a female head felt that the body was ready to produce young, she would initiate the coupling. Usually she would wait until they were near another flock, and pick one of that flock for her partner. If she couldn't wait, then she would pick one of the rukhs in her own flock, avoiding inbreeding by following the advice of the elder rukhs who kept a memory of the genealogy of the flock.

"Harrier have baby. Soon," said Uppereye, concluding.

"What number days?" asked Sandra.

"Three times sixty times sixty plus thirty times sixty," replied Uppereye. Sandra had found out early that the rukhs used a base-sixty number system, like the Babylonians, and rather than forcing Uppereye to learn the human decimal system, she counted on Jeeves to give her instant translations.

"About twelve thousand of their days. Fifteen Earth years, or half a Saturnian year," Jeeves informed her.

Sandra had been hoping that they would still be around when the baby came, but it was not to be. The long gestation time made sense for creatures this large, and the long Saturnian year stretched it even longer. She had learned that the flock crossed over to the southern hemisphere at the equinox so they could hunt the food prey there as the prey rapidly multiplied in the southern summer season, so a birth cycle of half a Saturnian year made sense. There were two young "dependent" rukhs in the flock. Buzzard had a fuzzy "baby," Owl, who was always kept well tucked into the feather forest along the leading edge of its parent's wing, while Merlin had a "child," Osprey, who would often venture out to "glide" in the rush of air over its parent's wing, where it could swallow smaller prey that its parent had expertly underflown so the prey was directed by the slipstream directly into one of Osprey's maws. Within half a Saturnian year, Osprey would be big enough to hunt on its own, Buzzard's baby would be the "child" of the flock gliding along on Buzzard's bow wave, and Harrier's new youngster would be the flock "baby."

A month passed. They now had fifty tons of meta. The language lessons were going well, information about the lifestyle of *Rukh raptosaturnus* copied from Jeeves's ever-accepting memory was flowing back to excited scientists on Earth, and the crew was beginning to have renewed hope that they would be able to make it back home to Earth. Their previous thoughts about how they would spend their individual billion dollars had faded as each was forced to realize that life was more precious than money—even a billion dollars of money.

Rod, trying to be a good symbiote, was vermin-hunting out on the surface of Peregrine, so he was the one who felt it first—a strong multitone "twang" vibrating the surface of the balloon body beneath his boots. The flock was halfway through the daylight hunting dive. Something fast and heavy had struck the tether trailing the nuclear reactor below Peregrine.

"That was a strong one," Rod muttered worriedly to himself, turning off his meta torch and casting aside the charred crisp of another feather louse. "I'd better get back and help Seichi with the tether repair. We may have to operate both Kitty and Mouser if a lot of lines need repair."

He was wending his way back, carefully reeling in the "Hansel and Gretel" line he had left behind to mark his way through the feather forest, when a booming warning from Jeeves made him break into a bounding trot, following the line without trying to reel it up.

"REACTOR DAMAGE! INITIATING EMERGENCY SHUT-DOWN!"

There was some static and the radio link went dead for a moment. The silence in the helmet earphones drove Rod's adrenaline glands and legs into high gear. Mercifully, the radio link was soon restored.

"BACKUP POWER NOW OPERATIONAL."

"Who's on the bridge?" Rod panted as he slowed to a steady trot.

"Seichi here, sir," came the calm reply. "The strike was directly on the reactor secondary loop cooling fins. All lines are now showing zero overpressure. I am presently using Tabby to survey the extent of damage. I will report the results as soon as I have them."

Rod, bothering only to drop off his backpack and helmet in the airlock, climbed the ladder up to the command deck in his bright yellow saturnsuit. Seichi turned from the holoviewport, which now had an image of what Tabby was seeing. It looked somewhat like a rotary card file except the cards were badly bent.

"The situation is not good, sir," said Seichi grimly. "The last secondary cooling loop has developed a fracture leak. In Saturn's gravity field, the sodium-potassium coolant in the portion of the line above the leak has drained out. Even if we could use Tabby to weld the fracture, there wouldn't be enough coolant in the line for it to function."

"How about fixing one of the lines and using the leftover coolant in the other two lines to top it off?" suggested Rod.

"A most ingenious suggestion, sir," replied Seichi, but he wasn't smiling as he said it, so Rod knew there was something wrong with his idea. "It was one of my first thoughts. Unfortunately, the sodium-potassium eutectic alloy reacts spontaneously when it encounters moisture, and there is a great deal of moisture in the clouds of Saturn. I have yet to think of a method whereby the mechbot could accomplish the necessary transfer without exposing the liquid to the atmosphere."

By this time Pete and Chastity had joined them on the control deck. Dan and Sandra, who had stuck their heads out of their habitat doors during Jeeves's warning, had gone back to sleep once they knew somebody was working on the problem. They knew it was important that some of the crew be fresh and alert when darkness came again in a few hours.

"Maybe we don't need to fix the cooling loop," said Pete. He turned and looked to the two pilots. "Can we make it with the fuel we have? I'd guess we have about fifty-one tons by now."

"That would barely get us into low orbit," said Chastity, rejecting the idea at once.

"He might have an idea there," said Rod. "Jeeves! Suppose we stripped the ship of all nonessential items. How many tons of meta would it take to reach our refueling supply in Titan's orbit?"

There was a pause as Jeeves went through the options. "Are you willing to go without washing water for the year-long trip back to Earth?"

"Sure!" they all replied.

"Can you go without habitats, bedding, hammocks, and all clothing except one jumpsuit?"

"Sure," they all replied, although slower this time.

"Can you make do with one toilet?"

"Sure . . ." came the reply, but Pete was not part of the chorus.

"Then the mass of *Sexdent* can be stripped from fifty to thirty-six tons, and the amount of meta fuel needed at liftoff is approximately sixty-five tons."

"Damn!" said Rod in disgust. "That's so far from fifty-one tons there's no use in working along that line any longer. Looks like we've got to find some coolant and get that reactor working again."

"How about using another coolant to replace the 'NAK'?" suggested Pete. "The chemsyns in my lab can make practically anything organic. How would you like a few dozen liters of ethylene glycol?"

"Only six liters of coolant would be required," replied Seichi politely, but Rod noticed that Seichi still wasn't smiling. Something was wrong with Pete's idea too. "Unfortunately, the reason the sodium-potassium alloy was chosen was, not only does it remain liquid down to minus eleven C, it is highly conducting and can be circulated around the loop by an electromagnetic pump. Electromagnetic pumps contain no moving parts and require no physical access to the interior of the pipe containing the coolant. Both aspects contribute to long-term reliability and resulted in the selection of the alloy over other coolants, including ethylene glycol."

"One thing ethylene glycol ain't is conducting," agreed Pete. "I could spice up some water with some ionizable stuff, like salt, to make it conductive."

"For the electromagnetic pumps to work, the coolant must be highly conducting and remain liquid at the below-freezing temperatures the radiator fins experience here on Saturn," replied Seichi. "I have looked carefully through the physical properties listings in Jeeves's chemistry files, and the only known candidates are alkali metal alloys, certain gallium alloys, and mercury. Mercury would be ideal since it would not react with Saturn's atmosphere."

"Fat chance of collecting six liters of mercury up here in the clouds," commented Chastity, her engineering brain trying hard with them all to find a solution to their problem.

"I have thought of one way to repair the reactor," said Seichi solemnly. Again Rod noticed that Seichi wasn't smiling. If anything he was looking even more somber.

"What!" exclaimed Pete and Chastity simultaneously.

Seichi replied slowly and solemnly. "Although I am unable to think of a method whereby Tabby could accomplish the necessary transfer without exposing the sodium-potassium alloy to the moisture in the atmosphere, I can think of a method whereby a human being could accomplish the task. This reactor is of my design. The design failed. The failure is therefore my fault. So it is necessary that I be the one to carry out the repair."

"No way!" said Pete angrily.

"We can't let you do that!" exclaimed Chastity, moving forward to touch him on the arm. "There *has* to be some other solution."

"Chass is right," said Rod, frowning. "Anything you can do, Tabby can do!"

"I think, in time, you will find my analysis is correct," replied Seichi firmly.

* * *

In time, they all had to agree that Seichi was right. It took a number of days before all the alternate solutions were thoroughly examined by both the crew and hundreds of thousands of concerned people back on Earth, with suggestions coming in from South African youngsters new to the SolNet, to Brazilian auto mechanics working on the latest Grand Prix race cars, to nuclear engineers at reactor facilities in every major nuclear nation.

First, Sandra got Peregrine to leave the flock after a night's climb to altitude and instead of joining in the hunting dive, to continue to climb to higher and colder altitudes. Although Uppereye had been able to elicit the cooperation of Lowereye for this departure from Peregrine's normal way of life, it didn't mean that Lowereye liked doing it. Lowereye had managed to learn a few words and he used them on this occasion. They had been climbing only a half-hour when Lowereye's head flew its way up to the clearing to join Sandra and Uppereye. Lowereye was in charge of Body Peregrine, so he was experiencing the feelings of the body.

"Cold!" Lowereye announced. "Down now?"

Sandra looked up at the holoviewport above her, where Seichi stood at the scottyboard. "What's the temperature, Seichi?"

"Minus twelve C in the air," replied Seichi, "but only minus eight C on the radiator fins. There is still some residual heat stored in the mass of the reactor-radiator system. He needs to fly higher."

"Up more," said Sandra firmly, then added, "please."

Lowereye activated his canards and flew his head back to its perch on the lower notch in Peregrine's keel, where at least the head and eye would be partially protected by the warm feathers that surrounded the nesting site. As he disappeared from sight over the black feather forest canopy, Sandra heard the head rumble something, while at the same time the body below them echoed the rumble with many additional overtones.

"What Lowereye talk?" Sandra asked Uppereye.

Uppereye didn't want to tell Sandra all of Lowereye's list of complaints; how cold, hungry, tired, bloated, and bored he and Body Peregrine were, and how annoyed he was at being told what to do by an insignificant four-legged squinty-eyed blue-pink gizzard-worm.

"Cold," Uppereye lied.

An hour later Seichi announced that the temperature of the radiator section had dropped to minus fifteen degrees centigrade. "The alloy should be frozen solid now. You can have Tabby start working on loop number two, Jeeves." As he watched on the holoviewport, Tabby used the tools Seichi had made for it with the mechfab to cut the tubing of the two most damaged secondary cooling loops at their lowest points, clean the hardened sodium-potassium out of the end of the tubes, and crimp the tube ends tightly shut. To maintain the reactor's neutron-scattering profile, the portions of the secondary cooling loops that passed through the heat exchanger section were also crimped off to prevent the alloy from leaking out once the reactor was heated up again. Next, the fins on the least-damaged cooling loop were cut loose at a straight portion of the tubing. The fins were warmed up with a meta torch until all the alloy dripped out. With the alloy gone, the fractures could be welded shut. The repaired fins were then reattached to the tubing with a mechfab-made butt-joint threaded tube coupling. The repaired loop now only needed refilling through the fill port at the top end of the radiator stack.

That night Seichi was just preparing his bed for sleep when he heard a tapping on his habitat door. He swung the door open to see Chastity—quite a bit of Chastity.

"I was wondering if you'd like a little company tonight," she asked, reaching in a braceleted arm to scratch his cheek with her brightly colored long fingernails.

"I would be greatly honored," Seichi replied. "But I am afraid the antiradiation drugs and the sleeping pill Dr. Horning gave me have made me very sleepy. Perhaps tomorrow night?"

"Sure. Tomorrow night . . ." said Chastity, tears welling in her violet eyes as she gave his cheek a last pat and withdrew. Both of them knew full well that even if Seichi wasn't killed on his mission, and managed to survive until "tomorrow night," he would be facing months of pain, nausea, and probable death from the whole-body dose he would have received, and even if Doc pulled him through the first crisis period, he would likely die young from cancer.

Fifteen hours later as the dim sun rose behind the thick layer of water clouds high above, a well-rested Seichi with a deliberately very empty stomach stepped onto the "rungs" of the Hoytether that led to the

now-cold reactor hanging below Peregrine. Although Body Peregrine also had a nearly empty gizzard and sent hunger signals to Lowereye, he kept the giant body moving in a slow circle as Uppereye
had been making it do all night instead of climbing to altitude. They
were well down in the atmosphere and the air was warm and moist.
Occasionally the searching sonar from Peregrine's wing would notice a larger-than-normal morsel of prey and Lowereye would
smoothly adjust the trajectory of the giant body to swoop it into one
of the rukh's maws. The bits of food kept Petru's hunger pangs down.

Seichi started down the Hoytether, followed closely by Chastity
and Dan, with Rod and Pete staying on the wing edge, monitoring
a well-anchored belaying line attached to all three of them. Seichi
moved slowly and heavily. His backpack had extra bottles of gas attached to it, and the curved metal body shields on his helmet and
underneath the torso of his saturnsuit added to his weight.

When they reached a point about two hundred meters above the
reactor-radiator complex, Dan called a halt.

"My helmet dose meter is reading about five rems per hour," said
Dan. "Chass and I had better wait here for now. We'll come down
closer to help you up just as you finish the job."

"Thank you for risking your lives to help me," said Seichi. "If it
had not been for my faulty design, you would not be placed in such
a harmful position."

"I told you once and I'll tell you again!" roared Rod over the radio
link. "You designed that radiator system perfectly for the job of floating under a balloon. Just because the fins weren't able to cope with
incoming jellyfish traveling at jetliner speeds is *not your fault!*"

"You are very kind, sir," replied Seichi. "But even if it is not my
fault, it is still my duty to make the repair." Taking a deep breath, he
started down the last two hundred meters, moving as rapidly as he
could to minimize his exposure time.

Tabby was waiting for Seichi when he arrived at the top of the
three-lobed radiator stack. Precariously balancing on the top of the
array, Seichi unfastened his safety line from a ring on the belaying
line to Chastity above and replaced it with a hook leading from a
package of folded gold-coated plastic film taken from insulating panels that had protected the walls of the meta factory from the heat of
the rocket engines that had landed them on Saturn. He shook the
package and a long tubular bell of glittering golden film fell all about

him and down around the radiator stack and the reactor below, flashing brightly as mirrorlike film reflected his helmet light again and again until the whole interior of the bell was illuminated. Under the control of Sandra and Jeeves back on *Sexdent*, Tabby scurried down and around to unhook the skirt of the golden bell whenever it hung up on a snag. Tabby then drew in a drawstring at the bottom to turn the bell into a bag with a small exhaust hole at its base. Seichi reattached his safety line to the inside top of the golden bag, then removed two large tanks from the top of his backpack, and with a sigh of relief hung the tanks from the tubular frame that supported the radiator stack and opened the tank valves. The bag billowed out and stiffened as the tanks added their contents to the inside air.

"Dry nitrogen on. Humidity should be at acceptable levels shortly," he reported brusquely as he moved quickly to his next task. He hauled up one of the two cooling loops that Tabby had previously disconnected from the reactor. Turning it end for end inside the closed confines of the bag was a complex task, but he had practiced it on a virtual simulator many times and completed the maneuver without tearing the bag or getting the radiator fins caught in the support frame or the fins of the other two cooling loops. He quickly opened the fill valve on the repaired cooling loop, then slowed himself down as he put the filling cone of the damaged loop up next to the filling cone of the good loop and slowly opened the valve on the damaged loop. He allowed himself a smile of satisfaction as he watched the bright silvery stream of sodium-potassium alloy trickle out and into the filling cone of the good loop.

The second loop went even faster because of the experience with the first one. As the stream of silver poured out and spiraled down the cone, Seichi clung to a glimmer of hope that he might get out of this without too much damage. The smile that was starting to appear on his face suddenly disappeared as the silver stream stopped and the last droplets fell through the hole in the bottom of the filling cone. He stared at the empty cone that was silently demanding more of the precious silver metal. He shook the cooling loop on his shoulder, but nothing came out.

"I have emptied the second cooling loop, but the fill cone is not full," he reported.

"Shut the valve and get the hell out of there!" exhorted Chastity.

"That will not result in a repair," Seichi replied. "The fill cone must have liquid in it when the valve is closed, otherwise there will be an air bubble in the line and the pumps will not work. More alloy is needed."

Seichi's brain, sleeted through with a constant barrage of ionizing particles, tried to think its way past the random noise generated within itself to find a solution to the problem. It found one.

"Jeeves!" commanded Seichi. "Have Tabby follow me, saw claw at ready."

"What are you going to do?" asked Chastity, frustrated that the golden bag prevented her from seeing what was going on.

"There is more alloy in the reactor," replied Seichi.

"Don't do it!" yelled Dan, now extremely concerned. "Every meter closer you get to that reactor means your chances of survival decrease."

"I am aware of that," said Seichi calmly. "I will move rapidly." He needed a container to carry the liquid alloy. He thought of using his plastic water bottle, but that would not work. If he emptied it inside the bag, the humidity would rise and the sodium and potassium in the alloy would react with the water to produce a slag of sodium and potassium hydroxide that would clog the channels in the cooling fins. Also, if any drops of water clung to the walls of the bottle, when the alloy contacted the water drops there would be a burst of flame that would probably burn its way through the plastic. He took the metal plate off his helmet. It was a shallow bowl, but it would do. Sending Tabby ahead to start sawing, he clambered down the tubular frame that connected the reactor to the cooling tower, his gloved fingers and booted toes using the clawholds built into the frame for Tabby's use. His stomach was starting to churn and his arms and legs were feeling weak as he reached the bottom of the reactor.

His eyes had trouble seeing through the ionization flashes from the high-energy particles traversing his retinas as he reached the bowl out under the pinched-off secondary cooling loop tube extending out from the reactor. It took Tabby a number of seconds to finish sawing away the tube and precious drops of alloy were lost, but Seichi did not want to risk having any stainless steel filings contaminating the cooling loop so he waited until the stream of silver ran clear before capturing a half-bowlful of the precious alloy.

He vomited as he rose and started his way back up the rungs in the enervating pull of Saturn's gravity. His helmet stank with bile as he poured the bowl of liquid silver into the filling cone, filling it to overflowing. Dropping the bowl he turned the valve that shut off the filling cone.

"Filling complete." He coughed and retched again.

"Get him out of there, Tabby," commanded Dan, starting to climb down to his patient, while Chastity, safely anchored above him, tightened up on the line that led to Seichi. Under the control of Jeeves, Tabby ripped open the golden bag and added its claw power to the pull of Chastity and the weak efforts of Seichi as he tried to climb the slippery lines of the Hoytether.

"I'm coming, Seichi," said Dan as he made his way down. "Just hold on!"

"What is the reading on my helmet dose meter, Jeeves?" replied Seichi. "I can't read it. I'm blind."

There was a long pause, and when the reply came, it came from Dan. "Eighty-three thousand rem. But you're out of the danger zone. Keep climbing and I'll meet you."

"We both know what that reading means, Doctor," said Seichi. "Do not injure yourself further by foolishly attempting to rescue me. I must go now."

"No, Seichi! *No!*" screamed Chastity, pulling hard on the line, trying to drag Seichi bodily to safety.

"Tell my parents that I hope that I have brought honor to my family name, even though I failed to complete my mission successfully."

Chastity burst into tears as the line went slack in her hands.

That evening the remainder of the crew were all waiting on the lower deck as Pete cycled back through the airlock from the meta factory.

"Everything is up and running, and optimized for maximum meta production. We're now making about two tons a week," he reported. Both Chastity and Rod did quick calculations in their heads.

"Fourteen weeks to make twenty-eight tons and we're out of here with our clothing, beds, and both washrooms in full operation," said Chastity, a tone of hope and optimism coloring her voice.

"That'll only give us eighty tons of fuel, Chass," replied Rod. "I think we ought to wait another two weeks to make sure we have enough margin."

"You're the commander," replied Chastity. "Although you didn't think we needed much fuel margin when we came down. Sixteen weeks it is."

"In the meantime, what'll we do to keep ourselves amused?" asked Pete.

"There's a more somber job we need to do right now," said Rod. "Although the Space Unlimited monitoring team are aware of Seichi's death, I have asked them to hold off telling his parents until I can inform them myself, and I wanted you all here with me when I did so. Now is a good time, since it is early morning in Japan. They should get our video message well before noon.

"Let me comb my hair," said Sandra, patting her normally neat gray-streaked coif with both hands and finding a few stray hairs. "I wouldn't want to distract things by looking out of place." She ducked into one of the toilets. Chastity went into the other and soon returned with her eye makeup and lipstick now more subdued and her uniform zipper pulled all the way up to her neck.

The five remaining crewmembers arranged themselves in back of Rod on the bottom deck, while Puss, holding on to the airlock hinges, used a portable imager to record their message. Dan had retrieved Seichi's keyboard and programmed it to play the "Saturn Suite" from Holst's *The Planets* for background music.

"Mr. and Mrs. Takeo," Rod started. "I would like to tell you about a very brave man . . ."

The light on Puss's imager went off and the solemn group broke up. Chastity blinked back some tears and forced a smile on her face.

"I don't think Seichi would have liked seeing us this gloomy," she said. "After all, he did save our lives. We ought to feel happy!"

"Chass is right!" said Pete. "Let's have a wake! I'll go get the laser juice."

Chastity was going to object, but then decided to let Pete go ahead—a good stiff drink was what they all probably needed right now.

Dan programmed Seichi's keyboard to play some polkas and they danced awhile, sometimes forgetting that it wasn't Seichi playing for them as he had done so many times before. The closeness of his recent death clouded the atmosphere, however, so when Pete got drunk again, they called an early halt and went to bed—separately.

The next night Sandra resumed her language lessons with Uppereye Peregrine. As she exited the airlock, she noticed there was a rukh close overhead, flying in formation with Peregrine. It didn't look familiar to Sandra, so it was probably a visitor from some other flock. Sandra suspected it was here for purposes of interflock mating.

"Where Seichi?" asked Uppereye, looking around as she glided into the clearing on her head canards, neck claws grabbing an anchor hold on the surrounding feather forest canopy. "Seichi talk to rukh name of"—instead of an English word at the end of the sentence, Uppereye had generated a chordal pattern. It sounded like a name chord to Sandra, but she wasn't sure. Seichi would know instantly, and would have probably been able to extract the root chord that indicated the visiting rukh's flock name. That was not to be. Their rate of learning about the language and culture of the rukhs was going to slow drastically without Seichi's ability to understand and "feel" the rukh language.

"Seichi not here," replied Sandra. "Seichi"—she paused, for she had not yet taught Uppereye the English word for "dead." She would have to come up with an alternate phrase that would indicate the finality of Seichi's nonappearance. "Seichi dive down. Seichi not fly up in future time."

Uppereye emitted a chordal pattern and the giant bird above pulled in its eyes and lifted upward and away. Sandra and Uppereye then started their daily language lesson. Sandra was now teaching Uppereye about Earth geography. She activated the portable console and sat down on the edge of the lowered airlock door, her back to the giant eye. Uppereye moved up behind her until the one-meter contracted iris on the ten-meter eye was looking over Sandra's shoulder. They could now both see the screen at the same time. Uppereye's two lower foreclaws held on to the edge of the platform to steady the head, while the two giant upper foreclaws joined Sandra's tiny gloved hands on the touchscreen as they activated the icon labeled "Planetary Geography." Uppereye was fascinated with the idea that a planet could have a solid surface that stayed the same shape all the time, and that "flocks" of humans could set up "national borders" on those surfaces that could keep other humans out. The rukh flocks had their own "hunting territories," but those fluctuated with the winds and the seasons. What really interested Uppereye, though, were the many "things" that the humans had. She kept getting distracted by new "things" showing up in the image, and Sandra would have to explain what they were and how they were used. A few nights ago Uppereye saw a brightly colored bow tie on a human neck and really coveted it. Sandra sacrificed the cloth in her dancing skirt, and soon Uppereye's neck was sporting a bright red bow tie in addition to its string tie.

The planetary geography continued with a zoom from outer space toward Earth. The zoom took place over Cape Canaveral in Florida since pictures from above that point were readily available.

"What that big thing?" interrupted Uppereye as they came to a picture of a rocket ready to take off from the cape. Fortunately, since Peregrine itself was jet powered, it was easy for Sandra to explain how the rocket worked. She even got "bodyguard" Pete to stop watching blue movies on the inside of his holovisor and come out of the airlock with the meta torch to show how the flame "jetted" from the nozzle. During this demonstration, Uppereye had backed off, foreclaws carefully closed and tucked away.

"Meta made from wind," Sandra explained, waving at the atmosphere in front of her. She then realized that she could use this most-recent topic to help explain why the humans had come to Saturn. "Much wind on Air. Humans come to Air to make meta. Find rukh here. Rukh need wind. Humans not take wind to make meta. Humans go back to Earth."

"Humans not go back to Earth. Humans stay. Humans teach Uppereye. Humans teach other rukhs. Humans bring 'things' for all rukhs."

Sandra didn't want to get into the real reason why the Earth authorities had decided to cancel the Saturn meta project. Without the motivation of a commercial return from the production of meta, there would be no permanent base orbiting Saturn, and no realistic way to maintain communication with the rukhs. There would be the occasional robotic scientific orbiter or balloon probe, but nothing like the back-and-forth interactive communication that Sandra and Uppereye were engaged in. It looked like the budding friendship between the rukhs and the humans was coming to an abrupt end. She decided to tell Uppereye just part of the truth in order to keep it simple. She repeated what she had said before.

"Rukhs need wind," she said. "Humans not use wind to make meta."

"Much wind," argued Uppereye. "Much wind for rukhs and humans. Humans stay. Humans use wind to make meta. Humans teach rukhs. Humans give rukhs things."

"Sandra talk to humans on Earth," she promised, then started in on the Earth geography lesson again.

After many weeks of discussion with Uppereye and other rukhs in the flock and nearby flocks, and much debate on Earth, a solution was found. Although the rukhs traveled from hemisphere to hemisphere, following the Sun back and forth over the equator during the thirty-Earth-year-long seasonal period, they never went anywhere near the poles.

"No light. No heat. No food. No go there," Uppereye summarized succinctly. The Earth scientists agreed. Now that they knew what infrared bands to look in, it was easy for them to use the science satellites orbiting Saturn to detect the existence of the microscopic planktonlike lifeforms in Saturn's atmosphere that formed the base of the food chain, with the rukhs at the top. There was plenty of plankton near the equator, but none at the poles. Without plankton to feed on, there would be no advanced lifeforms in the polar regions, so the plutonium-powered floating meta factories could be safely operated at the poles without either the reactors damaging the alien lifeforms or the alien lifeforms damaging the reactor, meta factory, or balloons. With the orbiting space stations paid for and maintained by the profits from the meta operation, the scientists could come along for the ride and maintain close contact with the rukhs below. It was Art Dooley who solved the last problem—the disposal of the nuclear reactors.

"We'll just use a meta rocket to haul the reactors back out at the end of their useful lifetime and put them into a holding orbit around Saturn. That and the extra cost of landing the factories at the poles instead of the equator will up the price of meta a few percent, but Saturn meta in Earth orbit will still be fifteen times cheaper than Earth meta in Earth orbit. The only uncertainty is the cost of those 'things' the rukhs want in payment. They can't be serious—pink silk underpants and giant bow ties?"

"Buying the polar regions of Saturn for some 'things,' " remarked Dan when he heard about the proposed solution. "It sounds to me like the deal the Dutch did to the Indians—buying Manhattan for some beads."

6

TURN FOR THE WORSE

EMERGENCY! REACTOR SHUTDOWN IN PROGRESS!

Rod's eyes didn't even blink when Jeeves's loud warning blared throughout the control deck. Ignoring Chastity as she scrambled up out of her habitat in her blue nightgown and powered up the scottyboard, he went into his test-pilot-in-trouble mode as he methodically scanned the indicator icons on his pilot console.

"Plenty of time," he reminded himself, keeping physically calm while his brain raced through his various options. "Think first, act later." A few seconds prior to Jeeves's warning, Rod had felt the deep "twang" that came every time a bubblefloater or other prey animal struck the Hoytether hanging below Peregrine. A strike happened at least once every hunt dive. Almost all of the strikes hit the tether directly. The failsafe design of the Hoytether kept the multiline structure from parting, and usually the worst that happened was that Mouser would have to climb down and replace damaged lines in that sector of the tether. This time, however, the bubblefloater must have struck the reactor complex at the end of the tether.

Rod waited until Jeeves had completed the reactor shutdown and connected the capsule power lines to the onboard meta-powered thermoelectric generator.

"Status report, Jeeves," he said quietly, once he had completed his scan of the screen.

"Strike on radiator fins of sole remaining secondary cooling loop," replied Jeeves. "Cooling loop pressurization lost. I have Tabby inspecting the damage."

Both Rod and Chastity had their eyes glued to the screens in front of them, trying to make sense of the moving video images coming from one of the camera "eyes" of the mechbot down on the reactor. Tabby came to a halt and the video image stabilized on their screens. Through the wet guck of the innards of a smashed bubble-floater dripped a silvery trickle of liquid sodium-potassium alloy droplets. The drops flashed brightly as they traveled, leaving behind a trail of desiccated burnt flesh covered with white streaks of sodium-potassium hydroxide.

"That blows it!" growled Chastity. "Good thing there's no oxygen in Saturn's atmosphere or all that hot hydrogen being generated would have added an explosion and fire to our list of problems."

"Jeeves. Any chance of Tabby fixing the leak?" asked Rod, knowing full well the answer—for Seichi had tried hard to find a way before finally deciding he would have to go down himself.

"The mechbots are not capable of making the repair," replied Jeeves. Both Rod and Chastity felt the heavy hand of fear tighten around their hearts as they faced the grim realization that it might take another human sacrifice to enable the survivors to return home.

"Is a human capable of making the repair?" asked Rod, facing the fear head on. The fear changed to despair at the reply.

"The cooling loop cannot be repaired. There is insufficient coolant to recharge it."

There was a long pause as both Rod and Chastity thought in vain for alternative solutions to their predicament. Chastity punched at the keyboard as she asked Jeeves to compute something for her. The nimble trimmed fingers of her right hand moved gracefully over the letter and number icons on the touchscreen, their rapid dance alternating with the taps of her long left index fingernail at the Shift and Function icons.

"The backup power system is burning sixty kilos of meta a day," she remarked as she noticed the indicator at the top of the scotty-board. "We can't afford that. We need every bit of meta we have for powering the main rockets if we're going to get off this godforsaken planet. Jeeves! Can you bring up the reactor and operate it without the cooling loop? Every watt of electricity the reactor can supply means that much less meta will be lost."

"The reactor is not designed to be operated without the secondary cooling loops operational," replied Jeeves.

"She didn't *ask* you that!" yelled Rod, beginning to lose control in the face of what looked like an increasingly hopeless situation. "Bring up the reactor without the cooling loop and get every watt you can out of it!"

"Such an option is not allowed by safety regulations," replied Jeeves in a level voice.

"Why don't you work on trajectory options, Rod?" suggested Chastity, trying to get the situation back on track. "Assume you'll have available all the meta presently in the fuel tanks. I'll work with Jeeves and the Mission Control people back on Earth, and get that reactor up one way or the other."

Three hours later, the five remaining crewmembers of *Sexdent* met in the galley. It was dinnertime, but no one was particularly hungry. They just picked at their food as Rod and Chastity reported what they had been able to come up with.

"The reactor is up and running," reported Chastity. "With the secondary cooling systems nonfunctional, it's operating at internal temperatures well beyond what it was designed for. The Mitsubishi engineers predict a random failure in the reactor control system producing either a meltdown or an irreversible shutdown within an estimated mean time to failure of about one year. Of course, since the failure would be a random event, it could happen sooner than that, or later than that."

"With the string of bad luck we've been having, it'll probably be sooner," said Pete dejectedly. "I was really looking forward to spending my billion. Too bad I can't use it to buy a new reactor."

"How much electricity is it generating?" asked Rod. "Is there enough to power the capsule and still make meta? I'm going to need every drop."

"Sorry," Chastity replied, biting a recently crimsoned lip and blinking eyelashes black with fresh mascara. She had deliberately taken the time to freshen her makeup before their communal dinner in order to brighten things up. There was no need for her to look dowdy even though the news she was bearing was bad. "We barely have enough to run the capsule. I've shut down all the mechbots, turned off the high-power transmitter link to Earth, and shut down or reduced everything else I thought I could get away with."

"I noticed it was colder in here than it used to be," said Sandra.

"We're still having to burn a little meta in the backup generator to carry the load," replied Chastity. She turned to Pete. "I know the main part of the meta factory is shut down," she said. "But the scottyboard says there is still some power being drawn."

"Air circulators and chemsyns," replied Pete. "I leave the chemsyns on all the time and have them producing ethanol when I'm not using them for something else."

"Right after we finish eating, go out and close everything down," said Rod. "We can't afford to waste meta making booze." He paused, and a grim look came over his face. "Although we might as well use the meta for making booze. I certainly can't use it to get us out of here." He took a deep breath and everybody stopped to listen to their commander.

"To get to Titan's orbit, where our return fuel waits for us, requires a launch velocity of thirty-seven kilometers per second, counting air drag and gravity losses. We're at twenty-one degrees north. Since Saturn is rotating and we're moving with it, we're already traveling at nine klecs, so we need the meta rockets on *Sexdent* to boost us an additional twenty-eight klecs and we can get out of here. But that only puts us in an elliptical orbit with its peak altitude at Titan's orbit. To circularize the orbit and come to a stop at the fuel depot will require another burn at apogee of four klecs. The total mission delta vee we need out of the rockets is thirty-two klecs. Unfortunately, to do those two burns requires that we start out with ninety-six tons of meta in our fuel tanks and we only have sixty tons."

"How about Space Unlimited sending a rescue ship?" asked Sandra with a perturbed frown. "They got us into this mess, they should get us out."

Chastity was tempted to remind Sandra that she was getting paid a billion dollars *because* it was a risky mission. Instead, she replied, "Art Dooley and the Space Unlimited crew back in mission control are working on the problem. Don't forget that *Sexdent* was a custom-made ship, especially the extralarge first two stages. It looks like it would take almost a year before a vehicle with a similar ability could be cobbled together, and then it would take another year before it could get here. So rescue is at least twenty-four months away. Even after they get here, they can't rescue us without us doing our part. No ship exists that could drop all the way down into Saturn's cloud deck to pick us up and fly back out again without refueling. We landed with empty tanks. We're going to have to meet them at least halfway, by getting ourselves into as high an orbit as possible."

"Well, at least we've got sixty tons of meta," continued Sandra. "How far will that sixty tons take us?"

"Out to the G ring, just outside the joint orbit of the twins, Janus and Epimetheus," replied Rod. "Good enough for a rendezvous with a rescue ship, but a *long* way from Titan and our fuel resupply."

"Can we pull a tether whip around Janus like we did on Helene on the way in?" asked Sandra.

"Yeah!" said Pete. "Once we get to one of the lower moons we can use the tether to climb up out of Saturn's gravity well just like we climbed down."

"Unfortunately, we've only got one penetrator left," replied Chastity. "And the maximum boost we could get from Janus won't be enough to get us to Titan's orbit."

"We can still use the tether at the top of our trajectory to latch on to Janus and circularize ourselves so we don't fall back into the atmosphere and burn up," said Rod. "Of course, we don't want to do that until the rescue ship arrives, since we'll have to leave the reactor behind when we take off and live off our leftover meta."

"I've been doing some calculations myself," interjected Dan, the features of his face taking on an even more somber countenance as he continued. "We have food left for only eighteen months"—he paused—"and that estimate takes into account the fact that Seichi is no longer sharing meals with us."

"We can stretch it out . . . make it last twenty-four months," said Sandra bravely.

"I'm sure we could make the food last," replied Chastity. "Perforce, if nothing else. But the real difficulty is making the reactor and Hoytether last. Even if the reactor doesn't fail on us, one of these days a really big bubblefloater is going to hit the tether and snap it, and we'll lose the reactor power that way. Combining the reactor failure probability with the tether failure probability, the Space Unlimited engineers and I calculate the estimated combined lifetime is less than six months. The minute either one of them goes, we've had it. We'll have to start burning meta to keep alive, and pretty soon we won't have enough fuel left to make it up to a decent altitude so the rescue ship can reach us."

"How about lightening the ship—throwing stuff overboard?" suggested Sandra.

"Not a bad idea," said Dan, brightening up. "We've already taken some mass off already. I'll have to ask Jeeves to get the exact figure, but I would guess that I hauled almost two tons of shit off *Sexdent* before we started our drop down the rings."

"That's a start," said Rod, also brightening up. "I'd forgotten about that. I'd been assuming that *Sexdent* massed fifty tons dry. If the correct number is forty-eight tons, then the amount of fuel we need to finish off the mission is only ninety-two tons. We're at that point in the exponential of the rocket equation curve where each ton of ship mass we can dump means almost two tons less fuel we need."

Sandra looked at Dan. "Those bags of waste you got rid of used to be food at one time. How much more food have we 'converted' since we've been down here?"

"Yeah!" said Pete. "We certainly don't need to haul shit to orbit."

"There's more than food to consider," said Rod, also turning to look at Dan, more seriously this time. "How much of *Sexdent*'s mass is consumables? They're the easiest thing to dump."

"I'll have to work with Jeeves to get the exact numbers," said Dan. "But from what I can recall, we started out with about six tons of water, five tons of air, most of it nitrogen, and five tons of food. We ate about two tons of food on the way out and I got rid of that in Titan's orbit. We've probably eaten about another ton in the six months we've been down here and we can certainly dump that."

"Do we really *have* to carry all that water and air, Doc?" asked Rod. "Can't we keep just a small amount and recycle it?"

"We do recycle, of course," answered Dan. "But there's a minimum needed just to fill the recycling systems so they'll function. Let me check with Jeeves." Putting down his dinner, he went to the engineering sector, opened the door, and started punching at the icons on the console inside.

"While you're at it," said Pete, "why don't you ask Jeeves how much equipment we can dump. There are a bunch of spare parts and nonessential pieces of equipment in the storage and engineering sectors. Make sure you include the weights and steps in our habitats that we used for our morning exercises when we were in free fall."

"Include the habitats, too," said Rod. "We don't need beds in free fall."

Dan turned around with a frown on his face. "The habitats and the exercise equipment are essential to our long-term health—"

"Doc!" interrupted Rod with an annoyed bark. "To *hell* with our long-term health. It's our short-term health I'm worried about. The first Russian cosmonauts stayed in free fall more than a year without gee-stress exercises. Sure . . . their bones shrank and their muscles got so weak they couldn't stand up when they came back to Earth, but they recovered after a few months. We can do the same."

While Dan took Jeeves through the ship's mass budget, item by item, the others picked at their dinners. Finally, Dan turned from the console. His face was not happy.

"We can strip two tons of spares and nonessential equipment from the storage and engineering sectors. By reducing the water and air reserves to two tons each, we can cut another seven tons. Cleaning out the waste tanks and reducing the food supply to the minimum required for the one-year journey back will result in another three-and-a-half-ton saving. Then, assuming that we dump the habitats, saturnsuits, and spacesuits, we can shave off another ton. The stripped mass is thirty-six tons."

"That doesn't sound like enough," said Rod. "What did Jeeves say?"

"The required fuel at takeoff is sixty-nine tons."

"We only have sixty," said Rod, pausing before he put another bite of his dinner in his mouth. "Not good enough." He finished his bite and started to chew mechanically at his food, his flickering eyes showing that his brain was still in high gear. "Got to do something about that burn at apogee. It's costing us four klecs." He swallowed and turned to Chastity. "Think you can harpoon one of those ice blocks at the Trojan point and brake us to a halt, Chass?"

Chastity, who had been uncharacteristically silent for a long time, brought herself back from her own self-induced problem-solving trance.

"Already looked at that earlier," she said. "Even assuming that I hit my target, the penetrator doesn't pull out under the strain, and the tether doesn't snap under the four-gee stress, to get rid of the four-klec velocity difference before we run out of tether requires getting rid of over two-and-a-half gigawatts of heat. The radiators would melt almost instantly. Can't stop that way."

"If we can't use the tether, then why take it along?" asked Pete. "I don't remember you mentioning that in your list of cuts, Doc."

"I didn't!" said Dan, his face brightening up. "There must be tons of mass available there. Jeeves and I didn't include it in the first round of cuts because the tether is being used to hold the reactor." He headed back to the console inside the engineering sector door.

"If we leave the tether behind, then that means we leave Peregrine stuck with the burden of the reactor," said Sandra, a disturbed frown on her face.

"I'm sure if you were to ask Peregrine, she would be glad to bear that burden rather than have her good friend Sandra die of starvation," said Rod in an irritatingly patronizing tone, made all the worse by the fact that the speech was delivered with Rod's eyes not looking amicably at Sandra, but instead focused firmly on Dan's back, seemingly trying to pull a solution to their predicament out of Dan by sheer willpower.

When Dan finally turned back from the console, Rod instantly knew the answer. "Got four more tons off," said Dan. "*Sexdent* is down to thirty-two tons total mass."

"How much did we miss by?" asked Rod.

"To get our required burn of thirty-two klecs, we need sixty-one tons of meta," replied Dan.

"And we have sixty . . ." said Rod in a resigned tone. He looked around at his crew, taking command with his personality. "You can't fight the cold reality of the rocket equations. It looks like we're not going home anytime soon. We'll just have to wait for the rescue ship to get here, then use the last of our fuel to go up to meet them."

There was a long silence as the crew faced the seriousness of their situation.

"It sure doesn't look good," Dan finally said. "Even if the tether and reactor survive the two years it will take for the rescue ship to arrive, we'll be close to death from malnutrition. The chemsyns can make simple carbohydrates, but they can't make all the vitamins we need."

"And every liter of carbohydrate costs us about three liters of meta," Pete reminded them.

"We have to meet the rescue ship at least halfway," Rod reminded them. "If we have to start using meta to keep us alive, then we're as good as dead."

"When the time comes to die," said Sandra, "I hope we can be brave enough to end our lives properly."

"Wha'dya mean?" said Pete. "I'm going to fight on to the bitter end."

"Before we die, we should relieve our host of the burden we placed on it. We should cut the lines that hold *Sexdent* on Peregrine's back, have Peregrine roll us off, and use the last of the meta in the ship to unwind the Hoytether from around Peregrine's body," said Sandra.

"You're right," said Dan. "If we don't, then we'll be condemning the poor creature to carry us around for the rest of its life—like the albatross around the neck of the Ancient Mariner."

Sandra rose, a determined look on her face. "But until that time comes," she said, "I'm going to make myself useful by learning as much as I can about the rukhs and the other lifeforms on Saturn and send it back to Earth so the follow-on mission gets off to a good start in their relationship with the lifeforms on this planet."

Rod also rose, his face even more somber than Sandra's. "Things don't look good. I would recommend that each of you make sure your affairs back on Earth are arranged properly to take into account the possibility of your death." He then smiled grimly at them as he headed up the ladder to his habitat. "But we're not dead *yet!* Carry on . . ."

The Sun set. The partially eaten dinners were carefully put away, to be finished another day. They now couldn't allow a single calorie to go to waste. Chastity, scheduled for night watch, cycled Pete out the airlock. There, Pete explained to a waiting Uppereye that she would have to educate herself by talking with Jeeves through the portable console, since Sandra wasn't coming out for language lessons this night. Pete then ducked in between two of the engines at the base of *Sexdent* and squirmed into the meta factory airlock.

After resetting the airlock so it was ready for Pete's return, Chastity dropped by the ladies' before she started her night watch duties. She opened her private locker, and after touching up her makeup, she slid the cluster of jangling bracelets off her left wrist and replaced them with the solid-silver-hinged bangle from the locker. The bangle was her private "fat" detector. When the two heavy half-circles of solid metal closed neatly around her wrist, and the heavy catch clicked solidly shut like a handcuff, then she was at just the right weight. This time, however, she had to squeeze hard on the two halves before the clasp caught.

"Half rations for you for a while, Chastity Blaze," she chided herself. She left the bangle on her wrist to remind herself to avoid eating any snacks during her night-shift coffee breaks.

Five hours later, Rod rose with the Sun, brain full of ideas that might possibly be a solution to their problem. As he climbed out of his habitat, he saw Chastity busy at the scottyboard console, working some tether trajectory problems. She too had obviously been coming up with new ideas all night, and was busily working on them, her silver bangle occasionally clicking on the console edge as she manipulated icons on the screen. Rod went to the toilet on the deck below. When he came back up the ladder, Chastity was still engrossed in working with the calculations and diagrams that covered the scottyboard screen.

"Time for me to take over," Rod said as he sat down at the pilot console with his squeezer of coffee. "Why don't you take a break?" Chastity broke from her concentration, looked around the control deck, then out the window at the dawn.

"Where has the time gone?" she remarked, violet eyes blinking tiredly. "Think I'll get some coffee and reheat my dinner from last night for breakfast—can't afford to waste a calorie now."

Chastity was halfway through breakfast when a call came through the emergency speakers on the control deck.

"HELP!"

"It's *Pete!*" yelled Chastity, suddenly springing alive and dashing toward the ladder. "He never came back in from closing down the meta factory." In her haste, her foot slipped halfway up the ladder and she fell heavily back down onto the facilities deck, breaking her fall with her left arm. She picked herself up and climbed the ladder again, more carefully this time. As she climbed, she favored her left wrist, which was turning black and blue under the bangle.

"HELP!" came the call again.

"Jeeves!" commanded Rod. "What's wrong with Pete?"

"I do not know the cause of his cry," replied Jeeves. "Until a few moments ago he was walking through the feather forest. Suddenly he called 'Help!' and I switched his cry to the emergency channel."

"I thought he was in the meta factory, closing it down," said Chastity angrily. "What the hell is he doing wandering around in the forest at night?"

"Help!" came the cry again. "Sh'ave me!"

"He's drunk!" snarled Chastity in disgust.

"The important thing is to get to him as soon as possible," said Rod. "Where is he, Jeeves?"

"I can get a position location by analyzing his radio link signals," replied Jeeves. "But there must be some problem with either the signal reception or the position-finding algorithm, because his indicated position is illogical."

"Illogical or not, show it to me!"

The screen in front of Rod filled with a schematic drawing of Peregrine. There was a flashing red spot at a point above the leading edge of the wing.

"This is the point where the first cry for help came from," said Jeeves. "That position is logical. It is at a position on the surface of the wing." A second flashing light appeared below the first one—at a point in empty space below the leading edge of the wing.

"This is the point the position-finding algorithm finds for the present location of the cries. That position is illogical."

"He's slipped off the front edge of the wing and is hanging below it on something," said Chastity. "I guess he wasn't too drunk to realize he should be using a safety line. Jeeves! Wake Mouser and have it meet us at the airlock door exit with all the climbing lines and hardware we used during the reactor expedition." She turned to look at Rod. "This is going to be like a mountain rescue attempt. I'm going to need all the help I can get."

"Right," said Rod, activating the icon that broadcast announcements inside the habitats.

"Sandra! Dan! Up and at 'em!"

With Sandra staying behind on command watch, Dan, Rod, and Chastity—backs to each other in the airlock—rapidly dressed in their saturnsuits. Chastity found that the catch on her silver bangle had been damaged in her fall off the ladder. Try as she might, she couldn't get the clasp to open and the bangle was much too tight to slip off over her hand. With Pete's life literally hanging by a thread, she quit trying to get it off and just pulled her elastic jacket on over the bangle and folded the cuff back out of the way.

Once out of the airlock door, Chastity checked out her climbing team. Each of them was loaded with as much line as he could carry, plus pockets full of belaying rings and anchor lines designed to encircle featherroots. Chastity had brought along a pocket full of some of her thicker bracelets and finger rings in case she needed to improvise something. They then set off in a bouncing lope across Peregrine's taut balloonlike skin, Jeeves guiding them to the leading edge just above Pete's location.

A half hour later, Chastity found herself rappelling down a large black feather tree right at the edge of Peregrine's wing. Her helmet light on high, she looked over and down.

"I see him," said Chastity.

"You don't sound very pleased," remarked Dan.

"I'm not," said Chastity. "He's hanging on to the tip of a feather tree and it's blowing like crazy in the wind. What's worse, it looks as though he wasn't using a safety line. The minute he loses his grip on the feather, he's a goner." She raised her voice. "Pete! Can you hear me?"

"Yesh . . ." came the strained response. "Hurry . . . I can'd hold on much longer."

"Still drunk!" Rod swore loudly. "You'd think by now he'd be scared sober."

"Really great!" complained Chastity. "He's going to be no help at all in that state. I'll have to rescue him as if he were unconscious." She started to fashion a crude sit harness from the free end of a spare line, laboriously cutting off lengths of tough macropolyhextube line with the less-than-razor-sharp blade of her Swiss Army knife, then tying them together into leg loops, belt loops, and connecting harness. As she was working, she became aware that something was moving toward her over the top of the feather canopy. It was Uppereye, crawling over to see what Chastity was doing. For a second, Chastity thought their problems were over. When they first met, Uppereye had picked her up and Chastity had been forced to hold on to a climbing rung to keep from being hauled off. Although Pete weighed more than she did, perhaps Uppereye could just reach down and pluck Pete from his precarious perch. She instantly rejected the idea. She wasn't sure that Uppereye had the strength needed, and besides, with Pete drunk and scared, it was highly likely he would fight off his alien rescuer and end up dropping to his death.

She then had another thought and stopped what she was doing to unhook another spare line from her backpack.

When Uppereye arrived, Chastity lifted a hand to the creature. Uppereye responded in the usual way by putting the tip of one of her foreclaws in Chastity's gloved hand. Chastity pulled the creature closer until she could reach the "string tie" still hanging around Uppereye's neck above the more-gaudy red bow tie. She grasped the loose end of the tie and lifted up the bowline knot there. If Uppereye was able to tie that knot once, she could do it again.

"Uppereye tie knot," Chastity said, then heard the outside speaker on her backpack repeat her words in an ultrabass growl. Chastity knew that Sandra had taught Uppereye the human word for "tie," but wasn't sure the creature knew the word *knot*. In any case, Chastity had an example of the knot in her hand and Uppereye wasn't dumb.

"Uppereye tie *this* knot," blurted the neck segments of the giant eye, pointing a foreclaw at the knot in Chastity's hand. "Uppereye tie this knot *good*."

Chastity proceeded to tie a large bowline knot lasso around her body just under her arms, making sure that Uppereye could see her exact motions as she did so.

"Chastity tie knot to Chastity," she said as she completed the task. She undid the knot and placed the loose end of the line in one of Uppereye's foreclaws, then pointed down to Pete hanging below.

"Uppereye tie knot to Peter," she said, then added, "Please?"

"Okay!" boomed Uppereye. It crawled off down the feather canopy covering the leading edge of the rukh's wing, the line whipping along behind in the wind. Chastity, now somewhat relieved, controlled the payout of the line while watching in bemusement as the multitude of neck segments marched by her position. The inflated neck was being buffeted about by the incoming air blast, and she noticed that each approaching claw carefully secured its hold before the preceding claw released for the next step.

"Wha' the hell you doin'? You big bug!" came a yell from Pete over the radio link. "You're gonna knock me off! Go 'way!"

"Pete!" shouted Chastity over the radio link. "Uppereye is only trying to help."

The giant eye soon returned, deflating its neck backward in a reverse procedure that had claws stepping backward by Chastity until Uppereye was once again facing her.

"Uppereye tie knot to Peter," the eye reported.

"Good!" said Chastity. She reached into a pocket and pulled out one of her bracelets. It made a nice-fitting "ring" for Uppereye's slightly smaller second left foreclaw.

"Thank you," said Uppereye, holding the foreclaw up so she could admire her new "thing." She inflated the canards on her head, and diving into the wind coming over the leading edge of the wing, flew her head back to its perch on the top of the rukh's keel. As Uppereye left, Chastity could feel deep rumbles coming from the bowels of the great body beneath them. Uppereye was probably calling to her flockmates to come see her new possession.

"Thank *you*," replied Chastity softly to the receding alien.

"How do things look down there?" asked Rod, his view hidden by the feather canopy between them.

Holding on to her safety line, Chastity leaned forward and peered over the edge again at Pete down below.

"The end of the line is now attached to Pete," she replied. "So even if he loses his grip on the feather and falls off, he won't go far." She paused. "Wait . . . there's something funny—"

"What?" asked Rod, concern once again in his voice.

Chastity switched the image intensifier lens in her helmet to high magnification. "Pete must have given Uppereye a hard time. The loop doesn't go under both armpits," she reported. "It goes under his left armpit and then around the right side of his neck."

"Blasted bug trie'ta choke me," muttered Pete over the radio link. "Hurry up! Armsh gedding tired."

"Just hold on with your feet and keep that left arm down as far as you can, so you don't slip out," said Chastity. "I'm going to pull in the slack and see if I can take some of the weight off you with the line." She pulled on the line leading to Pete, taking in meters of it through her belay loop. The line stiffened, then tightened until she could haul in no more. When she looked down, however, she could see that the portion that connected to Pete was still slack.

"Snagged!" she said in disgust.

"What now?" asked Rod.

"I'll have to think," said Chastity, then added loudly, "Don't worry,

Pete. We'll find some way to get you out. Just keep hanging on and don't let go." She reached to the control panel on her chest and punched in a code that switched her radio link to a private channel between herself, Rod, and Dan.

"It's not good," she reported. "The line has lots of slack still left in it. If he lets go, then there's a good chance the jerk at the end of the fall will cause him to slip out of the loop. Even if that doesn't happen, there is also a chance he will either dislocate his left shoulder or break his neck."

"Serves him right, the *jerk!*" exclaimed Rod.

"What now?" said Dan, repeating what Rod had said previously, trying to defuse the situation by getting Rod to return to his normal logical thinking.

"I'll have to get down to him as fast as I can and get him into a sit harness," said Chastity. "I'll need one of you down here at this position to belay me and work the high end of Pete's line."

"I've been having Jeeves feed me a mountaineering video while I've been waiting here in the dark," said Dan. "I've never done a belay before, but at least I've seen the movie."

"It's really pretty simple," said Chastity encouragingly. "Just remember to *never* let go of the slack rope. You'd better climb up the adjacent feather tree. I don't know if this one can hold both of us. Once you get up here, we can pull them together and lash an anchor ring to both of them. Two quill roots are better than one."

Soon Chastity was rappelling down through the tops of the feather forest, following the line leading to Pete and releasing it from its snags between feather barbs as she went. By the time she came to the last snag, she was just twenty meters above Pete. The line she had freed was now draped all around Pete's body. Before she had Dan pull in the slack, she should be down there making sure Dan didn't pull Pete off his precarious perch. With Dan's belay giving her extra security, she started to rappel her way down through the gust-filled air to Pete.

"It's a good thing these saturnsuits have an ultratough skin," she remarked to herself as she saw how deeply the thin macropolyhextube line was pressing into the insulated suit where it passed between her crotch and her thigh. "What I wouldn't give for a nice fat eleven-millimeter kernmantle right now." She found that if she wound the upper portion of the line once around her left arm and let it press against the heavy silver bangle on her wrist, she could relieve a little of the pressure on her thigh region.

"You're shure a schight for sore eysh," said Pete when she came level with him. "I'd like to give you a great big hug and kish. But I'm too busy hold'n on. Jus' like you tol' me."

"You keep doing that," said Chastity reassuringly as she quickly tied two Prusik loops to her main line and stood up in them so she could safety herself to her waist ring with a couple of half hitches of her slack line. "We'll have you out of here in no time."

Her first task was to replace Uppereye's almost "hangman's noose" emergency harness with a decent sit harness that wouldn't kill Pete if he happened to fall. It wasn't going to be easy, since he had both arms and legs wrapped tightly around the feather tip.

"Now, don't think I'm getting fresh," she said. "I'm just going to put a harness around you. First your waist." As she cinched the waistband tight she made sure it was above the roll of fat around Pete's waist.

"There," she said with a sigh of relief as she dressed the knot so that it lay flat. "Your butt may be too skinny to hold up a belt, but even if you fall upside down, you aren't going to slip out of that." She was tempted to give his butt a friendly pat, but considering what she would have to do next, she figured that might send him the wrong signals—especially considering his condition.

"Now come the leg harnesses," she said. She started one knot wrong and was glad her left glove had its special molded plastic nail extensions on the ends of the fingers. The fine nail ends made it easy to pick apart the knot.

"Next, we readjust Uppereye's chest loop," she said, pushing up on her Prusik loops to raise herself to that level. Pete's arms and head were covered with tangled loops of line that had fallen from above. She was reaching through the tangle to get to Uppereye's bowline knot when Pete disappeared!

Chastity looked with bewilderment at the coils of line around her, swirling downward like water going down a drain. With a hissing sound, the loosely flowing line wrapped itself three times around her left arm. The moving, sinuous shape and the hissing sound reminded Chastity of a "Cleopatra's asp" forearm bracelet she had left back on Earth. Slowly becoming aware of the danger, she tried to brush the hissing snake off her arm with her other hand, but the coils piled up against the heavy silver bangle. There was a jerk—

Chastity screamed as her shoulder was nearly pulled from its socket. The last thing she saw, before her eyes filled with tears of pain, was the glitter from the silver bangle as it tumbled off into space, illuminated by the beam from her helmet light.

"Chass! Pete! Are you okay?!" asked Rod over the radio link.

"I think they are, Rod," interjected Dan, when there wasn't an instant reply. "I have tension on both of my belay lines, so there is still a body at the bottom of each line."

"Let's hope there's more there than bodies," said Rod. "Chass! Pete! This is Rod. Report in!"

"Ow! That hur'sh!" came Pete's voice. "Wha' happened?"

"That's one heard from," said Rod.

"Chass! Are you all right?" yelled Dan, now almost annoyed with Pete for being alive. If Pete survived and Chastity died, Dan would never forgive the drunken bum. He was greatly relieved to hear a shuddering sob as Chastity regained her breath.

"I'm alive. But I'm upside down and my shoulder is hurting" came Chastity's reply. "I'll give you a damage report as soon as I get myself upright." There was a long pause. "There's something wrong . . . red splotches on my visor . . . I can't seem to get my left hand to grab the rope . . . now I see the problem . . . I don't *have* a left hand . . . feel faint . . ."

"Quick!" yelled Dan. "Grab your wrist with your good hand before you bleed to death!"

"Good idea," replied Chastity in a faint dreamy voice. "Got it," she reported a short while later. "But now I can't climb my line."

"I'll be right down," said Dan.

"Wait until Rod is there to belay you," replied Chastity, becoming more alert as she began to be concerned about Dan's safety. "Don't rappel. You've never done it before and you can kill yourself. Use Prusik loops instead. Takes longer, but it's safe and sure."

"But—" protested Dan.

"Safety first," replied Chastity. "I'll hold on. You just make sure you get here. I'll be waiting for you."

"Shay!" came Pete's voice over the radio link. "Wha' about me?"

"You can just *hang* there!" yelled Dan.

While he was waiting for Rod to climb the feather tree to him, Dan had Jeeves show him the section of the mountaineering video that showed him how to tie and use Prusik loops. He sort of wished, however, that Chastity had let him rappel down. From what he had seen in the video, it looked like fun.

When Dan finally arrived at Chastity's level his first task was to seal the wound. Chastity had already figured out that the stump was less likely to bleed if the end was covered, so while he was coming down she had loosened the grip of her right hand on her left wrist for a moment, pulled up the end of the elastic saturnsuit sleeve, folded it over the stump, and tightened her grip again. Dan approved of the arrangement as it was and replaced her grip with a couple of tight loops of hextube line.

"How do you feel?" he asked.

"Woozy," she replied. "Strange thing. My shoulder hurts real bad but I don't feel any pain in my hand."

"Shock," he replied. "We'll have to get some painkillers into you quick before the pain really kicks in."

Now that she was safely stabilized, Dan considered his next move. In her present condition, Chastity wouldn't have the strength to make the climb to the top herself, even if he moved her Prusiks for her. He would have to do the climbing for the two of them.

"Cross your wrists over each other, while I tie them together," he commanded.

"Sure," she said agreeably, leaning forward in her harness with her arms outstretched. She was woozy from shock and giggled when a thought struck her— "Strange time for bondage games."

He ducked his head between her now-bound arms and lifted her off her loops. Her body lay limp along his front between him and his main line.

"Hug me!" he commanded, boosting her higher on him with one hand. "Arms and legs both!"

"Sounds like fun," she replied as she squeezed him tight and cuddled her helmet into his neck.

"More like work," said Dan as he shifted their combined weight to his left lark's-foot loop, moved the right Prusik knot upward twenty centimeters, and then stepped up into that loop for the start of the long upward climb. He noticed, however, that the feeling of her body lying across his brought his manly hormones out in force. He found himself performing much better than he would have expected.

"Say, Rod," he called through the radio link after a few steps.

"How about a little boost help with the belay line."

"Sure thing," said Rod. Soon he was doing deep squat leg boosts in synchronism with Dan's steps from one loop to the next, adding the lift of his leg muscles to that of Dan's.

On the way up, the three heard a strange rumbling noise coming from the radio link.

"What's that! Thunder?" asked Dan, a little concerned since he was so exposed and so encumbered.

"Sounds like a rukh talking," said Rod. "But it's coming over the radio link instead of from outside."

"It's Pete snoring," said Chastity sleepily. "Heard it plenty of times."

Dan knew that was probably true. He also knew that it was none of his business what Chastity and Pete did together. But he still didn't like it.

"We need to get her to *Sexdent* as fast as possible and get that wound cleaned and stitched up properly," said Dan, as Rod helped him get Chastity down the feather tree to the rukh's surface. "But we also need to take care of Pete."

"He's not suffering like Chass is," said Rod. "I say let him hang there and sleep it off."

"But—" protested Dan.

"I'll stay here and reassure him in case he wakes up," said Rod. "You take care of Chass and come back as soon as you can. I'm not climbing down there without a belayer up top."

When Dan and Chastity arrived back at the ship, Sandra was waiting for them in the airlock. The minute Chastity had her helmet off, Sandra gave her a pain pill, then waited, hypodermic in hand, for Chastity's shoulder to be bared as Dan cut the top half of the saturnsuit off, leaving only the lower sleeve portion that was wrapped over her stump. Sandra had set up a sick bay on the lower deck using Seichi's bedboard as an operating table, with all of the medical kit's operating tools lined up in a row on the galley counter.

The operation didn't take very long. The loops of fine macropolyhextube line had sliced neatly through the skin and flesh when they had tightened, while the pressure of the bangle had neatly pulled apart the wrist intercarpal joints. Fortunately, there was a nub of metacarpal bone, some muscle tissue, and a portion of palm skin left on the little finger side of the hand, and Dan was able to fashion a small "finger" at the end of the stump that Chastity would be able to use for activating icons on a control screen.

The next day Chastity exited the ladies', face pale with pain. She was still dressed in her blue satin nightgown and was planning on going back to her habitat to continue her recuperation. Even with Sandra's help, the one-handed climb down the ladder had been tiring and she wasn't looking forward to the climb back. First, however, she had to get a drink of water to take the pain pill that Doc had prescribed for her. She needed it. Her shoulder ached, and although it was no longer there, the thumb on her left hand was pulsating in pain. The way to the galley was blocked by Pete, who was opening one galley door after another, looking for something. He turned to face her, eyes bloodshot, chin covered with stubble, hair unkempt, and jumpsuit wrinkled and sweaty from being slept in.

"Where are they?" he asked grumpily. "I always kept the ethanol squeezers in the top locker. I need some 'hair of the dog that bit me.' They're all gone."

"I don't know," replied Chastity, glad that she really didn't know where the alcohol had gone, although she remembered hearing Doc and Sandra discussing various hiding places to keep it away from Pete. "And I don't care!" she concluded venomously, her violet eyes glaring at him, furious with suppressed anger.

Pete was sober enough to realize that an apology was in order. "Chass," he started. "I'm really sorry for what I've done." He reached clumsily toward her. "Let me give you a big hug and—"

"Don't you *dare* touch me!" yelled Chastity angrily at him. *"Ever again!"*

Chastened, Pete backed off. He didn't blame her one bit. There was no apology sufficient to make up for what he had done to her. Sandra came down from her watch station on the control deck to back up Chastity, and Pete retreated to the men's under their combined stare. Sandra helped Chastity get the pain pill out of the bottle so she could take it, then assisted her up the ladder by climbing up one side of the ladder while reaching through to support Chastity's back as she climbed up the other side one-handed. After she had Chastity safely tucked back into her habitat, Sandra returned to her lonely watch duties. She would be "acting commander" of *Sexdent* for a number of hours yet, as Dan and Rod, physically exhausted from hauling Chastity and Pete to safety, both took an eight-hour Saturnday sleep period.

After a week and a half of rest, Chastity got herself dressed, and over Dan's objections insisted on starting to pull her share of watch shift duties. She pretended she didn't notice that every time she was on watch duty, Dan or Rod or Sandra "just happened" to be out of their habitats and busy doing something or other, so she was never left alone. Pete, thoroughly chastened and essentially ignored by the others, spent most of his time in his habitat watching old videos recalled from Jeeves's immense memory.

During this particular nighttime shift, Chastity found that her "guardian angel" was Rod. Rather than forcing Rod to come up with some excuse for his being awake when it was dark outside, she enlisted his help by asking his advice.

"I'm still trying to find a way to fly us out of our predicament," she said to him as she came down the ladder to join him in the galley for a cup of coffee. Now that her arm was not so sore, she was becoming quite proficient at using the little bit of wrist she had left in her left hand to "hook" the side rail on the ladder. "I know we've been through it dozens of times and proven mathematically it can't be done, but I keep thinking that we've just not thought of the right set of trajectories."

"I do the same thing when I'm on watch duty," admitted Rod, leaning his back against the corner of the galley and lifting his squeezer. "Sometimes even when I'm not on watch duty."

"I thought if you and I worked on it together, then perhaps we might come up with some new idea that we wouldn't have thought of separately." She joined him at the galley counter and picked up her squeezer from Kitty. The deck and countertop, like everything else on *Sexdent*, was now tilted at a slight angle since Peregrine was on its nightly climb upward. The tilt of the deck brought their bodies together, shoulder-to-shoulder and thigh-to-thigh. Rod stiffened slightly at the close contact and turned to look closely at her. She had obviously gone through a long session in the ladies' before she started her watch shift, for her makeup was perfect and not a hair of her gorgeously curly black hair was out of place. He didn't have to look down to notice the position of the zipper on her coveralls; his peripheral vision was sufficient for that.

"What I was thinking," she continued, putting her squeezer in the crook of her left wrist to keep it from sliding across the countertop while drawing on the counter with her right index finger, "was that instead of trying to get out to Titan in one big jump, we try climbing out from moon to moon, using a rocket burn at each one, and saving the tether for the moon where it will do the most good."

Rod, instead of looking at the moving fingertip, found his eyes staring at the stump and its strange little wormlike appendage, both still mottled with purple-red scars where the stitches had been.

"We both know that it probably won't work," said Rod. "It's always best to do your burns deep in a gravity well, and the gravity well of Saturn is the deepest one we've got. But . . . you never can tell until you work out the equations. Let's go on up to the consoles and take Jeeves through his paces." He was relieved when the close contact was broken and even more relieved when they got to the control deck where they would be working at separate consoles. His body had enjoyed the contact with her body, but his brain had recoiled at the injury, leaving him in a highly confused emotional state. Now that they were working together on a technical problem and he could think of Chastity as a pilot instead of as a woman, the fact that she had no left hand was no longer important.

For the next four hours, the two pilots worked the problem intensely, trying one option after another. Chastity felt really alive again, the pain in her shoulder and wrist forgotten as her brain concentrated on trying to solve the impossible problem.

Finally, they ran out of variations on Chastity's original idea. Unfortunately, none of them offered any route to escape from their present predicament.

"Well," said Chastity, almost cheerfully, as she shut down the trajectory computation program and put the pilot console back on its standard display. "It didn't work, but it was a good try."

"Let me know when you have another idea," said Rod. "One of these days one of them is going to work." He yawned and looked at the time on the display clock. "Where did the night go?" he said, getting up and stretching. "I'll be on night-shift duty in five hours, so I'd better take a shower, hit the sack, and get a few winks so I'll stay awake."

"I'll be off shift duty in half an hour," said Chastity softly, swiveling in the pilot console chair to smile invitingly up at him. "Would you like some company tonight?"

A frightened, almost panicked look appeared on Rod's face. "Gee, Chass," he spluttered. "I'd love to, but didn't Doc say you're supposed to take it easy and rest?"

Chastity had been expecting that answer and was going to reply, "I was planning on just lying there and letting you do all the work." When, however, she saw that Rod's eyes were focused not on her cleavage, but on the stump of her left arm, she suddenly grew angry.

"What's the matter, Rod?" she snarled, raising her stump and thrusting it at him. "Don't like the idea of fucking a 'crip'?" Rod didn't try to answer, but quickly turned and scuttled down the ladder to the safety of the shower. "And don't bother coming back and saying you've changed your mind," she yelled loudly at his retreating back. "The last thing I want from *you* is a 'pity fuck.' "

A few days later, as the long nighttime climb of Peregrine and the rest of the flock was reaching its end, Sandra noticed that Uppereye had stopped paying attention to the language lesson. She then realized that the normal low level of booming "gossip" among the members of the flock had increased in volume and quantity. Uppereye had been communicating with Sandra in the "upper register" using the air sacs in Uppereye's neck, but at the same time Uppereye had been talking to other members of the flock by generating chordal tones with Peregrine's body that Sandra felt mostly with her feet and gut. Sandra knew from experience that the chordal patterns were different from the usual flock gossip and once again sadly missed Seichi. If he had stayed alive and had spent the last many months learning rukh talk, he could probably have told her what the sounds meant, not only in content, but feeling. As it was, she was restricted to getting a translation in pidgin English from Uppereye.

"Peregrine makes much talk," Sandra started. "Flock makes much talk. Talk is different. Talk this night not same as talk other nights. Why talk different?"

"Eagle not okay," replied Uppereye, handing the portable console back to Sandra and raising its eye up on its neck to leave. "Uppereye go now. Uppereye go help Eagle." Sandra, slightly bewildered, and wanting to ask more questions, watched as Uppereye left, using a combination of claws and canards to make its way back to its niche in the prow of Peregrine.

"What happened?" asked Dan over the radio link from his watch station on the control deck. "Why did Uppereye leave early?"

"I don't really know," said Sandra as she prepared to enter the airlock. "Something about Eagle not being okay. I guess we'll know more once the Sun comes up and we have more light on the subject." As the airlock platform rose up, she heard loud rising tones coming from the front of Peregrine's body. The humans normally only heard those tones when the flock was in a daylight hunting dive. Something strange indeed was going on in the flock.

Petra settled into her niche and chirped a strong signal from the ranging sacs along the front edge of Petru's wing, aiming them at the distress cries coming from Galru far above. She made the chirp high in tone so as to allow her to extract the maximum detail from the return. When the return came, the image it brought was not a good one. Although Galru flew straight and steady, and Galra was in her proper place on the top of Galru's keel, there was something wrong with Galro, for the long neck that supported Galro's eye had come loose and was hanging down from the base of Galru's keel. What was worse, Galro's eye was only half-open and stayed that way.

Petra increased Petru's thrust rate and climbed upward to help. All around her in the dawning light she could see other members of the flock joining her as they hurried to assist one of the more-respected elders of the flock.

"It's Eagle, all right," said Dan, as Sandra, still dressed in her saturnsuit, scampered up the ladder from the airlock. Dan was looking upward through the holoviewport with the biviewer. "I can tell from the white band of feathers near the head of the keel. There's something wrong with Eagle's lower eye. It's hanging down limply. Doesn't look good to me." He froze the pantograph holding the biviewer and stepped aside so Sandra could take a look.

"The brain of the lower eye must have died during the night," said Sandra as she studied the light-amplified image through the biviewer. "But the upper brain must be all right, because the body is flying along normally." There was a long silence as they both thought about the implications.

"It must be like being married for decades and having your spouse die," said Dan somberly. "I've heard it's like losing half your personality. This is bound to be worse. Eagle has lost half its brain."

"At least you can survive without your spouse," remarked Sandra somberly. "Eagle is doomed. Sooner or later its upper eye is going to have to go to sleep."

By the time Petra had brought Petru close to Galru, Petro was awake. Galru was surrounded by other members of the flock, so their help wasn't needed, but they decided to stay in formation with the stricken rukh and its helpers. Since Petra could see better from their position below Galru, Petro let Petra continue flying Petru. There would be no hunt this daylight period.

As the flock moved lazily in a large circle, those in the flock just below Galru lifted up the lifeless neck of Galro and carefully tucked it into its feathered niche at the base of Galru's keel, closing the lifeless, stiffening pincers about feather quill roots to hold the neck in place. A large quill from someone's tailfeather was stripped and used to fasten Galro's head into position by weaving the quill through the white feathers on either side of the keel. With the drag of Galro's neck gone, Galru flew easier, and there was now time to comfort Galra.

"I tried to thinklink again and again, and he doesn't answer," wailed Galra in chordal tones that brought sadness to all in the flock.

"I'm afraid he will never answer," boomed Conro, the eldest of the flock, the balding keel allowing the rich tones of wisdom and authority to rumble unmuffled into the air. "I have seen many such in my lifetime. When the eye stays half-open, the brain behind the eye is dead."

"But what am I to do?" cried Galra, the tones of the sad cry now laden with overtones of fear. "I cannot stay awake forever, and without someone to control it, Galru cannot fly."

"In time, the end must come for all of us," boomed Conro in tones again of wisdom and authority, with additional tones of finality added.

"I'm afraid!" wailed Galra in abject tones of despair.

"We'll stay with you," reassured Falro with tones of sympathy and comfort.

"And sing to you," said Petra, who started up the cheerful "Circling in the Sun Glow" song.

```
              r  r  r  r  r  r  r  w w s  s  s  s  s  s  s
                    a  a  i  i                 o  o  a  a
              i  i  i  i  i  i                 a  a  i  i  i  i
              ngngs  s  s                       r  r  l  l  ngng
              i  i  i  i  i  i  i  i  i  i  i  i  i  i  i  i  i  i
              ngngngngngngngngngngngngngngngngngngng
S  S  S  S  S  S  STST                         G  G  G  G  G  G  G  G
U  U  U  U  H  H  R  R                         L  L  L  L  L  L  L  L
N  N  N  N  I  I  E  E                         E  E  A  A  O  O  O  O
            A  A                               A  A        W  W  W  W
      N  N  N  N  M  M                          M  M  R  R
   I  I  I  I  I  I                             I  I  I  I  I
   NGNGNGNGNGNG                                 NGNGNGNGNGNG
         C  C  C  C  C  C                       WHWHWHWHWHWH
         Y  Y  O  O  U  U                       I  I  O  O  E  E
         C  C  I  I  R  R                       R  R  R  R  E  E
         L  L  L  L  L  L                       L  L  L  L  L  L
      I  I  I  I  I  I  I  I  I  I  I  I  I  I  I  I  I  I  I
      NGNGNGNGNGNGNGNGNGNGNGNGNGNGNGNGNGNGNG
```

When Dan checked for messages before going to sleep, he found there was a return-receipt net-letter waiting for him. It was the one he had been dreading. It was from a court clerk in Houston, informing him that the court had granted Pamela the divorce. The decree would become final after the mandatory two-week waiting period. There was also a video message from Pamela. When the video started, only Pamela was in view of the camera. This didn't surprise Dan, for he had noticed in the header that the video had been sent late in the evening Houston time, long after the kids should have been in bed, for they had school tomorrow. Pamela was quite calm, and had a self-satisfied smile on her face.

"I just called to say good-bye," she started. "And to let you know that in two weeks you will be free to play Buck Rogers for as long as you like. You no longer have to worry about me or the children. We will be well taken care of." Her smile grew more vindictive. "Especially me. I have found someone who *really* cares about me." She reached out and drew a handsome young man into view. The man put his arm possessively around Pamela, and with an arrogant smile, stared challengingly at the camera.

"Dan," said Pamela. "I'd like you to meet Mike Travolta. I believe you know who he is. We are planning on getting married as soon as the divorce is final."

Dan knew who Travolta was, for he had received many return-receipt net-messages from him over the past many months. Travolta was Pamela's divorce lawyer. He probably had started to court his client as soon as he had found out how rich she was. It was no wonder that all of Dan's attempts to negotiate a reconciliation with Pamela had ended in failure. Dan could tell by Travolta's smirk and the fact that he was still at Pamela's house well after midnight that he was already living with her. Travolta started to say something, but Dan, feeling betrayed, turned off the console. He tried to take it bravely, but secure in the knowledge that the habitats were sound-proof, he purged himself of his loneliness and misery by crying himself to sleep. That night he again dreamed about winning the Solar Lottery, but the minute he accepted the check, everyone vanished and he was left alone, with no one to share his riches with.

Two dark periods later, Galra's eye blinked shut once again as the sun set and dusk came to the skies. This time the blinking eye stayed tight shut in sleep. The flock could have wakened her, but that would have only prolonged the inevitable. As the giant body of Galru, no longer under conscious control, slowly slipped into a downward spiral, the voices of the flock rose into the "Death Dive" song as they escorted Galru along the first stages of the long dive down into the darkening depths.

```
d  d  d  d  d  d  d  d  d  d  d
e  e  e  e  e
s  s  s
c  c  c  p  p  p  r  r
e  e  e  a  a  a  o  o  o  i  i  i
n  n  n  r  r  r  p  p  p  p  p  p
d  d  d  t  t  t  p  p  p  p  p  p
i  i  i  i  i  i  i  i  i  i  i
ngngngngngngngngngngngng
         D D D D D D D D D D D D
         E E E
         P P P R R R
         A A A O O O I I I I I I
         R R R P P P P P P
         T T T P P P P P P V V V
         I I I I I I I I I I I I
         NGNGNGNGNGNGNGNGNGNGNGNG
                D D D D D D D D D D D D
                R R R
                O O O I I I I I I Y Y Y Y Y
                P P P P P P
                P P P P P P V V V
                I I I I I I I I I I I I I I I I I I
                NGNGNGNGNGNGNGNGNGNGNGNGNGNGNGNGNGNGNGNG
```

The first indication the humans had of Eagle's demise was the downward tilting of Peregrine at the start of the hunting dive the next morning. During the hunting dive, Sandra and Dan used the biviewer on the control deck to take a careful inventory of the flock as Peregrine shifted positions within the hunting cone. They looked carefully for the telltale white-feathered neck of the elder rukh, but Eagle was no longer among them. The elder rukh had obviously died sometime during the night.

When night came again five hours later, Sandra was already outside on the airlock door, waiting to start the daily language lessons with Uppereye. She had a long list of questions to ask, and hoped that the rukhs didn't have a cultural taboo against talking about the subject of death.

"Eagle is not with flock," started Sandra the minute Uppereye arrived. "Is Eagle okay?"

"Eagle not okay," replied Uppereye. "We sing song to Eagle. Song of leaving forever and diving forever and sleeping forever. Eagle not return, not climb, not wake, ever."

"Why did Eagle die?" asked Sandra.

"Eagle old," explained Uppereye. "Eagle very old. Only Condor

older. When rukh get very old, upper eye or lower eye stops working. Body still working. Other eye still working. Eye soon gets tired
and sleeps. Body dies, air gets too hot. Rukh dies. All old rukhs die
someday."

Sandra knew that the rukhs were at the top of their food chain
and had no natural enemies. Now was her chance to ask some
oblique questions about their physiology and their society.

"How old was Eagle?" she asked. Uppereye paused as it tried to
remember.

"Uppereye not certain. Eagle old when Peregrine was child on
wing of parent. Eagle about sixty plus twenty dimmings of Sun."

"Eighty dimmings?" queried Dan over the radio link from the
control deck where he was on watch duty. "Eighty Saturnian years?
These rukhs live over two thousand Earth years!"

"Not really surprising considering their size, and the thirteen
years it takes between conception and birth," replied Sandra over the
radio link. She then returned to speaking to Uppereye through her
backpack speaker.

"Do all rukhs die when old like Eagle?" asked Sandra.

"Nearly all rukhs die like Eagle," replied Uppereye. "Some rukhs
die other ways. Sometimes body hit by lightning or meteor and stops
working. Rukh falls and dies."

Sandra knew that the various flocks stayed well separated from
each other so they didn't intrude on each other's feeding territories,
but she wanted to find out if they ever fought over territory. "Do
rukhs ever die other ways? Does a rukh ever make another rukh die?"

Uppereye's neck bobbed in surprise. "Words of Sandra not understood by Uppereye. Rukh cannot make other rukh die. Rukh too
big for other rukh to eat." Uppereye paused for a brief moment as
she thought a thought that she had never thought before. "Big rukh
could eat baby rukh . . . but *no* rukh *never* do that!"

"So, rukhs never die by getting eaten," confirmed Sandra. "All
rukhs die from either an accident or old age."

There was a very long pause before Uppereye replied. "The elders say that sometimes rukhs get eaten. A whole flock of rukhs get
eaten at the same time by . . . Uppereye have no human word for
creature. Our thought for creature is large, many mouths, rising,
everywhere, fear, despair, capturing, swallowing, everything."

"How large?" asked Sandra.

"Very large. From horizon to horizon to horizon," replied Uppereye, looking far to the north, south, east, and west with its eye as its neck sacs talked. "Rising up everywhere at the same time, capturing everything, swallowing everything. No escape."

Sandra reserved judgment. "How many mouths?"

"Very many mouths" came Uppereye's quick response. "Sixty times sixty. Maybe more."

"This is getting ridiculous," said Dan. "A creature with thirty-six hundred mouths? It makes biological sense for a creature to have a lot of feet—millipedes for example—but a lot of mouths?"

"At least you've given me a good name for Uppereye's mythological creature, Dan," said Sandra over the radio link. "Millipede means 'thousand footed,' so we'll just use the Latin for 'thousand mouthed,' *Millistoma mythicus*." She switched to the backpack speaker. "We will name it the 'millistoma,'" she said to Uppereye. "Have you ever seen a millistoma?"

"No," said Uppereye.

"Has an elder of the flock seen a millistoma?"

"No," replied Uppereye. "Elders learn about millistoma from elders before them. Millistoma comes once every dimming, when Sun is dimmest. The time when Sun is dimmest comes soon, so millistoma comes soon. Millistoma lives near equator. Flock is flying north to stay far away from millistoma."

Sandra decided to leave it at that. It was obvious that the *Millistoma mythicus* was nothing more than an ancient mythological creature invented by the rukh culture. It was probably invented to explain the occasional disappearance of a flock of rukhs to a violent storm. Although the humans had yet to see a tornado on Saturn, Sandra didn't doubt that they could be generated. Any tornado on Saturn would be bound to be a big one—big enough to tear a flock of flimsy balloon-bodied rukhs to shreds.

It was now time for Uppereye to ask questions. "Do humans die?"

"Yes," said Sandra. "Most humans die old. For same reason rukhs die old. Part of body stops working. Sometimes brain behind eyes stops working. Sometimes part of body stops working." She used the portable console to display an image of the inside of the human body and showed Uppereye some of the major parts that could fail. "Sometimes humans die young. A thing hurts the body and it stops working before it gets old. Seichi was hurt by things from the reactor and died young."

"Things can make you die?" asked Uppereye. She lifted the end of her "shoestring" necktie and looked at it quizzically.

"A human can make a weapon out of anything," muttered Dan over the radio link. "Even a shoestring necktie. Makes a good garrote."

"Things used the wrong way can make you die," said Sandra to Uppereye. She suddenly had horrible visions of future flocks of rukhs engaging in warfare using sac-rupturing rapiers made from sharpened radio antennas, garrotes and slings made from macropolyhextube line, and high-altitude-dropped flechettes made from anything small, sharp, and dense. She would have to make sure that the things the rukhs got from the humans in exchange for their polar helium were carefully screened for the weapons potential—although she had to admit Dan was right. Given enough ingenuity, anything could be turned into a lethal weapon. Sandra was afraid that Uppereye would ask her whether humans killed other humans, but fortunately the line of questioning went off on another tack.

"What number of dimmings when old human die?"

"Humans get old and die at about sixty plus twenty Earth years—not quite three dimmings," replied Sandra.

"That makes Uppereye sad," came the reply. "Uppereye like Sandra. Uppereye want to be friend of Sandra for whole life, but Sandra will soon get old and die."

Sandra thought for a long while before replying. Although the humans were working and hoping that they would survive their present predicament, the chances of their dying for one reason or another before the rescue ship got there were realistically quite high. She finally decided that it was important that Peregrine be prepared for their death if it finally came.

"Sandra may die before she gets old," she replied. "Sandra may die soon. All humans on *Sexdent* may die soon." She used the portable console to generate a cartoon picture of Peregrine's body with the reactor hanging below it on the end of the Hoytether. "This is reactor," she said, pointing at the glowing image on the screen. "Reactor not okay. If reactor stops, then humans not be able to go home. Humans must stay on Saturn. Humans soon eat all human food. Humans cannot eat rukh food. Humans die. To not die, humans must go home."

"Uppereye not understand word. What does word 'home' mean?"

" 'Home' is the place where a person lives," said Sandra. As she said it, she suddenly realized that what was obvious to a human was completely unknown to a rukh. The flock had no "place" to call "home." They wandered from thermal to thermal, drifting along with the trade winds, moving slowly with the seasons back and forth over the equator. She then realized that the rukhs did have a home—it wasn't a mere "house," however, it was something bigger than that—a whole planet. Sandra looked upward at the sky. The five-hour night was nearly over. During their session together, Uppereye had flown Peregrine steadily upward, gaining altitude for the next day's hunt. They were now well above the water clouds and the ammonia clouds above were sparse. In the east, there was a brightening of the sky, heralding the imminent arrival of the Sun. "My home is out in that direction," she replied, pointing to the east. "Although it is hidden by the light from the Sun. My home is Earth. You call it 'Parent,' the larger globe of 'Parent-and-Child.' You have a home too. It is Air." She activated the portable console again and brought up the diagram of the solar system. After showing Uppereye where on Earth she had her house, Sandra showed her pictures of her relatives—Sandra's equivalent of Peregrine's flock.

"Okay," replied Uppereye finally. "I now understand. Home is where you are happy, have much to eat, and have many friends to talk to. If Sandra stay here, Sandra will have only a few friends to talk to, Sandra will not get enough to eat, and Sandra will die. Uppereye not want Sandra to die. Uppereye want Sandra to go home."

I only wish you could fly us there, thought Sandra to herself as she started to put away the portable console. Above her on the control deck, Dan started the airlock cycle that would let Sandra inside. He gave a yawn. It had been a long night. It was time for him, Sandra, and Uppereye to all get some sleep.

Sandra exited the airlock onto the facilities deck, where Dan was having a light supper before going to bed. Dan looked worried.

"I think Chastity is having problems," he said. "She's supposed to follow me on watch duty and she's not out of her habitat yet."

"That's not a good sign," replied Sandra.

"Tell Rod when he gets out of the men's that he'd better take over the watch," said Dan, taking his medical kit out of the engineering sector locker. "I'll go check on her."

When the hatchdoor slowly opened to his tap, Dan was dismayed at what he saw. Chastity's countenance was contorted with pain and her eyes were red. It was obvious she had not slept much during the night period, if at all. He quickly slid inside to join her and shut the hatchdoor behind him to give them some privacy.

"I keep telling myself that it's all imaginary," said Chastity bravely. "But it still hurts. Hurts so bad I can't get any sleep."

"What hurts?" asked Dan sympathetically, stroking perspiration-wetted wisps of errant jet-black hair from her forehead.

"My fingers," replied Chastity. "The fingers I don't have. They feel like they're being crushed in a red-hot vise. Yet they can't be hurting. They're not there."

"They're called phantom pains," said Dan in a professional tone. "But they're real enough. The injured nerve endings in the stump are sending messages back to your brain, which is misinterpreting where the pain is. You should have come to me earlier instead of trying to tough it out." He pulled a hypodermic out of his kit and gave her a shot. "Sometimes massage helps," he said, taking the stump between both his hands and gently kneading it with his fingers.

"Stop!" she cried, pulling her arm away. "How can you stand to do that! It's so ugly . . . *I'm* so ugly . . . I don't blame Rod for not wanting to sleep—"

"*Wait* a minute, there," interrupted Dan loudly, trying to get her to think logically instead of emotionally about her condition. "You're not ugly . . . you're *beautiful!* You have one of the most beautiful faces on Earth—you know yourself that you are now as beautiful as Elizabeth Taylor ever was. If you had not been such an excellent space pilot, you could have *easily* become a video star. Yes, you have lost a hand, but you still have one of the most desirable curvaceous bodies a man could ever wish for."

"Are you positive about that?"

"Yes," replied Dan with certainty, allowing his eyes to stare at her cleavage to emphasize the point.

"Then sleep with me!" said Chastity almost desperately, pulling him toward her with her good hand.

"I would be honored to sleep with you," he said, giving her a strong, long hug and a lingering kiss. "There is nothing I would enjoy more than making love to you, passionately and fiercely and softly and naughtily and adoringly and lovingly." He pulled back and looked her straight in her deep violet eyes. "But I can't. I'm still technically married, and I may yet be able to win Pamela back and save my family. I could never do that if I had been unfaithful."

He reached again for her stump and continued to massage. "The shot should be taking effect by now," he said.

"It is!" said Chastity, surprised that she hadn't noticed that the pain had gone. A pleased smile brightened up her otherwise sodden face. "Thanks for all those nice words about how beautiful I am. They really cheered me up. I won't argue with you about them, but just pretend you really meant them."

"I *did* mean them," Dan replied. "Chastity, you are the most beautiful, most desirable, most wonderful woman in the world. You're smart, you're fun, and God knows you're sexy . . ." He let go her stump. "I'd better go."

Chastity stiffened and pulled back her stump. "Of course you'd better go! Of course! How could I have forgotten? How could *any* of us have forgotten! You're married. Married to a mewing little cat with the face of a doll and about as many brains! That selfish little idiot has all your loyalty—all your love!" Frustration rose in her throat, choking her.

"God no!" Dan spat out angrily, shaking his head in vehement denial. "Don't you get it? It's you I love! I love you totally . . . completely . . . I want you more than I have ever wanted anything in my life . . . but I'm not going to trade in the love I feel for you just to become another roll in the hay when your ego needs petting."

Chastity looked at Dan's angry face in amazement. She had seen Dan argue with Rod, fight with Pete, even suffer through Pamela's tirades, but she had never seen him truly angry.

"I have been watching you. Wanting you—as you made yourself available to each man you met, as the mood suited you. At first I burned—God, how I burned with jealousy. But then I saw that it didn't matter. It didn't matter to *them*. It didn't matter to *you*. It was just sex. It wasn't important. But the way I feel about you. That's important. You're important. You deserve a man who is free, really free, to give you the kind of love you need, and the kind of respect that *you* can respect."

Gently, Dan took her into his arms and whispered in her ear. "Soon I will be free. Out of this mess of a marriage. And when we *do* make love . . . it's really going to matter." He didn't let go and

Chastity returned the embrace, holding on tight to him in return.

Later that night Chastity lay with her head on Dan's sleeping chest, listening to his heartbeat through the rough material of his coverall. She was still in a state of wonder. *This is the first time,* she thought, *that I have spent the night with a man and kept my clothes on.* Yet she felt more satisfied than she had been in a very long time. Chastity had first learned about sex on top of a cemetery bench on Earth, looking up at the stars. Now looking up at those same stars through a viewport on top of a giant bird on a planet halfway across the solar system, she was finally learning about love.

"How come no one ever told me?" she asked them.

7

ESCAPE FROM THE WELL

Position: 22.22 degrees north, 108.52 degrees east.

The repeated number 2 for the latitude on the console screen drew Rod's attention.

"That's funny," he mused. "I thought we were at twenty-one degrees north." Later, at dinner with the rest of the crew, Rod asked Sandra about it.

"The flock seems to be slowly drifting northward," he mentioned to her. "We passed over the twenty-two-degree north latitude line yesterday. What's going on? Every degree north we move will make it that much harder to get off this gasball when the rescue ship arrives."

They all knew the chances of their still being alive when the rescue ship arrived were minuscule, but the only thing keeping them going was hope, so those negative thoughts were never mentioned aloud. They always said "*When* the rescue ship arrives," not "*If . . .*"

"It's because the rukhs are afraid of the millistoma," replied Sandra. "It's coming up to the time in the year when the millistoma is supposed to rise up out of the depths and swallow everything in sight. Since it supposedly lives near the equator, the flock has gone far north to stay away from it. The rukhs actually prefer hunting near the equator. There's more food available there. Later on in the Saturnian year, when the threat from the millistoma is less, they'll be heading back south."

"Say! That may be the solution to our problem!" said Rod excitedly. "Chass and I have been doing all our trajectory calculations
assuming we were going to have to launch from twenty-one degrees
north. If we can get Peregrine to fly us to the equator, then we
might be able to get off this planet all by ourselves, without having
to wait for a rescue ship. The gravity force is weaker at the equator and the rotational velocity is higher, so we get more of a boost
from the planet." He put his dinner aside and headed for the ladder to the control deck, the others following. Settling himself at the
pilot console, he tapped an icon on the screen. "Jeeves! If we take
the nonessential mass off *Sexdent,* but keep the tether so we can
unwind the reactor from Peregrine, how much delta vee will our
sixty tons of meta give us?"

"Approximately twenty-nine kilometers a second" came the reply.

"And how much delta vee do we need to reach our fuel tank in
the orbit of Titan if we launch, not from twenty-one degrees north,
but from the equator?"

"Taking into account the J-sub-two gravity term, subtracting off
the rotational velocity of the planet, and adding the drag and gravity losses, the velocity increment needed at launch to enter an elliptical orbit with an apoapsis at the orbit of Titan is 27.5 kilometers
per second," replied Jeeves.

"And we have twenty-nine," said Rod. "More than enough, with
plenty to spare."

"And to circularize the orbit at the Trojan point in Titan's orbit
that contains the fuel tank, another burn at apogee of four kilometers per second, for a total delta vee requirement of 31.5 kilometers
per second," concluded Jeeves.

"Right . . . forgot about that burn," said Rod with a dejected shake
of his head. "Even if we strip *Sexdent* bare we can't meet that target." He turned around and looked apologetically at the crew. "Looks
like the gain we got from going to the equator wasn't as much as I
thought."

There was a long silence as the implication of the numbers sank
once again into the assembled crew. For a while it had looked like Rod
had found a way out of their predicament, but now it seemed their
hopes had been dashed once again on the harsh cold rocks of the
rocket equation. But Rod and Chastity were not the type to give up.
Both had gone into their test-pilot-in-trouble mode—twitching eyes

staring blankly, body motions and breathing slowed to glacial pace.
"Use Titan to help us stop—" Chastity finally said.

"Of course!" said Rod, coming out of his trance. "Jeeves, instead
of stopping at the Trojan point of Titan, how much delta vee do we
need to stop using Titan's gravity well? Once we circularize our orbit
there, we can drift over to the Trojan point."

"The required burn for a circular capture orbit around Titan is
three kilometers a second, for a total mission delta vee of 30.5 kilometers a second."

"Fifteen hundred klecs short," said Rod, discouraged again.
"Might as well be a billion."

"Wait!" said Chastity. "We don't want a circular capture orbit
around Titan. Our fuel depot isn't at Titan, it's out at the leading Trojan point. What we want is a highly elliptical orbit around Titan that
stretches out to that Trojan point."

"Good thinking," said Rod, cheering up again. "Jeeves. Recalculate the capture delta vee about Titan assuming the capture orbit
is one that is just a fraction of a klec of an escape trajectory."

"The required periapsis burn at Titan is now two kilometers per
second," replied the level voice of Jeeves, "with a total mission burn
requirement of 29.5 kilometers per second."

"Damn!" said Rod. "Still half a klec short. In orbital mechanics,
a near miss is as bad as a mile." He turned to Dan. "We're going to
have to strip more mass off *Sexdent*. To get those last five hundred
meters per second of velocity, we're going to have to leave another
ton of something behind. Which is least important, food, air, or
water?"

Dan frowned and paused, not wanting to make the decision.
"You're already assuming a stripped ship where all three of those are
cut past safe limits. We can't cut any one of them any more—"

"Then our only alternative is to leave the tether behind," said
Rod, driving the point home by adding, "leaving our best friend on
Saturn with a heavy burden it will have to carry for the rest of its
thousand-year lifetime—unless, of course, that heavy burden short-
ens that lifetime." He paused to look directly at Dan with eyes half-
veiled by lowered eyebrows at the base of his brow, a brow deeply
furrowed by the demands of command responsibility. "As our physi-
cian, you are the person most qualified to make decisions that affect
the future health of the crew. Which should it be, Doc? Risking Pere-

grine's future health or risking *our* future health? One or the other has to be put at risk to get us that last five hundred meters per second." Rod didn't help Dan out by making reassuring noises, but continued to look gravely at him, patiently waiting for an answer. Dan looked down at the deck, avoiding the intent, demanding stare from Rod's eyes. The seconds ticked on . . . Suddenly Dan's eyes blinked wide as he thought of something. He looked up at Rod.

"Five hundred meters per second," repeated Dan. "That number reminds me of something. Did Jeeves count in the winds?"

"Winds?" asked Sandra, turning to Dan with a slightly puzzled look.

"No, I did not," replied Jeeves.

"The equatorial trade wind bands that blow in the same direction as Saturn's spin," explained Dan to Sandra. "I remember reading that they often reached velocities as high as five hundred meters per second."

"Jeeves!" said Rod, switching his voice tone to command. "Recalculate required mission velocity assuming a wind-assisted launch at the equator."

"The required mission velocity increment from *Sexdent*'s rockets is now estimated at twenty-nine kilometers per second," announced Jeeves.

"Wonderful!" cheered Sandra. "We can go back home without putting either us or Peregrine at risk."

"Zero margin," muttered Rod grimly. "But at least it isn't a negative margin anymore. I don't like it, but we'll have to live with it." He turned to Chastity, who had come out of her trance. "We'd better both go over all of Jeeves's calculations and assumptions."

"They'll probably hold up," Chastity said. "Jeeves is no dummy." She turned and activated her console screen, the single digit at the end of her left arm alternating with the five digits at the end of her right arm. With Dan's love and emotional support aiding her already strong personality, Chastity had come to terms with her disfiguring injury. Although the fingernails on her right hand were still kept trimmed so they could operate the joyball controller precisely, they were now each brightly painted, this week with miniatures of the five most picturesque planets—Earth, Mars, and Jupiter with their surface features, and Saturn and Uranus with their rings—on a jet black matte background. She had also completely adjusted to the limitations of her left arm and now casually but affectionately referred to its grublike appendage as her "pinky." In addition to punching icons on her console, her left-hand pinky was useful in tasks like painting the fingernails on her right hand—using nail polish brushes modified with a close-fitting "thimble" for a handle.

"Then we'd better work on the timing," said Rod. "The only way we're going to keep that margin from going negative is to make sure we launch from Saturn at exactly the right time from exactly the right place."

"It isn't going to be easy convincing Peregrine to fly us south to the equator," warned Sandra. "Although you and I know the milli-stoma is a myth, the monster is real to the rukhs."

"Convincing Peregrine is *your* job," said Rod gruffly, turning away from her to face the pilot console. "I'll tell you where and when, and you make sure Big Bird gets us there."

Sandra looked dismayed. There was no way that she could make the creature perform to schedule.

"We should have a launch window about every eleven hours," Chastity said to her reassuringly. "When the launch point is on the opposite side of Saturn from Titan. You just get Peregrine to take us to the region with the highest east wind velocity and fly along it for a few days, and Rod and I can work out the best timing."

"There's the little matter of damage to the launch pad," said Dan. "After getting all this cooperation from our alien friend, it just doesn't seem like a proper way to say good-bye—frying it with our exhaust when we leave."

"That won't be a problem," said Sandra. "In order to make sure Peregrine didn't dump us off its back, one of the first words that Seichi and I learned was their word for doing a roll maneuver. I got both Uppereye and Lowereye to promise that they wouldn't roll us off Peregrine's back. When the time comes, I'll ask for the roll and we'll be launched."

"Hmmm," said Rod. "We'll lose a few hundred meters in altitude before we can start our engines safely. We'll have to put that in Jeeves's launch model."

"We want to start at as high an altitude as possible," said Chastity. "How high can Peregrine take us?"

"I don't know," said Sandra. "I'll make it a point to ask during my next session with Uppereye."

"Actually, it's a combination of both launch altitude and launch velocity that needs to be optimized," said Rod. "I know that Peregrine can reach over two hundred klours in a dive. That amounts to fifty meters a second. With zero margin, every meter-per-second helps. How fast can Uppereye fly Peregrine when she really puts her mind to it?"

"I'm sure she doesn't know," said Sandra. "But if Pete or Doc can rig up a way to measure our velocity with respect to the air, I'll talk Uppereye into trying bursts of high-speed flying at various altitudes."

"I'm going to be pretty busy disconnecting the meta factory from the ship," said Pete.

"I'll come up with an airspeed indicator," said Dan. "Probably along the lines of an anemometer. Uppereye or Lowereye can hold it up in the airstream near the prow."

"They'll like that," said Sandra. "Another 'thing' for them to keep after we're gone. Can you make it so they can read the speed? They would love that—probably try harder to fly at top speed to make the indicator read higher."

"If it'll inspire them to do that, then I'll definitely make sure they get a speed indicator. Should it be digital or analog?"

"Something like a thermometer probably would be easiest for them to interpret—the longer the red line on the indicator, the faster they're going."

"Thermometer it is!" said Doc. "I'll just steal the electronic one on the food freezer and replace the thermocouple voltage input with voltage from a jury-rigged anemometer. Hope they don't mind measuring their flying speed in 'degrees C' instead of 'klours'. . . ." He got up, opened up the door to the galley storage compartment, and started looking at the fastenings for the thermometer on the freezer compartment.

Now that they had a definite plan, everyone cheered up as they went into action, trying hard not to let themselves think too much of the slim margin that they had.

At the language lesson the next night, Sandra talked to Uppereye about their new plan for returning to Earth. Fortunately, having the pictorial capability of the portable console made it easy to explain, especially since Uppereye, being jet powered, knew firsthand about the concept of action and reaction, and being an astronomer, already knew that objects moving in free fall moved along elliptical orbits.

". . . then, after we fill *Sexdent* with flame juice, we dive once again around Saturn, use the flame juice to push *Sexdent* so it flies even faster, then we fly off home to Earth."

"Sandra go home," said Uppereye. "That make Uppereye sad."

There was a long pause as the two highly dissimilar creatures thought about how much each would miss the other. Sandra tried to think of something reassuring to say. She expected that one day she would come back to Saturn as part of the Space Unlimited crew assigned to the orbiting space station monitoring the polar meta factories. The monitoring crew would need to have someone knowledgeable assigned to be "liaison" to the rukhs. But all of that was far in the future, and Sandra couldn't promise that she would return. Even if she did return, it was doubtful that she would ever again come eye-to-eye with her friend. The cost and the risk of visiting the deep gravity well of Saturn were just too high. The best the two could ever hope for would be a video link through a radioisotope-powered transponder parachuted down to the flock once the orbital space station had been set up.

It was Uppereye that broke the poignant silence. "Uppereye more sad if Sandra die. Uppereye happy Sandra go home and not die. Uppereye help Sandra go home."

Initially it was easy for Uppereye to convince the rest of the flock to head back south again. The hunting was better there and they would be doing that anyway in the not-too-distant future once Saturn had passed its aphelion and the Sun, having reached its farthest point and being its dimmest, started to brighten again. But as the flock drew closer to the equator, the instinctive fear of the millistoma grew ever stronger.

"The flock is slowing down," Rod complained to Sandra one evening. "We've been stuck near ten degrees north for the past three days. Can't you get them to keep moving south?"

"Uppereye has been doing her best," said Sandra. "But the elders of the flock are advising caution. Can't we launch from here? Surely the difference in Saturn's rotational speed at ten degrees north can't be that much different from the speed at the equator."

"It isn't," replied Rod. "Only one hundred and fifty meters a second. But what we need is that five hundred meters a second from the equatorial winds. If we don't have that, we have negative margin."

Dan spoke up. "Don't forget we've got plenty of food, now that we know we don't have to stretch it out for two years. As long as the reactor and tether hold up, we can mark time here until the flock feels better about moving farther south."

"I don't like it, but I guess I'll have to live with it," muttered Rod. He turned to Sandra. "Just keep reminding Uppereye every chance you get." Sandra didn't reply. She was glad that Chastity was on watch duty that night instead of Rod. He would have kept reminding her all night to bug Uppereye about heading south. She finished her meal and headed for the airlock door to go outside for the nightly language lesson.

"Dawn comes soon," said Uppereye as they neared the end of the lesson. "This lighttime flock not hunt. Flock help Kestrel instead. Kestrel be having baby. Sandra ask Uppereye many times about baby rukhs. Would Sandra like to see baby rukh born?"

Sandra, whose eyes had been beginning to blink tiredly as the night drew on, suddenly was wide awake. "Yes!" she cried. "How?"

"Uppereye once pick up Chastity. Chastity heavy, but not too heavy. Chastity hold on to *Sexdent*. Uppereye not carry Chastity away."

"You're damn right you didn't!" murmured Chastity over the radio link from the watch deck.

"Sandra not as big as Chastity . . ." continued Uppereye.

"Humph," muttered Chastity.

"If Sandra not hold on to *Sexdent*, Uppereye can carry Sandra. Uppereye can carry Sandra to Kestrel. Sandra see baby born."

"Hey! Wait a minute!" yelled Chastity over the radio link. "Sandra! As acting commander I forbid it!"

"Let me get some new oxygen tanks," Sandra replied to Uppereye, ducking inside the open outer airlock door. Once inside, she switched to radio link and argued with Chastity.

"Chass! It'll be my *one* chance to see a baby rukh being born. It'll be the one chance of anyone in the *whole human race* seeing a baby rukh being born. I'll take *two* safety lines and make sure one of them is always snug around Uppereye's neck. Sooner or later Uppereye has to come back to Peregrine and I'll come back with her."

"Okay . . ." said Chastity reluctantly, only wishing that Uppereye had the strength to carry two humans so she could go along too. Initially Uppereye had planned to carry Sandra in her claws, but Sandra had another idea. She had Uppereye bend her eye down next to the airlock door platform. With Uppereye's help, she looped one safety line around Uppereye's first neck segment and cinched it tight. She then climbed up on Uppereye's head and sat down just behind her eye, legs astraddle her neck, holding on to the cinched safety line with one hand like a cowboy riding a bull. For extra security, in case she lost her grip, she hooked her other safety line to the cinched one.

Feeling as if she were riding a dragon, Sandra watched below her feet as the canards inflated from the side of Uppereye's head, lifting them both high in the air. Once elevated, Uppereye simultaneously air-surfed and crawled across the tops of the feathers, the long neck moving in a sinuous fashion across the feather forest somewhat like a sidewinder snake moving across the desert sands. They soon reached the niche in the keel where Uppereye rested. For the next number of minutes Sandra got to view what it was like being a rukh—master of the air—gazing outward toward the distant horizon. The experience was slightly marred by the occasional splat of a miniature roundfloater on her helmet, but it was exhilarating nevertheless. Fortunately, everything she was seeing was being recorded by the video camera on her helmet, where it was transmitted back to *Sextant* by her radio link to be stored in Jeeves's cavernous memory.

Peregrine's jets pulsed harder and soon the rukh caught up with the rest of the flock, who were gathered in a clump, flying in formation all at the same level. Peregrine's body rumbled and the flock parted, letting them through. At the center of the flock was Kestrel, whom Sandra recognized by the anomalous single black feather in its otherwise colorful tail.

"Hold line good!" rumbled the warning from the neck sacs below Sandra. "Uppereye fly to back of Kestrel."

Sandra rechecked her safety line as the canards inflated once again beneath her feet. This time the flight of Uppereye's head was across the gap between the two cruising birds and Sandra got a chance to look down. This was the view that Lowereye normally had. As Sandra lifted her glance to look ahead to their landing place, she realized that she was quite willing to let Lowereye keep his monopoly on that long scary view downward.

They landed well to the rear of Kestrel's back. The region where Uppereye brought them down was very similar to an analogous region on Peregrine's back. In this rear portion of the upper body of a rukh, the "trees" in the feather "forest" grew shorter, finer, and softer, producing a large oval "meadow" of black down. Running down the center of the "meadow" was a single "furrow." The furrow was Kestrel's vagina, located on the upper, female side of the rukh body. Normally, the furrow was tightly closed—just a long sharp-cusped shallow depression in the black down meadow. Today, however, it was slightly open and moist. Pushing its way out through the opening was an eye! It was a rukh eye on a rukh neck, but it was only two meters in diameter instead of ten.

"We arrived at right time," said Uppereye. "Baby is coming."

Sandra looked around. She and Uppereye were not the only ones watching. A number of the flock had flown eyes over to Kestrel's back to witness the event. Both of Kestrel's own eyes were watching too. All of the rukh eyes were keeping a good distance away, watching from positions near the edge of the meadow. All around her, Sandra could hear rumbling through the air as the rukhs talked to each other.

"What are members of flock saying?" Sandra asked.

Uppereye paused before replying. "Members of flock not singing logical thoughts. Singing feelings like: *Baby nice. Eye of baby pretty color. Baby strong.*"

"Baby talk, in other words," said Chastity over the radio link.

The single small eye was joined by another, and both started to crawl forward through the meadow using the claws along the bottom of their necks. The wind over the back of their parent was quite strong, but the baby eyes held tight to the roots of the down "bushes," the claws along the emerging neck instinctively grabbing and releasing their hold on the roots as they moved along. The neck sacs behind the two baby eyes were not inflated as they normally were in an adult. This puzzled Sandra a little, but rather than trying to interrupt Uppereye with a query about that, she decided to just wait, watch, and learn. The two eyes initially made good progress across the meadow, their two-meter-diameter necks moving along side-by-side through the short down. All this time, the adult eyes maintained their distance while continuing their rumbling comments. The rumbling increased in volume as the base of the baby's necks came in view, dragging behind them a long wrinkled mass of moist downy flesh.

"So that's what a deflated rukh looks like," said Chastity over the radio link.

Soon the hundred-meter-long body was out on the meadow and dragging through the down "bushes." The going now got harder for the two necks. The constant wind soon dried out the down feathers on the body, which increased the drag. The ends of the long deflated wings started flapping in the gusty wind, making the task of the two baby necks even more difficult. Still the adults kept their distance and let the baby continue the struggle unaided.

"Notice . . ." said Sandra, adding comments to the video feed being transmitted through the radio link. "The tips of the wings on the baby rukh have tiny hooks on the end. There are no such hooks on an adult rukh. This must be a juvenile organ like the 'egg tooth' on the beak of some reptiles."

The formation of rukhs around Kestrel shifted slightly, changing the wind patterns across the meadow. One of the eyes of the baby, buffeted by a turbulent gust of wind, lost its grip. Its head end was blown into the air, causing the neck to be "unzipped" from its grip on the meadow and to go flying to the rear. The other eye was able to maintain its grip and the windblown neck came crashing down on its back, its claws waving ineffectually in the air. The shock caused the deflated main body to lift, allowing the wind to get under it and lift it up. The other eye started to lose its grip. Despite the baby's obvious plight, the adults did nothing, although the rumbling talk of the adults changed in tone and decreased in volume.

"Why doesn't somebody *do* something!" yelled Sandra. She slid down off Uppereye's neck, slowing her ten-meter fall by letting her safety line slide through her gloved hands. She hit Kestrel's inflated back with a thud, bounced up, and started leaping across the meadow toward the base of the baby neck that still had a grip. The neck of the baby rukh was bigger around than she was, but she knew that she was much more dense. If she could just grab a couple of the loose neck claws and add her weight to the effort, the two of them could maintain a hold until the other neck could right itself and get its claws gripping again. She had almost reached the baby when she was grabbed in mid-leap by four strong foreclaws.

"*NO!*" said Uppereye in the loudest and most emphatic tone Sandra had ever heard the neck sacs utter. Sandra found herself carried swiftly back to the edge of the meadow, where she and Uppereye rejoined the waiting, watching ring of adult eyes.

"Sandra not help baby. No person help baby. Baby must be strong. Only strong babies are good babies."

Sandra was ashamed of herself. She had allowed her emotions to overcome her scientific detachment. Fortunately, Uppereye had gotten to her before she had interfered too much. The grip of Uppereye's foreclaws hurt where they pinched her waist and limbs, but Sandra decided now was not the time to complain.

Fortunately, the overturned baby rukh head was able to regain its grip on the meadow and together the two heads resumed their crawl toward the front of its parent. The only help the adults gave the baby was that Kestrel's two eyes parted a path through the larger feathers as the two eyes left the down "bushes" of the meadow and entered the forest of feather trees. Sandra could see the need for that. If one baby eye went on one side of a large feather root while the other eye took the other side, the baby would get stuck where the two necks joined at the keel of the still-deflated body. Once inside the protection of the forest, the wind abated and the two necks made good time. It only took a few hours for the baby to make its way across the kilometer of distance from the meadow to Kestrel's prow. There, Kestrel's upper eye had arranged a nest for the baby, right at the front, where it would be constantly under the eye of the female half of its parent. Once the baby was settled in its niche, it opened its two maws for the first time. The onrushing wind filled the maws with air and the baby started to fill its body sacs. Soon its wings were inflated. They stretched out widely from the sides of Kestrel's keel and could be a problem in turbulent weather. It was then that Sandra found out why the baby rukh had hooks on the end of its wing. Kestrel's upper eye reached down on each side of its keel, selected a strong feather, and slipped the feather into the hook at the tip of each of baby's wings. Baby was now securely fastened to Kestrel's keel. Both eyes of the parents started visiting the gullets in the maws on each side of Kestrel's keel, picking out little tidbits with their foreclaws and feeding them to the hungry little one, who was emitting high-pitched hungry sounds from its newly inflated body sacs. One after another, the "aunts" and "uncles" of the other members of the flock took turns visiting the new baby and feeding it bites gleaned from their gullets. Uppereye didn't get to join in. Her foreclaws were burdened with Sandra.

"Sandra see enough?"

"Yes," replied Sandra. "Thank you."

Uppereye tilted its canards and flew back to *Sexdent,* with Sandra trying to apologize all the way back.

The day finally came that they had all been dreading. The reactor control system malfunctioned. The reactor started to heat up past safe limits, but the safety rods quickly shut the reactor down before a meltdown started.

"That's it," said Pete, after checking the reactor status at the scottyboard. "We've got a choice of two states: either we leave the safety rods in and the reactor is cold, or we pull the safety rods out and the reactor heats up until it melts. We're now on the meta-heated backup power generator. I've cut the power consumption as much as I dare, but we're still burning about twenty kilos of meta a day."

"We can't afford to do that very long," said Rod grimly. He turned to Sandra. "It's time to put pressure on the rukhs to fly us south to the equator."

That night, Sandra had a long discussion with Uppereye, who in turn had long discussions with the rest of the flock, especially the elders. Condor, the eldest of the elders, advised continued caution about approaching the equator, for the time when the Sun was dimmest was still many days away and the risk of the millistoma rising from the depths was still strong. The flock, accustomed to following the advice of their elders, decided to stay where they were.

The sun rose and Lowereye awoke to join the discussion. Although Lowereye was less interested in the welfare of the humans than Uppereye, not having spent as much time with them as Uppereye had, he was very much in favor of getting rid of the weight of *Sexdent,* and the weight and drag of the reactor and its long tether. Their burden really spoiled his prowess as a hunter. Peregrine was a relatively young member of the flock. But because of Peregrine's lowered mobility during the hunting dive, Lowereye had found himself relegated by the other young members of the flock to the "Elders ring" surrounding the central feeding portion of the hunting cone. Those holding that position during the hunt would always get plenty of food to eat without having to exert themselves too much. Thus, despite their fear of the millistoma, Uppereye and Lowereye jointly decided to help the humans by leaving the flock and taking them to the equator. Uppereye informed Sandra of their decision.

"Peregrine not want Sandra to die. Peregrine fly to equator so Sandra can go home. Peregrine fly fast. Fly to equator and fly back before millistoma come."

"Before we leave," replied Sandra, "we must say good-bye to the flock and give everyone some presents to remind them of us after we are gone."

"Uppereye not understand word. What is 'presents'?"

"Things," said Sandra. "Pretty things."

"Uppereye like things."

"You will get the most things and the prettiest things," promised Sandra, who had already decided that she didn't really *need* to wear underpants under her coveralls.

Now that a definite course of action had been decided on, the crew got ready to leave. Farewell presents were prepared for all the members of the flock. Pete went outside and removed the rest of the evaporated-gold-covered high-temp polymer multilayer film from the outer walls of the meta factory, where it had insulated the walls from the heat and flame of the rockets during their landing. The sheets of film were turned into large golden bow ties that flashed brightly in the sunlight. Sandra taught Uppereye how to tie a number of different bow patterns, and soon every neck in the flock was sporting a decoration, with designs varying from long flowing single sashes that fluttered in the wind, to tight neck rings of multiple tiny rosettes.

Dan and Pete solved the problem of maintaining future communication with the flock by turning *Sexdent*'s three mechbots into semi-intelligent video transponders. There were three laser communicators on *Sexdent* that had been used out in space for high-speed data links back to Earth. Soon all three cat-sized mechbots assigned to *Sexdent* had the thirty-centimeter-diameter parabolic optical dishes from the communicators installed on their backs while the laser transmitter and receiver modules were connected into the mechbot's computer. The eyes of the mechbots served as the video input to the communicator, while the video output was produced on small displays salvaged from monitor consoles in the meta factory which were attached to the top of the mechbot's head, just above the eyes. Although the display was minuscule in size, during prototype testing Uppereye assured them that its large eye had no problem seeing Sandra's image in the display. Uppereye was especially pleased with the quality of the sound system. Pete had arranged for the optical surface of the dish to be protected from weather and round-floater strikes by an inflated "radome" of tough clear plastic that also doubled as a bass speaker.

The real problem was power. The mechbots had rechargeable batteries, but they had no prime power source. They had depended upon *Sexdent* for periodic recharging. Pete solved that problem by using the optical dishes to collect sunlight during the daylight periods. At Earth, the light flux from the Sun is fourteen hundred watts per square meter. A thirty-centimeter-diameter dish near Earth would collect almost one hundred watts, which would be enough to burn out the communicator's photodetector, so the photodetector had a narrow-band optical filter in front of it that kept out the sunlight, but let in the narrow-band laser signal. On Saturn, ten AU from the Sun, the light levels were lower by a factor of one hundred or more, depending upon the cloud cover that day, so there was no danger of burnout. Thus, by removing the narrow-band filter, Pete could use the communicator's photodetector as a solar cell to convert the collected sunlight into a half-watt or so of electrical power to recharge the batteries in the mechbot. After five hours of collecting sunlight, the batteries would have enough energy stored for a few minutes of video communication.

Because of the multiple cloud layers on Saturn, the communication sessions would have to wait until just before dawn, after the flock had finished their nightly climb to altitude and were well above the water cloud layer. The mechbot would adjust its position on the prow of its rukh host until the dish could establish a laser link with one of the orbiters around Saturn. The orbiter would dump the latest message it had received from Earth, then pass back the rukh's reply. Soon Uppereye was communicating with many new friends on Earth. With Uppereye able to show them how, two other members of the flock were assigned mechbots and started taking long-distance language lessons. Fortunately, the scientists back on Earth had learned a lot about the rukh "language" from listening in on Sandra's and Seichi's language lessons. After Seichi's death, Sandra, who had to work in real time and didn't have a method of reproducing rukh chords, had been reduced to conversing with Uppereye in pidgin English. The Earth scientists had the luxury of time, sound-generating equipment, and computer help, so the language lessons with the new rukhs progressed rapidly despite the fact that the two alien races could only communicate for a few minutes every ten-hour Saturnian day.

Tabby, the mechbot assigned to the now-defunct reactor, was too radioactive to leave with a rukh. Instead, it was recalled to take Kitty's place as outside mechbot, while the humans took over Puss's inside tasks, which had mostly consisted of making coffee and washing dishes.

With an anxious Rod reminding them almost hourly about the dwindling meta supply, the crew completed their preparations. After a hunting dive where the flock had allowed Peregrine to stay at the feeding point of the hunting cone until its gizzards were full, Peregrine flew around to each member of the flock to say good-bye and left for the equator. Since Uppereye now had its own video monitor on its mechbot, one of the last things the humans did was to bring in the portable console that Sandra and Uppereye had been using for language lessons and reinstall it back at the commander's position. *Sexdent* was now ready for liftoff as soon as Peregrine got it into position.

"Say," said Chastity as she turned over the watch duty to Rod two days later. "Peregrine is really moving along. With Lowereye hunting at high speed during the day to make up for Uppereye's slower climb at night, our speed has been averaging a hundred kilometers per hour, which adds up to a thousand kilometers a Saturnian day. We should be at the equator in another eighty hours."

"Good," replied Rod grudgingly. "The faster we get there the more meta we'll have."

They spent the next daylight period pulling in and storing the habitats. Rod wanted to leave them behind, but Dan objected on medical grounds. "We each need a separate tube to get our daily gravity exercises. Besides, having your own place, where you can get away from everyone else for a while, is going to be essential for maintaining our sanity on the journey back. I know for sure I couldn't stand to see *your* ugly mug nonstop for a whole year."

Since the thin-walled habitat tubes only weighed eighty-five kilos each and they had identified a couple of tons of other pieces of equipment and hardware that could be unbolted and dumped, Rod reluctantly agreed. Seichi's habitat and all the other nonessential equipment were then cycled through the airlock and placed outside on Peregrine's back to decrease the mass *Sexdent* had to haul into orbit. Plumber Dan then spent a day replumbing the air and water tanks, adding dump valves leading to the outside on some of them.

The time to leave came sooner than they thought. Four Saturnian days later, as the light from the rising Sun was turning the ammonia clouds above them a bright reddish-orange, Rod checked in on the control deck after breakfast, taking over the pilot console to give Chastity a chance to have something to eat too. "How's it going?"

"Real good," said Chastity, relinquishing the pilot seat. "We're approaching four degrees north."

"Only a few days more and we'll be at the equator and can head for home," said Rod.

"Actually, we might be better off if we make our run today," said Chastity.

"How so?" said Rod, somewhat surprised.

"I've been having the orbiters obtain detailed Doppler maps of the horizontal wind speeds along the limb," said Chastity. "Right now, the eastward velocity of the winds increases as the latitude decreases, but instead of peaking right at zero latitude, there seems to be a double peak in wind speed on either side of the equator. The maximum wind velocity is now at about four degrees north and south. Another orbiter should be coming over soon. Its Doppler should be able to get a good measurement of the wind speeds right at our position. We should be close to the peak." Rod took her seat as she climbed down the ladder to the galley. She was halfway through her breakfast of biscuits and sausage gravy when Rod called down.

"You were right, Chass," he said. "We're smack-dab on the peak.

We can go today as soon as Saturn rotates us around to the proper takeoff point on the opposite side of the planet from Titan. I figure three-and-a-half hours." There was a pause. "That's funny . . ."

Chastity didn't like the tone, so she left her breakfast to cool in the galley and was back up the ladder in seconds.

"The video picture coming from the satellite shows there's a big white spot growing under us," said Rod, pointing to the screen. The console had a small blinking dot that indicated the position of the *Sexdent*. Surrounding the dot was a large white region that showed up in sharp contrast to the typical "Saturn-orange" color of the rest of the equatorial band.

"That white cloud wasn't there five hours ago when we went into darkness at the beginning of my shift," said Chastity. "I distinctly remember, since I was having the orbiter make wind velocity measurements as we crossed the terminator."

Rod now had an enlarged version of the white spot on his screen. "It's really growing fast," he said. "Looks like a gathering of thunderheads building up in the afternoon after a long hot muggy summer day."

"That must be the Great White Spot that the scientists have been asking us to keep a lookout for. According to them, it comes once every Saturn year, right around aphelion. Looks like it's early this time. I'll ask Sandra, she's out saying good-bye to Uppereye since it's almost time for Uppereye's daytime nap." She slipped into the scotty chair and activated the comm link to Sandra's helmet. She didn't talk immediately, since she could feel the rumble of Peregrine's voice through the floor of the capsule, so she knew Sandra was busy listening to the version frequency-shifted by Jeeves.

"What is the problem?" Sandra was saying to Uppereye. There was another rumble, then Uppereye left rapidly, its eye blinking nervously and its multitude of claws pushing against the feathertops to assist the contraction of the inflated neck as Uppereye headed toward the prow of the bird. With Uppereye gone, Chastity spoke.

"What *was* the problem?" asked Chastity. "Although I think I know what the answer is going to be."

"Uppereye got a mind link from Lowereye right after he woke up," said Sandra. "Something about the mythological millistoma."

"I don't think it's mythological," said Rod from the pilot console. "Here's a max-res video image from the orbiter of what is right down below us." He punched icons on his console, and the holoviewport in front of Chastity and the holovisor on Sandra's helmet both lit up with a strange sight. The entire screen was filled with a myriad of cloud columns that looked like a pot of oatmeal boiling on the stove, rapidly rising higher in the pot and about to boil over.

"What a storm!" said Sandra, awed. "We're in for some turbulence."

"More than that," said Rod. "This is a max-res radar scan taken by the orbiter that shows what's beneath those clouds, and rising up with it."

The image in the holoviewports now had superimposed on the visible cloud image a speckled artificial radar image of a pattern of circles. The circles were very close together and formed a semiregular pattern that covered the image from side to side.

"What is it?" asked Chastity. "Looks like the spots on a leopard skin—although they're all of different sizes."

"I've seen something like that before," said Sandra, in a bemused scientific tone. "Remember the ribbonswimmer that Dan and I dissected after it hit the tether? It consisted of nothing but a lot of mouths, each a separate primitive animal, but all connected together into one larger creature, like a sponge or a coral reef. The pattern here is similar. Simple basic element . . . different sizes . . . semiregular pattern . . . but this is so much bigger than a ribbonswimmer. How big is it, anyway?"

"As big as a small state," said Chastity. "Nothing but a lot of mouths, stretching from horizon to horizon to horizon to horizon—"

"Mouths," said Rod grimly. "Thousands of mouths, wouldn't you say, Sandra?"

"Looks like I'd better change the name from *Millistoma mythicus* to *Millistoma gigas*," said Sandra. "Next time Uppereye tells me something, I'm going to believe it, no matter how mythological it sounds. But it's beginning to make some sense," she added, her scientist brain trying to comprehend the meaning of what her eyes were seeing. "All the lifeforms in the clouds eventually fall into the depths—a constant 'rain' of food. This creature probably normally lives down in the boiling hot depths, just like an algae mat at the bottom of a hot spring on Earth, living off that falling detritus. Has to stay simple to be able to survive in such hot air. The rising air column has lifted it up to our altitude."

All of them could feel the acceleration surges beneath their feet as the jets on either side of Peregrine increased their tempo and strength as the giant bird climbed in altitude in an attempt to escape the uprising millistoma.

"You'd better get in here, Sandra," commanded Rod. He met her a few minutes later in the airlock. Instead of turning his back to let her strip down and get into her coveralls, he took her helmet from her hands the minute she raised it from her head. "Forget about changing into something comfortable. I'm going to need you to raise Uppereye on the mechbot communicator right away. You *have* to convince Uppereye to keep Peregrine on a due east course until we get to the right launch point."

Fortunately, the radar images from the orbiter showed that the best escape route lay to the northeast, so both Rod and Lowereye were adequately satisfied with Peregrine heading in that direction. Uppereye brought the air-speed indicator down to where Lowereye could see it, and soon Peregrine was on a course that slowly increased in altitude while maintaining a high speed. Lowereye protested that he could make Peregrine fly much higher and faster if the humans would hurry up and leave. Uppereye passed his concern on to Sandra, who promised that they would leave as soon as they could, and immediately if the danger got any greater.

"You shouldn't have made that promise," growled Rod as Sandra closed down the laser link to the mechbot. "I'm the one that has command responsibility for the crew." Sandra turned to face Rod, her face clouded with exasperation.

"The crew you are responsible for is not made up of just us humans," she said forcefully. "It includes Peregrine. If it weren't for the hard work and bravery of that volunteer member of your crew, we humans would now be slowly starving to death at twenty-two degrees north!" She didn't wait for an answer but headed for the ladder. "I'm going to get out of this sauna-suit and into something more comfortable."

"She's right," agreed Rod in a chastened tone as she left. "We're all in this mess, humans and rukh together, and I'll do my damnedest to get us *all* out." He turned to Chastity. "How does the situation look? Can Peregrine escape the millistoma at its present speed?"

Chastity started tapping on her pilot console, the pinky on her left arm punching Function and Shift icons while the five fingers on her right hand tapped at the letter and number icon keys. The bodies of the crew rocked slightly at each accelerating jet pulse emitted by the giant body beneath them as they waited for Chastity to take Jeeves through the calculations. Soon she had on her screen a cross-sectional view of the surface of the millistoma as determined by the radars on the various orbiters circling Saturn. It contained gently curved "hills" where the upwelling warm air currents had raised the blanketlike body of the millistoma higher, with shallow "valleys" in between. Above the curving "terrain" was a line indicating the climbing slope of Peregrine's trajectory with a flashing white point indicating Peregrine's present position. The trajectory passed well over the highest "hill" on the millistoma surface. At a point farther along the trajectory, on the other side of the hill, was a reddish-purple flashing dot with the notation "Launch Point."

"Right now Peregrine is on an escape path," said Chastity. "We should reach the launch point in two hours." She paused as she studied the drawing more closely. "But the millistoma is still rising, so I'd better have Jeeves make some future projections." She started punching the icons on her screen again. Rod turned to Dan, who had taken over the scottyboard after Sandra had gone.

"In the meantime, Dan, you'd better get Tabby busy cutting all the lines holding us on Peregrine's back. We may have to leave sooner than we thought."

"It's going to be close," Chastity finally concluded. "There is a portion of the millistoma that is rising up right in front of us. According to Jeeves's projections, it might intersect Peregrine's trajectory before we get there."

"How about another trajectory?" suggested Rod. "Preferably one heading due east."

"Tried that option," said Chastity. "There's a 'pass' through the 'mountains' toward the east, but it could close before we get there. The projections are just not certain enough."

"As long as we're not in immediate danger, then we'll wait until the projections are firmer," decided Rod.

The minutes dragged on. When Sandra returned in her coveralls, Rod had her take over his command console so she could open up contact with Uppereye again.

"Explain the situation to her," said Rod. "Do you think she can understand Chastity's diagram?"

"I'm pretty sure she can," said Sandra. "She seemed to understand orbital trajectory diagrams when I drew them on the screen."

"And reassure her that I'm as concerned about Peregrine's safety as I'm concerned about my own . . . and that of the rest of the crew, of course."

Unfortunately, Chastity had to depend upon the radars in the orbiters to obtain accurate maps of the altitude of the surface of the millistoma, so the information on the present position of the millistoma only came sporadically.

"Damn," muttered Chastity as the latest map came in from a newly rising orbiter a half-hour later. Her fingers and pinky flew over the screen as she tried various other cross-sectional views. Rod came over to stand behind her to look at her display, his body swaying slightly as each pulse from Peregrine's jets pushed them ever higher. Chastity pointed with her pinky to the place on the screen where a millistoma "cliff" intersected Peregrine's trajectory. The reddish-purple blinking dot labeled "Launch Point" was on the other side of the "cliff."

"That must be the outer rim of the millistoma body," said Chastity. "The radar doesn't report anything beyond it. But since that edge portion isn't being weighed down as much, it's rising faster than the central portions and forming this long rising cliff in front of us."

"A rising bowl-like structure," muttered Sandra. "Good design for a predator. Drives the prey toward the middle where *all* of it is eventually swallowed. No wonder whole flocks of rukhs disappear with no survivors left to tell the story."

"Looks like the millistoma has us cut off at the pass," said Rod grimly. "If we stay on top of Peregrine, both we and Peregrine will be swallowed. Our chances will be better if we separate and each make a run for it using our individual jet systems." Now that the decision time had come, Rod's commands were loud and swift.

"Dan! Make sure all connections are severed between *Sexdent*, the meta factory, and Peregrine except for the nose tether to the reactor."

"Already done," replied Dan quickly from the scottyboard.

Rod turned to holler down through the grating.

"Pete! Activate the dump valves on the consumables tanks."

"Roger," came the response from below. Soon they could hear the hiss of water and air escaping from the bottom of the capsule.

"Sandra! Tell Uppereye that we'll be leaving shortly. As soon as we leave she should be able to increase Peregrine's speed and out-climb the millistoma. To get us launched she needs to turn Peregrine east and switch to level flight at the maximum speed she can get Peregrine to fly at."

A few minutes later the view from the upper windows of the capsule tilted to the level and the crew could see what was ahead of them.

"Mouths . . ." said Chastity in a voice soft with fear.

"Thousands of mouths," added Dan, his voice echoing her fear.

"A cliffside of mouths. Each ready to swallow us up," said Rod, a brave determined grin on his face. "But we're not going to wait around to get swallowed. We're going to get out of here, even if the time isn't right." He turned to Sandra, who was still using the commander's console to communicate with Uppereye. "How's our speed?"

"Near the maximum Peregrine can attain carrying us on its back," said Sandra. "Uppereye is very concerned about the rate that the edge of the millistoma is rising. She now has grave doubts that Peregrine will be able to fly over the top of the cliff even after we leave. She sang me a final farewell, since she does not expect to survive, but she hopes that we will keep our promise and come back to bring things and knowledge to her flock and to all the flocks on Saturn."

"We'll give her the best escape chance we can," said Rod. "Everybody! Into your acceleration couches and strap in!"

It was less than a minute later when Rod turned sideways in his couch to look at Chastity beside him, the pilot console suspended above her waist.

"Main rockets primed and ready for ignition," she said, anticipating him.

Rod turned to Sandra on the other side of him. Since she still needed to communicate with Uppereye, he had relinquished the commander's console to her.

"Tell Uppereye to roll us off and then get Peregrine out of here as fast as she can," he ordered. "And say 'Thanks and good luck' from all of us," he added belatedly.

As Peregrine started the long slow roll to one side, they felt the tilt on their backs first. Then the black feathers that could be seen out the viewport windows began to move. Soon they were sliding through the feather forest, the feathertops whipping swiftly by the viewports. Suddenly, the moving feather tips were gone and they were in free fall, followed by the pieces of hardware they had abandoned.

"Got it," said Chastity as she activated the vernier jets to fly them away from the falling junk. There was a jolt as the meta factory separated and fell free. Gravity returned as she flew *Sexdent* high up above Peregrine, pulling the long Hoytether loose from the black forest top as she climbed. Verniers thrusting, *Sexdent* raced ahead of Peregrine and dropped down in front, pulling more tether loose from the orange feather forest underneath as Peregrine moved rapidly overhead.

"Don't want to give Lowereye a 'wedgie,'" said Chastity, verniers flashing as she made sure the unraveling tether didn't get hung up on Peregrine's trailing waste appendage. They were soon a number of kilometers away from the giant bird because Chastity was keeping the tether under tension as it unwound. They could now see all of the creature they had resided on for so long. Chastity kept *Sexdent* moving in its great arc until they were high overhead and in front of the leading edge of Peregrine's wing.

"Reactor falling free," reported Dan from the scottyboard.

"Then let's get out of here!" said Chastity, punching the main engines icon with her pinky and lifting the joyball controller with her right hand. The twelve giant magnoshielded meta engines at the base of *Sexdent* burst into a roar and they were pressed into their seats by the acceleration.

"Good-bye and thank you, dear friend," said Sandra through her link to Uppereye. "Now go! As fast as you can!" She closed down the video link to the mechbot and pushed the command console over above Rod. The first thing Rod noticed when he scanned the console was that *Sexdent* was still attached to the reactor through the tether. Its drag was tilting the capsule to one side, causing Chastity to use both the main engines and the vernier jets to keep them on course.

"Cut the tether, Chass!" yelled Rod. "You're costing us apogee!" He started punching the icons on his commander's board to switch control of the tether cutter to his console. "I'll get it for you!"

"*No!*" yelled Chastity. "I'm going to use it!" She turned the other way and hollered at Dan at the scottyboard. "Dan! Pull out the safety rods and bring that reactor up to meltdown! I'm going to give that monster ahead of us something that's too hot for it to swallow! That should take its mind off catching Peregrine!"

Now that he understood, Rod removed his hands from his board and let Chastity take them on up. The main engines roared at full thrust, driving them ever faster toward the distant horizon in their almost horizontal escape from the gigantic planet. The minutes passed, the gee level in the control deck built up as the fuel load the rockets had to push diminished, and they were all pushed into their seats. Sandra looked out first one viewport above her, then the other.

"My god . . ." she whispered softly. "It's filling up the sky!" Ahead of them, the millistoma cliff edge was rising rapidly, as the monster used its jet propulsion to augment the rapidly rising column of air driving the rise of the Great White Spot. The rising cliff looked like a sped-up movie version of the buildup of a thunderhead cloud— except this was the horror movie version where the cloud consisted of thousands of maws, slowly opening and closing, swallowing everything in front of it.

"There are mouths everywhere!" said Sandra, starting to panic. "We're going to be eaten! There's no way we can avoid them!"

"That's right!" replied Chastity cheerfully. "See that big mouth right in front of us just below the clifftop? I've been timing it and we should fly right into it just as it's wide open!" Twisting the joyball slightly, she shifted their attitude slightly so she would hit the mouth dead center.

Sandra turned to look at Rod. "Stop her! *Do* something!"

"It's our only way through the enemy lines, Ms. Ruby," said Rod, laboriously turning his head away from the horrifyingly gripping scene out his viewport to give Sandra a smile and a wink. "You forgot these creatures are all air. Chass is giving us our best shot by flying through an open mouth, so we avoid hitting the front skin of the creature. We're going so fast now we should have no problem busting through the backside of the mouth and out the other side. The ride may be a little rough, though, so hold on tight!"

"The reactor is starting to melt," reported Dan. "I can see it glowing below me out the lower viewport windows. It's almost reached the mouths down below us."

"Good!" said Chastity, cutting loose the tether by tapping on the icon with her left-arm pinky. The reactor, dropping glowing molten drops of metal behind it, smashed into a half-open mouth, pulling the trailing tether behind it. The kilometers-long tether sawed its way through one mouth after another. Spreading away from the widening wound was a slow rippling of the inflated flesh that connected the mouths into one gigantic creature. Reacting to the pain, the millistoma started to collapse in on itself, its mouths automatically closing as the pain message was passed on to the rest of the body so it would avoid eating another painful morsel.

The high-speed capsule beat the pain message to the mouth opening before them. Chastity flew them into the multistory maw, the ultrahot flames from *Sexdent*'s roaring jets melting away an ever-widening hole behind them. There was a sharp twist of the capsule cabin as the nose of *Sexdent* hit the back wall . . .

"Stars!" said Chastity, as they burst out the other side of the giant cloud-creature into the darkening sky. "Let's go visit them!" Minute after minute the twelve engines in the base of *Sexdent* roared reddish-purple flame to the rear, pushing them skyward.

"Thirty klecs . . . thirty-two . . . thirty-four . . ." Rod counted evenly.

"Thirty-five," replied Chastity a short time later, as she pulled down on the joyball and the ship went into free fall.

"We're on our way home!" said Pete loudly, echoed by sighs of relief from Sandra and Dan. But then all three noticed that both Chastity and Rod were strangely silent.

"What's the matter?" asked Dan, turning to Chastity.

"Right speed, wrong direction," she replied brusquely. "Rod and I need to think." The capsule grew silent.

"I'll check fuel level," said Rod. "Okay to rotate capsule?"

"Yes," replied Chastity as she brought up some alternate trajectories on her screen. "Apogee is over three days away. We've got plenty of time before we have to make a burn decision."

The electric motor between the crew cabin and the fuel tank slowly started the cabin rotating one way and the fuel tank the other. Still harnessed in, they felt themselves sliding outward under the small amount of centrifugal acceleration.

"Less than three tons," Rod finally announced. "Enough to give us just over two klecs of delta vee."

"Just as we had planned," replied Chastity. "That two klecs was exactly what we needed at apogee to put us into an elliptical orbit around Titan. Only when we reach apogee, Titan isn't going to be there."

"What happened?" asked Sandra, frightened and bewildered.

"The millistoma forced us to leave too early," said Chastity. "We needed to wait another hour and a half until Saturn had rotated so that our takeoff point was exactly on the opposite side of where Titan will be three days from now when we reach apogee. As it is, our apogee will peak right at the same altitude as Titan, but Titan will be sixty degrees ahead of us. Our orbit will peak at the trailing Trojan point instead."

"Isn't the Trojan point where we want to go anyway?" asked Sandra.

"Our fuel is at the other Trojan point, the one leading Titan," said Rod.

"It wouldn't make any difference anyway," added Chastity. "We can't stop at either one of the Trojan points. Don't have enough fuel."

"Isn't there anything we can do?" said Sandra, almost whispering in her despair.

"I'll have Chass do enough of an apogee burn to make sure we don't burn up in Saturn's atmosphere when we come down again three days later," replied Rod. "But that will just postpone the inevitable." He looked around. "Chass and I'll continue to work the problem. You three can unstrap your safety harnesses and take a break. Just be ready to come back in a hurry in case we think of something to do."

"I think better on an empty bladder," said Chastity, unstrapping her harness and floating off to the ladder leading to the toilets below.

A short time later, Sandra reported good news from the scottyboard, which she had set up as a science console.

"Peregrine escaped from the millistoma!" she cried. "I'm getting a strong signal from the telemetry transponder on the mechbot. The accelerometers are reporting regular jet thrust pulses, strong and fast, while the position indicator has Peregrine at high altitude and moving northward at high speed toward the rest of the flock."

"How did Peregrine manage to escape?" asked Dan, who was having a squeezer of coffee down below. "We were surrounded by mouths."

"I had Jeeves backtrack the telemetry signal," said Sandra. "Peregrine flew out through the gap that Chastity burned through the millistoma cliff edge using the reactor and *Sexdent's* rockets."

They had three days to climb up out of the gravity well of Saturn and three days to fall. Although Rod and Chastity, indeed all of them, thought about various things they might do, none of them promised to get them out of the predicament the millistoma had put them into. It now looked as if the only survivor of the millistoma was going to be Peregrine. Sandra was able to establish communication with Uppereye through the mechbot laser link, but the communication intervals were so short because of the energy limitations of the mechbot solar power collector that there was little she could do except tell Uppereye the bad news and reassure her that humans would be coming back to Saturn even if Sandra wouldn't be able to make it herself.

"Might as well be comfortable on our deathbeds," said Rod grimly as he had the crew reinstall the habitats. He also knew that the activity would help keep their minds off their predicament. Sandra also helped by insisting that everyone take turns helping her take more images of the rings and moonlets as they passed over them on the way out. The scientists on Earth helped by giving them targets to look for. They had carefully scanned the ring images that Sandra and Dan had transmitted back during their climb down the rings and had predicted the locations of a number of "shepherd" moonlets. Soon the catalog of the "Moons of Saturn" exceeded one hundred, many of them now named for inhabitants of Saturn. In addition to names such as Peregrine, Falcon, and other members of the rukh flock, there was one moonlet seemingly completely covered with small craters of various different sizes that now sported the name "Millistoma."

Two days later, they had left the rings behind, and Chastity and Dan were up at the science console taking high-resolution pictures of the region around the trailing Trojan point that they were approaching. Rod and Sandra were having a dinner together down in the galley.

"Haven't you found anything that can get us out of this spot, Rod?" pleaded Sandra.

"Doesn't look good," said Rod with a shake of his head. "We're in an elliptical orbit with the apogee at Titan's orbit, but Titan isn't going to be there to stop us. After we come down, the perigee penetrates the upper atmosphere, and when we hit that, we burn up."

"Can't we fire our rockets?"

"As I said before, we can," said Rod. "And unless Chastity or I can think of something else to do with the remaining fuel, I will have her do an apogee burn, which will raise our perigee slightly and keep us from burning up. But I can't raise it too much, or in our next pass we'll smack into the C or D ring. Even if I stay below the D ring there's a four percent chance we will hit a rock spiraling inward from the D ring. Even if that means that our chance of survival is ninety-six percent, those odds are multiplied each seven days, as we go through the ring passage segment of the orbit. Multiply that probability up over enough weeks and we'll be holed before a rescue mission gets here. Even if we are lucky enough not to be holed, we'll soon use up all our meta. Right now it looks like we'll either starve or freeze to death. Compared to those lingering deaths, a fast hypersonic burnup doesn't sound like a bad way to go."

"What are we going to do!" wailed Sandra, looking up to him for comfort. "I'm scared!"

"Why don't we two go upstairs and take a little break in my tube," said Rod, putting a comforting arm around her. "I've got some laser juice stored there. We can have a little party, just the two of us, and think about something else for a change."

As he followed Sandra up the passageway, he looked up at Chastity and Dan, scanning the space ahead of them with *Sexdent's* telescope. Rod had wanted to leave the telescope behind, but Dan didn't have the proper tools to remove the specialized bearings from the welded frame.

"We've found some icebergs at the Trojan point," Chastity said. "Should be easy enough to avoid them."

"Can't we use those icebergs to stop?" asked Sandra, turning around on the ladder to look down at Rod floating by one hand behind her.

"Won't work," said Rod. "Chass and I looked at that long ago. Let me show you." They ottered to the top of the ladder and drifted over to Chastity's console. After admiring the picture of the iceberg, Rod punched some icons and brought up a diagram and some tables.

"When we arrive at apogee, we'll be traveling at 1.7 klecs, while the icebergs at the Trojan point will have Titan's orbital velocity, which is 5.6 klecs. We'll be going 3.9 klecs slower than Titan. It would be nice if we could use the tether to just swing around the iceberg. We would end up going the other way, only this time we'd be going 3.9 klecs *faster* than Titan. We'd soon catch up with it, and if we aimed our trajectory right, we could spiral into Titan's gravity well, use the last bit of our fuel to do the perigee burn at Titan, as we had originally planned, and come out on a trajectory that would float us off to our return tank full of meta at the leading Trojan point."

"Then why don't we do it that way?" asked Sandra, puzzled.

"Playing 'swing around the iceberg' at the end of a two hundred-kilometer tether while you're moving at a velocity of 3.9 klecs means pulling nearly eight gees," interjected Chastity. "Although we humans can take it, the tether can't. Can't be done that way."

"We also looked at using the rockets to slow *Sexdent* down before we start the swing. If we lower the initial velocity enough so the tether isn't snapped by the centrifugal acceleration, then there isn't enough fuel left to do the perigee burn at Titan. It just goes to prove the old rocket pilot adage that it's best to do your burns in the deepest gravity well you can find."

"How about slowing *Sexdent* down using the electromagnetic brake on the tether—like we did at Helene?" asked Sandra.

"Won't work," said Chastity. "Remember? We did those calculations long ago, before takeoff, when we were trying to figure out a way to stop at the leading Trojan point. If we tried to slow down from an initial velocity of 3.9 klecs, the radiators would melt instantly. Even if we used the rockets to slow *Sexdent* down as much as we could before starting the braking process, the calculated radiator temperature is above four thousand kelvin, and tungsten melts at thirty-four hundred. That option is so far from being feasible, I stopped thinking about using it long ago. Tether braking is only useful when you're moving at low velocity, like coming to a stop at the iceberg that's shielding our return tank."

"But before, when we were trying to find a way to reach the fuel tank at the leading Trojan point, we were trying to brake all the way to a stop," said Sandra, not wanting to give up. "Now that circumstances have sent us to the trailing Trojan point, we no longer want to stop. We want to leave with enough velocity to get to Titan and the leading Trojan point. Have you tried combining braking, swinging, *and* rocket burns?"

Rod looked at Chastity, who looked back at Rod.

"Out of the mouths of babes . . ." said Rod. He turned to Sandra, took her head in both hands, and gave her a big kiss. "And what a babe she is!" Leaving Sandra floating in midair he turned and settled himself down at the commander's console to join Chastity as they took Jeeves through another round of trajectory calculations. Dinner that night was a celebration, with Pete staying sober enough to prepare cherries jubilee again for them.

"Chass and I are calling it Sandra's 'Swoosh, Slide, and Swing' maneuver," explained Rod, sipping his after-dinner coffee from his squeezer. "It's complicated, but if everything works, we're on our way home." He held up an ice cube rescued from his predinner "scotch on the rocks" squeezer, and a baking powder biscuit saved from his special southern fried chicken dinner. The biscuit had a hole poked out of the center. He carefully placed the ice cube in free fall. "This is the iceberg at the trailing Trojan point." A meter away he placed his globular coffee squeezer in midair. "Here is Titan . . ." A meter farther he carefully placed the donut-shaped biscuit so it too was floating. "And here is our return fuel tank with the meta we need to take us home." He took a cherry out of Sandra's cherries jubilee and held it between his fingers. "And this is *Sexdent.*"

He moved the cherry below the "iceberg." "As *Sexdent* and the iceberg pass each other going in opposite directions, I first use the rockets to slow down *Sexdent,* in the process using up nearly all of our fuel." The motion of the cherry slowed. "Then Chass fires the penetrator . . ." From the hand holding the cherry he pulled out a length of dental floss he had been palming and brought it up to the ice cube. "And spears the iceberg. But only half the tether has been deployed." Holding the floss taut, he started to swing the cherry around the ice cube. "*Sexdent* then starts swinging around the iceberg, but instead of keeping the tether locked, Dan allows it to unreel, while using the brake to extract energy from *Sexdent.*" He moved the cherry up above the ice cube, pulling out more floss as he did so. "It takes us about two-and-a-half minutes to swing around the iceberg. By the time *Sexdent* has completed a half-circle, braking all the time as the tether is getting longer, it is moving much slower than it did when it arrived, and is going in the opposite direction—toward Titan." He moved the cherry over to the squeezer. "It arrives at Titan a few days later, dives down the gravity well, I give a small perigee burn"—he twirled the cherry around the squeezer and then moved over to the biscuit with a hole in it—"and we end up at our fuel depot at the other Trojan point, where one tiny little jet burst brings us to a stop." He looked around at his crew. His face, usually furrowed with the burdens of his command responsibility, was, for once, calm and at peace.

"But we've got a lot to do to get ready," he ended, taking charge again.

A day later they reached the peak of their escape trajectory from Saturn. Everything was in readiness to carry out Sandra's "Swoosh, Slide, and Swing" maneuver. The habitats were stored, everyone was in their acceleration couches, the radiators for the electromagnetic tether brake were unfurled to the sky, and Tabby had the last penetrator checked out and ready in the open port of *Sexdent*'s nosecone. Rod watched the display on the commander's console as the blue dot that indicated the approaching iceberg rapidly caught up with the much more slowly moving red dot representing the position of *Sexdent*. Rod lifted up on the joyball in his controller and the main engines at the rear of Sexdent ignited again. The red dot on the screen grew a reddish-purple tail and started moving faster in the same direction as the iceberg dot.

"One point five . . . one point six . . ." counted Rod, then pulled the joyball down. "One point seven klecs," he finished, his voice echoing in the silence that followed the loud roar of the engines. "That's nearly all our fuel. It's your turn now, Chass." He switched the joyball to vernier jets and turned the capsule around so it was facing back along their direction of travel. In the viewport windows above them, the crew could now see the rapidly approaching mountain of ice. The holoviewport above Chastity grew partially opaque as cross-hairs appeared, superimposed on a long-distance image of the iceberg. Chastity, her right hand in her controller, used the joyball to align the cross-hairs on the target, then activated an icon with her pinky. There was a swooshing sound from the nose compartment above. Spouting a reddish-purple meta flame from its rear, the penetrator jetted off into the distance. While Chastity guided the penetrator, Dan read off the length of tether deployed.

"Ten kilometers . . . twenty . . . thirty . . ."

The holoviewport above Chastity now showed the view from the video camera in the nose of the penetrator. The ice mountain began to fill the screen as Chastity focused the cross-hairs on the center of a medium-sized crater.

"Ninety-five . . . one hundred . . . and five . . ." continued Dan.

"Got it!" yelled Chastity as the screen above her went black. "Now hold!" she pleaded in a softer voice.

It was now Dan's turn. Although Chastity had operated the electromagnetic brakes previously, handling both the tether and the brakes simultaneously required two hands, so now she controlled the tether while he controlled the brakes. Watching the displays on the scottyboard carefully, Dan slid the tether brake icons down with his fingers until the acceleration level in the capsule built up to almost four gees.

"If the penetrator pulls or the tether snaps, this'll be the time," muttered Chastity. The acceleration level slowly began to decrease as the tether rapidly unreeled, giving their swing around the iceberg a longer arc. Above them arose a brilliant light from the now whitely glowing radiator fins sticking out from the nose of the ship. The viewport windows darkened, protecting their eyes from the intense light, but soon the heat from the infrared began to make itself felt through their clothing.

"Three thousand K . . ." said Dan, reading the temperature indicator on his display, ". . . thirty-one hundred . . . thirty-two hundred."

"Isn't that getting a little high?" asked Rod, slightly concerned. "The melting point of tungsten is thirty-four hundred. I thought we were going to keep the radiator temperature below thirty-one."

"That was the plan," muttered Dan. One of the three fingers on his hand made a tiny adjustment to its icon that controlled the amount of electric current flowing to that radiator. Above each icon were indicators showing their temperature and current ratio. "But one of the radiators isn't working right and I'm having to ask the other two to carry more of the load so the braking power stays constant—"

"You're making the right decision," Rod assured him. "If we leave this iceberg moving too fast I won't be able to stop us with the fuel we have left." The seconds passed slowly. The acceleration level slowly fell as the temperature inside the capsule rapidly rose.

"Just one more minute," said Rod, trying to encourage his crew. "Then we can turn this sauna off."

The light above them grew until it was brighter than the Sun . . . Suddenly there was a flash and then darkness—

"Brake, Dan!" yelled Chastity. "We've not completed our swing!"

"Brakes are gone," replied Dan grimly. "And I can't activate the tether clamp while the tether is moving. Just pull off the nosecone if I tried. That's why the end of the tether isn't tied to the reel."

As the viewport readjusted to the lowered light level, the crew could now see a cloud of glowing red specks streaking by the viewports, viewports now permanently dim with a silvery-gray film of evaporated tungsten on the outside. Above them they could hear the tether reel whirring freely as the tether flowed out unchecked. They came to the end of the tether and dropped into free fall, the only sound the whir of the still-rotating tether reel above them.

Rod, saying nothing, was quickly analyzing the situation on his commander's console. Chastity soon was doing the same.

"We got about three-fourths the way around," said Chastity, explaining things to the rest of the crew while Rod concentrated on trying to figure out their next move. "We're in a climbing trajectory. It'll take us high over Titan's orbit, then back down through it again, but when we get there Titan will still be ahead of us."

"What happens then?" asked Sandra in a small, scared voice.

"We go into an elliptical orbit around Saturn," said Chastity. She looked at the trajectory diagram on her screen. "Fortunately our perigee will be outside the ring system so we don't have to worry about being holed by a ring particle."

"Then that means we'll come back up to Titan's orbit again," said Sandra. "How long before we meet up with Titan again?"

"According to what Jeeves just told me, two hundred and thirty-seven days," replied Rod.

"That's not so bad. We'll still have food left," said Sandra.

"We run out of meta in nine days," said Rod grimly.

Rod and Chastity finally had to admit they couldn't think of anything to get them out of their predicament. *Sexdent's* initial speed in its new orbit had been slightly faster than that of Titan, so they had caught up with the moon slightly as their trajectory took them high over it. Titan would move ahead of them again as *Sexdent* slowed at the top of its trajectory. Chastity had used the science telescope to obtain a high-magnification image of the leading Trojan point. On the screen were fuzzy images of the iceberg mountain protecting their donut-shaped return fuel tank from meteorites. The fuel tank itself was just barely visible behind the large rendezvous stage protecting its opposite side. Chastity had brought up the image of the ice mountain in the hopes that the sight of their goal would somehow inspire either Rod or herself to find some way out of their predicament.

"It doesn't look good," Chastity finally said. "There's a thousand enemy soldiers between us and the mountain. We lost our bayonet taking the last foothill and we're down to our last five hundred and forty bullets."

What made the problem unsolvable was that they only had 540 kilos of meta left, and they were using it up fast. At *Sexdent*'s normal consumption rate of 60 kilos a day, it would only last nine days. The crew had faced this problem before and soon had everything nonessential turned off, even putting most of Jeeves "to sleep" for most of the time. Even after all their economies, they still faced a short lifetime. The meta-powered generator would run out of fuel and stop supplying electricity in less than a month. Without electricity, all the life support systems would shut down. After that, their bodies would have to start coping with bad air, bad water, and freezing cold. Dan passed out "termination" pills. Everyone hesitated before accepting them, but all did, tucking them away somewhere out of sight in their habitats.

Sandra thought about sending a farewell message to Peregrine, but decided that she wouldn't even bother to ask Rod for permission to use the energy to do so. With the heat turned off in the capsule, the crew now spent most of their time in their habitats. Pete was given the password to the ethanol stores in Seichi's habitat and soon was off on a month-long binge, keeping warm by burning ethanol. The other four paired off and shared habitats, partially to keep warm and partially for intellectual stimulation, for they had limited themselves to four-hours-a-day access to Jeeves's library. No video—that took too much power—text only, saved by the memory feature of the console screen between pages. Most of the crew didn't use their allotted reading time—usually finding something else to do instead.

Chastity awoke in her habitat. She was alone. Dan must have gone back to his own tube. Despite being well tucked under her bed covers, she was cold. She smiled. She knew how to take care of that problem. She reached up to the ceiling and activated the communicator. "Jeeves?" she asked. "Is Dan awake?"

"Yes" came Jeeves's reply.

"Connect me to him, please," she asked. She soon heard the soft sounds of Dan breathing.

"Good morning, lover boy," Chastity started. "How would you like to start the day off exploring a couple of mountains and a warm cozy forested valley?"

She heard him give a tired sigh. "Gee, darling. I'd love to. But I'm not sure I'm up to it. After all, the last time was only two hours ago. I think I'd better rest some more."

"You do that," she replied, pushing off the bed covers and reaching for the latch to the habitat hatch. "If Mohammed is too tired to come to the mountains, the mountains will come to Mohammed."

Dan heard the intercom switch off and started trying to think the right kind of thoughts to psych himself up for the upcoming visit. It wasn't hard, for the past few days had been the most enjoyable Dan had ever experienced. His wildest fantasies about making love to Chastity had been exceeded by the reality, except for one thing—the feel of long fingernails scratching lightly down his bare back.

The minutes passed with no tap on his hatchdoor. "She must have stopped by the ladies' first," Dan thought to himself, but the minutes continued to drag on with no tap on his hatchdoor. Dan was puzzled, and beginning to worry a little, when suddenly he heard the commotion of a hatchdoor clanging open and loud conversation. He struggled out from under his warm covers, pushed his hatchdoor up, and peered out. Across the deck, peering out from Rod's habitat door, was a bewildered-looking Sandra, a blanket wrapped around her naked shoulders. Sitting at the pilot console on one side of Sandra was Chastity, still in her blue nightgown, punching icons and talking loudly to Rod. Sitting at the command console on the other side of Sandra was Rod, punching icons and giving commands to Jeeves. As far as Dan could tell from his deck-level viewpoint, Rod was sitting in the commander's seat stark naked, his lanky thighs starting to turn blue and sprout goose pimples in the cold air of the control deck. Chastity saw Dan peeking out his habitat door and gave him a cheery smile from across the deck.

"I thought of a way to get us out of here!" she said, excitedly. "Instead of us trying to figure out a way to fly over to our fuel tank, I'm going to fly the fuel tank over here!"

"Jeeves. Back off rendezvous tank," said Rod. On both their screens were two images obviously collected by distant video cameras. One camera was on the donut-shaped fuel tank that contained the meta that would take them home, while the other was on the empty rendezvous tank stage that they had left as a meteorite shield. The camera on each tank stage was transmitting an image of the other stage. The two images shrank simultaneously as the two tanks separated, the small vernier jets on the large empty shield tank flashing occasionally as Jeeves backed it away. When the two tanks were well separated, Rod turned to Chastity.

"It's all yours, Chass," said Rod. "Fly that meta tank over here and hook us up!" Chastity reached her right hand into the controller box under her console. The image of the donut-shaped fuel tank sprouted a fine necklace of tiny purple-red meta flames as the vernier jets started the massive tank on its way.

Rod turned to look around the control deck. The face of a bleary-eyed Pete had now appeared in his hatchdoor, so everyone was present.

"Because of Chass, we're going home!" he announced with a smile. "The fuel tank should be here in a day or so. Although technically the hole in the center is big enough to pass over the habitats, the last thing I want is an accident, so everybody get dressed and clean out your habitats, we're going to have to pull them all in and store them during the docking maneuver." Pete, head pounding from a hangover, groaned at the thought. "At least the exercise will keep us warm," continued Rod. He then looked down at his blue legs and realized that he had nothing on. His face and chest blushed reddish-blue. "Say, Sandra," he said with an embarrassed tone. "Pass out my kleins and coveralls, will ya?"

A week later, *Sexdent* was completely checked out and ready. Now that the danger was over and the stress level had lowered, Pete stopped drinking, sobered up, and once again became a help rather than a hindrance to the rest of the crew. Chastity was especially surprised to find that when she came on shift duty at the command console, Pete was usually working away at the science console, using the high-resolution wide-screen color display capability of the large holoviewport.

"What are you working on that you need the holoviewport for?" asked Chastity, who had partially forgiven Pete now that he had mended his ways.

"Helping design a video game," said Pete cheerfully. "My brother is in the video game business. He thinks our recent adventures would make a great video game. He already has decided on a name for it— 'Climbing Saturn's Rings.' There are so many different options available. There are dozens of ways to climb down and up the rings using combinations of rocket burns and tether whips. There are all the alien creatures that you have to find on Saturn to get points. And most of the game options will not have a rukh eating the balloon or the reactor failing—"

"In a video game, when you get in trouble and 'die,' all you have to do is press the Restart button and you're alive again," said Chastity somberly. "It doesn't work like that in real life."

"Yeah . . ." agreed Pete. His creative momentum lost, he closed down what he was doing and stored it. Chastity noticed the lengthy file title before it disappeared from the screen: TECHNICAL BACK-GROUND FOR VIDEO GAME "CLIMBING SATURN'S RINGS."

"Let's go home, Chass," said Rod, when they were finally ready. "Just follow the course Jeeves and I plotted. Slide *Sexdent* over sixty degrees from this Trojan point to Titan, drop into Titan's gravity well and do a little perigee burn that leaves us falling inward toward Saturn, then in Saturn's gravity well do a big perigee burn that drops us inward to the Sun—and home."

"Can we delay our departure for just two hours?" asked Chastity.

"No problem," said Rod. "It's going to take us a few days to catch up to Titan, then another few days to reach Saturn. An hour or two different starting time doesn't make any difference in the energetics, only the timing. But why?"

"I want to wave good-bye to a few friends."

❖   ❖   ❖

A week later, after a safe ring passage, Rod lit the candle over the dark side of Saturn. He kept the gee level of the burn at a quarter gee, while rotating the capsule at the same time, so the rest of the crew could sit on the windows of their habitats and look out at the gigantic orange and white clouds rolling past their viewports six hundred kilometers below them, illuminated by their twelve-gigacandle purple-red meta exhaust.

After the main burn ended, Chastity climbed up out of her habitat against the centrifugal gravity, sticking her stump out the hatch door for Rod to pull on to help her "up." He switched ship control to her pilot console, and leaving her in command, dropped down into his own habitat. With her right hand in the throttle-hole, she tapped the icons on the touchscreen with the pinky on the end of her stump, and soon had a map of Saturn on the screen. Their perigee had occurred on the dark side of Saturn, below the equator. They were now coming up on the terminator, but they had passed over the equator and were now climbing upward over the midlatitudes of the northern hemisphere. It was in this band, between the turbulent equatorial wind band and the bleak and cold northern cap, that the rukhs flocked. In that region, the display on the touchscreen showed a tiny blinking dot—a weak beacon signal coming from the radio transponder on the mechbot they had left on Peregrine. Their giant friend had been climbing to altitude all night, so as to get ready for the start of the next day's hunting dive. It would be the astronomer half that would be awake at this time of the Saturnian day. Chastity only hoped that the sky was clear enough that Uppereye would be seeing the stars. Taking the throttle control in her fingers, Chastity raised it slightly three times, timing the burns with the slow rotation of the capsule, finishing off the last of the burn that Rod had started. Doing the burn this far from periapsis was slightly less efficient of fuel, but they now had fuel to spare. In the habitats, each crewmember in turn got to see the cloud patterns light up below. They had once lived there—and one of them had died there. Now they were going home to where you lived under the clouds, rather than *in* them.

Down below, Petra could feel Petru getting tired and hungry. But soon it would be morning, and she could get some rest and let Petro fill the empty gizzard. The sky was clear of clouds above, and Petra could see Parent-and-Child rising over the horizon, soon to be followed by Bright. Parent was the home of the humans. The last she had seen of the humans was the brilliant purple-red light coming from the base of their strange wingless flyer as they entered one of the gigantic ravenous maws of the Swallower.

Just then, a light appeared in the sky above. Petra, with her long experience of gazing at the patterns of light in the sky, marked its position in her memory map of the heavens. The new light was brighter than any star and moving. At first, Petra thought it might be an incoming meteorite, but instead of coming downward and getting brighter, it went outward and stayed constant, until it stopped and faded away. She knew it wasn't a meteorite when the light turned back on again. She now recognized the reddish-purple color of the light—it was the light emitted by the humans' flyer!

Voices came out of the darkness around her from the rest of the flock. "Look up there!" "Did you see that?" "Is it a meteor?" "Strange color for a meteor." "What is it?"

"That light is from the flyer of the humans," Petra boomed out to the others around her. Seeing the humans leave, she felt a sense of loss, similar to what she felt when one of the flock entered into the death dive.

"Where are they going?" asked Hakra from below.

For a third time, the bright reddish-purple light glowed, then faded again. Petra was now able to determine the direction of travel of the pulsating light. It was headed in the direction of Parent-and-Child.

"They are going home."

TECHNICAL BACKGROUND FOR VIDEO GAME "CLIMBING SATURN'S RINGS"

by
Pete Stewart

SATURN DATA

Orbital Semi-Major Axis	9.53884 AU = 1.4270 Tm
Eccentricity	(9.008 to 10.07 AU) 0.05565
Inclination to Ecliptic	2° 29″ 22″
Sidereal Period	29.4577 yr = 10,759.22 day = 0.9295966 Ms
Synodic Period	1.035136 sidereal yr = 378.09 day
Axial Tilt	26° 44′
Mean Daily Motion	0.033460 °/day
Mean Speed Along Orbit	9.64 km/s
Radius , Equatorial (1 bar)	0.845 R_J = 9.46 R⊕ = 60.33 Mm
, Polar	54.88 Mm
, Core	30.3 Mm
Dynamic Oblateness (1 bar)	0.0982
Volume	744 V⊕
Mass	0.30 M_J = 95.26 M⊕ = 5.688x10²⁶ kg
J_2 Gravity Oblateness Term	0.016479
Specific Density	0.69
Sidereal Rotation Period (radio)	10 hr 39 min 24 s = 38,364 s
(equatorial atmosphere)	10 hr 10 min = 36,600 s
Equatorial Rotational Velocity at 60,330 km	9.881 km/s
Peak Wind Velocity	+0.500 km/s
Escape Velocity Required (including J_2 term)	
Pole	36.999 km/s
Equator	35.542 km/s
Eastward 45-degree Latitude Launch	29.697 km/s
Eastward Equatorial Launch	25.661 km/s
Wind-Assisted Eastward Equatorial Launch	25.171 km/s
Gravity (including J_2 term and centrifugal acceleration)	
Pole	1.238 gees = -12.137 m/s²
45 degrees latitude	1.089 gees = -10.671 m/s²
Equator	0.925 gees = - 9.067 m/s²
Effective Temperature	95 K
Internal Heat Flux	2.0 W/m²
Sun as seen from Saturn	3′22″ = 0.056°
Insolation Solar Energy Flux	15.4 W/m²
Solar Light Flux	2.06 W/m²
10 Optical Depth Sub-Cloud Flux	9.3×10⁻⁵ W/m²
Earth Surface Full Moon Flux	2.8×10⁻⁴ W/m²
Heat Emission/Solar Insolation	1.78
Albedo (Bolometric Bond)	0.328
Magnetic Field (North Pole)	0.84 Gauss
(South Pole)	0.65 Gauss

SATURN RING AND SHEPHERD MOON DATA

Name	Width (Mm)	Distance (Mm)	Distance (R$_s$)	Orb Vel (m/s)	Optical Depth
Clouds (1 bar)		60.33	1.00	9,881[V(rot)]	
D Ring		66.97	1.11	23,806	
C Ring Inner		74.51	1.235	22,570	0.08
C Ring Center	17.55	81.4	1.35	21,600	
Maxwell Gap	0.25	87.48	1.450	20,830	
C Ring Outer		92.06	1.526	20,305	0.15
B Ring Inner		92.06	1.526	20,305	1.21
B Ring Center	25.46	111.6	1.85	18,440	1.76
B Ring Outer		117.52	1.948	17,971	1.84
Huygens Gap	0.43	117.70	1.951	17,958	
Cassini Div	4.54	119.76	1.985	17,802	0.12
A Ring Inner		122.17	2.025	17,626	0.70
A Ring Center	14.60	126.7	2.10	17,310	
Pan		133.57	2.214	16,857	
Encke Gap	0.33	133.57	2.214	16,857	
Keeler Gap	0.03	136.53	2.263	16,673	
A Ring Outer		136.77	2.267	16,659	0.57
Atlas		137.67	2.282	16,604	
Prometheus		139.35	2.310	16,504	
F Ring Center		140.39	2.327	16,442	
Pandora		141.70	2.349	16,366	
Epimetheus, Janus		151.42	2.510	15,832	
G Ring Center		169	2.8	15,000	
E Ring Inner		180	3	14,500	
Mimas		185.54	3.075	14,303	
Enceladus		238.04	3.95	12,627	
Tethys, Calypso, Telesto		294.67	4.89	11,349	
Dione, Helene		377.42	2.74	10,028	
E Ring Outer		480	8	8,900	
Titan		1,222.86		5,570	

SATURN SATELLITE DATA

Name	Distance (Mm)	(R_s)	Period (days)	Eccentricity	Radius (km)	Escape Velocity (m/s)
S18 Pan	133.58	2.21	0.58		10	
S15 Atlas	137.67	2.29	0.60	0.002	19×15×13	
S16 Prometheus	139.35	2.30	0.61	0.003	70×50×37	
S17 Pandora	141.70	2.35	0.63	0.004	55×45×33	
S11 Epimetheus	151.42	2.50	0.69	0.009	70×58×50	
S10 Janus	151.47	2.50	0.69	0.007	110×95×80	
S01 Mimas	185.54	3.08	0.94	0.020	200	185
S02 Enceladus	238.04	3.95	1.37	0.004	255	205
S03 Tethys	294.67	4.89	1.89	0.000	530	438
S13 Telesto	294.67	4.89	1.89	trail	12×11×10	
S14 Calypso	294.67	4.89	1.89	lead	15×12×08	
S04 Dione	377.42	6.25	2.74	0.002	560	500
S12 Helene	377.42	6.25	2.74	lead	18×17×14	
S05 Rhea	527.10	8.74	4.52	0.001	765	660
S06 Titan	1,222.86	20.25	15.9	0.029	2570	2638
S07 Hyperion	1,481.00	24.55	21.2	0.104	205×130×110	
S08 Iapetus	3,560.80	59.02	79.3	0.028	730	586
S09 Phoebe	12,954.00	214.7–550		0.163	110	

SATURN RINGS AND SATELLITES

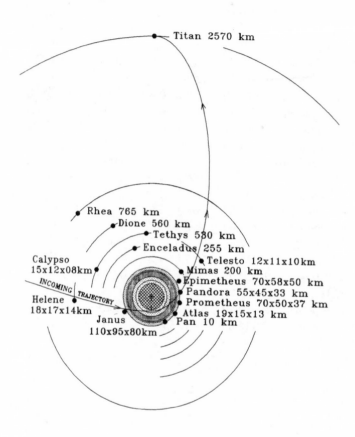

Titan 2570 km

Rhea 765 km
Dione 560 km
Tethys 530 km
Enceladus 255 km
Telesto 12x11x10km
Calypso
15x12x08km
Mimas 200 km
Epimetheus 70x58x50 km
INCOMING TRAJECTORY
Pandora 55x45x33 km
Helene
18x17x14km
Prometheus 70x50x37 km
Atlas 19x15x13 km
Janus
Pan 10 km
110x95x80km

SATURN RINGS AND SATELLITES

THE *SEXDENT* PLANETARY
EXPLORATION SPACECRAFT
INSTALLED ON BOOST AND
RENDEZVOUS STAGES

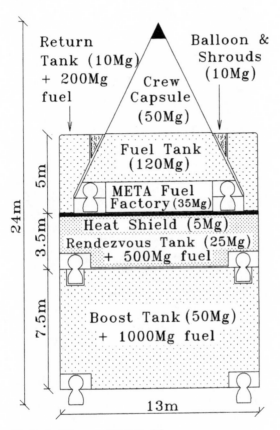

Return Tank (10Mg) + 200Mg fuel

Balloon & Shrouds (10Mg)

Crew Capsule (50Mg)

Fuel Tank (120Mg)

META Fuel Factory (35Mg)

Heat Shield (5Mg)

Rendezvous Tank (25Mg) + 500Mg fuel

Boost Tank (50Mg) + 1000Mg fuel

24m

5m

3.5m

7.5m

13m

Total Mass 2005 Mg

HIGH-SPEED ARRIVAL OF *SEXDENT* AT SATURN; PERIAPSIS BURN UNDER RINGS; STOP AT TITAN

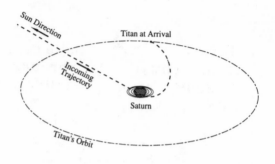

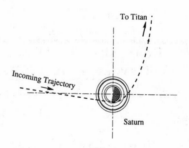

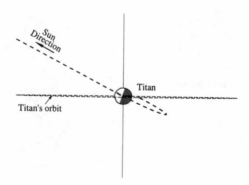

"CLIMBING DOWN SATURN'S RINGS"

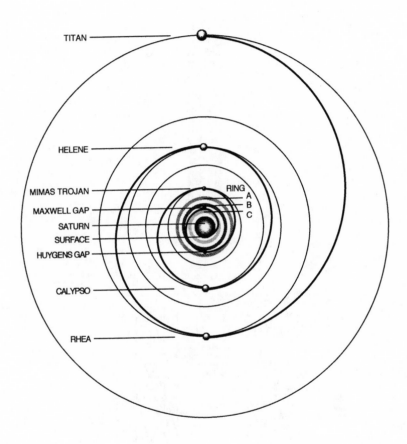

TITAN

HELENE

MIMAS TROJAN

MAXWELL GAP

SATURN

SURFACE

HUYGENS GAP

CALYPSO

RHEA

RING
A
B
C

HIGH-STRENGTH, FAILSAFE HOYTETHERS "REPAIRING" THEMSELVES WHEN A LINE FAILS

Tubular Hoytether

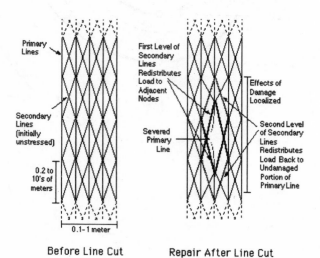

Primary Lines

Secondary Lines (initially unstressed)

0.2 to 10's of meters

0.1–1 meter

Before Line Cut

First Level of Secondary Lines Redistributes Load to Adjacent Nodes

Severed Primary Line

Effects of Damage Localized

Second Level of Secondary Lines Redistributes Load Back to Undamaged Portion of Primary Line

Repair After Line Cut

SEXDENT

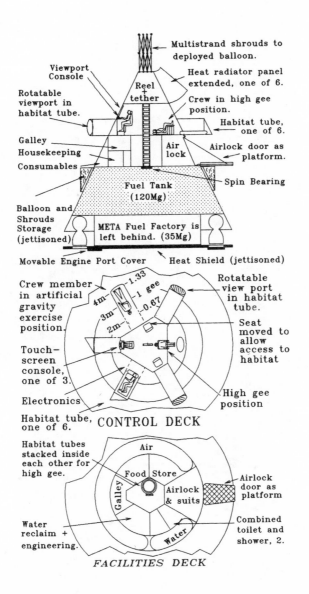

Multistrand shrouds to deployed balloon.

Viewport Console

Heat radiator panel extended, one of 6.

Rotatable viewport in habitat tube.

Reel + tether

Crew in high gee position.

Habitat tube, one of 6.

Galley
Housekeeping
Consumables

Air lock

Airlock door as platform.

Fuel Tank (120Mg)

Spin Bearing

Balloon and Shrouds Storage (jettisoned)

META Fuel Factory is left behind. (35Mg)

Movable Engine Port Cover

Heat Shield (jettisoned)

Crew member in artificial gravity exercise position.

1.33
1 gee
0.67
4m
3m
2m

Rotatable view port in habitat tube.

Seat moved to allow access to habitat

Touch-screen console, one of 3.

Electronics

High gee position

Habitat tube, one of 6.

CONTROL DECK

Habitat tubes stacked inside each other for high gee.

Air

Food Store

Galley

Airlock & suits

Airlock door as platform

Water reclaim + engineering.

Water

Combined toilet and shower, 2.

FACILITIES DECK

BIBLIOGRAPHY

C. W. Allen, *Astrophysical Quantities* (Athlone Press, London, 1976), pp. 140, 141.

Tom Gehrels and Mildred Shapley Matthews, eds., *Saturn* (University of Arizona Press, Tucson, 1984). Saturn data, p. 942. Satellite data, pp. 653, 655, 673. Ring data, pp. 473, 477, 497, 523.

Patrick Moore and Garry Hunt, *Rand-McNally Atlas of the Solar System*, 2nd ed. (Rand-McNally, 1984).

Carl Sagan and E. E. Salpeter, "Particles, Environments, and Possible Ecologies in the Jovian Atmosphere," *Astrophysical Journal Supplement Series*, Vol. 32, pp. 737–755 (December 1976).

E. C. Stone and E. D. Miner, "*Voyager 1* Encounter with the Saturnian System," *Science*, Vol. 212, pp. 159–163 (10 April 1981), and following articles.

E. C. Stone and E. D. Miner, "*Voyager 2* Encounter with the Saturnian System," *Science*, Vol. 215, pp. 499–504 (29 January 1982), and following articles.

ABOUT THE AUTHOR

Dr. Robert L. Forward writes science fiction novels and short stories, as well as science fact books and magazine articles. Through his scientific consulting company, Forward Unlimited, he also engages in contracted research on advanced space propulsion and exotic physical phenomena. Dr. Forward obtained his Ph.D. in gravitational physics from the University of Maryland. For his thesis he constructed and operated the world's first bar antenna for the detection of gravitational radiation. The antenna is now in the Smithsonian Museum.

For thirty-one years, from 1956 until 1987, when he left in order to spend more time writing, Dr. Forward worked at the Hughes Aircraft Company Corporate Research Laboratories in Malibu, California, in positions of increasing responsibility, culminating with the position of senior scientist on the staff of the director. During that time he constructed and operated the world's first laser gravitational radiation detector, invented the rotating gravitational mass sensor, published over sixty-five scientific publications, and was awarded eighteen patents.

From 1983 to the present, Dr. Forward has had a series of contracts from the U.S. Air Force and NASA to explore the forefront of physics and engineering in order to find breakthrough concepts in space power and propulsion. He has published journal papers and contract reports on antiproton annihilation propulsion, laser beam and microwave beam interstellar propulsion, negative matter propulsion, space tethers, space warps, and a method for extracting electrical energy from vacuum fluctuations, and was awarded a patent for a Statite: a sunlight-levitated solar-sail direct-broadcast spacecraft that does not orbit the Earth, but "hovers" over the North Pole.

In addition to his professional publications, Dr. Forward has written over eighty popular science articles for publications such as the *Encyclopaedia Britannica Yearbook, Omni, New Scientist, Focus, Aerospace America, Science Digest, Science 80, Analog,* and *Galaxy.* His science fact books are *Future Magic, Mirror Matter: Pioneering Antimatter Physics* (with Joel Davis), and *Indistinguishable from Magic.* His science fiction novels are *Dragon's Egg* and its sequel *Starquake; Rocheworld* and its four sequels, *Return to Rocheworld* and *Rescued from Paradise* (with his daughter, Julie Forward Fuller), and *Ocean Under the Ice* and *Marooned on Eden* (with his wife, Martha Dodson Forward); *Martian Rainbow, Timemaster, Camelot 30K,* and now *Saturn Rukh.* The novels are of the "hard" science fiction category, in which the science is as accurate as possible.

Dr. Forward is a fellow of the British Interplanetary Society and former editor of the interstellar studies issues of its journal, associate fellow of the American Institute of Aeronautics and Astronautics, and a member of the American Physical Society, Sigma Xi, Sigma Pi Sigma, the National Space Society, the Science-Fiction and Fantasy Writers of America, and the Author's Guild.